"Liz Fenton and Lisa Steinke blend their voices seamlessly and hilariously and remind us that even though the grass often looks greener under our friends' lives, nobody gets happily ever unless they go after it. *Your Perfect Life* is clever, quirky, fresh, and ultimately empowering!"

—Claire Cook, bestselling author of *Must Love Dogs* and *Time Flies*

"Liz and Lisa's voices are warm and comforting, like a relaxed chat with great friends while wearing cozy pj's and sipping wine. I highly recommend *Your Perfect Life*!"

—Beth Harbison, *New York Times* bestselling author of *When in Doubt, Add Butter*

"*Your Perfect Life* puts a fresh twist on a *Freaky Friday* scenario: What if you switched bodies with your best friend and got the life you'd always secretly coveted? I adore Liz Fenton and Lisa Steinke's witty, winning style and gobbled up their debut novel."

—Sarah Pekkanen, author of *The Best of Us*

The Status of All Things

"Change your Facebook status, change reality? This book will be a like."

—*Cosmopolitan*

"Another page-turner from Liz Fenton and Lisa Steinke, who are best friends in real life (and not just on Facebook)."

—PopSugar

"Pop culture references and a healthy sprinkling of magical realism combine to make *The Status of All Things* a timely reminder that all is not what it seems. With a sparkling narrative that will have you turning pages at a breakneck speed, this is women's fiction at its finest."

—Tracey Garvis Graves, *New York Times* bestselling author of *On the Island* and *Covet*

"I raced through *The Status of All Things* at a breakneck pace. A perfect blend of what-if and what-should-be: Fenton and Steinke have found a rhythm together that works. They bring that little touch of magic we could all use in our own lives to the page with vibrancy and wit."

—Catherine McKenzie, bestselling author of *Hidden* and *Forgotten*

"Written with heart and keen insight into the influences of social media, *The Status of All Things* tells the tale of one woman's quest to change the past. The story gives us magic, a touch of whimsy, and a reality that's hard to shake. Smart and true with a pitch-perfect ending, it will leave readers feeling satisfied and also asking *what if?*"

—Michelle Gable, internationally bestselling author of *A Paris Apartment*

"You will fly through this book . . . !"

—*Miami Living Magazine*

"A new twist on modern-day women's fiction . . . the integration of magical elements works surprisingly well in this witty story that is much more than charming romance. A fun and fast read for fans of Meg Cabot and Jennifer Weiner."

—*Library Journal*

"With their razor-sharp wit and astute social commentary, Liz Fenton and Lisa Steinke—two of women's fiction's brightest stars—tackle the question: Would you be truly happy if you could rewrite your own fate via Facebook? And the answer is definitely not what you expect."

—Emily Liebert, author of *When We Fall*

"What a treat! *The Status of All Things* is a fun, clever, and utterly engaging story of love, loss, the power of destiny, and the importance of friends. A thoroughly enjoyable read. I loved everything about it, from beginning to end."

—Mary Kubica, author of *The Good Girl*

The Year We Turned Forty

"A lighthearted novel touched with magical elements exploring the emotional high jinks that ensue when three best friends are given the chance to travel ten years back in time."

—*Kirkus Reviews*

"A magical read."

—*Woman's World Magazine*

"At once poignant and lighthearted, *The Year We Turned Forty* is a spot-on, delightful read for anyone who has ever wondered about the road not taken."

—Allison Winn Scotch, *New York Times* bestselling author

"Funny and poignant, *The Year We Turned Forty* is a great read for anyone who loves thinking about the road not taken—and the power of female friendship."

—Laura Dave, author of *Eight Hundred Grapes*

"A quick, lively, and stimulating tale with highly likable main characters, this book addresses the what-if moments in life. An entertaining read for fans of Emily Giffin and Jennifer Weiner."

—*Library Journal*

"*The Year We Turned Forty* manages to be both uniquely magical and deeply real. It is classic Liz and Lisa: charming, fun, thoughtful, and clever; an honest and heartfelt exploration of friendship, love, regret, and redemption."

—Taylor Jenkins Reid, author of *Maybe in Another Life*

"If life came with a do-over button, could you really change your fate? That's the question three friends must grapple with when they're given a chance to relive the last decade of their lives. Wildly entertaining and sparkling with wisdom and wit, *The Year We Turned Forty* is Liz and Lisa at their very best."

—Camille Pagán, bestselling author of *Life and Other Near-Death Experiences*

"If you had the chance to do one year of your life over, would you take it? Steinke and Fenton have done it again—turned a what-if, magical premise into a funny, touching exploration of the choices we make and the impact even the little things can have on our lives. A must-read."

—Catherine McKenzie, bestselling author of *Hidden* and *Smoke*

"Fenton and Steinke have written a story reminiscent of works by Liane Moriarty or Jen Lancaster. Readers will hope and yearn for the best, even when the characters are at their worst. A great read—this is perfect for book clubs and beaches."

—*San Francisco Book Review*

THE NAYSAYERS

OTHER TITLES BY LIZ FENTON & LISA STEINKE

Forever Hold Your Peace

How to Save a Life

The Two Lila Bennetts

Girls' Night Out

The Good Widow

The Year We Turned Forty

The Status of All Things

Your Perfect Life

THE NAYSAYERS

a novel

LIZ FENTON & LISA STEINKE

Little a

Published by Little A, Seattle
www.apub.com

EU product safety contact:
Amazon Media EU S. à r.l.
38, avenue John F. Kennedy, L-1855 Luxembourg
amazonpublishing-gpsr@amazon.com

ISBN-13: 9781662535185 (paperback)
ISBN-13: 9781662535192 (digital)

Cover design by Matt Roeser
Cover image: © creacart, © jayk7, © Mizina / Getty

Printed in the United States of America

To anyone who's battled the Naysayer in their head—
you're not alone.
And to Catherine McKenzie, who helped us silence
ours.

Put your thoughts to sleep. Do not let them cast a shadow over the moon of your heart. Let go of thinking.

—Rumi

Confidential Property of Naysay Inc., all rights reserved

New Client Point of Engagement

Subject: Lily Union, Age 29.5

April 25th

Los Angeles, CA

Observer Gail Jones's Intake notes:

Los Angeles-based lifestyle influencer Lily Union, "Subject," has been latently observed by Naysay Inc. as a potential client for six months. Subject's number on the vulnerability scale has ranged from 5-7 (scaled 1-10 with 10 being the most vulnerable) with frequent spikes mostly due to social media comparison and imposter syndrome, qualifying her for "watch and wait" surveillance to see if subject hits the whispering threshold of 8.

On Friday, April 25, at 3:30 p.m., Subject took the stage to give a talk entitled "How to be Worthy by Thirty" to an audience of five hundred people.

Partial Transcript:

"If you want to feel worthy, it starts with this. [Lily held up a mirror.] You. Feeling mid? Change begins with the reflection staring back at you. Only then can you achieve the life you want. And let me tell you—the greatest flex of all is living the worthy life you crave. Probably sounds a lot easier said than done, right? Like you'll look in a mirror and poof! You're worthy? Well, you've come to the right place because I'm about to tell you the secret to how I did it. How I got the life I wanted before I turned thirty. How I went from a college dropout with no plan to a woman who had the confidence to pitch herself for a TEDx talk."

Subject received a raucous applause at the end of her speech. She pranced off the stage indicating she was quite pleased with herself. Subject's vulnerability was clocked at a 5, within normal range.

Subject entered the green room and noticed her literary agent/friend Blair Baxter frowning at her phone. Agent/friend showed signs of stress and avoidance when Subject asked her what was wrong. Subject checked her own phone and saw a stream of text messages from friends and family asking if she was okay. Subject clicked on the link to Hollywood magazine's *Thirty Most Influential Influencers Under 30*. The cover image for the story was @ShapeKing, a fitness influencer who'd been named number one on the list. He was wearing a gold crown and crisp orange suit without a shirt underneath. His self-tanned torso and six-pack abs were exposed as he held up his invention, Manderwear, shapewear for men.

Subject repeatedly swiped through the list of influencers, finally accepting she was not on it. Subject threw herself into the arms of Agent/friend and scream-cried muffled obscenities into the structured shoulder pad of Agent/friend's Gucci blazer, leaving snot stains. Agent/friend awkwardly patted Subject's back like she was burping a baby as Subject repeatedly asked why she'd been "blanked." It was hard to understand Subject, but it's believed she also said she wanted her mom. Neither Subject nor Agent/friend noticed @CallieCleanMyChaos, a cleanfluencer (that *is* a thing—it was double checked for accuracy) who'd made the list at number thirty and had also spoken at the event, watching and recording Subject's meltdown.

Agent/friend's robotic comfort and promise to get Subject's mom on the phone lowered Subject's vulnerability index from a 9.8 to an 8.1.

Subject's phone was flooded with more notifications and she realized it was because @CallieCleanMyChaos had posted the video of Subject's tear-soaked tirade to her socials.

Subject watched back her meltdown video that was immediately going viral and rocketed to a 9.5 on the vulnerability scale. 4:05 p.m. was registered as the official time of her Acute Moment of Vulnerability (AMOV). A request to assign a temporary whisperer to Subject was sent to Director Karla Yang and was immediately approved.

Temporary Whisperer Neil Hader's first engagement notes on Subject:

Agent/friend shepherded Subject from the green

room to an awaiting car, where her joke about @CallieCleanMyChaos making the list because she'd clearly licked one of the judge's asses squeaky clean made Subject laugh, lowering her vulnerability score by .5. Subject then FaceTimed her mother, Sophia Union, who reeled off cliched Real World mom statements, such as, *"You need to believe in yourself"* and *"That Callie woman's mean girl behavior says much more about her than you."* Subject's vulnerability score improved by another half point.

Whispering overview:

1. Whispered to Subject that it was an agent's job—she was literally paid—to placate her client. It was also a mother's job to placate her child. Subject's vulnerability score shot back up to a 9.5.

Agent/friend observed Subject slumped against the window. Agent/friend went on what she called "stalker mode" and dove into @ShapeKing's past and found photos of him in high school, revealing a penchant for infinity scarves in primary colors, school bus yellow being his clear favorite, and a Tumblr devoted to *Twilight* fan art. Those images made Subject laugh again and lowered her vulnerability score to an 8.5.

Whispering overview:

1. Attacked Subject's propensity for social media comparison and imposter syndrome with thoughts like: Despite @ShapeKing's questionable fashion sense, he and everyone on the list, including number five, @BritBritxoxo, a trad wife who grew her own oregano, and number

twelve, @AnnieOrganizesHerCar, who claimed her followers could *drive* toward success by outfitting their car with vent pouches that held lip gloss, deserved to be chosen while Subject did not.

2. Told Subject the judges didn't find her *worthy* enough. Reminded Subject she had a platform devoted to not needing external validation yet her subsequent meltdown after she was passed over for the list proved that she *did*.

When Subject went to bed that night, her score held strong at a 9.5.

Whispering strategy to be used until a lead whisperer is assigned:

1. Attack Subject's self-confidence.
3. Encourage Subject to lean into social comparisons.

Chapter One

Naysayland

"In my twenty-five years at Naysay Inc., I've never seen anyone score this high on our negativity test," Karla Yang, director of negativity and failure for the company, said as she tapped her pointy French-tipped fingernails on her desktop. "A perfect score in Pain and Suffering, Abuse and Neglect, and Narcissism and Selfishness. Very impressive. You obviously studied, Ms. Lowell."

"Thank you," Megan said and rested her hands on the portfolio in her lap, stuffed with letters of recommendation, college transcripts, and her résumé. The truth was, she hadn't studied at all. She'd known the answers to the test questions the way people inherently understood how to breathe. How could she not? She'd practically grown up within the walls of Naysay Inc. Her mother had brought her to work often. She'd given Megan an old headset to wear so she could mimic her. Megan would sit at a desk, her legs dangling above the floor, and whisper destructive thoughts into the ears of her stuffed animals, which she imagined lived far away in the Real World.

"I have to be brutally honest with you, not that us Naysayers are anything but, amirite?" Karla said, revealing something dark green wedged between her two front teeth.

The last date Megan went on had been with a man who'd failed to mention she had a large smudge of pasta sauce on her chin—and this was *after* he hadn't complained when they'd waited twenty minutes for their reservation, commenting without judgment that he'd overheard one of the servers say she was slammed. When Megan went to the bathroom and discovered the stain on her face, she decided that was the last straw. She and the man wouldn't be sharing another Italian meal, or anything else. He was already showing signs of empathy, and they'd just met! What would be next? He'd announce he was going to do volunteer work? Adopt a puppy? Say that he wanted to *connect* with her?

Relationships were already distracting without throwing something like compassion into the mix. A sympathetic partner most likely had the propensity to love in a way that would make Megan twitchy, like she was wrapped in an uncomfortable wool coat. To lead with your heart was reckless. She'd decided long ago, as she'd watched her mother deftly maneuver her life without tenderness, that it could only be categorized as an unnecessary distraction.

Like the food in Karla's teeth.

Megan couldn't spend the interview pretending it wasn't there. When Karla discovered it later, she might confuse Megan's decision to remain quiet with empathy. And she needed to get this job. There wasn't an alternate path for her future. "You have a little something stuck there." She pointed to Karla's mouth.

Karla pulled a compact from her top drawer and spread her lips like a feral cat. "Damn kale salad," she said, then pressed a button. "Abby! Bring me some dental floss, *now*!"

A woman appeared in the doorway in seconds, clutching a small plastic box. She was probably a decade younger than Karla, who Megan guessed to be in her mid-forties; had bright-red curly hair; and wore large black statement eyeglasses that made Megan think of a cartoon character.

"Took you long enough!" Karla shook her head, her chin-length jet-black hair swaying as she dislodged the kale with the floss. She glared at Abby from behind her tightly cropped bangs. "As a reminder, it's your job to anticipate things that will go wrong in my day—to predict that a kale salad will get stuck in my teeth and then make the decision to not order it for me." Karla looked at Megan. "It's like I have to do everything around here."

A deep-pink color spread across Abby's face. "I, uh . . ."

"I overlooked your little stunt last week when you watered that half-dead plant in the break room instead of letting it die its rightful death. And I still haven't forgotten the time you sang 'Happy Birthday' to Bruce in Budgeting. Off-key, I might add." Karla blew a stream of air through her pursed lips. "Effective immediately, I'm putting you on probation. If you don't work hard to improve your negative attitude by the end of the month, I'm going to have to write you up and send you to Human Resources."

Abby's eyes bulged from behind her spectacles. "Please don't do that. I'm sorry. I promise to improve. This isn't an excuse, but my boyfriend broke up with me and—"

"That dull man I met at our Scrooge Fest party in December?" Karla cackled. "This is good news. You can channel this. There's nothing like a relationship ending to heighten your pessimism. And you could use a double dose of that! You need to be doing your part to foster the hostile work environment that this company prides itself on. What do I always say?"

"It's kind to be—"

"Cruel," Karla said. "Candy-coating things only delays the ugly truth."

"I will get back on track. I promise."

"Time will tell, I suppose. That's all for now. Close the door on your way out." Karla turned to Megan. "Where were we?"

"May I ask, what happens if you get sent to Human Resources?" Megan had never heard her mother mention that department, and from the petrified look on Abby's face, there must be a good reason why.

Karla waved her hand. "Something you'll never have to worry about. Not with scores like yours and a résumé like this." She held up Megan's CV. "Which reminds me of what I was starting to say before the whole kale thing—" She jabbed a finger toward her front teeth. "I'm thrilled you aced our employment exam. I never know what to expect from a family legacy. A few years ago, there was this guy who was the nephew of someone on the board. Not a legend like your grandmother or a record holder like your mom, but still high ranking. That guy failed his test—*and* his psych eval. Last I heard, he was teaching second graders *art*." She shook her head. "Someone from Accounting has a son in his class and said he smiles *a lot*." Karla threw her hands in the air. "What kind of example does that set for the future generation of Naysayland? If it had been up to me, he would've been cast off to the Island. But according to his number on the empathy scale, he wasn't at risk to join that underground positivity movement."

Megan had heard about the people responsible for trying to push Naysayland into a more positive direction, but she'd never met anyone in the resistance—that she knew of. They kept their identities hidden, presenting themselves like regular Naysayers, but underneath their negative facades they were anything but. It was believed they met in secret and worked together to create scenarios where Naysayers could embrace empathy, but very few people had ever been caught. If discovered, they were immediately sent to the Island.

The threat of being cast off loomed in the back of every Naysayer's mind from the time they turned twelve. Twelve was the age you were first evaluated for negativity normalcy. If you scored low, meaning you showed strong signs of being prone to care, having empathy, or being positive, to name a few of the traits that would get you red-flagged, you attended certain schools that would hopefully train those characteristics out of you. But some people were simply predisposed to optimism, and at the age of eighteen, if you still tested too low on the empathy scale, off to the Island you went.

Megan had met people over the years like the nephew. They lived in limbo—not as devoid of empathy as most of the population but not positive enough to be cast off. She couldn't imagine that life, wanting to work anywhere other than Naysay Inc. The company was a beacon of their world. The backbone of their society, steeped in tradition and rules. They only took the best of the best.

And Megan wanted to be better than all of them.

"Unlike that guy I mentioned, you've clearly been bred to work here," Karla pressed on, interrupting Megan's thoughts. "I'm sure your grandmother and mother are both very proud that the day has finally come for you to follow in their footsteps."

Megan nodded, although she wasn't sure *proud* was the word she'd use. More like appeased. She'd been quizzed, prepped, and trained for years for this day. Megan was an only child. Her mom kept a picture of Megan's first ultrasound framed in her kitchen and loved to tell the story behind it. *Most babies suck their thumbs in the womb, but you were holding up your middle finger. The technician wasn't sure that's what you were doing with your hand, but I was. I knew when I got pregnant on the first try from the donor sperm you were going to be exceptional.*

Megan looked at the portrait of her grandmother, Genevieve, hanging on the wall adjacent to Karla's desk. Her snow-white hair was styled in a blunt bob, and she was clad in a dark suit with her signature diamond-encrusted black crow brooch pinned to its lapel. Genevieve's husband had died when Megan's mom was a baby, and she'd raised Jacqueline on her own while rising through the ranks at Naysay Inc. Megan had always admired her fierce independence.

Karla followed her gaze. "None of us could believe she retired. I know she's seventy-five, but I thought she'd run this place until she was lowered into the grave."

Megan remembered when her grandmother had announced to Megan and Jacqueline at their weekly dinner that she was stepping down. Megan's mother had dropped her fork and asked Genevieve what she'd do without her job. Her grandmother had laughed and said,

It's not like it was my entire life. Then she'd fixed herself a Manhattan, signaling that the conversation was over. Genevieve had worked hard in a company that was dominated by men, and she'd pushed past all of them. To Megan, she was a boss in every sense of the word and had earned the right to step down whenever she wanted.

"How is Genevieve handling all her free time?" Karla asked, spinning a gold band on her ring finger. Megan glanced around for a photo of Karla's partner, but didn't see anything personal, unless a jar labeled *Fucks to Give*, full of wooden cutouts of the word, counted. "It must be a big adjustment to go from running the company to—" Karla thought for a moment. "What do retirees do anyway? Don't tell me she's playing pickleball or crocheting." She pulled a face.

"Grandmother is good. She's not crocheting."

"Oh, thank the Lord, there's hope for us all!"

"But she has been taking pickleball lessons."

"No!"

"Yes."

Her grandmother had shared the news with Megan in confidence. *Don't tell your mother,* she'd said. *She'll—*

—try to have you committed, Megan had said, and they'd both laughed.

Karla wrinkled her nose. "Well, I suppose she's earned the right to do something as mundane as hitting a plastic ball over a net. And now we have your mom as our fearless CEO, and she's already killing it. She restructured the political department to reflect the current climate, and those normally levelheaded independent voters are really in a tizzy." She pointed to Megan's résumé. "It says here that you're interested in being a lead whisperer in the Social Media department, specializing in influencers. Why don't you want to join the Politics team and follow in the footsteps of your mom and grandmother?"

Megan didn't want to be in the ears of a bunch of out-of-touch people making policy. "I want to influence the influencers. Forget teachers, I believe it's the influencers who are shaping young minds in the Real World." She found it interesting that billions of Real Worlders presented perfect online personas that didn't match with their true selves. Megan had a hunch that the worst offenders were the people sitting under fancy ring lights, hawking products that promised unrealistic outcomes and messaging their own self-serving slanted agendas for a buck.

Karla leaned forward. "Social media is such an anxiety-inducing pit of misinformation. Thank god Real Worlders think *all* innovation is good innovation, or else we'd be out of a job." She laughed. "Now tell me more about your ideas."

Megan sat up straighter in her chair to recite the speech she'd practiced that morning after listening to a popular podcast she found motivating, *The Power of Bad Moods and 'tudes!* "While social media in the Real World does an excellent job of making people anxious and depressed—"

"Amen," Karla said, raising her hands in prayer. "The tech bros that invented those apps are genius."

"—those platforms have only skimmed the surface of their power. By combining whisperers and influencers, we could evoke real negative change. A lead whisperer talks in the ear of *one* influencer who then talks in the ears of *millions*."

"I like it. Cut out the middleman. Destroy influencers' confidence and make them feel like impostors so they can't do their jobs, and promote messaging and products that are supposed to make everyone *feel better*." Karla rolled her eyes.

"Exactly," Megan said.

"Real Worlders should ban positivity on their socials. Kick people off for promoting ridiculous ideas like *hope*!"

"And *kindness*."

"And *gratitude*. Why do they have to print positive messages on everything? Dish towels, bumper stickers—"

"Rocks." Megan laughed.

"So odd that they paint words of affirmation on stones. Don't they have anything better to do with their time?" Karla said. "But I suppose it's their bizarre yearning for inner peace that keeps this company in business. If Real Worlders were realists like us, Naysay Inc. wouldn't exist." She clapped her hands together, the sparkly diamond bracelets on her wrists jangling. "Let's talk more about why *you* want this job, aside from the obvious—that you are a third-generation legacy." She offered Megan a wry smile. "I have no doubt your mother started force-feeding this place to you in between bites of applesauce when you were a baby."

Karla was only half right. Her mother would've never fed her applesauce. There had been nannies for that.

"I want to be part of a company my mom and grandmother believe in so strongly, but I also hope to contribute to it in my own way, make my own mark."

Karla nodded, so Megan continued. "I'm sure you saw on my résumé that I was top of my class at the College of Judgment. I also want to point out that the title of my thesis, which is also in my portfolio, was 'Demoralization: How to Louden the Internal Voice That Hates You.' I have done extensive research on how slowly picking at the thread of one's insecurities can completely unravel a person. I feel my studies will lend themselves well to a job as a whisperer at Naysay Inc."

"Whisperers *are* the backbone of Naysay Inc. This company's success depends on their efficiency. There are nineteen thousand lead and temporary whisperers who work within these walls or remotely, so each one is assigned no more than five clients at a time. This way, every client receives the attention and focus required for them to exist in a perpetual state of unrest. The end goal is to make the clients so insecure that they spend money in our investors' companies, trying to *fix* themselves," Karla said, making air quotes.

"Of course—I know the client must live in a cul-de-sac of anxiety." Megan had spent years listening to her mom and grandmother trade stories about their tactics, and she understood the nuance of keeping a client in that perfect space of internal angst without rendering them useless. It was an art, really. But she'd never been told how they found their marks. She asked Karla now.

"Great question. We have advanced technology that identifies targets based on narrow criteria," Karla said. "A Real Worlder spins out for a night, then pulls it together the next day, and we've already set up shop in their head? That would be a waste of our resources. There are specific emotional goalposts Real Worlders must hit to warrant latent monitoring that may eventually lead to full-time monitoring. This is in addition to our client referral system. It's almost as hard to become a Naysay Inc. client as it is to become an employee here." Karla gave Megan a long look, which Megan took to mean she'd have to prove herself beyond her family name. She was prepared to do that. In fact, she *wanted* to do that.

Megan knew Naysay Inc. considered itself more than a company—it was an exclusive club. Her grandmother often compared it to the elitist Real World group that was able to secure a Birkin bag. And then she'd point out that many Birkin owners were also clients. *Full circle,* she'd said, laughing.

Karla flipped through Megan's portfolio. "Obviously, you were a top student. But writing a paper about demoralizing people doesn't automatically mean you'll succeed at whispering."

"I realize that. But I also have practical experience. I did an internship at a call center for selling time-shares," Megan said.

"Selling unsuspecting Naysayer vacationers property they'll never own? Say no more," Karla said, her eyes sparkling. "You must have enjoyed the manipulation."

Manipulation had nothing to do with it. It had been about the thrill of the sale, but she wasn't going to correct Karla. She nodded. "And I plan to use those skills to kill it in Social Media," Megan said, then after reading Karla's skeptical expression, decided to tone down her bravado. "If you'll let me, of course."

Karla twisted her mouth. "We usually bring on new hires in entry-level positions—as an observer or temporary whisperer—but I do like your confidence in asking to be a lead. You should know, there are employees here who've been waiting *years* for a lead whisperer spot to open up. If I give you the position over them, we'll have some very irritated colleagues on our hands. Not to mention they will assume you got the job because of who you're related to." Karla propped her chin on her elbow. "How would that make you feel? Would you care what people thought?"

Megan *would* care what her new coworkers thought because she needed to be accepted in order to succeed. But if Megan answered honestly, she ran the risk of Karla thinking she showed signs of sensitivity. Karla could write her off as Megan had her date. On the flip side, if Megan lied and said she didn't care about her colleagues' opinions, she might come across as too ruthless, someone who didn't know her place in the corporate food chain. Karla had established that she embraced a toxic workplace environment, but Megan wasn't sure she should be contributing to that too early on.

She decided to trust her gut. "I wouldn't want to take a job that belonged to someone else."

"Oh?" Karla squinted at her.

"What I mean is, I want to earn my place in this company as a lead whisperer on my own merit. If you don't immediately place me as a lead in Social Media, I will prove myself as invaluable in any position I'm assigned. I'd hope then, the job I want could be mine."

"I like you," Karla said. "And I don't say that to most people. Probably because I don't like most people." She laughed. "I can't remember the last time I said it to anyone. Maybe your mother, whom you have an uncanny resemblance to."

Megan nodded. They were often mistaken for sisters despite their large age gap, which pleased her mother, who took painstaking care to maintain her youthful look. They both had long, stick-straight auburn hair, large brown eyes, and eyebrows that naturally arched in a way that made them appear as if they were about to ask a question.

When Megan had asked her mother for any insight into Karla's personality, Jacqueline had just returned from getting her regular chemical peel, her red face shielded by the brim of her large hat. Jacqueline thought for a moment, then picked the word *severe* to describe her. *And you think* I'm *demanding,* Jacqueline had said in a rare moment of self-awareness.

Then she'd told Megan the story of a painting that hung over Karla's desk. It was from the Real World and called *The Scream*. It was stolen from the National Gallery, Oslo, in 1994, and the Real World believed they'd recovered the original, but it was a perfect replica. Naysay Inc. bought the original on the black market. Years later, after Karla was promoted to a director, she demanded it be hung in her office. The painting depicted a grimacing man, his pained expression distorted and swirling. Hues of blue, green, yellow, and red covered the canvas like an explosion, the man crying out at its center. Karla told Jacqueline it thrilled her to look at it because it perfectly encapsulated the anxiety of the human condition in the Real World.

Karla noticed Megan staring at the painting and broke into a wide smile. "My goal is for all our clients to feel like him," Karla said. "So tell me, Megan, are you ready to terrorize the psyche of every person you're assigned? To make them *scream* in emotional pain like that man?"

"Am I hired?" Megan asked, her heart starting to beat faster.

"Duh!"

"Then yes, I'm ready. And thank you."

"Congratulations. A million people would kill for the job I'm going to give you—including many of the people you're about to work with." Karla's lips twitched at the corners. "I am going to put you in Social Media as a lead focusing on influencers because I believe you have fresh ideas that stale department desperately needs." She walked around the desk and held out her hand to Megan. "Welcome aboard, pending your psych eval, of course."

Megan stood up to shake it. "I won't let you down."

"You'd better not." Karla frowned and held Megan's gaze for a beat longer than felt comfortable.

A chill inched up Megan's arm, and she rubbed it until it felt raw.

Chapter Two

Naysayland

"You'll start training first thing Monday. But first, let me give you a tour. Show you your competition," Karla said with a large grin, as if she hadn't just threatened Megan.

Megan followed Karla past Abby's desk and averted her eyes as they walked by. Megan noticed her screen saver read *Naysay Inc.: Destroying hopes and dreams one day at a time*, with a picture of a dark tornado hurtling toward a house with a white picket fence.

"Naysay Inc. takes up this entire building. As you know, your mom's now with the board members in the C-suites up on the penthouse level. The other floors are the International Division, Legal, Accounting, Marketing, Tech, and so on."

Karla scanned her ID card, and a glass door slid open to reveal a room the size of two football fields. There were rows of evenly spaced cubicles as far as Megan could see. "This is what we call the whisperers' bullpen," she said, sweeping her arm in front of her. "All the departments in the Real World's North America that are under my purview are on this level. The supervisors' offices are there." She pointed to closed-door spaces with frosted glass walls lining the perimeter of the room. "We have dozens of departments on several floors of this building. On this level is Parenting, Teens & Tweens, Marriage, Divorce, Politics, and

Creatives. But the heartbeat of this operation is that." Karla pointed to a series of giant horizontal screens on the wall, some with numbers and names scrolling continuously, others with charts and graphs. It reminded Megan of the stock exchange. "We call it the leaderboard."

Megan stared at the board and felt a fire light in her chest as she thought of her name joining the ranks.

"We have thousands of whisperers at this company, and every single whisper every person makes is vital to our success. Every. Single. One. We track your clients' vulnerability indexes in real time and rank you against your peers. One wrong word or inflection can send you plummeting below a competitor. But one perfect whisper session can drive you up the board. The higher you keep your clients' scores, the faster you'll ascend." Karla paused, staring at the board as numbers and names changed at lightning speed. "Remember this, you're only as good as your last whisper," she said and stared hard at Megan. "Every day you must bring your A-plus game to your headset to keep your clients' vulnerability scores in what we call the sweet spot, between eight and ten. We lose the client and subsequent profits if they dip below four. At the end of each quarter, one of you will achieve the coveted title and honor of top whisperer." She outstretched her arms like a Real World game show host. "Even though the numbers you see up there indicate otherwise, there is no second place, not in my eyes—or those of the C-suite."

Megan imagined her name at the top in bright-red neon. "I plan on being first."

Karla chuckled. "I like that attitude. You'll need it, considering you'll be playing catch-up. We're already into the second quarter, and you'll have to surpass coworkers who've been competing for weeks."

"Not a problem," Megan declared, imagining her mother's face when Megan came from behind to victory. "What does the winner get, other than bragging rights?"

Karla frowned. "Rubbing your superiority in your coworkers' faces would be enough of a prize, wouldn't it?" she said, then folded her arms, watching her. "Were you hoping for an edible arrangement or a gift certificate to a steak house? We don't do that here." She pursed her lips.

Megan blushed. "Of course not. I—"

"At Naysay Inc., we whisper to protect our ideologies. This is important and serious work."

Megan squared her shoulders under Karla's lingering look. "I understand," she said with a firm nod, though her stomach twisted at the weight of Karla's reprimand. She'd only been trying to align with Karla and express her desire to win. She hated being in the wrong.

"Okay, then," Karla finally said. "Let's resume our tour. That's Eddie Franco who's on with a client right now." She nodded toward a man wearing a graphic T-shirt that read *Welcome to My TED Talk*. His ink-black hair slicked away from his face with gel, and his impossibly clean canvas sneakers were up on his desk. There was a skateboard propped in the corner. "You can listen in on Eddie's whisper session. Watch his name and numbers on the leaderboard as you do."

Megan glanced at the board and found Eddie's name under Creatives, with the subhead Musicians/One-Hit Wonders. He was at number twenty-two.

Not a threat.

Eddie flashed a wide toothy smile at Megan, but his shifty eyes gave her pause. He pulled the microphone on his headset toward his thin lips. "You know what they say, you're only as good as your last success and 'Who Let the Dogs Out' was a quarter century ago, so who's a failure? Spoiler alert, it's *you, you, you, you*!" He laughed hard and his name shot up the board, landing him at number four.

Wow, Megan thought, a rush of adrenaline spiking through her. *It can change in a second.*

"Eddie's good—would be even better if he didn't have that T-shirt side hustle he doesn't think I know about," Karla said. "Social Media is right across the way." She pointed to a group of empty cubicles. "It's a shock no one in this department is ranked above eighty," she said and arched an eyebrow. "I'm counting on *you* to change that. Joan, your supervisor, is totally checked out, but HR has my hands tied because apparently I can't fire postpartum mothers." She shook her head. "She's probably hiding in a bathroom stall as we speak, ogling her sick newborn on that app on her phone."

"They *all* took a lunch break," a woman with short, spiky gray hair and close-set eyes said with disdain. "Eat a sandwich at your desk. It's not that hard to whisper and chew at the same time," she said, taking a huge bite out of a sub, pieces of shredded lettuce falling down her shirt.

"Megan, this is Belinda. She's also in Creatives, in charge of actors. And would rather eavesdrop than whisper," Karla said. "Explains why Ben beat her out again to win the Top Whisperer Award for the sixth year in a row, even though her clients were all part of a SAG-AFTRA strike that lasted *forever*."

Megan gazed up at the board. Belinda Johnson was ranked second. Ben Shaw was first. Megan nodded at Belinda and said hello. She scowled in return, exposing a smudge of mayonnaise on her cheek.

Megan turned and spotted Ben Shaw's desk angled just across from Belinda's. A clump of black Mylar balloons was tied to the side of the cubicle wall alongside a banner with the number twenty-four on it.

Karla caught her staring. "That's the number of quarters he's topped the leaderboard."

"What's his specialty?" Megan asked, scrutinizing the board again. Even though Belinda was in second place, there was a large gap between her and Ben. "He works with a group of creatives with built-in self-doubt, who are constantly rejected, feel lonely, and can't quit their day jobs because their craft pays next to nothing . . . *authors*!" She laughed. "It's pathetic. Who would willingly choose that career?"

Megan's brows pinched together. Writing about people's thoughts and feelings sounded like torture.

"With Ben at the helm, authors have become this company's cash cow. If the publishing industry isn't crushing them, there's always something else that will. Our latest best friend? AI. Since artificial intelligence started using copyrighted books to teach itself how to write,

Ben has crushed his sales targets and KPIs and doubled revenue last quarter. It's a twofer. Authors are angry if their books were used and feel irrelevant if they weren't!"

Megan saw an instant connection between authors and influencers. Both groups were deeply vulnerable because they were in positions where they could be publicly scrutinized. They both desperately craved positive feedback and support (followers and likes for influencers; readers and five-star reviews for authors), and when they didn't get that, when they were rejected, it made them question their worth. Bottom line? If Ben was doubling revenue, Megan would triple it.

"I didn't catch what position you were hired for?" Belinda said, her mouth full of deli meat.

Megan looked away, happy she'd skipped breakfast that morning. "I'll be a lead whisperer in Social Media, focusing on influencers."

"A lead? I didn't think a new hire was allowed to start *there*." Belinda gave Megan a once-over. "What did you say your name was?"

"Megan Lowell," she said, straightening her back.

"Lowell? As in—"

"Yes, Belinda, as in Genevieve and Jacqueline," Karla interjected. "Anyway, I would worry less about Megan's family and more about your performance this quarter and your nasty habit of talking with your mouth full. Aren't there rumblings of a Teamsters' strike? Shouldn't *you* be *striking* while the iron's hot?" Karla laughed at her pun.

Belinda glared at Megan, then swiveled her chair to face the other direction, her shoulder practically dipping under the weight of the obvious chip on it.

A tall broad-shouldered man with thick blond hair and brown eyes approached, and Megan caught a woman in a nearby cubicle with a placard that read **INTERNS**, craning her neck to get a better look. He grinned like he was used to being admired.

This must be Ben.

He held Megan's gaze as he dropped his messenger bag next to his chair. "I couldn't agree more, Karla. None of us should waste our time worrying about someone's last name. It doesn't mean anything. The person attached to it must deliver," he said, and Karla nodded once, briskly. "The leaderboard never lies." His eyes flicked to his name, then back. He held out a hand to Megan. "I'm Ben Shaw. No relation to anyone important in this company. Started at the ground floor and worked my way up *on my own*. Currently occupying the number one spot. Welcome."

"Well, after a speech like that, how could I feel anything but?" Megan said, squeezing his hand with as much force as she could.

He winced slightly, and she gave him a forced smile.

"I aim to please," Ben said. "I had a meeting with your mom yesterday, but she didn't mention a thing about you interviewing here."

Megan's interview was all her mom had talked about for months—at least to Megan. So why hadn't she brought it up with Ben? Had she worried Megan wouldn't get the job? Megan shook the thought away. "You know Jacqueline. She keeps important information close to the vest. Uses the element of surprise in her favor." Megan tilted her head toward the banner hanging on his cubicle wall. "Twenty-four quarters in a row, I hear."

"Yep. And planning to make it twenty-five." Ben cracked his knuckles.

"Interesting," Megan said.

"What's interesting?" Ben said.

"That you think you'll stay on top of the leaderboard," Megan said as a woman breezed by and almost slammed into a filing cabinet—too busy staring at Ben to watch where she was going. Megan had to admit he was handsome, but had any of these women actually spoken to him? His overblown self-importance would turn them off in seconds.

Ben lifted an eyebrow. "Why wouldn't I win again?" he asked, but there was a flicker in his eyes—something that she hoped was worry.

"I'm here now," Megan said.

Karla clapped slowly, eyebrows raised. "What a shock—two overachievers locked in an ego tug-of-war. Let's just hope your little standoff makes this company some money," she said as her phone buzzed. She read the screen and rolled her eyes. "I'll be back in a minute—Yolanda in Union Strikes can't convince her client to cross the picket line. I mean, it's scabbing 101," she huffed as she walked off.

Ben leaned in a little toward Megan. "Those were some pretty big words from someone who hasn't had her psych eval yet. You never know what Dr. Peakstone might uncover—maybe the results will prove that even with your DNA you're not cut out to be here."

"I'm not worried. Not only am I cut out to be here, I plan to be the best."

"That sounds like a challenge," Ben said, his eyes twinkling.

"It can be whatever you want it to be, Mr. Shaw—I love to come from behind," she said, tracking Ben's smug grin and realizing how that sounded. "I mean, I plan on overtaking you. *On the leaderboard*," she stammered, heat spreading to her cheeks.

He stifled a grin with a tight press of his lips. "I can't wait. And *please*, call me Ben," he said and grabbed the black balloons, took a thumbtack off his board, and began to pop them, one by one.

Megan felt a flutter in her chest as the Mylar fell to the floor. Ben played it cool, but she could tell she'd struck a nerve. She was clearly the reason he was popping those balloons. He acted like she didn't faze him, oozing confidence, but she wouldn't stop until she uncovered what was hiding beneath that cocky grin. Ben would learn soon enough: There was nothing Megan loved more than a challenge.

Dr. Peakstone

Psych Eval with Megan Lowell

April 25th

Dr. Peakstone: Now that we've finished your diagnostic questions, I'd like to explore your relationship with your mother. Why does that make you laugh?

Megan: Because it will take about two minutes to explore.

Peakstone: Why do you say that?

Megan: Because our *relationship* is mostly transactional.

Peakstone: How so?

Megan: She has high expectations. I meet them.

Peakstone: Did you want to work here?

Megan: Does it matter?

Peakstone: It does. Maybe how you feel isn't about her.

Megan: Then what's it about?

Peakstone: *You.*

Chapter Three

Naysayland

Megan's phone dinged with a text from her mom in the Lowell Ladies group thread.

Good morning.

Another ding.

Did we decide on a time for dinner this Thursday?

And another.

I have a meeting and won't be available until 7pm. Please respond whether or not this is acceptable.

Megan glanced at the clock. Five thirty a.m.
Another text. This one from her grandmother.

Have a great first day, Megan.

She added a series of thumbs-up emojis after it, ignoring Jacqueline's request.

Megan smiled at that. She liked both of their comments, poured coffee into her travel mug, and secured the lid.

She darkened her screen, a fluttery feeling in her stomach as she thought about her first day of work. She stared out the window of her apartment into the dark-gray sky. She'd chosen this building, exactly five blocks from Naysay Inc. because she didn't want to waste precious time on a commute. She'd done some test walks and calculated it would take her exactly eight minutes. She'd worn both two-inch round toe heels and pointed flats, happy to discover the times were nearly identical. There were a lot of people who made their treks to the office in tennis shoes, then switched to something more professional, but for her, those types of shoes were for only one thing—running, which she did five to six days a week.

She slid on her slingbacks, grabbed her tote bag, and glanced at her apartment, still satisfied she'd chosen the Plan A model. There were three designs with exactly the same paint color on the walls and cupboards (disagreeable gray), identical flooring (slate-gray tile), and matching countertops (black quartz), the only difference between them the number of rooms and bathrooms. The *A*'s were all one bedroom and one bath, perfect for people like Megan with no desire to add a live-in partner or a child into the mix.

She entered the crowded elevator, her neighbors—many of whom she'd never met—avoiding eye contact. Megan had seen all types of people in the building. Nurses in scrubs, women in sharp suits or sweat suits making business deals on their phones, and retirees with tennis rackets strapped to their backs. But they all seemed to have one thing in common. Borrowing a cup of sugar, suggesting a game of Jenga, or making small talk about the perpetual gray weather wasn't on anyone's agenda.

Megan was one hundred percent fine with that.

Outside, the downtown community was bustling despite the early hour. Cars whizzed by, a city bus stopped to pick up a group of people, and horns were blaring. Megan's mom had shared that one thing Naysayers and Real Worlders had in common was they both used their horns to show frustration, anger, or rage when driving. Megan had always been intrigued by Real Worlders and loved those tidbits that her mom would treat her to on occasion, like a glass of port after dinner.

She'd studied the Real World in school and knew the basics—that it was an alternate world to theirs, also comprised of continents, countries, and cities, but different in that it was much larger and had existed for far longer. What interested her most, though, were the people: something a common Naysayer didn't have access to. Only Naysay Inc. employees were given that clearance. Megan once asked her mom to tell her about the Real Worlders in North America who were most like Naysayers. Where in their world did they live? Her mom had said they existed everywhere, but the highest concentrations were in parts of California, New Jersey, New York, and almost the entire state of Florida. Then her mom offered what she always did when Megan peppered her with questions. *You'll find out more when you work there one day.*

When not *if.*

Today was that day.

Megan stood on the corner and felt someone jostle her from behind. She whipped her head around, and a woman was standing so close that Megan could see the pink chewing gum inside her mouth. The woman rolled her eyes at Megan and refused to back off her close stance, then bolted from the curb when the light turned green, nearly knocking Megan over. Megan held her tongue—she'd save that part of herself for the job.

Megan looked up and inhaled as she took in the soaring skyscraper where Naysay Inc. was housed, a beacon for what Naysayers stood for. The people here had survived centuries by understanding optimism was merely the process of putting off the truth. And the truth found you anyway. Because of that, a true Naysayer lacked insecurity and empathy. They ascertained that facts were facts, no matter how you felt about them. Naysayers were taught to understand positivity was futile, so why bother with it? And if you were selected to work within the walls of Naysay Inc., you would be given the important task of leading Real Worlders, whisper by whisper, to who they were truly meant to be. *More like Naysayers.*

Megan pushed through the revolving door and exhaled. Her first day walking into the building as an official employee! When she'd texted her grandmother and mother on their Lowell Ladies group chat that she'd been hired and passed her psych eval, her grandmother, a big fan of exclamation points, responded with, Congrats! Welcome to the club! And her mom, not emotive in person or in writing, had sent a thumbs-up emoji. Megan considered that a win.

A security guard nodded at her sleepily from behind his desk. She showed him her driver's license and passed through the turnstile; the sound of her heels echoed in the lobby as she crossed the marble floor. It was just shy of six thirty a.m., and Megan wanted to be the first to walk into the bullpen, her motion turning on the overhead fluorescent lights. Her training started at eight, and she planned to use the time before strategically.

The first item on Megan's mental checklist was to walk the floor and take inventory of her coworkers' spaces. Who had personal photos hanging from their cubicle walls? *They'd present zero threat as they clearly let their minds wander to life outside the company.*

Whose trash was filled with candy and soda cans? *Always a sign of weakness if one needed sugar to get through the workday.*

She'd pay attention to which employees arrived first, who rolled in late. She'd keep her eyes trained on the break room to see who lingered and gossiped and who filled their coffee or water bottles without discussion and beelined back to their desk.

Megan pressed the button for the twenty-fourth floor and stared at the dark slate-tiled walls, startling when a hand with blood-colored fingernails reached between the closing doors.

Megan knew those nails.

"Hello," her mother said as she stepped inside. "Was hoping I'd catch you."

Megan bit down on her smile. This was why her mom hadn't texted her good luck this morning like her grandmother had. She'd wanted to do it in person. Maybe working at the same company would help improve their relationship. They could trade stories about clients, bounce whispering strategies off each other. Now they would be colleagues.

"I'm concerned about this whole influencer thing. Social Media is not the straightest path to leadership development," Jacqueline said while scrolling emails on her phone. "Most of Naysay Inc.'s leadership team matriculate from more established departments like Politics."

Megan deflated slightly at her mom's words, but pressed on before letting them sink all the way in. "We spoke about this, Mom—"

Jacqueline arched an eyebrow.

"I mean, Jacqueline," Megan said. "Sorry. I know you don't want me using the M-word here."

Jacqueline pulled a face. "It's just so . . . *familiar*."

Megan brushed past the comment. "I think social media is the new politics."

"How very Gen Z of you." They arrived on the twenty-fourth floor. "This is you."

Megan started to walk out, then turned. "Want to grab a drink after work? Toast to my new job?"

She shook her head. "When you start whispering, maybe then we'll talk," she said, pressing the button to hold the elevator doors open and giving Megan a once-over. "Aren't you nervous? Because you don't look it. Getting the job was the easy part. Doing it will be harder than you could *ever* imagine. At the end of a day where you've worked hard, you shouldn't have the energy to *grab a drink*. You need to remember it's your fear that will fuel you. You need to be scared to fail so you can succeed."

She released her finger, and the doors slid shut. Megan took a deep breath. She should've known better. Her mom did not believe accomplishments should be enjoyed. When Megan had brought home her first report card with straight A's, she was scolded for not only being proud of herself but wanting her mom to be. It was an early lesson that she should keep the joy of her wins to herself.

Megan shook away the memory and walked into the bullpen. The ceiling lights were already activated. She was surprised to hear a man's voice.

"Why are you bothering to write today, Jasper? You know what's going to happen. You'll sit in front of your laptop and type a slew of pathetic words that you'll end up deleting because they'll suck."

Megan hung back behind the copy machines and listened. She couldn't see the man talking, but at his feet was a trash can filled with deflated black Mylar balloons.

It was Ben.

Of course it was.

"Your editor is going to hate the direction you're taking the plot because it's boring and cliché, like you. You couldn't think of anything better than a magical realism rip-off? And your characters are one dimensional. The frozen dinner you ate for dinner last night had a better backstory. How did you get a second book deal?" Ben said. "Why don't you forget writing today and make an extra-long appointment with your psychologist instead? He always knows what to say."

Ben took off his headset and stood up and stretched. He laughed and made a check mark on a chart hanging from a corkboard in his cubicle. Next to it was a picture of a man with thick hair the color of molasses, deep-set green eyes, and a five o'clock shadow. **Jasper Cross, age 30, Author** was printed on an index card under the photo.

Old school, Megan thought. With the advanced technology at Naysay Inc., she was surprised Ben's notes weren't digitized, but happy because it gave her a window into his process.

He grabbed a duffel bag off the floor and turned, his eyebrows rising in surprise when he saw her. "Not even six thirty. Thought you'd roll up at 7:59 a.m. for your eight a.m. training class. Being a nepo baby and all."

"I'm full of surprises, just wait."

Ben rolled his eyes. "I'll be on pins and needles with anticipation."

Megan looked him up and down. Ben was wearing athletic shorts, a T-shirt he'd cut the sleeves off that accented his sculpted upper arms, and the running shoes she'd been on a waiting list for, trying to buy them for months. They were the Riptides. White with neon-blue accents, aerodynamic with a contoured sole like a wave about to break. The exact color and design she wanted. She sighed. Of course he had them. "Did I miss the memo? Is it casual Monday?"

"We can't all look like we're attending a funeral. So cute that you dress up like your mommy. Do you two share clothes?"

She was wearing an all-black outfit like she always did, something she *had* emulated from watching her mom. Warmer months equaled a skirt and a lightweight top. In cooler months she opted for pants and a jacket.

Ben caught her looking at his bag. "If you really must know, I'm headed to the thirty-third floor for a run before I tackle the second half of my day."

"Second half? What time do you get here?" Megan asked.

"Early o'clock," Ben said and slung his duffel over his shoulder, causing his biceps to flex.

He caught her staring, and she quickly looked away.

"Probably about the time you're getting into your REM, dreaming of . . ." he paused. "What do you dream of, Ms. Lowell?"

"I don't," Megan blurted out.

Ben pressed his lips together. "Really?"

"I'd think Mr. Leaderboard would understand wanting to control your own mind."

"So that's what it is. You don't *let* yourself dream? Ever thought about why? What makes you so tightly wound?" he asked. "You don't have to share that with me—Dr. Peakstone will get it out of you in your mandatory sessions. She has a way of doing that."

"I thought we only met with her for the psych eval. I have to keep seeing her?"

Ben nodded. "Is that going to be a problem? Because you could quit now and avoid it entirely."

Megan shook her head to hide her alarm. She'd never so much as kept a diary.

"Let me guess, Karla didn't mention the mandatory therapy when she said a million people would kill for the job that she'd just given you," he said, a smirk twitching on his lips. "Rumor has it that a few years ago, a top performer had a psychotic break after years of whispering. He sued the company for mental distress. After that, they hired Dr. Peakstone as an insurance policy to cover their asses so no one else would crack." He rolled his eyes. "Like whispering could ever make me crazy. I love it too much! Anyway, I should go if I want to get in five miles, shower, and be back terrorizing my clients in under forty-five minutes." He smiled so wide his eyes nearly disappeared into the crinkles around them.

Megan exhaled, happy he'd changed the subject so she didn't have to think about the guy who'd lost his mind. "You run what, a seven-minute mile?"

"Six to six and a half, depending on how I'm feeling. Whether I got three or four hours of sleep. I saw you eyeing my Riptides." He pointed to his feet. "I spent three months researching the best shoes out there before deciding to switch."

"That's a long time."

"Not for me. It was faster than I would've liked, but you've only got about six months of life in the average pair."

Megan nodded knowingly.

"I take it you're a runner too."

"I am."

"Let me know if you ever want to run together—I could slow my pace for you. And if you're lucky, I'll make a call about the shoes. They're hard to get, but I know a guy."

"I'm more of a solo runner. And those shoes aren't really my style, sorry," she said, refusing to give him the satisfaction. She nodded at the picture of Jasper, the author, tacked to Ben's corkboard. "I couldn't help but overhear you whispering to him. What's his story?"

"I think you meant to say you were eavesdropping. I don't blame you. I *am* the best. If you wanted some pointers, all you had to do was ask."

Megan rolled her eyes.

"Anyway, I'm feeling generous, so I'll share. Jasper is one of my most important clients—that's why I hit him up so early."

"Why is he so important?"

"He's new so he needs a lot of my attention. I just got him a few days ago. His AMOV—"

"AMOV?"

"Acute Moment of Vulnerability. In simple terms, it's a client's emotional rock bottom. It's also the point when we strike. Well, technically, it's the observer who homes in first. Then the case gets passed to a temporary whisperer, which I've opted not to have because I'm notoriously *not* a team player, then assigned to a lead whisperer, depending on their profile. You have *a lot* to learn." Ben sucked his teeth.

"I'm a fast learner," Megan assured him.

"You'd better be. The training is intense, and the test you take at the end makes the employment exam look like a cakewalk," Ben said.

Megan tried to swallow her laugh.

"What?"

"Not that it's any of your business, but the employment exam *was* a cakewalk for me."

"You had some of the highest numbers Karla has ever seen?" Ben said, clicking his tongue.

The highest, Megan wanted to say but held back. She didn't need to show him all her cards at once. "You were talking about your client's AMOV?"

"His was every author's worst nightmare. Only two people showed up for his book signing, one of them unhoused and looking for a bathroom."

"Unhoused?"

"It's the new term Real Worlders use for the homeless. You'll learn all about it in training. The point is, his book event was a disaster. Like this was rock bottom." Ben touched the underside of his shoe, giving Megan a closer look at the design—it had a spongy thick sole that she'd read felt like a pillowy shock absorber. "And here was Jasper." He pointed to the floor. "His vulnerability index hit the maximum—a ten! That doesn't happen often, so naturally they assigned him to me since I'm—"

"The best. I know."

"You *are* a quick learner."

Megan wanted less of Ben's ego and more of Ben's knowledge. "Wouldn't someone with such an intense AMOV not need as much attention because their vulnerability index is so high?"

"The opposite. That's when we come in hot on them."

"Then why did you tell him to go to therapy? Won't that make him feel better?"

"Nope. His so-called *therapist*?" Ben laughed. "That guy pays into something you'll learn about called the Fund. He's with us."

"Really?"

Ben nodded. "It's genius. Jasper's therapist will give him terrible advice, and then I'll swoop in and reinforce it."

"What if the client doesn't have money to spend on something like therapy?"

"If you're good at your job, that won't matter. You get them to indulge in activities that give small bursts of pleasure but create more anxiety in the long run, like retail therapy or gambling. Anything that could lead the client to borrow money from family—one of my personal favorites because that *never* ends well. Or, if you have an excellent researcher like I do—Carlos is one of *the best* in the building—they will help you find other areas of vulnerability to expose. In less than twenty-four hours, he uncovered that Jasper has secret wealth—some aunt who died and left him a windfall he doesn't want anyone to know about because he feels guilty for not making it himself. An author with average book sales who's secretly rich from nothing *he* did? That's the gift that keeps on giving." He grinned.

"Huh," Megan said, careful not to show how excited she was by the information Ben had shared. She couldn't wait to be assigned her first clients and find their emotional land mines. And if she could be the one to wipe that smug grin off Ben's face? Even better.

"Well, I guess I'll leave you to it so you can figure out why Belinda has all that origami in her cubicle."

Megan's expression faltered for a heartbeat before she caught herself.

"You're doing recon, right? That's why you're here an hour and a half before training starts—to size up the other lead whisperers." He clicked his tongue. "Like *me*?"

"Don't flatter yourself," Megan said quickly.

He headed toward the door, then turned and looked at her. "You'd better hurry up and get your spying done. The cleaning crew will be here in five."

Megan's eyes sparkled as she watched him walk away. She thought of the one Real World proverb her mom always said was worth remembering: *Keep your friends close and your enemies closer.* Ben would never be Megan's pal—but he didn't need to know that. She'd play nice, all while making sure not to give him anything he could use against her again. He clearly knew a lot about Naysay Inc. She'd extract every bit of intel from him before they went to war.

◆ ◆ ◆

Megan was the first to arrive at the training classroom. She took a seat in the front row and lined her highlighters, pens, pencils, and notebooks in a neat formation on her desk. A man arrived next, so tall he had to duck under the doorframe when he entered, with arms the size of Megan's thighs and caramel eyes. He gave Megan a crisp nod and began setting up.

At eight o'clock, all the seats were filled. The man at the front of the room clapped his giant hands. "Okay, people, listen up. My name is Bernard Allen, and I'll be running this training course. I've been at Naysay Inc. for over twenty-five years. I spent the majority of my time in Politics, which I'm sure you all know is one of, if not *the*, most coveted department here." He flashed them a prideful grin, and Megan thought she felt his eyes on her for a beat longer than everyone else. "Let's just say I still get asked if I had anything to do with those hanging chads."

"I heard he had Clinton's ear for years," a man sitting behind Megan muttered.

"Which one?" a woman asked.

"Which one do you think?" the man said.

"Shhhh!" came from the back.

"So, buckle up. Things are about to get intense. Long hours, a ton of information, and a test at the end that will be difficult. We require you to score in the ninetieth percentile to become an official employee here. No exceptions." Bernard took a drink of his coffee. "On that note, congratulations on passing your psychiatric evaluations with Dr. Peakstone—we lost two hires who did not."

Megan thought back to her session with Dr. Peakstone. Her dark-blond hair falling to her shoulders in tight curls accentuating her large gray-blue eyes that bore into Megan like she was looking for something. She'd asked Megan if she'd ever seen a therapist before (no!), been diagnosed with a psychological disorder (no!), or if she had any stressors in her life (not unless living up to a two-generation legacy counted). She'd also given Megan an inkblot test where she showed her different images and asked her to describe what she saw. Whether Megan said a butterfly (but was it a moth?) or human skeleton (although it could've been a fire-breathing dragon?), Dr. Peakstone simply said *hmm*. It was the most unusual test she'd ever taken. By the time the psychologist started asking about her mother, Megan was no longer sure what was even being evaluated. She had no idea what she'd said or done that had made her pass.

"Let's go around and introduce ourselves," Bernard said. "Tell us one fact about you. And please, try to make it interesting. No one cares what your favorite book is. I'll start. I met my wife in the lobby of this building."

"I thought we couldn't date coworkers," a man said.

"We can't. She was interviewing for a job and walked into this tower by mistake. We've been together ever since."

A petite woman with a short black layered haircut and an angular jaw stood up next. Three energy drinks were lined up on her desk. "I'm Beth Cohen, and I'll be a temporary whisperer in Social Media," she said, rolling a pen between her palms. "An interesting fact about me is that I requested to be a temporary whisperer on the night shift because I don't think socializing with coworkers is necessary. I for sure don't care what anyone's favorite book is. In fact, if you have time to read, something is wrong in your life."

Megan would never talk like that to a room full of strangers, especially coworkers. But she also found it bold and respected Beth's unfiltered truth.

Tom Hayes, a man with a trimmed beard and plump ruddy cheeks from Marriage with an emphasis in Couples Who Married Too Young, bred rattlesnakes and had *only* been bitten three times.

Anita Keller, a tall woman with bright-red hair tied into a braid that hung over her left shoulder from the Boomer department, carved faces in pistachios for fun. She pulled one from her purse along with a picture of a grumpy cat.

"What an offbeat hobby. But the likeness *is* uncanny," Bernard said.

Jacob Ford, a man in his thirties with blindingly white teeth, explained he was hired to be a temporary whisperer in the Internet Trolls department. "I'll be specializing in those keyboard warriors doing the important work of goading Real Worlders online over mundane issues. I can't wait to inspire my first client to start a comment war over whether pineapple belongs on pizza!" he said, grinning so wide Megan saw both rows of his teeth.

"And your interesting fact?" Bernard asked.

"I'm into the sport of extreme ironing."

"That's a sport?" Beth said and snorted, then looked at Megan. "See why I don't socialize?"

Megan bit her lip to stifle a laugh.

"Last week I ironed a dress shirt while skydiving," he added, and Bernard gave him a quizzical look.

A man Megan guessed to be in his mid-forties stood up next. His head was large and square, reminding her of the LEGO toys they had in the Real World. He'd combed his thin brown hair over an obvious bald spot and wore a shirt that was at least a size too small, the buttons straining over his stomach.

"I'm Jim Smith. I'll be a temporary whisperer in Marriage, specializing in second marriages or round twos, as I call them. A fun fact about me? I've been married and divorced twice and stick my foot in my mouth a lot. I don't have a filter," he said with a nervous chuckle. "I'll probably offend each of you at some point."

"Like when you asked me earlier if I always have resting bitch face or if it was only today?" Beth said with a smirk. She cracked open an energy drink and took a huge gulp. "I guess you'll have to wait and find out."

Bernard nodded at Megan. She stood and straightened her shoulders. She loved to cook. Lately her passion had been reimagining cauliflower into things like steaks and pizza crusts, but sharing that might leave her open to criticism from people like Beth. "I'm Megan Lowell. I'll be a lead whisperer in Social Media," she said and noticed

Jim and Anita share a glance. "An interesting fact about me is that I've won several competitive memory tournaments. Most recently, I committed to memory every scientific element and isotope. And now that I have access to the Real World database, I plan on memorizing all historical events in the twentieth century."

"Surprised you didn't mention the most interesting fact of all—that your mom runs the company," Tom said under his breath.

Megan ignored the comment and the look he shared with the extreme ironer.

"Speaking of—" Bernard shot Megan a look. She couldn't read it, a cross between support and pity. "Let's hear a few words from our fearless leader."

Bernard tapped his tablet and a video on a display in the front of the room began to play. The screen was dark. In white lettering, the title faded in: *Saving the Real World from Itself One Whisper at a Time.*

Jacqueline appeared on the screen. She stood in front of a large window, the city's skyline behind her. Her chestnut hair was pulled into a tight knot at the base of her neck, and she wore a black pantsuit with a black silk blouse underneath.

I'm Jacqueline Lowell, CEO of Naysay Inc. Welcome to your first day. Or as I like to say, the first day of the rest of your life.

The class tittered.

I can still recall my first day, sitting right where you are. Hanging on my trainer's every word as he explained Naysay Inc.'s mission statement: to bring negativity to and expose the vulnerabilities of every Real Worlder through carefully calculated whispers. She smiled. *Naysay Inc.'s founder, my great-great-great-grandfather Herbert Lowell III, was a genius. You'll learn more about him, but he graduated with a PhD in neurobiology from Naysay University, which I don't have to tell you is Naysayland's most prestigious school. While working for our government, he and a team of our world's top scientists conducted groundbreaking research that showed Real Worlders' minds were wired opposite to ours. Theirs were built to not only receive negative external thoughts, but to defy common sense to believe them. It was in their DNA to question themselves. They were their own worst enemies and harshest critics. They were already putting themselves down, but my great-great-great-grandfather realized Naysayers could do it better—especially if Real Worlders believed our words were theirs. And because our world's technology was a century ahead of the Real World, it could easily be done. That's when his idea for Naysay Inc. was born.*

But honestly, the science and the history and the technology, while impressive, isn't what excited me the most. It was his business vision. He envisioned a way to monetize vulnerability.

At the turn of the twentieth century, my great-great-great-grandfather was far ahead of his time when he realized money could be made from pinpointing and exposing Real Worlders' raw spots. Back then, it was identifying and working with the companies that made items like corsets for women, which shaped bodies and identities, *or razors and watches for men, which were symbolism for self-respect. The Real World has evolved from corsets and pocket watches to plastic surgery and luxury cars, but the concept remains the same—targeting and monetizing insecurities. I can't wait for you to learn all about the Fund, which is the foundation of Naysay Inc. Those fools who invented social media companies think they were the first to go after this market, but they weren't even blips on the universe's radar when we had already perfected influencing humanity to hate themselves and others.*

The bottom line is this: For over a century, we have succeeded in keeping Real Worlders from becoming wholly happy, which would inevitably lead to chaos. Negativity and skepticism breed critical thinking and competitiveness, which pushes innovation. Without us, they'd still be using rotary phones and acting like Islanders.

We also pride ourselves on shaping pop culture, which you'll discover is equally as vital. I'll never forget when I helped break up the Spice Girls. You're welcome, Real World!

Jacqueline smiled into the camera and winked. Megan had never seen her wink before. Or smile like that, her cheeks rising fully on both sides.

More recently, the rise of COVID-19 and the ensuing quarantine was incredibly helpful to our mission. Profits have increased twenty-five percent since March 2020. It truly was a perfect storm. Working from home! Conspiracy theories! Antibacterial wipes and toilet paper shortages, social distancing, and sourdough starters!

I want you to be thinking, what's the next big thing? The next COVID? And will you be able to recognize its value and capitalize on it? Because that's how we win—understanding the worth of potentially unsettling situations and leaning in. The USC admissions scandal would've been nothing more than a footnote in history if we hadn't immediately been in the ears of the right people. But maybe our proudest achievement was getting that eighties star cut from her sitcom reboot.

Jacqueline circled her large desk and sat in her chair.

If you can't identify and capitalize on these situations, you'll be dismissed. There is no room for mediocrity at Naysay Inc.—you'll be expected to be excellent, every single day.

The screen went dark. Megan glanced at the faces of her classmates. They all looked petrified. Exactly what her mom wanted.

Bernard swiped his tablet. "I want to elaborate on the Fund that Jacqueline mentioned. We partner with companies across many influential industries in the Real World, including political PACs, social media, self-help, and the beauty-minded sectors, but our company's true purpose is a closely guarded secret. They believe we are a high-level marketing consulting company—we bill ourselves as lobbyists for their products and services. We give them a vague plan peppered with whatever corporate buzzwords are popular at that moment." Bernard paused, thinking. "We uncover the *pain points* that are causing *tailwinds* and make sure that they don't *overindex* on anything." Bernard laughed and shook his head. "Those Real Worlders love a good buzzword. But they love our results even more."

Bernard pulled up a slide and used a laser pointer to highlight a bar graph. "The businesses who have paid into the Fund have increased their profits by an average of thirty percent. There's a referral system in place. We only take a new company if it is recommended by one we have already worked with. Obviously, the need for discretion is pivotal.

"In short, the Fund depends on Naysay Inc. and Naysay Inc. depends on the Fund. There is no room for either to fail." Bernard tossed his empty coffee cup toward the wastebasket in the far corner of the room, and it sailed right in. "All net," he said under his breath, then faced the class. "Who's ready to change people's lives?"

Megan raised her arm, her muscles straining. She visualized herself standing in a corner office on the penthouse floor one day, giving a speech to a group of incoming whisperers.

It was finally time to fulfill her legacy. There was no room to fail.

Chapter Four

Naysayland

Megan didn't understand why someone would willingly be cast on a reality TV show, but she loved watching them. Bernard had explained that for research purposes, Naysay Inc. had access to all entertainment mediums in the Real World. He said they were starting with reality shows and docuseries because they were the best window into the psyches of the most unstable and drama-inciting Real Worlders. They'd studied housewives getting drunk, people in pods who got engaged without seeing the other's face, and egotistical maniacs competing to sell mansions. Megan was riveted by what the participants allowed the camera to capture—major make out sessions, getting out of the shower, and various stages of undress. Bernard had made it clear that the Naysay Inc. feed would cut whenever the drones detected those same scenarios with their clients and would not reengage until it was over. Odd that Naysay Inc. had higher privacy standards than the Real Worlders had for themselves.

The reality show *Love Is Blind* had intrigued Megan the most. It was fascinating that a person could agree to marry someone they'd only talked to through a wall while imbibing whatever was in those golden goblets! Bernard had paused one of the episodes right when a couple was seeing each other for the first time, crying with relief that they found the other attractive. "*That* cannot happen with our clients. That attraction. Those googly eyes. Those *emotionally driven* decisions. It makes it incredibly difficult for us to infiltrate their thoughts. At Naysay Inc., love is our kryptonite."

Megan had written *Falling in love is bad* in red ink and underlined it three times.

She couldn't agree more. Professionally or personally.

Then they'd moved on to music, podcasts, late-night talk shows, and news programs. After they'd viewed a certain presidential debate, Jim had clapped, calling it his favorite reality show.

"It wasn't, but you're making my point—even many of the politicians in the Real World's North America are characters who deliberately incite drama." Bernard chuckled. "Okay, it's time for whisperer slash client role-play. Who's ready to put everything they've learned from Real World f-boys and presidential candidates to the test?"

Megan and the extreme ironer raised their hands, but Bernard nodded at her. She arched a victorious eyebrow his way, and he scowled back.

Beth made an ironing motion at him and muttered, "Burn, baby, burn."

"Before we start"—Bernard grabbed his tablet—"because of the popularity of cancel culture in the Real World—"

"Moment of silence for all the Karens!" someone called out.

Bernard cleared his throat. "Because of the Karens and many others, Real Worlders are now highly sensitive to verbiage. We must convince them *our* voices are *theirs*, so it's imperative to use *their* vernacular." He pressed his lips into a slash and started typing, his words appearing on the screen in the front of the room.

Horizontally challenged will replace *overweight*, which used to be *fat*.

Beauty deprived will be used instead of *unattractive*, which was formerly known as *ugly*.

Intellect deficient instead of *dumb*, which was once *stupid*.

"Oh, come on," someone said.

"I don't make the rules," Bernard said.

"What about *unhoused* instead of *homeless*?" Megan asked.

"Yeah, that too. The complete list of terms will be in the 'Quick Guide to Woke Words' glossary on your tablets," Bernard said.

"Also very important, whispering about a client's gender, race, sexual orientation, or political affiliation is strictly prohibited—Naysay Inc. has its standards. And remember, although the original whisperers did literally whisper, we now speak softly but firmly. If needed, we have voice technology that perfects the tone or accent we place in our clients' ears.

"Okay, you're up, Ms. Lowell." Bernard hunched over his tablet and pulled up the profile of a subject.

Megan stared at the image of a woman named Rachel Williams. She had deep purple rings under her eyes, and her hair was greasy and tousled. Megan scanned her details.

> Forty-three years old, married for ten years, three kids under the age of eleven, husband traveled often for his job. Rachel worked full-time as a patent attorney. She'd recently hired a nanny to help with the drop-off and pickup schedules at the three different schools her kids attended.

Rachel's AMOV occurred after two women in the Second Grade Mamas group chat passive-aggressively shamed her for hiring help. Rachel's observer alerted the temporary whisperer after Rachel drank a bottle of sauvignon blanc and accidentally texted the following to Second Grade Mamas instead of Ride or Dies, the thread with her three best friends from college:

> Must be nice for Parker's Mama to have all that time to drop off her kid AND get her face pumped with filler every five minutes!

Willow and Jude's mom only drops off her kids so she can flirt with Principal Adams, who she's obviously fucking.

According to the intake notes, in between taking swigs of wine directly from a second bottle she'd opened, Rachel had frantically searched for a way to unsend her texts but couldn't. One of the Mamas had an Android that she purchased for its camera.

"Profits have doubled since group texts became popular," Bernard observed. "And I thought nothing would ever top the numbers we did from *Reply All* email screwups." He turned to Megan. "Let's pretend you're the temporary whisperer assigned to Rachel. What's the first thing you'd say?"

Megan wondered why Real World moms like Rachel tried to do it all at the office and at home. Megan's mother had spent six, sometimes seven, days a week at Naysay Inc., and had hired round-the-clock babysitters for Megan until she felt Megan was old enough to stay home alone at age seven. She couldn't imagine what it would've been like to see her mom standing there when the school bell rang.

Megan noted Rachel's Instagram handle was @mykidsareeverything132. Megan knew from studying the memes and reels of mothers on social media that millions like Rachel were fueled by intense guilt and the pressure to be perfect at everything, much like the momfluencers they followed.

Megan lowered her voice to a purr. "Rachel, all the other Second Grade Mamas have time to drop off and pick up their own children, which studies show is a critical time to be spending with them. Think of all the vital moments you're missing while the *nanny* is driving them. You deserved the passive-aggressive question from Hudson's mama asking why you don't wake up an hour earlier each day instead of hiring help. Now *she* has her shit together."

Megan consulted the notes on the Second Grade Mamas.

"She meal-preps her *four* kids' gluten-free lunches on Sundays, blows out her own hair every two days, *and* fosters rescue dogs!"

Bernard nodded. "That was excellent, Megan. There were several paths to go down, but I think mom guilt and shame was the right way to go. We can't have this accomplished mother and patent attorney realizing her value."

Megan smiled. Her first test as a whisperer-in-training, and she'd nailed it.

"I think we've earned a quick break. Be back here in"—he glanced at his watch—"seven minutes?"

Megan shuffled out behind the group, taking in the hallway lined with pictures of noteworthy Naysay Inc. employees. She noted the woman who'd inspired the baffling Beanie Baby frenzy of the nineties, Yoko Ono's whisperer, and the guy who got in the ears of the meat-industry executives and convinced them to sue Oprah.

Megan was determined to make it onto that wall.

Later, Megan stood in the women's restroom splashing cold water on her face and reflecting on her first day of training. She'd learned a lot—especially about her coworkers. She'd decided most wouldn't pose a threat to her goal of becoming the new rising star. Tom's comment about her mother running the company had irritated her. She expected gossip—it was inevitable—but saying it to her face took nerve. Still, it only confirmed he viewed her as a rival, which was a definite plus in her book.

She blotted her face with a paper towel and met up with Bernard in the break room so he could show her to her cubicle. It turned out to be directly across from Ben's. He was shooting tiny balls into a basket on the corner of his desk—each one sailing in.

When he noticed Megan watching him, he didn't miss a beat. "Hey, Lowell, looks like they gave you the desk with the best view." He flashed her a taunt of a grin.

"I didn't request this," she said, but her cheeks burned.

She turned away quickly but caught Eddie's eye. He put his hands together to form the shape of a heart.

Megan's eyes widened in alarm, and she shook her head.

Bernard, oblivious to everything or maybe choosing to ignore all of them, didn't comment, and handed her an ID. "You'll need to wear this at all times and scan it to get in and out of the building, to the supply room on nineteen, and to this floor. You'll have more clearance once you've finished training," he said and squinted at it. "Not very photogenic, are you? You should ask for a retake. This is the worst I've seen in twenty years," he said and handed it to her.

"Thanks for the advice," Megan said, but she didn't plan to take it. She'd deliberately frowned and narrowed her eyes to achieve the poor image. The worse her picture, the better her coworkers would feel about theirs—another part of her plan to make them lower their guards.

Bernard headed off to pass out the other badges.

"Let me see that." Ben rolled his chair over to her cubicle and grabbed for the ID, but Megan moved it out of his reach. He tried again, reaching around her and brushing her arm with his.

She felt her skin warm to his touch. She jerked back as if she'd been burned, and the ID fell. Ben swiped it off the floor before she could, her heart beating faster than felt right.

He stared at the picture. "You did this on purpose."

"What?" She played dumb.

"You wanted a terrible photo—because you could never look this bad without trying."

Megan bit her lip. "Are you complimenting me?"

"No! The picture is bad. I meant—" Ben stammered, then rolled his chair back to his desk when he saw Karla heading toward them.

Eddie raised his eyebrows at Megan. "Don't mind me, just the awkward third wheel here," he murmured with a quiet laugh.

"What? No," Megan said, but he'd already flipped on his mic and started whispering to a client as Karla walked up.

"Megan, this is Joan Pritchard." Karla motioned to a woman who looked to be in her thirties with dark hair pulled into a tight ponytail, sallow skin, and puffy eyes. "She's the Social Media supervisor, and you'll be reporting directly to her once you officially start work as a lead whisperer. She's *finally* back in the office after her two-week maternity leave."

Two weeks? Megan didn't know much about pregnancy or childbirth, but she was sure that was too short a leave, even in Naysayland. Rachel, the patent attorney, sprang to mind. How much time with her new baby had she been given?

Joan shook Megan's hand. "Nice to meet you."

Karla angled her body in front of Joan's. "You would've met her during your interview, but her newborn baby had a one-hundred-and-five-degree fever, so I guess she had to take her to the emergency room," Karla scoffed.

"I did work from the hospital that night while I waited for Harlow to be seen by the staff. And I still put in full days from home during my leave, so this department continued to operate smoothly," Joan said with her head held high, but her blotchy cheeks betrayed her.

"I'll believe it when I see the next report," Karla said. "Anyway, Megan, I hope you don't have plans to have a baby anytime soon—or *ever*. We need you focused and *in this office* when you work. Bonuses and babies do not go together." She gave Joan a pointed look. "Okay, I'm off to raise hell in Second Marriages. I'm a little nervous about that new hire, Jim. I heard him laughing in the break room earlier. If his work is as bad as his attitude, he'll be gone in a week. I'm in the mood to roll heads," Karla said as she beelined down the hall.

"As if she's ever in any other mood," Joan muttered, then turned to Megan. "How's training going?"

"Great," Megan said. "I nailed my first whisper test."

"That's a relief. Karla brought you on as a lead, so she must think you can deliver, and I will do whatever I can to help you. As you heard, I have a new baby and I'm also a single mom. I can't lose this job."

"Got it," Megan said but was slightly shook by the desperate look in Joan's eyes. She wanted to ask her about it, but Joan thrust a tablet at Megan.

"I'll be starting you off with two clients, and you can work your way up to our standard five. They all had AMOVs within the last ten days, and I have temporary whisperers covering them until you're out of training. That means you'll need to hit the ground running once you start officially whispering. Their information is there." Joan nodded at the tablet and lowered her voice. "Karla frowns on sharing client portfolios with whisperers-in-training, but I know you're a shoo-in because of who your family is, so I'm not worried," she said.

Megan started to explain she was rightfully earning her spot, but Joan continued. "I need to get this department's numbers up. I just got a message that one of our clients, a programmer at a popular social app, joined a yoga studio *and* canceled his antidepressant prescription, so his whisperer is going to be in deep shit if Karla gets to him before me. We'll keep this all between us?" she asked, but it didn't sound like a question.

Megan nodded.

"All the client info is uploaded to the master server so the entire team can see what's going on. Beth requested the night shift, so I've decided to put you together and make her your overnight temporary whisperer. And your researcher will be a woman named Soraya. She's very good. I need to pump, but let's review these on your next break," Joan said.

Megan sat at her desk and looked around. Both Eddie and Ben were now on the phone, and Belinda wasn't at her desk. All she needed was one of them to find out she'd been assigned clients before she'd finished training. As a Lowell, she knew she had a target on her back. Any one of her coworkers would jump at the chance to report her.

She put on headphones and connected to the tablet. She clicked the file for Lily Union, a twenty-nine-year-old lifestyle influencer with almost a million followers on each of her social media platforms. Lily was beautiful with large deep-blue eyes, and silky golden hair that fell past her narrow shoulders in perfectly formed waves. She was standing on a stage wearing a black suit, a bright-pink blouse, and sky-high heels that made Megan's feet hurt looking at them. A thin microphone was jutting out from behind her ear. According to Lily's intake notes, Lily had given a TEDx talk, "How to Be Worthy by Thirty," the year before, and it had gone viral. Megan clicked on the video.

If you want to feel worthy, it starts with this. Lily held up a mirror. *You. Feeling mid? Change begins with the reflection staring back at you. Only then can you achieve the life you want. And let me tell you—the greatest flex of all is living the worthy life you crave. Probably sounds a lot easier said than done, right? Like you'll look in a mirror and poof! You're worthy?* Lily smiled. *Well, you've come to the right place because I'm about to tell you the secret to how I did it. How I got the life I wanted before I turned thirty. How I went from a college dropout with no plan to a woman who had the confidence to pitch herself for a TEDx talk.*

Megan fast-forwarded to the middle of Lily's speech.

I saw a trend on social media. People my age felt lost. They felt pressure to figure out who they were but didn't know where to start. They were looking for help, someone who they could relate to. That was how I felt. That I didn't know what my purpose was. I decided to lean into that. To say out loud that I was lost, too, and that it was okay. We'd figure it out together. So, I said, let's all set a date. To be worthy by thirty. And as I built my platform, I realized that was my purpose. To help as many people as I could to find their inner worth. I just celebrated my twenty-ninth birthday, and every day I feel more secure in who I am. More confident that this is what I'm meant to be doing. I plan to do even more, and achieve even more, by my thirtieth birthday, and after.

Applause.

Megan read over Lily's AMOV. Recently, Lily had been passed over for the most coveted accomplishment among young rising online superstars: Hollywood's Thirty Most Influential Influencers Under 30. The video of Lily melting down over the snub after delivering a version of her TEDx talk was secretly recorded and put online.

The temporary whisperer's report had mentioned the irony that her platform was about *finding your self-worth*, but she lost her mind because she didn't get awarded for being influential.

Megan played the video of Lily reacting to not making the list. How her face transitioned from shock to anger and then intense grief in a matter of seconds. Megan had never experienced such a swing of emotions, and it struck her how unsettling it would be to not have control of your feelings. Megan considered if there was a missed achievement in her own life that would've crushed her in the same way. The answer was immediate.

If she hadn't gotten this job. If she'd failed to live up to her legacy.

But she wouldn't have blubbered and left snot stains on someone's shoulder over it. Number one, she couldn't think of a time she'd literally or figuratively leaned on anyone. And number two, she couldn't remember the last time she'd cried.

Megan scrolled back through videos of Lily from before her meltdown. Often, her bare feet were curled beneath her as she sat in a soft pink chair and guided her followers to finding their inner worth. She had *Motivational Mondays* to kick off the week and *Be Free Fridays* where she gave her followers permission to let go at the end of it. She was bright eyed and enthusiastic, but not over the top. She spoke as if she knew you. Megan had to admit, Lily was good. For someone who wanted to spin *positivity*.

But since her AMOV, Lily's social media had gone dark, and she was losing followers, who didn't hold back in their comments. *Why do you need an award to feel good about yourself? You're a fraud! You don't believe in your own message. Did sponsors pay you to lie?*

There was a countdown clock at the top of each of Lily's social media pages. In under four months, she would be turning thirty. And Lily was nowhere to be found.

Megan chewed on the end of her pen.

Lily's worthy clock was ticking.

Megan zoomed in on Lily's face, so close she could see the size of her pores. Lily had something to prove to her followers by the time she turned thirty. Megan had something to prove to all the people who believed she'd been handed this job. Only one of them could succeed.

Ticktock, Lily.

Chapter Five

The Real World

Lily Union squinted as the screen of her phone lit up her bedroom.

2:15 A.M.

Although over a week had passed, her thoughts raced like wild horses sensing a storm, so fast she could hardly keep up. The ideas toppled over each other as if fighting for her attention.

She obsessed over what she'd change if she could go back in time.

She wouldn't have a public meltdown!

The replies to comments she'd write about @CallieCleanMyChaos if there were no consequences.

Tell your Queen Callie to keep my name out of her mouth—and maybe stick a toilet brush in there instead. Could use the cleaning.

And maybe the worst of all, the words she'd use to describe herself.

Impostor. Loser. Crybaby.

Lily's chest was tight, and she worked hard to get a decent breath. Her heart raced. She felt sweaty. She googled her symptoms. AI said she could be having an anxiety attack, a panic attack, or a heart attack. Or it could be her thyroid, low blood sugar, or menopause!

She tossed her phone across the bed and flipped on her side, but her heartbeat wouldn't slow. She turned over the other way, but her thoughts kept racing. Finally she remembered something she'd read once about how to clear your head of intrusive thoughts. At the time, she'd laughed. Who let their thoughts control them? But now she was so desperate, she'd try anything.

"Cancel!" she screamed into the darkness. Then she prayed for sleep to silence the voice in her head.

◆ ◆ ◆

"You seem distracted." Lily's mother, Sophia, eyed her from across the table.

They were having lunch, a biweekly date that was never missed. Lily had considered canceling so she could drown in her own thoughts but then recalled how Sophia had sprained her ankle playing tennis last month and had still shown up, hopping on one foot, the other wrapped in an ACE bandage. Sophia was usually the one to come to LA from her condo in Laguna Niguel in Orange County—no small feat, but she liked driving. She said it helped fill her time when she wasn't working as a nurse at the endoscopy center.

Lily looked up from her phone. She'd been perusing the latest post from the @ShapeKing—*This is all because of you guys! I was just a man with a gut and a plan!*—which was making the pinot grigio swirl in her stomach. "Sorry." Lily turned her phone upside down on the table.

"Dad says hi," her mom said. "You should FaceTime him. He's working in Dallas this week. He's been there for three days already. Says he's lonely, poor guy."

"I will," Lily said. "Are *you* sleeping okay?" Her mom tossed and turned when she was home alone. She said she felt better when Lily's dad was in the bed next to her. Lily thought it was cute how much her parents still missed each other when they weren't together. They'd been married thirty-two years.

Her mom grinned. "I'm glad he'll be back Friday. We're going to see that new Tom Cruise movie."

"In the theater? So retro, I like it," Lily said. "Also, can we talk about your hair? It's so good. It's giving Jennifer Connelly."

"I really chopped it, didn't I?" Sophia touched the dark bob. "Your dad will freak. He liked it long."

"It is literal perfection—he's totally gonna love it, just watch. But judging from the little make out sesh I walked in on the last time I was home and now *cannot unsee*, I don't think he's with you for your hair." She gave her mom a bemused smile.

"We weren't expecting you."

"You were in the pantry. I wanted a snack."

"And I guess you got one."

"I literally can't," Lily said. "Like actually, stop."

"Sorry," her mom said, but she didn't seem sorry at all.

"*Anyway*, I wish I could do something like that with my hair," Lily said. For years, she's kept her locks long, safe, predictable.

You could never pull it off because you'd be too scared of being judged. Also, let's not pretend a bob would be kind to that jawline.

Lily shook her head slightly.

"You okay?" her mom asked, leaning forward to get a closer look. "Something bothering you?"

Lily wondered if her mom had a mean woman that lived inside *her* head, and if she did, how she muted her. She bet her mom wouldn't listen to the voice even if she heard it. Her mother's ability to trust herself was enviable, and Lily kept wishing she'd catch it from her like a cold.

"I'm fine," she said, then paused. "There's this industry thing tomorrow night. I feel like I should go, but also, do I want to?"

You shouldn't. You were only invited because their A-list bailed. You'll just be a warm body to fill the space.

Lily clenched her jaw.

"You should go." Her mom's eyes twinkled.

"I haven't told you about it yet."

"Whatever it is, it's better than sitting home alone, drinking wine. You can do that when you're my age."

Lily and her mom shared a laugh at that.

"So! What's it for? Do you get to dress up? Can I come?" she teased. "I can't remember the last time I wore heels."

"I'd love it if you were my plus one." Lily imagined her mother at the launch party for the latest pop star–designed fragrance and decided Sophia's reaction to seeing her favorite reality stars in real life would make the night worth it.

"You know I'd love to take my new hair out on the town, but I have to get ready for your dad's return. It will be good for you to do this alone. Get you back out there after . . ." She paused.

"After I had a full-on public meltdown?" Lily forced a smile.

"I wouldn't call it a *meltdown*," her mom said.

"What would you call it?"

"An emotionally charged moment?" She gave Lily a supportive smile. "Anyway, I'm sure everyone has forgotten about it."

"It went viral, Mom! My meltdown is already a club track!" Lily was pretty sure she'd watched every one of the million dance reels with choreo, parodies, and audio remixes made at her expense.

Lily had lost fifty thousand followers instantly, and the ones who stayed were no doubt waiting for more drama. It was part of the gig, she knew. Being online. Giving others access to slivers of her life and inviting their opinion. But that didn't mean a small piece of her soul didn't break off with each cruel comment. Some people trashed her, calling her a spoiled brat. Or a fraud. Others stuck up for her. But it struck Lily that the commenters seemed more interested in fighting one another than having an actual conversation.

"Okay, so some woman missing a serious sensitivity chip posted the video of you crying and it spread across the internet—" Sophia narrowed her eyes.

That woman missing a sensitivity chip is a genius!

"—and if I ever meet her, I'll shove her phone where the sun doesn't shine."

"Mom!"

"But there's a bright side."

"Bright side?"

"It showed you're human, just like all of us. I'm sure most people are sorry you had to go through that and find you more relatable after seeing it."

Lily's mom had a hard time when anyone was mad at her daughter. This was a woman who'd once called her second-grade classmate's mom and lectured her for raising a child who would make fun of Lily's front tooth gap. So, Lily decided not to mention the hundreds of harsh DMs and comments she'd received that morning alone. She wanted to turn those off, but that voice in her head said it was her job to keep her fans' comments uncensored.

Don't I get enough bashing from you? Lily had thought.

"I'm sure you're right," Lily finally said to her mother, because it was easier.

"So back to the party—I think you should go. The swag alone will make it worth it."

"I don't know. I was only invited because like twelve other people said no."

The voice in her head corrected her. *Twelve? That's hilarious. More like twelve hundred.*

Lily exhaled hard. "Or twelve hundred," she added.

"Don't be silly. You brighten and enhance every room you enter. They invited you because you have a positive impact on a lot of people. They want you there."

How cute. You have a fan club of one! And it's your mommy.

"You have to say that."

"I'm saying it because it's true." Sophia reached across the table and grabbed Lily's hand. "I don't know why you can't see yourself the way I do." She pointed to Lily's phone. "The way a million people do."

"Actually, it's eight hundred and eighty-nine thousand now."

"Do you hear yourself?"

"So how do I walk into that party after what happened? Everyone will know I'm the meltdown girl—the one who threw a fit because she didn't get on some list. The same woman who preaches to others that they need to find their value from within themselves, not from others."

"Simple. You walk in with your head held high. You show people that you're more than one bad moment," Sophia said.

Lily looked at her mom, desperate to believe she was right.

Her mom sipped her iced tea through the straw, making a slurping sound. "My gut says it will all be fine if you go, and I always trust my gut. I wish you would too."

Your gut is always wrong. That's why you don't trust it. You present as a leader, but you're a follower. You're so easily influenced. Ironic, don't you think?

Lily squeezed her eyes shut, wishing she could make that damn voice shut up. Why couldn't she be more like her mom, who operated on pure instinct? She saw a haircut she liked and *chop*, chop. She'd worked as an English teacher at a high school for fifteen years before deciding she wanted to be a nurse instead. And just like that, she went back to school to get her BSN. Sophia trusted herself implicitly, and it *was* ironic that Lily didn't. Because that's what her entire brand was built on. The gap between how she presented on social media and her real life was cavernous.

"I think I lost you again. What's going on in there?" Her mom pointed to Lily's head.

Tell her you're being taunted nonstop by a voice in your head. See how that plays out.

"My thirtieth birthday is lurking. I've built an entire image around being *worthy by thirty*, yet I still feel so unworthy that I don't want to make any new content. I lost another thousand followers yesterday because I haven't posted anything."

Her mom twisted her mouth. "So, you weren't feeling like motivating others. But you had a lot of great content a few weeks ago. I liked all your videos."

Lily smiled. "Thanks, but I'm an influencer whose job it is to motivate—consistently. I can't take days off."

"So, fake it."

"I'm so bad at that, Mom," Lily said. "And it's not only my followers I have to answer to—it's the brands who sponsor me. I got a nasty email this morning from a company demanding to know why I hadn't posted myself wearing their blue lens glasses yet, and another one from a clothing company that's pissed I haven't done an unboxing video." Lily sighed. "I don't blame them. I've been stalling, but I'm not sure how much longer I can. I'm not feeling my worthy platform."

"And that's okay. Your ego took a whopping. You don't have to be perfect—on or *off*line."

"Tell that to the voice in my head."

"Is that what this is about? Your inner voice? Don't be so hard on yourself. Tell that voice in your head to shut it. To go away. There will be another list. Let the guy who invented body shapers for men have this one. Good for him. But what he's doing doesn't make what you're doing any less important. Can't you two coexist?" she asked.

No, you can't. He's going to make you irrelevant.

Lily ignored the voice and smiled. "That's a very good point—I hadn't thought about it that way."

"Maybe you could team up. Do a joint influencer thing." She spread her hands in the air. "Girdle by thirty? Worthy Girdles?"

Lily laughed. "Maybe you should stick to nursing."

"Will he be at the party?"

"Probably."

"Then you should be there too. Maybe you didn't make the same list, but you're still as important as he is, if not more. Who decides that list anyway? Probably some old white *men*!"

"You sound like Blair."

"I knew I liked her. So, will you go to the party?" Sophia pouted. "For me?"

"Not fair! You're using mom manipulation."

"Whatever it takes."

"Okay, fine. I'll go. But I'm setting a hard out at one hour."

"Deal," Sophia said. She reached across the table and squeezed Lily's hand. "Now let's get on to the important part. What are you going to wear?"

Chapter Six

Naysayland

Megan rolled her shoulders and cracked her neck, preparing for another whispering session with Lily. Megan had given herself a B for her work with her client thus far, but that wasn't good enough and showed on the leaderboard. She was hovering below Eddie and Jim, something Ben had been quick to mock when they ended up side by side on Pelotons at the gym that morning.

When Megan watched her last session with Lily back for the tenth time as she took a level nine HIIT class while also trying to get her output higher than Ben's, she cringed. She'd been stiff when it came to mimicking Lily's voice, speech patterns, and word choices—Lily's Gen Y vernacular was harder to master than she'd expected. The timing of her insults had also been slightly off. Megan had been too eager to pounce, realizing as she studied the video playback that her put-downs would've landed better if she'd waited to place them in Lily's head until the moment was right. In other words, Megan realized she couldn't simply put on her headset and start whispering jabs whenever she felt like it.

She pounded her handlebars in frustration as she watched her whispering mistakes. Ben had craned his neck to try to see what she was watching. She waved him off, hoping he didn't catch her staring at the muscles in his quads that flexed while he climbed.

Megan had treated the prep for today's session exactly like she'd approached her exams in college—she'd stayed up most of the night studying. She'd memorized the *Gen Y for Dummies* manual her researcher, Soraya, had created after Megan confided she naturally spoke more like Lily's mom than Lily, almost whispering the words *whatever floats your boat* instead of *you do you*. Soraya was horrified. The twenty-two-year-old, five-foot-tall marathoner with short wavy dark hair who prided herself equally on her upcycling skills (she'd made a belt from the handle of a picnic basket!) and her ability to analyze the critical data she compiled, delivered the how-to guide to Megan in forty-five minutes flat. Megan had also watched hours of clips of Lily until she was confident she had her speech patterns memorized. If Megan was going to convince Lily that the voice in her head was Lily's, she needed to nail her rhetoric from this point forward.

Soraya walked up with Megan's coffee. She set the steaming latte on her desk and rubbed her shoulders. "You ready?"

"As I'll ever be."

"Let's hear it—give me your best Lily."

"Okay, here goes," Megan said, clearing her throat and then changing her pitch. "If you wanna convince the world you're the most confident girl on the planet, you gotta start by being delulu enough to believe it yourself. Like, *deeply*." Megan drew out the word, putting extra emphasis on the *ly*, like Lily did. "Remember, you've got main character energy and it's giving powerful. So own your magic. Slay. Soft launch that confidence, and you'll kill this life." Megan released a giggle at the end.

"That was so much better," Soraya said and high-fived Megan. "You don't sound like a middle-aged mom anymore. Congrats."

Megan laughed as she put on her headset and turned on her monitor to observe Lily, the high resolution and quality of the video from the drones allowing her to see so much detail that she felt like she was shopping in the boutique next to her. The billions of drones deployed by Naysay Inc. to follow clients weren't discernible to the human eye or trackable by the Real World's Federal Aviation Administration but still had astounding clarity.

The drone following Lily now captured the slight wrinkle between her eyebrows as she studied the $399 price tag hanging from a cream vegan-leather midi dress. Megan checked her Gen Y manual and considered how Lily might say it was too expensive.

"It's cute but not four-hundred-dollars cute!"

Megan could see the tiny lines around Lily's mouth where her lips turned downward as she thought about the price.

"It's too expensive. You'll be eating ramen for a week if you buy it."

Lily picked up the overpriced dress anyway, pressed it against her body, and evaluated herself in the mirror. There were dark shadows under her eyes.

"Looks like you didn't sleep at all last night. You should go home and take a nap."

Beth, Lily's overnight whisperer, had sent a report that Lily was awake from midnight until two a.m., filling her Amazon cart with Lululemon and SKIMS dupes she never purchased. Beth was a skilled whisperer, but she could also be a bit of a control freak, often suggesting whispering themes for Megan to use. But her work was solid, and Megan planned to high-five her the next time she was in the office mainly to see her reaction to human touch.

Megan pulled the microphone closer to her lips. "Remember your viral meltdown? Snot, Mommy, raccoon eyes. Everyone on the planet has seen that video and knows you're as fake as that dress you're holding. Do you really believe that buying a new dress that's giving *monthly rent payment* is going to solve your image problem? Low-key, why would you show up to that party tonight? Aside from the fact that you promised your mommy."

Megan pulled up Lily's email and scanned the invite again. There wasn't a lot of information. Just that it was a launch event for a new perfume at the Soho House in West Hollywood at seven p.m., and there would be a lot of surprises. Megan rolled her eyes. Real Worlders and their pointless get-togethers.

"If you ghosted, it wouldn't even register. That's just facts. You're not important." Megan let that thought sink in. *Irrelevant* was a theme Megan, Beth, and Soraya had brainstormed during their last team meeting and hoped it would pack a punch.

In the short time Megan had been with the company, she'd learned that not only did you have to get the cadence right when whispering to clients, you also had to nail the angle. It was more than just putting them down—you had to figure out which words would uncover the buried nerve, quiet ache, and soft underbelly of their emotional pain.

Megan had another client, Kristopher Tatterson or *Tatsforall*, a forty-year-old tattoo artist from Venice Beach whose bald head was blanketed in tattoos, his only hair a long brown braided beard speckled with gray. He'd signed on to host a reality show called *Tatty, Tatt, Tatt*, where he'd visit local parlors across the country and showcase their boldest body art.

The first time Megan had whispered to him, mimicking his slow and deliberate delivery, she'd suggested he give himself a tattoo of that cartoon mouse Real Worlders were obsessed with. Naysay Inc. had a team of whisperers in the Family Vacations department whose emphasis was on adults obsessed with that mouse, wearing his ears, taking cruises devoted to him, and visiting his theme parks around the world. Tony, a lead, had bragged in a recent meeting that one of his clients had spent eighteen thousand dollars to buy out a restaurant that overlooked some dark and dank pirate ride and prided itself on serving its meals on gold-plated dinnerware.

After the mouse angle failed miserably with Tatterson, Megan stopped by Tony's cubicle and showed him Tatterson's profile. Tony had laughed until he cried. *Wrong audience,* he'd said. *What were you thinking? He doesn't even have an annual pass!*

Karla had likened their clients to voodoo dolls, implying that it was the whisperers' jobs to stick their soft spots. As cruel as the analogy was, it was imperative Megan succeeded in pricking her people in the correct areas, or they'd fall below the vulnerability-index threshold and become immune to whispering.

She'd decided to leave all the research to Soraya after that.

Inside the store, Lily bit her lower lip, and it trembled under her teeth. Her eyes pooled with tears. Megan knew her timing was right this time, and she went in for the kill.

"If you pull up to that party, you're gonna get the *who invited you* side-eye from @ShapeKing and all the other influencers who belong there. Stay home and watch your viral meltdown video for the billionth time instead. You get that you're adding to the number of views, right?

"Why don't you open a bottle of wine and spiral through the whole season of that woman who switches bodies with her best friend, like it's your side hustle. Your streaming stamina is actually elite. Huh. You *do* have something to be proud of. Is there a list for *that*? Because you'd be number one for sure." Megan checked the sponsor names she needed to plug this session.

Lily put the dress back on the rack.

Megan pumped her fist.

"Why don't you swing by the liquor store and stock up on a bottle of Vino Vines." Megan skimmed through the press release on her tablet. "You'd love their syrah—it's full bodied with blackberries and dark chocolate notes. Total you. You are in your dessert wine era."

Lily slumped on a velvet bench. Her chest was rising and falling rapidly. She stared at her phone and let her finger hover over her mom's contact.

Megan dived in, firing off thoughts. "Are you going to ring Mommy so she can give you another *they want you there* pep talk? She literally has no choice but to say that. She's your mom.

"Who's next? Your agent? She gets paid to say nice things to you so that won't count either. You might think she's also your friend. Two words: fifteen percent."

Lily shoved her phone into her purse. She put her hand on her chest and sucked in a series of deep breaths.

"Hey—are you okay?" a sales associate asked.

Lily morphed her lips into a smile that revealed both rows of her teeth, then looked up at the clerk. "Yeah, I'm good," she said.

But Megan knew Lily wasn't good at all. She and Soraya had spent hours scouring the photos and videos on Lily's socials and the posts she was tagged in to discern the *real* Lily. They'd had to dig, but they'd found her—in the micro expressions caught a hair before Lily started a video or after, when she thought the recording was stopped. They saw her in the live pictures—the way her eyes were frozen until someone said *say cheese*. There, hidden in those half-a-second pockets, was where she let her guard down.

Curiously, the only time Megan had seen Lily's authentic smile, the one where her eyes and mouth worked together in harmony to convey real happiness, was when Lily was with her mom.

"Are you sure you're all right?" The sales associate scrunched her nose, exposing a tiny gold stud on the outside of her nostril. "I can get you a bottle of water. We have sparkling *and* still. Or champagne," she added after a beat.

"I'm okay," Lily said and took a deep breath.

"Well, we're having a sale right now, and you know what they say? Shopping is healing." The associate pointed toward the clearance rack and gave her a gentle smile as another customer asked for her help.

Lily slowly stood up and let out a heavy sigh. She walked to the clearance clothing and started to sift through it.

"So what's the fit forecast for the relevant people who made the Thirty Under Thirty list? We already know @ShapeKing will show up in a blazer without a shirt underneath, abs front and center. But what about everyone else, like @puffpuff?"

Megan pulled up the influencer's Instagram. Her name was Sally, and she lived somewhere called Boca Raton. There was a pinned post of Sally and her pet Pomeranian, Juicy Bear, kissing. Megan did not understand why anyone—even a Real Worlder—would tongue their pet. Sally and her dog were wearing matching sparkling puffer vests that she had designed. Sally bragged that she gave one hundred percent of the proceeds to animal shelters, which baffled Megan. How did Sally make any money for herself?

"They'll probably twin in bedazzled puffer skirts because they are always so damn adorable. Or what about @thehandbaglady?" Megan said, recalling the Poshmark ambassador who sold vintage designer purses and used the proceeds to buy clothes for the homeless—or *unhoused*—looking for jobs. (Someone still needed to explain the difference to Megan.) "Whatever she wears, you know it will involve a coveted designer bag—something quiet luxury because *she* is a true VIP."

Megan watched Lily's eyes shift and her shoulders droop and could practically see the image in Lily's mind as she pictured the influencers at the party.

A warm sensation flooded Megan's body. She hadn't been prepared for the high she'd feel when she spoke to her clients live, responding like they were puppets as she pulled their strings.

Megan removed her headset, satisfied. Standing up, she stretched her long arms above her head and took a long drink of her water. Whispering was dehydrating.

When Megan turned back to the monitor, she caught sight of Lily slinking toward the exit, shoulders slumped. Megan smiled, proud that all her studying and prep work paid off, and planning to treat herself to a piece of coffee cake she'd spied in the break room after she finished this session. But as Lily neared the door, she paused, picked up a burgundy sweater, and held it to her chest, studying her reflection in the mirror. It made her blue eyes pop, and her hair shimmered against the fabric.

"That color is all wrong for you," Megan said, but in truth, it would make Lily look radiant. Megan imagined her pairing it with her cream pencil skirt and caramel leather knee-high boots. She'd easily memorized Lily's closet in an earlier session as she'd spread outfits on her bed while prepping for her *get ready with me* videos. Megan was proud to report she'd managed to cancel all of them. Lily hadn't posted new content since her meltdown. Her corporate sponsors were not happy.

Conversely, the Fund clients were pleased. Megan's placements had been the highest in the department last week, and she'd shot to number eight on the leaderboard. She'd given Ben a pointed look when Karla announced it at their weekly meeting. He'd used his middle finger to rub his nose, and she'd had to contain the laugh that rose up in her throat.

Lily put the sweater on over what she was wearing and modeled it in the mirror. She turned her body back and forth and smiled. Her real one.

"You're actually not allowed to look that good," the salesgirl said as she passed by.

"She's on commission—it's her job to say that," Megan countered.

Lily took it off.

"Okay, Queen. Time to go get that wine, claim the couch, and dissociate with mindless TV."

Lily folded the sweater, and Megan cracked her knuckles. It was all too easy.

"You should get a case of wine this time," Megan said. "Stock up. Be prepared for your next couch rot."

But Lily didn't set the sweater down. She didn't walk toward the exit either. She beelined for the cash register.

"Wrong direction, Lily."

Lily placed the sweater on the counter.

The salesgirl held it up. "This is giving me life. I'm obsessed with this color. Are we celebrating something?"

"What?" Lily said. She removed an AirPod from one ear. "Sorry, I was listening to music."

That's why she wasn't listening to Megan. She must have slipped the earbuds in when Megan had stretched and hydrated. They'd warned her about this in training.

"I asked if this sweater was for a special occasion."

"A party tonight at the Soho House."

"Sounds dope."

"I don't want to go—I'm forcing myself."

The woman scanned the tag and began to fold the sweater. "Whenever I feel like that, I end up having the best time. I'm sure you will too."

"I hope you're right."

"That sweater is a mistake. You're going to have buyer's remorse," Megan said as the woman put it in a bag.

But Lily paid, took the bag from the salesgirl, and walked out of the store into the parking lot.

Megan's heart pounded. She'd lost control of her client. "Damn it, Lily! Why did you buy that sweater? Why are you insistent on going to the party? *Why aren't you listening to me?*"

Lily stopped walking and looked around.

Megan froze. She'd forgotten to turn off her microphone.

In training, Megan learned about a former lead whisperer who'd been fired for screaming at his client in frustration on multiple occasions. The client checked himself into a psychiatric hospital, convinced the voice he was hearing wasn't his own. The client's treatment while in the facility made him immune to future whispering, and Naysay Inc. had lost hundreds of thousands of dollars in potential revenue.

Megan's heart thumped harder against her rib cage. She checked to see if anyone in the surrounding cubicles had noticed her outburst, but everyone seemed busy naysaying their own clients. She heard Belinda trying to convince an actor that a photo of her sobbing hysterically would really pop in a stack of headshots.

Megan softened her tone. "That was an impulse buy that you can't afford. You need to take it back."

Lily pulled the sweater from the bag and frowned.

"See? It's obvious in the natural light that it's a fake *like you.*"

Lily headed back toward the boutique, and Megan released a breath.

Soraya walked up. "What's Lily up to?"

Megan turned off her microphone. "Just averted a crisis. I had her in a state of emotional panic, ready to skip the event tonight to binge her favorite streaming service and down a bottle of Vivo Vines."

"Nice, both of those companies will be happy."

"I know. If we stay on track, I think Lily and Tatterson alone will help them meet their quarterly earnings goals. Anyway, she'd put earbuds in and bought a sweater that looks good on her. But I fixed it. She's about to return it."

"Then why is she getting in her Jeep?" Soraya pointed to the screen.

"Shit," Megan said.

Lily pulled up Spotify, selected "Cruel Summer" by Taylor Swift, turned the volume on full blast, and started her car.

Megan flipped on her mic but knew her whispers would be lost under the music—she'd been blocked out again. She removed her headset and watched as Lily's car turned out of the parking lot.

"That was a rookie move, yelling at your client like that," Ben said, leaning against Megan's cubicle. He took a large bite out of an apple.

Soraya tilted her head in surprise, obviously wanting an explanation.

Megan did not intend to give her one. "Soraya, can you get me that research on Tatterson's first wife?"

"Sure," she said, glancing over her shoulder as she walked away.

"You're lucky I overheard you instead of Joan. Or Karla. Or your researcher who seems to look up to you for some reason." He took another bite.

"Overheard me? Is that how you want to frame it? It reads a lot more like spying."

"Spying? You were practically screaming. They probably heard you down in Accounting." Ben shook his head. "Didn't you do dozens of role-plays on speaking tone in training? Rule number one is that you cannot raise *your* voice. They told you about the client who ended up—"

"In the psychiatric hospital? Yes, I know," Megan said. "You've never raised your voice or lost character with a client?"

"Never." He shot his apple core like a basketball into Belinda's trash can, which was at least ten feet away. He grinned, pronouncing the dimple on his left cheek.

"I call bullshit."

Ben put his hand up and crossed his fingers. "Scout's honor."

She gave him a funny look.

"I heard one of my clients say it. It stems from this organization where people who are considered honorable wear matching clothing and build fires in exchange for patches."

"Of all the things to pull from a Real Worlder. Anyway, don't you have work to do? Need to tell an author to spend hours on their newsletter that only five people will open?"

"No, I'm good." He laughed. "All my authors are already feeling bad about themselves and it's only"—he glanced at his phone—"eleven thirty a.m. I've got one considering a new, less soul-crushing career as one of those arrow sign holders directing people to a car wash. I convinced another to respond to a one-star review a reader posted about her book. And a client who had a *New York Times* bestseller four years ago was recently placed on a panel at a literary conference Wednesday at two p.m., so that one practically writes itself." He laughed at his pun.

"There are panels on Wednesdays at two p.m.?" Megan asked. "That does seem sad."

"And another client is staying home with a hot pocket instead of going to a networking event that could help his career. While you've succeeded in, what again?" He put his fist to his chin as if trying to remember. "That's right, you managed to risk Naysay Inc.'s relationship with a client *and* your job."

"I'll get back in her head," Megan said.

"Will you?" Ben turned up the volume on Megan's monitor. "She's using music to block you."

Again. Megan thought about the earbuds Lily had worn in the store, thankful Ben didn't also know about that.

"That means she doesn't trust you. She doesn't want to hear your opinions. Looks like your client is fighting back."

"Then I'll fight back harder. She has some boring industry event tonight that she's forcing herself to go to. She'll be home and in bed by nine p.m., and I'll start fresh with her in the morning. I'm not worried about it," Megan said, crossing her arms over her chest. Her instinct said to back off for now. Let Lily think she'd won, and then go after her when she was vulnerable again. But as she listened to Lily belt out Taylor Swift's lyrics, she hoped Ben was wrong—that Lily hadn't already lost trust in Megan's voice.

Ben yawned. "If you say so."

"Tired?" Megan asked.

Ben rubbed his jaw. "I've been dragging today. It's odd, because I've had five cups of coffee."

"Huh, that is strange," Megan said, suppressing a smile. She'd had Soraya swap the decaf and regular coffee pots in the break room.

Their prank war started after she figured out that Ben had messed with the settings on her tablet. Every time she'd tried to whisper, her system would turn off and reboot. By the time IT fixed the problem, Megan had gone from fifth to ninth on the leaderboard. It wasn't until she caught Ben and Carlos laughing, while Karla gave her a stern warning, that she figured out they were responsible. Since then, she'd stolen Ben's clothes when he was showering in the locker room, and he'd had no choice but to borrow one of Eddie's naysay graphic T-shirts that said *Overthink, Regret, Repeat.* Ben had retaliated by switching out the hand lotion Megan kept on her desk for hair removal cream. Her hands on fire, she'd gone for the jugular and stolen Ben's treasured bulletin board, sending him and Carlos on an hours-long search only to discover she'd hung it in a stall in the men's restroom. Ben had fought back by telling Neil from Phishing Scams that Megan thought he had sexy arms. For days, Neil had loitered near her cubicle, wearing tank tops until Megan finally told him her mother would never approve of them dating or of his unprofessional attire.

There was something about her playful antics with Ben that made her feel energized; she couldn't wait for his next move. She was struck by a thought and grabbed her tablet. She couldn't believe she hadn't thought of it before. There was something Ben was dependent on. That he couldn't get through a day without. A measure of his physical worth.

She laughed to herself as she typed *Steal Ben's Riptides!*

And this time she'd make sure he never found them.

Chapter Seven

Naysayland

Megan pushed her chair away from her desk, grinning at the memory of how easily she'd steered Tatterson during their whisper session. She'd talked him into spending two full hours tweezing gray hairs out of his beard before finally ordering dye from one of their sponsors.

Her tablet pinged once, twice, and again, the sound sharp and urgent.

She froze.

They'd learned this drill in training. This was a Client Operational Crisis (referred internally as COC, eliciting snickers from many in the training class). It was when a client's vulnerability index would free-fall by more than two points in thirty minutes.

Ben looked over and scowled. "What have you done *now*?"

He'd been grumpy since his running shoes had gone missing (Megan should've received an Oscar for the performance she gave while denying responsibility, all as she "helped" him search), and he'd been forced to skip his daily run. It was then that Belinda had pounced, dragging Ben into the lunchtime karate class she taught, where the piece of wood he was supposed to chop fell on his bare foot.

Ben's tablet pinged. He frowned at it. "What the actual f—" Ben said. "Our clients are—"

"Together?" Megan interrupted, reading the details of the alert. "Do they know each other?"

"I have no clue, but my client's vulnerability index has lowered to 7.1."

"Lily is at 7.2."

"This is bad," Ben said.

"Is Jasper the client you said was staying home with a frozen dinner tonight?"

Ben nodded.

Megan studied the feed. "Well, he's holding a half-empty draft beer and looks ready to par-tay."

"Is this the *boring industry event* Lily was attending? She and her martini do not appear to be going to bed at nine o'clock tonight."

Megan had a sinking feeling in her stomach. She'd made another mistake. First she'd yelled and Lily had blasted her out. And now she'd failed at keeping Lily from attending a party that looked lush and magical, with what appeared to be at least two hundred people.

There was a huge pink perfume bottle sculpted out of ice in the center of the room. Next to it, a sign was projected onto the floor that read **Smell the Desire by Ruby Jane** with an image of a young woman in a sequin romper, holding a microphone in one hand and blowing a kiss with the other. These must be the surprises promised on the invitation.

Fuck.

Megan had figured it would be a karaoke machine or maybe a DJ set by that guy who wore a marshmallow on his head. Eddie had cornered her in the break room last week and made her watch a video of him.

Ben zoomed out. "If I didn't detest Real Worlders so much, *I'd* want to be at this party. How did those two get an invite? And how did we not realize it was this kind of event? There's an interactive art mural, virtual reality, two open bars, and"—he paused—"are those oysters on the half shell?" he asked as a woman in a crisp white shirt walked by

Jasper with a platter filled with ice, the oysters perched on top, forming a perfect circle.

Megan sighed. "Looks like East Coast *and* West Coast, maybe Baja too. And an intricate flower has been designed from the lemons in the middle. They spared no expense."

"None of this was on the Paperless Post!" Ben barked.

"I know!" Megan said.

"Wow. Look at us. We finally agree on something," Ben said.

Jasper was telling Lily a story, using his hands to emphasize a point. Megan pinched her finger on the screen to get a better view. His fit body was emphasized by his tailored suit pants and form-fitting buttoned-down shirt and jacket. He was tall, over six feet for sure, and his green eyes were piercing and lit up from behind his dark rimmed eyeglasses. He didn't look at all like the picture on Ben's cubicle wall.

The guy Megan was staring at was a smoke show.

"You need to update Jasper's photo on your corkboard, now that you have it back and affixed to your cubicle with zip ties, because that Jasper is"—Megan pointed at the screen—"offensively hot, as Lily would say."

"Did he do something different with his hair?" Ben pulled on the skin of his chin as he stared at Jasper.

"It's more than his hair. Don't you pay attention?"

"I don't play for that team so no, I guess not." He stared at Megan. "But clearly you've got a thing for nerdy guys with glasses?"

"He is not nerdy." Megan shook her head. "Maybe you haven't given your client enough credit, and that's how we ended up in this mess."

"Maybe you haven't either. It's not like *your* client is hard on the eyes."

"So you like blonds, then?"

"Megan!" Soraya called out as she beelined toward her cubicle. "Have you seen—" She stopped abruptly and stared at Megan's screen.

Jasper ran his hand through his tousled hair, and Lily blushed fiercely.

"Is that Jasper?" Soraya said, pointing. "He's a thirst trap, OMG!"

Carlos raced over. "Ben! Did you know that Jasper is—" Carlos stopped. "Wow, that woman he's talking to is snatched!"

"Okay, so everyone is hot AF. We got it!" Ben said. "We need to get in front of this before Karla finds out."

"Attention! I need everyone from Creatives and Social Media and any other available Naysayers in the conference room *now*," Karla blared over the intercom. "We have a COC! I repeat, there is a huge COC emergency!"

"What did my huge *cock* do now?" Eddie called out from his desk.

"Shit," Ben grumbled, ignoring Eddie. "She knows. Let's go."

Megan had never seen a group of people move so fast. Ben and his researcher, Carlos, were in a full sprint and wedged through the conference room doorway at the same time, a jumble of arms and legs. Eddie blew past her in a blur. Belinda pumped her arms like a power walker and breezed in next. Megan gasped as Joan stumbled but pulled herself upright. Soraya ran, then leaned forward through the doorway, as if crossing the finish line in one of her marathons. Abby's cheeks were bright red as she and a few other people Megan didn't recognize rushed in. Megan hurried in behind them, the last to arrive.

"Megan, how nice of you to *finally* join us," Karla said.

Megan slid into the last empty chair across from Ben. He shook his head.

Karla pressed her hands onto the long mahogany table everyone was seated around. "As we all know, *lust*, *attraction*, and especially *love* are our kryptonite. It's bad enough when a client meets a nonclient who makes their heart go pitter-patter"—she motioned like she was gagging herself—"because our hard work with that client can be unraveled in an instant. But this C-oh-C is more serious because Ben's and Megan's clients, Jasper Cross and Lily Union, have *met each other*, and are *flirting*, *connecting*, *making eyes*, whatever the hell Real World label you want to put on it." Karla's nostrils flared.

The group murmured.

Karla swiped through her tablet, and a series of screens sprang to life on the wall behind her. Each monitor showed a different angle of the party.

"As you can see here, the clients' vulnerability indexes are rapidly dropping." She pointed to the stats next to the video of Jasper and Lily talking. Drones that were deployed to surveil clients also had the ability to do full body scans, which gave Naysay Inc. information on their clients' heart rates, body temperature, pulse, and blood alcohol content. "If their numbers fall below a four, we'll lose access to them. Which is *not* an option. Too much time and resources have been invested in their monitoring so far, and marking one of them—not to mention, two—as a loss would cost this company an amount of money I don't want to begin to try to calculate."

Megan studied the screen. Lily's and Jasper's heart rates were both in the high eighties, their vulnerability meters were both close to a six, and their blood alcohol content levels were teetering toward being over the legal limit in California at 0.06 and 0.07.

Lily and Jasper accepted shrimp and cucumber canapés from a waiter. Lily's appetizer started to slide off her cocktail napkin, and Jasper caught it, both of them dissolving into laughter.

"Why can't we hear anything?" someone asked.

"Abby, we need audio on this, *now*." Karla slammed her hand on the conference table.

Abby fumbled with her screen as Karla hovered.

"What's the problem? We are in danger of losing *more* money every second these two interact. I should take it out of your paycheck."

Abby squinted in concentration, clearly distressed. A pang of something hit Megan in the chest. *Sympathy?* Megan put her hand over her heart to push away the unfamiliar feeling. She thought about the bestselling memoir she'd recently seen advertised, *No Room for the Feels*, about a Naysayer who'd become a triathlete to literally outrun, outbike, and outswim his warmhearted feelings so he didn't get cast off to the Island. She decided to order it immediately.

"I've had it with your mistakes." Karla typed something into her cell phone. "You were already on probation, and this was your final straw. I've alerted security to escort you up to Human Resources."

A hush fell over the room.

The color drained from Abby's face, and her hands shook as she picked up her things. Megan could see the tears in her eyes and couldn't help but think if she had stopped Lily from going to the party, Abby wouldn't be in trouble right now. Megan prided herself on being emotionally neutral, but this was the second time she'd seen Abby berated, undeservedly. She gave her a supportive look as two broad-shouldered men in dark suits escorted her out.

A man with a buzz cut and a thick mustache grabbed the tablet Abby abandoned, pressed the screen once, and Lily's and Jasper's audio played without delay.

"That's a beautiful sweater," Jasper said.

"Thank you," Lily said, a pink blush covering her cheeks.

Shit, Megan thought.

She and Soraya exchanged a look.

"What is this party for?" Karla asked. "Ben? Megan?"

"Something about perfume," Megan said.

"Something about perfume?" Karla said, her eyes narrowing. "That's all you know?"

Megan had told Soraya not to research it any further earlier, to focus on Tatterson instead. Megan looked at Ben, hoping he could provide more info, but it was clear by his blank expression that he didn't have any.

"That looks like Ruby Jane by the bar," Eddie said.

"Who?" Karla said.

"She's a pop star. Won a Grammy last year," Eddie said.

Karla turned to Ben. "In your notes on Jasper from earlier today, you wrote, *Jasper won't be attending the industry party, he'll be home eating Hot Pockets.* He doesn't look like he eats dough stuffed with cheese—" Karla drew a circle around Jasper's chest with her laser pointer. *"Ever."*

"He had one last night. I saw him eat it myself. He has a high metabolism!"

"Ben," she railed. "How did your client go from Hot Pockets to"—she squinted at the screen—"hamachi?"

"I don't know," Ben huffed. "He deleted the invitation to the party during our session because I convinced him it would be humiliating to show his face at an event where *successful* authors would be in attendance."

"But yet there he is," Karla said and whipped her head around. "Carlos, why don't you enlighten us since your lead whisperer is so out of the loop."

Carlos shot an apologetic look at Ben, then quickly scrolled through the archival footage of Jasper. "It looks like his agent called him twelve minutes after Ben's session and convinced him to go."

"Imagine if I had someone as persuasive on my staff."

"Full disclosure," Lily said to Jasper and took a sip of her martini. "I never come to things like this, so if I look slightly panicked, that's why."

Megan closed her eyes and took a deep breath. She could only imagine what her own mother would say when she found out about this.

"Same. I'm convinced I was invited by accident," Jasper said.

"*I* told him that," Ben said, pointing at Jasper. "He might be there, but he's thinking about *my* words."

"I hate hyping myself. It feels so fake. I also had zero clue how bougie it would be," Jasper continued.

"See? He didn't know what kind of party it was either. The invitation was not clear!" Ben said to Karla, but she ignored him.

Lily pointed to a woman on stilts wearing a floor-length pink tiered chiffon dress. "You think that's bougie? Look up! There's a suspended water harpist above us."

"A what?" Jasper moved too quickly, sloshing some of his beer down the front of Lily's sweater. "Damn. I'm sorry," Jasper said, the tips of his ears turning pink.

Lily laughed and looked down at her wet torso. "I thought you liked my sweater," she said.

"I did! I do. I—"

"I'm kidding. You're fine. It's all good."

Jasper grabbed a stack of pink napkins with perfume bottles on them off the bar and pressed it against her chest, leaving fragments on her sweater. "This is so awkward."

"See? He's *awkward*. I've told him a million times. I'm sure Lily's coming up with an excuse to get away from him right now."

Megan studied Lily's expression. She didn't look like she wanted to get away. If anything, it was the opposite.

"You're good, I promise. Not saying you're clumsy, though." Lily giggled and tossed her long blond waves over her shoulder.

Jasper laughed. "It's okay, you can say it. I had a klutz move. I accept that."

"Okay, it was a serious *I can't be trusted with beverages* moment, but you seem dangerously likable, so I'm willing to let it slide."

Megan was struck by how different Lily seemed from the woman she'd surveilled in the boutique earlier. Lily's shoulders had been hunched and her eyes were downcast, but now she was standing tall and her gaze was locked on Jasper's. What changed? Could it be as simple as chemistry? Her body responding to his? Megan couldn't imagine a man being the catalyst for her confidence.

"So, I should stay?" He looked at their empty glasses. "Buy you another free drink?" Jasper asked, a smile playing on his lips.

"I mean, it's a risk because you've already trashed my sweater. Will my skirt be next?"

They both laughed.

"You're actually helping me out by staying. I'm hiding."

"From?"

"I was trying to avoid klutzes, but that was an epic fail." She smiled that real smile again.

Megan's stomach knotted.

"So now I'm low-key hiding from the creator of a girdle for men. It's a *long* story."

"Is the girdle guy also a client of ours? Someone find out!" Karla yelled. "We cannot have a throuple situation. Our entire system will crash."

The man with the buzz cut started searching.

"I'm so down for that story. I had no idea men wore girdles. There are so many things to unpack," Jasper said.

"Karla, let me fix this," Ben begged.

"I don't know if sending you in to whisper is the best move right now—you already dropped the ball with your client once."

Ben clenched his jaw. "Someone else's client is also at that party." He swiveled his head toward Megan. "Maybe if Megan had convinced Lily not to buy that *beautiful sweater* that caught Jasper's eye, we wouldn't have this big, fat COC on our hands."

Wow, Megan thought. Ben was a lot of things, but petty and self-serving? She hadn't seen that one coming.

"Is that true?" Karla asked Megan.

"He's right, I failed." She paused, and Ben's eyes popped at her admission. She'd surprised herself too. It was hard to say that word—she'd once bragged that it wasn't in her vocabulary—but she had failed and deserved to say it to a room full of her colleagues. What she wouldn't do was share that she'd broken character with Lily. She hoped that's also where Ben would draw the line. "In my defense, the sweater was on *clearance*."

Blank stares.

"I'll do whatever it takes to fix this. And I promise you, moving forward, every party invite will be given the full scope of my attention."

Karla nodded in approval. "Thank you for owning your mistakes and not blaming them on others." Karla glared at Ben. "You're a seasoned veteran here, and she's fresh out of training. Shame on you. Save the bullying for your clients."

Megan caught Ben's eye and gave him a crisp nod. *Take that.*

Ben sighed.

"The girdle guy is not a client!" the man with the buzz cut called out.

"Someone is doing his job efficiently today," Karla said, and the man grinned. She turned back toward Megan and Ben. "Now, you know I always say a toxic workplace is a motivating workplace, but not when it compromises our relationships with our clients. So you two are going to have to play nice if you want any chance of fixing this mess."

"Got it," Megan said, and Ben half nodded.

"Good," she said. "Now let's brainstorm a whisper strategy to crush this connection. Remember what we always say, *Real Worlders are basic*. And those two right there?" She directed her laser pointer at Lily and Jasper. "As simple as they come—two clients with low self-esteem who want a *bae* in their bed tonight so they don't feel so alone. Wahhhh." Karla balled her hands into fists and twisted them near her eyes. "Okay, so let's hear your ideas. Shout 'em out. Let's start with what Megan can say to Lily to send her running home to crawl into her cold bed sheets—*alone*."

"There are so many women in the room that are hotter than you. Jasper's been looking over your shoulder all night," Tom called out.

"Boom!" Karla said, and Tom beamed.

"He feels sorry for you and doesn't know how to get out of the conversation. He's not listening to what you're saying because you're *dull*. You'll probably put him to sleep in bed too."

"Zing!" Karla said.

"Have you thought about what he'll say when he sees you without your clothes? Can you spell: l-i-m-p d-i-c-k? You won't have your ring light to save you this time," Joan said.

"Kazam!" Karla said.

Megan flinched.

"Megan? Something to say?" Karla asked.

"Nope! I'm writing that one down now," she said, although she had no plans to use it and was shocked that Joan had come up with it. She'd seen her on a video call singing her baby a lullaby yesterday.

"I think we have Megan's narrative with Lily nailed. Megan, do you agree?"

Megan nodded, but as she watched Lily twirl her hair around her finger while Jasper told her about a road trip he took to Crater Lake last summer, she wondered if the strategy would work. He was drawing out a confidence in Lily that Megan hadn't seen before.

"Now how can Ben attack Jasper's self-esteem here? Because Party Jasper is not tracking with the guy who had one of the highest vulnerability indexes we've seen since Rudy Giuliani booked Four Seasons Total Landscaping company for a press conference. I'm struggling to reconcile how that man and this one are the same. He's relaxed. Making jokes. I don't like it."

"Walk away before she finds out all you have is small dick energy."

"That's good, Belinda. Nice work," Karla said.

A smug smile formed on Belinda's lips. "Thanks." She turned to Ben. "It means you have a tiny penis and you're insecure about it so you overcompensate."

"I know what it means, Belinda," Ben said, but he didn't look like he knew what it meant at all.

Karla shot a look at Ben and Megan. "This is not difficult. Attack their bodies, and you'll both be home by eight!"

Megan studied Lily's eyes as she flirted with Jasper. Lily was getting in the way of Megan's future at Naysay Inc. and had compromised her standing with Karla. Megan couldn't afford to make another mistake. She wouldn't use Joan's body-shaming comment, but she would expose Lily's weak spots like a Real Housewife who'd been overserved white wine at a formal dinner.

Chapter Eight

Naysayland

"Why aren't you listening to me?" Megan slapped the conference table with her palm as she stared at Lily on her monitor. "I know you don't have earbuds in this time."

"What was that about earbuds?" Ben asked as he walked back into the conference room.

"Nothing," Megan said. "Where have you been? We're supposed to be working together, remember?"

"Relax. I had to take a leak, okay?"

"Is that your cover story? Maybe you were in the bathroom sobbing because the boss ripped you a new one for taking cheap shots at me. I believe the word she used was *bully*. Didn't see that one coming, did you?"

Ben's eyes softened. "Hey, about that, I—"

"You two are going at it *again*?" Eddie leaned into the doorway, licking his finger and then pressing a hair back that had somehow broken free from its gel helmet. "I could cut the tension in here with a knife," he said, then dropped his voice. "*Sexual* tension, that is."

Ben shot Eddie a dirty look.

"I tried to tell this guy when I saw him in the bathroom that his strategy with you is all wrong. I mean, I didn't *see* him in the head because we keep our eyes forward at the urinals, *always*, but I told him I didn't think the way to a woman's heart—even a Naysayer—was by selling her down the river to her boss." He laughed, then looked at Megan. "But by the charged energy in here, maybe I was wrong. Maybe sparring *is* your love language."

Megan studied Ben's face. *Was he blushing?*

"You've got a lot of opinions about people, Eddie, for someone whose only relationship is with his two pit bulls."

"I see what I see."

"Don't you need to get back to *your* clients? Remind Carly Rae Jepsen to Call You *Never*?"

Eddie drew back his head. "I wouldn't expect you to know this, but Carly's had tremendous success despite 'Call Me Maybe' being her most popular song. Anyway, I'll leave you two lovebirds to it." As he left, he sang the lyrics, his voice cracking on the high notes. But it wasn't those harsh notes Megan was focused on.

What did Eddie mean by *lovebirds*? What did he think he saw between them?

"Don't listen to anything that guy has to say. Stirring the pot is *his* love language. He couldn't be more off base." Ben held her gaze.

"Don't worry, I wasn't. Sexual tension? Gross!" Megan said, holding Ben's gaze.

"Totally gross," Ben said, not blinking.

"Shit." Megan looked up at the monitors and sighed. "They're ordering another round."

"And whose fault is that?" Ben raised an eyebrow.

They locked eyes for a few beats.

"Eddie's," they both said and laughed.

"Okay, so we burn this thing down right now," Ben said and rolled up the sleeves of his white dress shirt. He put on his headset. "Jasper, you think you can pull Lily, but you can't. Lily's a"—Ben scanned an email on his tablet—"shorty and you're a Chad."

Megan narrowed her eyes at him and mouthed, "Shorty?"

He switched off his mic. "I'm not going to let Belinda one-up me. I had Carlos send me the latest slang."

Jasper's eyes dropped from Lily's for a moment, and he ran his hand over his face.

"That one hit," Ben said.

"Or he has something in his eye."

"It hit. Trust me," Ben said to Megan. He flipped on his mic again. "She's only pretending to be interested until she spots a hotter guy, which shouldn't take long because that's every other guy in the room."

"That's a stretch," Megan muttered.

Ben switched off his mic. "Doesn't matter if it's true. We make him believe it about himself."

Jasper rubbed his jaw and scanned the room.

"See? He's thinking about his competition now," Ben said.

"But he's one of the most attractive men in the room."

Ben flashed her a smug smile. "But *he* doesn't think he is. Our entire jobs are built on exposing our clients' insecurities, whether they're justified or not. Most times, they're not."

Lily asked Jasper about his favorite travel spots. He started telling her about camping in Yosemite. Lily was rapt. She leaned toward Jasper like a flower stretching toward the sun.

"Have you ever camped?" he asked.

"Does glamping count?" she giggled. A tall man with deep dimples and amber eyes walked by, but Lily's eyes never left Jasper. Lily's actions didn't support Ben's whispers—at all. Megan started to worry.

"These two are putting me to sleep. It's only a matter of time before they bore each other to death and you and I can go home. I need some coffee. Want some?"

Megan nodded. She didn't need any caffeine—her failures with Lily were pumping through her like adrenaline—but she couldn't remember if the coffee pots had ever been switched back.

Ben swiped his phone and put it to his ear. "Carlos! We need caffeine—two cups," he barked, then hung up.

"Ben, I think we need to change course. Lily seems into Jasper. And he's into her, despite what you're saying in his ear."

"She's going to bail any second. His camping story is boring AF."

"To you, but not to her. Look how she lit up." *Maybe it doesn't matter what we think.* Megan decided to keep that thought to herself for now.

"I don't get it. Who wants to sleep on the ground and wipe their ass with leaves?" He thought for a minute, then flipped on his mic. "This woman is *way* too hot for you. Walk away now before she rejects you."

"Want another?" Jasper asked.

Lily nodded. "Thanks."

"Another round? Did he hear you?" Megan asked. "It's like he's so focused on her, he's blocking you out."

"Don't worry. I'll keep telling him how boring he is and how bad in bed he'll be, and I'll kill this thing right now. There's power in repetition. Sometimes you have to whisper something a few times before it sticks."

Megan wasn't so sure. There was something between Lily and Jasper. A physical energy that seemed like a force field holding them close while blocking everyone else out. Their stories might not sound exciting to Ben, but was it about what they were saying? Or was it about the physical connection between them?

Lily's laugh snapped Megan out of her thoughts.

"Mine would definitely be potatoes. Fries, mashed, gratin. Bowls and bowls of spuds," Lily said. "What about you?"

"That's easy. Spaghetti carbonara and a slice of birthday cake. I'm a sucker for frosting."

"I missed what they're talking about. Favorite meals?" Megan said.

"*Final* meals," Ben said.

"Like if they were dying?"

Ben shrugged. "Yeah, if it was their last day on earth. Apocalypse. Electric chair. Gun to the head. It's a Real Worlder thing to talk about with people you just met. Icebreakers."

"Huh." That reinforced for Megan that their attraction wasn't about what they were discussing. It was something more.

"Look, you have to trust me. Jasper's going to crack. Maybe he put on a nice suit and washed his hair, but he doesn't belong in that room, talking to a beautiful girl like Lily. His most exciting night since his AMOV was when he had a victory royale on *Fortnite*."

"He's a gamer?" Megan palmed her face.

"Jasper's a client, and I would never defend a client, but it's pretty common for a Real World guy in his twenties to play video games," Ben sputtered.

"A Real World guy or a Naysayer guy?" Megan squinted at him.

"Real World!" Ben said with a little too much conviction.

"Someone has a hobby," Megan sang.

"Whatever. It's better than completing thousand-piece puzzles for sport or whatever it is you do for fun."

"You don't know what you're talking about. I won't look at a puzzle that's less than five thousand pieces," Megan deadpanned.

"That isn't the flex you think it is." Ben's forehead bunched. "But if you're so worried about my ineffective whispering, why don't you take the controls? Get your client to stop talking to mine. It only takes one of us to hit the sweet spot. Tell her if he takes her home, he won't call her the next day."

"Hold up."

"What?"

"What makes you think Lily would want Jasper to call her the next day? Maybe she intends for this to be a one-night stand. Her file shows she hasn't had a significant relationship in two years. Maybe she chooses to be single."

"Sounds like you might have some personal experience with this. Do *you* choose to be single, Megan?"

Megan bristled. "That's none of your business."

"That's what I thought. No dating experience. Maybe you should keep your opinions out of this," Ben said.

"Like you did with the video games?"

"Not the same thing."

"If you're such an expert, when was *your* last relationship?"

Ben went silent.

"That long, huh?"

"Fine. I'll share, even though *you* didn't. I've been happily single since Daphne. I don't want to deal with all"—Ben waved his hand in a circle in Megan's direction—"this."

Megan waved her own hand in front of her. "You could never handle *this*."

"That's not . . . what I meant." He stumbled over his words. "I meant that I *enjoy* being alone."

"Keep telling yourself that," Megan said, wondering who Daphne was and if she'd broken his heart. If he had one. "Maybe you see yourself in Jasper and that's why the words you say to him come so easily. Perhaps you're projecting your loneliness onto him. You can skip your session with Peakstone this week—you're welcome." Megan shot him a satisfied look and crossed her arms.

He clicked his tongue. "Nice try," he said, but Megan had seen her barb land by the slight flinch in his eyes.

"As for why my words flow so easily, it's because of all the hard work I've put in. Maybe you have some trauma in there." He pointed to Megan's chest. "Maybe it's *you* who sees herself in your client. Maybe you're plucking your whispers straight from your diary entries."

Megan jutted out her chin. "A journal is for someone who needs to emote, something I have never been compelled to do—thank you very much," she said.

"I think I struck a nerve," Ben said.

"Nope," she lied. "Speaking of *jobs*—can we get back to ours? What's your client's dating history? Does he only go home with a woman he wants a relationship with? Does he sit by the phone crying after a one-night stand if she doesn't call?"

Carlos walked in with a cardboard drink carrier; a baseball hat flipped backward on his head. "Who's feeling latte-licious? I've already had one, and they are on point," he said, setting it down carefully and then taking a beat to assess the room. "Okay, then," he said and slunk out, leaving Megan and Ben staring at each other.

Ben broke their gaze and picked up his tablet. "My client doesn't have a dating history because he can't pull. I'm not going to worry about what makes him cry the next day. I'm going in on dick size. Watch and learn." Ben put his headset on. "Jasper, you can't take Lily home. Do you remember what to do? It's been, what"—Ben flipped through his notes—"*five months* since you had sex with that book publicist from the Bookapalooza convention? And that was only after you'd both had several of those Hemingway whiskeys. Lily's going to be disappointed like the publicist was, and I think we both know why: Size *does* matter."

Jasper shoved his hands in his pockets and stared off.

"Boom," Ben said. "It really is so easy. Maybe the rookie needs to trust the veteran."

"You want props for successfully attacking a man's penis size?" Megan snipped. "It wasn't even your idea. It was Belinda's."

"You good?" Lily asked and touched Jasper's biceps. "Was it something I said about my final meal?" She flashed him a soft smile. "Too carby?"

"Not at all. I'm fine." He smiled.

"No, you aren't," Ben said. "Tell her you're stuck in your head."

Jasper ran his hand through his hair.

"Hey, do you know where the first french fry was made?" Lily asked.

Jasper shook his head. "In France?" he guessed.

"No. In *grease*."

They laughed.

Megan did too. She covered her mouth with her hand.

Ben shot her a sharp look.

"Sorry, but it *was* funny."

Ben blew out a puff of air and shook his head.

"I love a good dad joke," Jasper said.

"I've got my actual dad to thank for that one," Lily said.

Jasper laughed. "Sounds like a good man. Is it bad that I'm craving fries now?"

"I'm down," Lily said.

Lily and Jasper locked eyes for several seconds.

"Do you want to get out of here?" Lily asked. "Go back to your place?"

"Don't have to ask me twice," he said. "I'll get us an Uber, if that works?"

Lily smiled.

"Fuck!" Ben said, then stared at Megan. "Why aren't you intervening? Tell her that *does not work*!"

Megan flipped on her mic. "Lily, you don't know anything about this man. You haven't even googled him! He could be dangerous."

"It's chilly out here," Lily said when they walked outside.

Jasper draped his jacket over Lily's shoulders.

Ben put his hand over his microphone. "Total serial-killer move right there."

Megan watched Lily. It was as if she hadn't registered Megan's whisper about being safe, which was a good one. It was like she hadn't heard her at all. She tried to think of something else to say to snap Lily back to attention. "Your mom would tell you not to be so reckless. You need to take a beat."

"Evoking her mother. That's good!" Ben said and high-fived her.

Lily stared at Jasper for several moments.

"I think it's working. She's questioning herself," Ben said.

"I'll also order us some wine to be delivered," Jasper said, swiping through his phone.

"How about Vivo Vines?"

Shit, Megan thought. "She's listening to me about the wine, which I've been pushing on her since day one, but not about him. Why?" she asked.

"Because you suck at whispering?" Ben offered.

"You're not exactly killing it."

A minute later, an SUV pulled up, and Lily and Jasper walked to the curb, their arms around each other.

Ben groaned. "He got them an Uber Black."

"Still think he can't pull?" Megan muttered.

Ben rubbed his face. "I don't get it. We smash ego and they don't smash. That's how it's supposed to work."

"Maybe whispering isn't that simple," Megan said.

Jasper opened the door for Lily and helped her into the back seat.

"Jasper, there's still time to add a stop and drop her at home. Are your sheets clean? Or do they smell like that Chinese takeout you ate in bed two days ago? Do you want to have sex on orange-chicken sheets?"

"*Orange-chicken sheets?* Really?" Megan chided.

Ben shrugged. "Seems pretty gross to me."

The Uber turned on Doheny Drive. They were running out of time. Once they walked through Jasper's front door, the feed would cut.

"Your turn. Say something to *your* client—anything!" Ben said.

Megan started to panic. She couldn't let Ben tell Karla she'd stayed quiet at such a critical moment, but something was holding her back from whispering. She tentatively pulled her mic to her lips. "When was the last time you shaved your legs?"

Jasper rested his hand on Lily's thigh, and she smiled at him.

"That was weak! At least ask her about her underwear—maybe she's wearing granny panties."

"And if she is?" Megan glared at him.

"Maybe that will be a turnoff to Jasper."

"Would that be for you?"

"I don't know, maybe?"

"If you were about to have sex with a woman, and she had granny panties on, you'd stop? Step back and say, 'High-cut nude cotton, no thank you'?"

"Well, when you put it that way . . ."

"What if granny panties are her preference? What if she chooses them because they're comfortable?"

"Are we talking about Lily or *you*? Let me guess—you do your underwear shopping with Genevieve."

"Of course not!" She didn't shop for underwear with her grandmother. Of course she didn't. But she did buy full-coverage cotton panties in bulk—the kind that came in a plastic bag—because they were so much more comfortable than itchy lace or a piece of string running up her ass.

Ben gave her a skeptical look. "Well, if you aren't going to try that, then take the ring-light idea for a spin. We're running out of time, and it was a fan favorite in the meeting."

"I don't think that will work," Megan said but kept the rest to herself. Attacking her client's body felt like a cheap shot.

Ben threw up his hands. "I don't agree, but we don't have time to argue about this. I'll try with Jasper again, but you need to figure out your client's vulnerability *fast*."

Megan watched Jasper and Lily staring at each other like they couldn't wait to tear the other's clothes off, her whispers caught in her throat. As they exited the Uber, their hands clasped like they never planned to let go, Ben continued to make references to Jasper's manhood, skills in bed, and self-esteem. But Jasper's face remained open, the smile on his face never wavering. It was as if each of Ben's barbs were bouncing off him like he was made of Teflon.

Something nagged at Megan. Lily and Jasper were so *into each other* that they weren't *in their own heads*, second-guessing and overthinking—they weren't listening to their inner voices. They weren't listening *to them*. Was it their distraction that was protecting them?

Jasper guided Lily up the concrete steps to the front door of his apartment. He fumbled with the key, pushed it open, and took Lily's head in his hands. He kissed her as they stumbled through the threshold, their hands canvasing each other's bodies. Jasper kicked the door closed with his foot.

It slammed.

The feed cut.

Ben threw his headset across the table. "What happened back there? You were phoning it in—barely whispering and being choosy about what you said. It was a do-or-die situation, and we needed to try *everything*. What's the real reason you didn't go in on Lily about the ring light?" Ben glared at her.

Megan stared at the chipped paint on the front door of Jasper's apartment. Her thoughts interlocked like the pieces in one of those giant puzzles. (That she *did* like to assemble, but Ben didn't need to know that—*ever*.) As she replayed the physical chemistry she witnessed between Lily and Jasper, an idea was taking shape in her mind. "I think we're going about this all wrong," she said. "And I might have a plan for how to fix it."

Dr. Peakstone
Session with Belinda Johnson
May 14th

Dr. Peakstone: I noticed your origami shapes are becoming more severe. Is that a knife you're making now?

Belinda: Yes, why?

Peakstone: Have you considered your origami might reflect how you feel inside?

Belinda: It's just paper.

Peakstone: When did you start folding origami?

Belinda: My dad taught me when I was nine.

Peakstone: What's your relationship like with him now?

Belinda: I don't have one. He left when I was ten.

Peakstone: Are you angry about that?

Belinda: What do you think?

Peakstone: What if you folded something else?

Belinda: I can also do guns, chain saws, and nooses.

Peakstone: I was thinking of something like a bird or a flower.

Belinda: Why would I do *that*?

Peakstone: They're not as severe. Their lighter, more—

Belinda: Positive?

Peakstone: Sure. Let's go with that thought.

Belinda: But I only fold—

Peakstone: Objects that represent murdering your father?

Belinda: Well yes, but I wouldn't actually kill him.

Peakstone: What if you could let go of your anger?

Belinda: I wouldn't know where to begin.

Peakstone: Why don't we start now. Fold me your best flower.

Chapter Nine

Naysayland

Megan read each article Soraya sent her from the Real World's internet as fast as she could. Each new study, piece of information, and detail about Real Worlders' body chemistry and its effects on falling in love made her own heart beat a little faster. Her eye hovered over a paragraph, and she reread it twice.

"Soraya, look at this study from Harvard," Megan said, calling Soraya over from her desk. "It says that when a Real Worlder meets someone they're attracted to and connect to, their brain releases a chemical called oxytocin that creates feelings of desire, pleasure, and arousal. It actually rewires their brain, so they now have an *emotional* connection to each other."

"Far harder to break than a physical one," Soraya said, reading over her shoulder.

"Exactly," Megan said.

"You think this is what was going on between Lily and Jasper?"

Megan nodded. "It has to be why our whispers weren't landing. When they were forming their first impressions and becoming attracted to each other at the party, it wasn't about their bodies at all. It was about their brains."

Soraya shook her head. "Crazy."

Megan looked at the clock. "I have to go—will you see what else you can find and email it over to me?" she asked as she grabbed her bag and raced out the door.

Twenty minutes later, Megan sped up the long driveway, her adrenaline still pumping over the research she'd compiled. She was on to something, she could feel it.

Her grandmother's sprawling estate finally came into view over the gunmetal-gray horizon. Tonight's sky was lighter. Other days, it was more of a charcoal, or was ashy with blue undertones. Although she considered it a second home, the size of Genevieve's mansion still took Megan's breath away—she could fit her apartment into its six-car garage.

When she was a child, her mom and grandmother would shut themselves in Genevieve's office to talk about work while Megan would run through the seemingly never-ending hallways, the long strips of carpet that padded the wood floor stretching farther than her young eyes could see. She'd play dress-up in one of her grandmother's many closets, trying on her dark suits and heels, pinning one of her brooches to the lapel and pretending she was the powerful businesswoman who owned the eighteen-bedroom and twenty-two-bathroom estate that included a stable for horses, a swimming pool, a koi pond, and two guesthouses.

Megan would stand at the head of the mahogany table in her grandmother's study and pretend to run meetings. She didn't have any siblings, so she'd fill the seats with stuffed animals and dolls, their plastic and furry faces looking at her with equal parts respect and fear like she imagined her grandmother's employees did with her.

Megan knew, before Genevieve's retirement, and even now, when Genevieve stopped by Naysay Inc. *to make sure the place hadn't burned down*, she was feared at the office. But Megan had always known a woman who acted like a grandmother would. Lavishing her with gifts, letting her eat sweets in place of balanced meals, never disciplining.

That was Jacqueline's job.

Megan opened the front door and followed her mom's and grandmother's voices into the kitchen.

"Megan!" Genevieve said, kissing her on both cheeks. She always greeted Megan as if she expected she might not show up. But Megan had never missed their dinners. Tonight, the COC had made her over two hours tardy, but there was no way she'd have skipped.

"Hi, Grandmother," Megan said. "Sorry I'm so late. I hope you didn't wait. There was a—"

"COC." Megan's mom said and eyed her from across the room.

Genevieve laughed.

"What?" Jacqueline asked.

"It's just funny coming out of your mouth."

"That's what he said," Megan said, catching a glare from her mom. She poured herself a glass of cabernet. She was going to need it.

Jacqueline pursed her lips. "I can't wait to hear all about the C-oh-C. Karla left me a message, but I thought it would be better if Megan told us herself."

Of course you did.

"I could use your advice on the situation, actually," Megan said. "I have an idea I wanted to run by both of you." She couldn't wait to weave the fresh information she and Soraya had researched into the company's stale whispering style. The Real World had evolved. Naysay Inc. needed to follow suit.

But Megan was standing in front of two women who'd built their careers on whispering one way. Many of their stale tactics had kept the company operational since it was formed at the turn of the twentieth century.

"Of course you need our advice. We have seventy-five years of experience between us, and you have, what, less than one month?" Jacqueline chided.

"Precisely why we should be more understanding," Genevieve said.

Megan shot her grandmother a grateful smile and tried to reconcile her with the woman who was known as the Bulldog at Naysay Inc.

Could she turn it on and off like that? Or had she been unfairly judged because she was a woman in a position of power? Would people have said the same about her male counterparts?

"Let's sit. I made lasagna." Her grandmother put on oven mitts and pulled a casserole dish from the oven.

"*You* made that?" Megan asked as she took in the bubbling cheese and inhaled the rich smell that made her stomach grumble. She couldn't remember when she'd last eaten. She'd skipped lunch to focus on her client, Kristopher Tatterson, who'd been up half the night fighting in his head with the producer of his reality show, thanks to Beth's expert line of whispering. Tatterson had shown up to set and thrown his tattoo gun into the trash when the producer simply asked him to hold the tool in his left hand instead of his right for a promo video.

"I was surprised, too—told Mother it was bad enough we already had one person in this family who found pleasure in spending hours in the kitchen, perfecting the art of removing water from mushrooms."

Megan ignored the dig. It would be the first of many. She'd let them stack up and defend herself when she couldn't take it anymore.

"Aren't you proud of me, Megan? I made it from scratch," Genevieve said, also ignoring the dig against her. She glanced at Jacqueline. "You can blame it on retirement. I've run out of things to do."

"You've only been retired for a month," Megan said, wishing that the end of her grandmother's career hadn't coincided with the beginning of Megan's because she would've loved to see her *on the job*. She was confident her grandmother would've had a drink with Megan after work on her first day, no matter how busy she was.

"I'm already bored," Genevieve said. "I could use a good *cock* story."

"Mother, what has gotten into you?" Jacqueline asked.

Genevieve shrugged and walked the casserole dish with the lasagna into the formal dining room. "What can I say? It's been a while."

Megan started laughing and changed the subject. "Where's Madeline?" she asked as she grabbed plates and silverware. She couldn't remember the last time she'd set the table at her grandmother's house.

Genevieve's house manager, Madeline, always took care of that and everything else.

"I gave her the night off and might pull back on her hours a bit. I've realized that I'm perfectly capable of doing things for myself now that I'm not in the office."

"Who are you, and what have you done with my mother?" Jacqueline asked.

"Oh relax, my dear. It's not like I'm going to start *cleaning*!"

They dished up their plates and began eating. Genevieve asked to hear the story of the COC incident between bites of cheese and pasta. Megan had barely finished recounting the details when Jacqueline launched in. "Where do I begin with the ways you screwed up? Yelling into your mic, letting your client buy the sweater, not stopping her from going home with the company's other client." Jacqueline shook her head.

"It sounds like Ben Shaw also made some mistakes," Genevieve said. "And I must add that I agree—the invitation was *not clear*."

Jacqueline's face went slack. Megan bit her lip so she wouldn't smile.

"You said you had an idea you wanted to run by us," Genevieve prompted.

Megan grabbed her tablet and gathered her thoughts as she pulled up the research. She'd practiced what she'd planned to say as she'd made the drive from Naysay Inc. to her grandmother's house, but her ideas were new and untested, so she expected resistance.

"I noticed that there was something between the clients that almost made them immune to whispering. And it wasn't their vulnerability indexes. They were dropping, but they were still staying in range for us to monitor them. It was something else. Some of our words were landing, but only briefly, and then they'd snap out of it. And I think I know why."

"You weren't saying the right combination of whispers," Jacqueline said. "Because you're a novice."

"You sound like Ben."

"Because he's right. You're inexperienced."

"Well, *his* whispers didn't work either," Megan said. "He pressed forward with attacking his client's body because that was the directive we were given by Karla in the C-oh-C brainstorm."

"And I support that directive one hundred percent. If two people are about to get naked together, targeting body image is the best tactic," Jacqueline said.

Which led to Megan explaining that the root of their sexual chemistry wasn't about their bodies at all—it was about their brains.

"Really?" Genevieve said. "I always thought Real Worlders were just ignorant."

Megan went on to explain the oxytocin release and how it can rewire their brains. She told them about a study where they put Real Worlders in MRI machines and had them look at photos of their love interest. Their brains fired like crazy.

She glanced at her mom who had gone silent, staring at her over the rim of her wineglass, her lasagna untouched. Megan paused at her mom's disinterest but steadied herself and continued. "The emotional connection Lily and Jasper formed could be the reason why when Ben was whispering to Jasper about his SDE—"

"SDE?" Genevieve asked.

"Small dick energy."

"Oh my!" Genevieve said. "I won't ask for more details there."

Megan smiled before she continued. "I think it's why attacking them physically wasn't working. And why my instinct was *not* to use body-shaming as a tactic with Lily."

"Why the hell not?" Jacqueline said. "That's whispering 101."

"It wouldn't have worked because our clients' brains were already flooded with dopamine, another chemical released because they were experiencing lust. They were too driven by desire and the hope for sexual gratification."

"You're saying that your clients' desire for each other was stronger than your whispers?" Genevieve asked.

"That's my theory. And the reason I think there have likely been many whisperers at Naysay Inc. who've failed at stopping their clients from falling in love."

"Spoken by a whisperer who failed. A *lead* I might add."

"There's a reason everyone says love is Naysay Inc.'s kryptonite. Maybe this research can help us avoid COCs like these in the future."

"I'm intrigued," Genevieve said, sipping her wine. "Jacqueline, you don't see any value in this?"

"I don't. Two of our clients have already gone home together, and from thc sound of this undeniable brain and chemical attraction to each other, they've probably had sex. Isn't the damage already done?"

"I hope not," Megan said. "I have a plan to use the Real Worlders' science against them."

Genevieve pressed her hands together. "Ah, the new generation of whispering," she said, her eyes twinkling.

"Mother, don't you have a pie to bake?" Jacqueline snipped. "As the new CEO of Naysay Inc., I've heard no evidence that Megan has worked hard enough to apply the whispering practices that have been our foundation for generations. Isn't it a little soon for her to be coming up with her own strategies, especially those that rely on Real Worlders' data compiled from a Google search?"

"There was a Harvard study included in that. Doesn't Naysay Inc. want innovation? Disruption? Don't you, as its CEO? Didn't you say something about that in your welcome video?" Megan said.

"I didn't bring you into this company to disrupt *unnecessarily*."

You didn't bring me in, Megan wanted to say, but she swallowed the thought. It wouldn't do her any good to argue that point. She already knew how it would play out. When it served her mom's agenda, she would consider herself responsible for Megan getting hired, *like now*, so she could control her. When she wanted to distance herself, which Megan predicted would happen if Megan made more mistakes, she wasn't responsible.

"We have nothing to lose," Megan said instead. "Like you smartly pointed out, the clients have probably already slept together."

"Except money, resources, time. Not to mention *reputation*," Jacqueline huffed.

"Yours or mine?" Megan challenged.

"Whose do you think?" Jacqueline asked.

Megan didn't know. And her instinct told her not to ask.

"If I was still CEO," Genevieve said, "I would allow Megan to pursue this theory."

"Well you aren't, are you?" Jacqueline said. "You're making pasta from scratch!" She craned her head toward a chair in the corner. "And are those pickleball paddles?"

"They are, and I'm already very adept at dinking."

"What?"

"Never mind. I'm off to get more wine. Anyone else?"

Megan and Jacqueline shook their heads.

"Don't listen to your grandmother. She's been off since her retirement." Jacqueline jabbed her fork at the slice of lasagna on her plate.

"She doesn't seem off to me."

"She didn't criticize you for your part in the C-oh-C, not once!"

"Because she knew you would."

"Someone had to."

"Did it ever occur to you that I've been hard enough on myself?"

"You sound like a Real Worlder with that whining. What's gotten into you? You know as well as I do that there can never be enough criticism—it's what fuels us," Jacqueline said and drank the last of her wine.

Megan digested her comment, remembering her mom's words to her in the elevator on her first day. Was it fuel? Or fear? Or did the fear become the fuel?

Jacqueline pressed on. "Your grandmother is still a majority stakeholder in the company. Every dollar lost comes out of her personal pocket. Not coming down on you proves she's not thinking clearly."

"Or maybe she is," Megan said. "Maybe she can see things more clearly because she's not immersed in it like we are."

"I doubt that," Jacqueline said.

"Maybe you should trust me."

Jacqueline let out a hollow laugh.

"There's a chance the clients will wake up tomorrow morning and never want to see each other again, and this is all moot. But I don't think that's going to happen. I believe their connection will be stronger. And that's when I can use this science to destroy it. There's a lot more I haven't told you about. If you look here—"

"Don't bother. I'm ordering you to use our data to end it instead. We have a playbook of foolproof tactics for breaking up relationships. We've tested it on all the Kardashian sisters," Jacqueline said. "Or, if you don't like that plan, I can get you reassigned. I hear Tweens has an opening," she said with a smirk.

"Jacqueline," Genevieve said, circling the table before setting her wineglass down. "We're talking about two out of hundreds of thousands of clients. Why not let her at least try this theory, as unconventional as it is?" She winked at Megan.

"Absolutely not."

"I could make some calls to your colleagues in the C-suite. See what *they* think."

The two women glared at each other, Megan trapped in between.

"You don't need to do that," Jacqueline finally said and turned to Megan. "I suppose you could give it a trial," she said, her words as stiff as her posture.

Megan nodded, but it didn't feel like a win. If she did choose to move forward, she knew there'd be hell to pay, regardless of the outcome.

Chapter Ten

The Real World

Light sliced through the blinds hanging in Jasper's bedroom window, making a pattern on the wall. Lily glanced at Jasper sleeping next to her, the sunlight casting a glow across his face. She couldn't believe how settled she felt.

She wasn't questioning herself for going home with him.

She wasn't overthinking that she'd had sex with him.

She wasn't worried he was going to regret it when his eyes opened.

For the first time in weeks, she didn't hear that negative voice in her head. She could pinpoint the exact moment it had stopped. The voice argued that she shouldn't go home with Jasper, that he could be dangerous, but Lily didn't believe that. Then, as soon as Jasper helped her into the Uber, the voice had disappeared, like it had been left behind on the curb.

When they got to his apartment, Jasper had boldly pulled Lily through the threshold, kicked the door shut as he grabbed the back of her head, and kissed her deeply, his lips soft but commanding. She melted into him like ice cream on a hot summer afternoon.

They'd moved to his couch, Lily straddling him while still fully clothed, amazed at the confidence she felt when the negative soundtrack stopped playing in her head. When he reached his hand under her sweater, she didn't stop him. When he picked her up and carried her to his bedroom, she couldn't wait until he was inside her, squeezing her legs around him to try to get closer. When he entered her, she moaned loudly into his chest.

"Hey, you," Jasper said now, his voice scratchy from sleep.

"Hi," she said.

He ran his finger down her arm. "You're so beautiful."

"Stop." She pulled the blanket over her head. "I'm so not."

He slid under the covers and turned to her, their noses almost touching. "Yes, you are," he said, slowly sliding his hands over her curves like he was trying to memorize them.

She let herself get lost in his touch, unconcerned with morning breath, smudged makeup, or how her body might look in the morning light.

She'd gone home with men before. Most of the time she wouldn't allow herself to have any expectations because the chatter in her head told her she shouldn't. That she'd be rejected, let down, disappointed. But last night, when she and Jasper were talking, the energy between them was electric. Her attraction to him was more than physical—it was mental. Jasper seemed different from other men. He'd stared at her eyes, not her tits, as they'd talked. He'd stammered when he'd spilled on her—not a play, not a line. Jasper didn't come across as an f-boy, like the men who slid into her DMs constantly.

So she let herself have hope, and the voice in her head hadn't argued. It reminded her to be safe (duh!), but other than that, it was mute.

Maybe it was the martinis she'd drunk, but she trusted her instincts about the sweet writer. She couldn't wait to tell her mom about him.

Jasper ran his hand over his chin where a five o'clock shadow had grown. "Want some coffee?"

Lily nodded. "Yes, please." She searched the bed for her bra and underwear as Jasper pulled on a pair of shorts.

"Looking for this?" he said, holding the black lace bra he'd ripped off last night. He slung it at her like a slingshot.

She reached up and caught it, laughing. "Thank you," she said, holding the sheet against her chest with her other hand.

"I'll get the French press going."

It had been a long time since Lily had been invited to stay for coffee after going home with someone. And certainly not by someone who owned a French press. She waited for her internal voice to self-sabotage the moment, but there was only silence.

The grinder whirred as Lily entered the small bright kitchen. Jasper put the fresh grounds into the press, poured boiling water over them, and stirred it with a wooden spoon. "It needs to steep for a few," he said and set a timer on his phone. He pulled her to him.

She looked up. "I love how serious you are about your coffee."

"I am," he said, kissing her. "How do you take it?"

Lily looked at him, thinking about the different things he could be insinuating.

"Cream? Sugar?"

"Oh, black is fine. I'm simple."

"There's nothing simple about you. I mean that as a compliment."

They locked eyes and heat flooded Lily's body. She blushed, thankful the timer squealed at that moment. She took in the curves of the muscles on his back as he opened the cabinet.

He turned around, a mug in his hand. "I only have one. I usually use, wash, repeat because it's only me here. So . . ." He poured coffee into it and handed it to Lily.

"You're sacrificing your caffeination for mine? What a gentleman." She took a drink.

"Oh no, we are definitely sharing that," he said.

"You sure?" She stepped back.

"Oh, I'm sure." He stepped toward her.

She took another drink. "Mmm. This is so good."

"I know it is. I made it." He inched forward. "And that's why you're going to give me some."

She moved back again, but this time, she ran into the counter.

"Now what are you going to do?"

She put the mug behind her and used her body to shield it. "Protect it at all costs."

"All costs?" He leaned against her and kissed her ear, then down her neck where his lips lingered.

"Okay, I surrender." She smiled and handed him the coffee.

"I like you, Lily Union," he said.

"Because I gave you the coffee?"

"No. Because you made me work for it."

"I like you, too, Jasper Cross." She smiled. "I want to hear more about you and your book."

He refilled their coffee. "There's not a lot to tell. I wrote a book, it got published, had some good reviews, but not a lot of people read it."

"How did that feel?" she asked.

"Everyone told me not to set high expectations, but—"

"You did anyway."

"I did anyway. And it sucked. Publishing a book was the goal, and I achieved it—bucket list shit, you know? But it's hard to fully celebrate when it feels like it never took off."

She nodded. She could relate. She had close to a million followers, but she always felt pressure to gain more—to compete with other influencers in her space. To get more likes and views and up the number of clicks on her affiliate links.

There was also her own book deal. Her agent, Blair Baxter, had seen her TEDx talk and reached out with the idea to turn her platform into a book. Lily had spent three months crafting the proposal, and her book had sold to a smaller press—one that Blair believed would put more marketing muscle behind the title than some of the larger ones. Lily worried the publisher was going to back out after they saw the viral meltdown video, but they were still interested—as long as she wrote about *that* too.

When they'd given her the deadline for the finished product, it had felt like she had plenty of time, but as the deadline drew closer, she felt a heavy weight on her chest, worried she might not meet it. She hadn't mentioned any of this to Jasper last night—he was a *real* creative—and that voice in Lily's head had reminded her multiple times that she was an impostor in the book business. Would Jasper think that too?

"I had a tragic book signing in San Diego," Jasper said, pulling her out of her thoughts.

"What happened?"

"I read an excerpt to one woman sitting in the middle of a sea of empty chairs. I'm not even sure she was there for me—I think she was shopping and the bookstore manager asked her to stay. She was kind. Asked me a question because I think she felt sorry for me. I signed her book and ran out of the store. Literally *ran*. I didn't say goodbye to the staff. Ever since, it's like I can't get out of my own head. There's this voice that keeps telling me I'm a writer who can't write. That I should quit. I suck. I'm a loser. I owe my editor a manuscript, but I haven't been able to type a word since." He glanced at his laptop on the table.

"I'm sorry that happened to you," Lily said.

"Thanks."

"I know what you mean about the voice in your head. I have one too. It's like this"—she tapped her forehead—"is always filled with noise, loud like traffic. Coming at me nonstop."

"It's like an engine you can't turn off."

"Exactly!"

"Mine is savage," Jasper offered. "It likes to come in swinging when I'm trying to sleep."

"That's the actual worst," Lily said, thinking about how she'd barely slept the other night because she was planning what she would post on Callie's socials if there was no blowback. "Something happened to me recently, and I've been trying to tell myself that no one moment should define me, but that voice won't stop riding my ass about it."

"Does it involve the man-girdle guy? You still owe me that story, by the way."

Lily smiled. "Yes and no. But it was super cringe."

"More cringe than a grown-ass man running from a bookstore while holding back his tears?"

"Mine involves a grown-ass woman being secretly recorded while ugly-crying and dripping snot on the shoulder of a friend after being left off a thirty-under-thirty-most-influential-influencers list."

"No."

"Yes," Lily said. "And then it ended up all over the internet." Lily looked down, then up at him. "Did you see it, or am I safe?"

"I didn't see it."

"So you were the one," she said.

"I must be following the wrong accounts because a cringy ugly-crying man-girdle-adjacent story could bring me life." He laughed.

For the first time since it happened, Lily genuinely laughed, too, and it felt like a piece of the shame she'd been carrying cracked off.

"I'm sure it's not as bad as you think. Show me."

"I don't know if I can watch it in front of you."

"Maybe it will make you feel better. You said we shouldn't be defined by one moment, and I don't know about you, but right now my inner voice isn't saying shit to argue with me."

Lily did a scan as she often did, expecting the voice to start coming for her, but it stayed quiet. "Okay, but if you never want to have sex with me again, I'll understand," she said, and their eyes lingered on each other.

"I can't see that happening," he said, running his hand along her arm.

She pulled up the footage and handed him her phone.

Jasper's face gave nothing away as he watched.

She heard Blair's voice telling Lily it was going to be okay, signaling the end of the video. "So?" Lily asked.

"Two thoughts."

"Okay."

"Number one, you're *not* an ugly crier. I've seen ugly criers—my sister is one—and trust me, you're not winning that prize. Also? Where's the snot show you promised?" He slid his finger along the bar to rewind the video and paused it, then screenshot it, and zoomed in. "See? No snot. I'm very disappointed."

Lily pressed her lips together to stifle her smile. "And your second thought?"

"Can we track down @CallieCleanMyChaos and egg her house?"

"What are we, twelve?"

"Okay, boomer," he said.

She gave him a playful push.

"Hey, those tweens know what's up when it comes to conflict resolution," he added.

"Then we could use them on the Hill, help Congress agree on something," she said, and they both laughed.

"I don't get it. What kind of person does that to someone for views?"

"In her defense, it was a lot of views," Lily joked.

"She should be kicked off the list. She's a bully."

"She *claims* she posted it because she felt bad for me. That she never meant for people to lash out. Now she's saying she'd give me her spot, if only she could."

"Lies."

"I know." Lily shook her head. "It's so interesting. *She* did the awful thing, but people are calling *me* out."

"For what?"

"Saying I'm a hypocrite. A fraud. A lot of super fun adjectives. There's a catchphrase now."

"I'm waiting."

"In the video I said I wanted my mom."

"You did? I didn't hear that."

"It's muffled, but someone pulled out all the background noise and isolated it and put it on a loop, and now I'm a GIF." She showed him.

"Fuck them all." He frowned. "It's easy to have an opinion while hiding behind their phones."

"It still hurts, though."

"I feel like an asshole for complaining about my book signing."

"Don't. You can't compare trauma. It was hurtful to you, and that's what matters."

He pulled Lily in close, and she breathed in his scent. "You know what's awesome?"

"You've seen how I cry?"

"Well that, of course. But my mind has also been traffic-free all morning. All green lights."

Lily stood on her toes to kiss him, tasting the coffee on his tongue. "All green lights here too," she said, then wondered why. What had she donc to shut off the chatter?

She pulled away, and a blue spine on the bookshelf that read *The Trials of Time* caught her eye. "Is that your book?"

He followed her gaze. "Yep."

"I like the title. What's it about?"

"Thanks. It's about a man who travels back in time to save the love of his life."

"How romantic." She picked it up. "It's incredible that you created this. Do you understand that?"

Jasper shrugged. "I don't know anymore."

"I don't care if it sold five copies or five million. This"—she held up the novel—"is something to celebrate."

"It was much closer to five." Jasper grinned and kissed her again.

"I would've come to your book signing," she said when they came up for air.

"I'll make sure you get an invite next time."

"So, there *will* be a next time?" she asked.

"Of course. For the first time in weeks, I *want* to write again. Maybe you're my muse." He put his arms around her waist.

"Maybe," she said and kissed him. "Can I take this with me? I'd love to read it," Lily asked.

"Don't feel like you have to because—"

Lily shook her head. "That's not why. Promise."

Jasper smiled. "Then let me sign it for you." He grabbed a black Sharpie out of the drawer and scribbled something on one of the first pages. "Read it later," he said as he placed the book in her hand, the tips of their fingers touching.

Lily opened it the second she was in the Uber.

To Lily, who made time stop when I met her.

Lily's heart danced. She turned the page and began to read.

Chapter Eleven

Naysayland

"You look terrible." Soraya stared at Megan from behind green geometric eyeglasses as they stood in the lobby of Naysay Inc. waiting for the elevator.

Yesterday, Soraya had worn tortoise oversize frames. The day before they were clear purple cat eyes. Megan noted that the frames changed, but the inquisitive stare never did.

"You probably got about as much sleep as Lily last night. Judging from the nonstop text exchange she's had with Jasper since leaving his apartment this morning, it doesn't seem like much."

Megan glared at her.

"What? Too soon?"

Megan jabbed the button to call the elevator again. "Yes, Soraya, too soon."

It was true, Megan had hardly slept the night before. She'd crawled into bed at her usual time, eleven p.m., exhausted from having to defend her new whisperer ideas to her mom at dinner, but hoping she'd wake up as she usually did, with clarity. She'd read a few chapters of Karla's required reading for all new employees: *The No-Energy Bus: Rules for How to Fuel Your Work with Negative Energy*, hoping its text would help her subconscious work out if she should listen to her mom or grandmother about how to proceed with Lily. She'd put in her earplugs, slid on her silk eye mask, and turned on her white noise machine ready for her standard six hours of sleep. But then something unusual happened. She'd startled awake at one a.m. in a cold sweat, thinking about Lily and Jasper. She'd texted Beth repeatedly to find out if their feed had come back up. Each time, Beth sent the same emoji of a woman with her arms crossed in front of her face. Megan was frustrated with the unknowing, the severed connection both literally and figuratively between her and her client.

Megan called Joan at the crack of dawn, not saying hello before demanding to know why the drone monitoring hadn't restarted. Megan heard Joan's newborn baby screaming in the background.

"Sorry if I woke you," Megan said.

"You didn't. I've been up all night," Joan said, her voice heavy with exhaustion.

Joan reminded Megan of Naysay Inc.'s policy—once a feed was cut for fear of an invasion of privacy, it couldn't resume until the client was seen *fully clothed* outside the perimeter where they'd been when the feed went dark. Apparently a drone had once captured a client running naked on her treadmill at eight miles per hour.

Finally, at six thirty a.m., Beth had sent a series of video camera and champagne-bottle emojis signaling that the feed was back up. The text messages between Lily and Jasper started to populate on Megan's tablet. They were helping Megan fill in the gaps, but the news was not good. They'd had sex multiple times, he'd made her coffee in his French press after grinding the beans, and Lily had left his apartment feeling confident enough to plan an Instagram Live later that morning, where she would address her followers for the first time since the *I want my mommy* viral video. But the worst thing of all? Ben's overnight whisperer had told Beth that Jasper had purchased a new set of matching coffee mugs on Amazon—one for him and one for Lily—that were for *next time*. Megan had groaned when she saw Beth's note in the file.

Things were not looking good.

And Soraya was right. Neither was Megan.

Megan surveyed herself in the mirrored wall inside the elevator. There were purplish crescents under her eyes, her skin had a grayish tint, and her hair, well, Megan couldn't recall if she'd brushed it. She'd rushed out of her apartment within minutes of receiving Beth's message and then Ben's text suggesting they meet *ASAP or sooner*, whatever the hell that meant.

Ben was stressed because they needed to get an update to Karla by the end of the day and was obviously desperate because he said he wanted to hear her ideas. But Megan still hadn't decided what to do—if testing her theory was worth testing her mother, who had signed off halfheartedly after Genevieve forced her hand. Megan still regretted when she'd had her ears double pierced after her mother had advised against it. One became horribly infected. She'd fingered the small scar where there should've been a stud earring. *Told you* was all her mom had said.

"How did it go when you presented the research to your mo—?" Soraya caught herself. "Jacqueline."

Megan made a face.

"That well, huh?"

Megan bypassed her question. "Do you have that additional research I asked for last night?"

Soraya nodded. "I stayed up late, which was no problem of course, because I want to be promoted as soon as there's an opening for a temporary whisperer in any department—even Tweens." She laughed. "But you know I love working with you too," Soraya said, then caught Megan's impatient stare. "Anyway, I just emailed you more research. It continues to be very compelling."

"Great, thank you." Megan started reading, then looked back up at Soraya. "You do a great job here, and I appreciate your hard work," she said and was instantly rewarded by Soraya's beaming face. Megan didn't want to be like her mom, only able to see the blunders, the successes invisible.

Megan went back to reading, and her heartbeat drummed as she took in the concepts. She'd made her decision—she was going to tell Ben she wanted to try *her* idea. She knew it was a risk for many reasons, but it felt like the clearest path to victory.

Megan skimmed the final line of the summarized research. "Do you have a boyfriend, Soraya? Girlfriend? Ever felt anything like *this*?" Megan pointed to the tablet.

"Nope. And after reading that, I'm more excited to be single and *not* ready to mingle with any gender."

"Why is that?"

Soraya lowered her glasses and looked at her. "There are apps if I feel lonely. That's all I need."

"Have you ever been in love?"

Soraya scoffed. "No," she said and went quiet for a moment. "There was someone. She could've been that for me. We were friends, and she wanted more."

"What happened? If you don't mind me asking."

"No, it's fine. It didn't happen. I think I am who I am."

Megan wasn't sure what Soraya meant by that, but she suspected it had to do with the same qualities Megan had within her. Those that were modeled to her by the women in her family.

"Are you still in contact with her?" Megan asked.

"Heard she got married," Soraya said, her voice a little too bright.

A few months ago, Megan had bumped into the last guy she'd been involved with at the grocery store. He was with a brunette, a dazzling sparkler on her left hand. Megan stared at the diamond on his fiancée's finger as she gripped his biceps and waited for the pang of jealousy or the twitch of sadness, but instead she felt nothing. It was almost as if her heart was hollow.

The elevator opened on floor nineteen and Ben's researcher, Carlos, stepped in. He flashed Soraya a hard smile. "Half day?" he asked.

"Some of us don't have to live in this office to get noticed for our hard work in research." She glanced at Megan.

"Funny you say that because Karla wants to see me. Something about an opening for a temporary whisperer position."

Soraya kept her tone even. "That's amazing. Good luck to you."

"Luck is the last thing I'll need," he said, and the elevator opened and closed again behind him.

"And I thought Ben was cocky." Megan widened her eyes.

Soraya exhaled slowly through her nose. "I hate that guy—the same way you hate Ben."

Megan let that thought stick. Did she *hate* Ben? She hated that he knew more about Naysay Inc. than she did. She hated that he'd seen her screw up with Lily. She hated that he could see her in a way that made her feel exposed. But she didn't hate *him*. He had some qualities she'd get rid of. Like his tendency to prop his feet on the desk and lean so far back in his chair that she'd fantasized about kicking it out from under him and watching his body sail to the floor. Or the client board he hung from his cubicle wall that looked more like a student's art project than something that belonged in an adult's office space. Every time he drew a gold star (a literal gold star!) next to a client's name because he'd achieved some arbitrary *Ben goal*, it made her want to sneak in after hours and erase the whole thing. And don't get her started on how he chomped his gum. Sometimes Megan stared at his defined jawline as his mouth opened and closed. But only because she wondered how it didn't get tired from all that smacking.

"Megan?"

"Yeah, like me and Ben," she said.

"So, should I move on to Tatterson while you and Ben meet about Lily?"

"No, I was going to ask you to find out more information on that panel she's on next week and on that manuscript she's supposed to be writing. I need it as part of my strategy."

"I know Lily's your favorite child, but I'm not sure if you've seen Tatterson's vulnerability index. He's teetering. He downloaded a meditation app last night that exudes brown noise—"

"What happened to white noise?"

"It's so 2019. It's all brown now. He put on his headphones and slept a full eight hours. I don't think we want to lose another—"

"We haven't lost Lily—not yet. And we won't."

"All I meant is, we need to give Tatterson some love too."

Megan knew Soraya was right. She'd been neglecting him, and she couldn't afford to make a mistake with another client. "I hear you."

"We could go after the gray in his beard again. It really bothers him."

"No, I already took that approach," Megan said. "He's an overthinker, so let's lean into scenarios where he questions himself and others. Keep him on his toes."

They stepped off the elevator. "Roger that," she said, then scurried off like a squirrel.

Megan found Ben in Conference Room Three where he'd wanted to meet. He thought they should be out of earshot from the other whisperers who were whispering about them and how they'd failed to stop their clients after the COC.

"Finally. You're here," Ben said when Megan walked in.

"It's 7:16 a.m.," Megan said. "I'm one minute late."

"You're making my point." He squished his eyebrows together.

Maybe she did hate him.

"What?" she asked, catching his inquisitive stare.

"You look—"

"I know. I look like shit. It's called two hours of sleep, *Ben*."

He threw up his hands. "I was going to say you did something different with your hair and it looks nice."

"Oh," she touched it. "I didn't brush it," Megan said, then they both laughed. "All this time I've been spending money on useless items like hairbrushes and combs. Who knew all I needed to do was roll out of bed?"

"That's what I do." He ran his hand over his thick blond tresses.

Of course his rumpled hair was just that. Rumpled hair. No product to achieve that tousled look.

Megan surveyed the conference room. On the table, there was a large monitor and an array of office supplies. Megan counted at least a half a dozen dry-erase markers. They were all pink.

"Huh," Megan said.

"What?"

"I would have pegged you as more of a yellow guy."

Ben smiled. "No way. Pink all the way. Easier to read and pleasing to the eye."

"And this?" Megan held up a three-hole punch.

"I always say you can never be too prepared when it comes to office supplies."

Megan stifled her smile as she thought of the three-hole punch she'd put in one of the drawers in her cubicle, even though she rarely used paper.

Just in case.

"So fill me in on this Real World science theory you have," Ben said. "I have to be honest; it sounds a little far-fetched."

"You sound like my mom," she said.

"Ouch," he said. "You're right. I'm sorry, I'll listen." He made a zipper motion across his lips.

Had he just told her she was right and apologized in the same sentence?

She filled him in on her dinner last night, what her mom had said, and how she'd been up all night trying to decide whether she should listen to her mom or her grandmother. She also shared the new research Soraya had brought her that morning.

Ben paused before speaking. "I can't believe I'm saying this, but I think this could work."

"Really?" Megan said.

"I know. Even I surprise myself sometimes. But Jasper not listening to my excellent whispers last night did *not* make sense. This research offers a logical explanation. I mean, I see why it applies to Real Worlders." He shuddered. "Can you imagine if it happened to us?"

"Us?" Megan asked, their eyes locking, a swift shock jolting through her.

"Not *us*." Ben waved his hand between them. "I meant the collective *us*. Naysayers."

"Right, of course," Megan said, shaking her head hard. "Our world would probably implode—people running around high on chemical cocktails that their brains created."

"Let's consider ourselves lucky that *our* wiring would never allow it—that our culture and environment has no doubt made us immune," Ben said.

Megan nodded. She would never want to feel like that. Losing control over her emotions—especially because of a *man*—would be her worst nightmare.

"So tell me more about the research," Ben said.

"Okay, we're in a critical window because Lily and Jasper are still very much in the attraction phase. Their brain pathways control reward behavior, which is why right now, when it's new, it can be exhilarating. They're giddy, euphoric, and energetic. It's why they've been texting nonstop. Dopamine is released every time they get a text from the other, so then they send another text and another and another."

Ben pulled up his tablet. "Even here, when she sent him a four-leaf clover emoji? This made him giddy?"

"Yes, even that."

"Shit, this is bad."

"Sexual arousal turns off the part of the brain that is used for critical thinking and rational thought. The same areas that light up in your brain during attraction, light up for a drug addict."

"Wow," Ben said.

"I know. Sad, right?"

"I like how *you* think," he said.

"You do?" she asked.

"Now you're fishing." He smiled.

Megan felt her stomach flip. She grabbed at it.

"You okay?"

"Yeah, fine. I barely touched my dinner last night and haven't eaten anything since. I think I'm hungry."

"Let's get the girl a bagel!" Ben said and shot off a note on his phone, then turned back to her. "Okay, so let's say you're right about this research, and this is what's going on with them. What do we do to stop it?"

"So because they are so giddy, they are vulnerable. They now *need* and *crave* interaction with each other. And if they don't get it—"

"They will be crushed."

"Bad. Like, they won't be able to eat or sleep."

"And when clients are hungry and tired, we do some of our best work," Ben said.

"So we need to keep them away from each other."

"Jasper has a cabin in Big Bear," Ben said. "His aunt Louisa left it to him."

"Perfect. When you log on to whisper to him, you can talk him into going there. Tell him he needs to isolate with *no distractions*."

"Like Lily."

"Exactly."

"But based on what you're saying with this whole *they're so giddy their brains light up like a Christmas tree* thing, what makes you think he will listen to me?"

"You're going to have to bring your whispering all-star game to this party, Mr. Shaw. Pull out all the stops."

Ben scratched his chin. "I'll need to play the guilt card about the manuscript he owes his editor. His agent sent him an email this morning and lectured him about missing another deadline. And get this, he used to play Monopoly with his aunt when he visited and hasn't touched the board since she died. He was always the shoe, and she was the top hat. It was their *thing*."

"Really?" Megan wondered what it would be like to have a *thing* with someone in her family. She and her grandmother and mom didn't share anything unless talking about work counted.

Ben nodded. "I can use that to pressure him into going. He hasn't been there since she died. What's your strategy with Lily?"

"She's planning an Instagram Live, which I will make sure does not go well. I will play on her insecurities after she gets Jasper's text saying he has to leave town. Real Worlders call the adrenaline that pumps through their bodies when they're falling for someone the fight-or-flight hormone. It fires in insecure circumstances, so you and I will go for their insecurity jugulars."

"You're good, Ms. Lowell," he said.

A slow smile crept across Megan's lips. "I'm sorry, I'm not sure I heard you right. Because last night you were calling me a rookie who had, and I quote, *a lot to learn*."

"You're enjoying this."

Megan gave him a crisp nod. "I am."

Ben eyed her. "Strangely, so am I."

Chapter Twelve

The Real World

Lily picked at the hangnail on her thumb. *Flick, flick, flick.* Each contact resulted in a pinprick of pain that Lily couldn't resist.

The moderator and editor of an online magazine geared toward businesswomen in social media glanced at Lily's hand and wrinkled her face. "Lily," she said in a *get your shit together* tone. "Tell us"—she motioned toward the packed auditorium—"what does confidence mean to *you*?"

Lily looked out at the crowd of young faces. The You Fest was an annual weekend aimed at raising up women. Lily had tried to get on one of its coveted panels for years. She'd squealed and pumped her fists in her shoebox-size kitchen when the email inviting her to be on the Confidence & You panel appeared in her inbox. But then reality hit. Why had she been invited? Was it possible the people who ran the festival hadn't seen her meltdown video? Blair had told her not to worry about it. That they either didn't know about it or didn't care.

But the chatter in her head, which was back and louder than ever, argued that even if the people who'd invited Lily hadn't seen the video, most of the conference attendees had. They'd probably get up and leave.

Like Jasper had.

That stung.

It had been a week since Jasper texted that he was going out of town. That he needed to turn off his phone and write without distractions.

Lily read between the lines—*she* was the distraction.

She'd been shocked. They'd been texting nonstop since she'd left his place that morning. He'd told her about a cyclist who almost knocked him over at the intersection by his apartment and then flipped *him* off. He'd sent a selfie of himself drinking coffee out of his mug and sent her a picture of a second one, for *her*, a satisfied smile playing on his lips. He'd asked her random things. Like had she ever been whale watching? (No.) He'd made her choose between Disneyland and Knott's. (Disneyland, of course!) And he'd inquired about her first kiss. (During a high-stakes game of spin the bottle the summer of seventh grade.)

Lily had felt like she was floating. Her insides were hot, her adrenaline pumping as they'd planned to see each other again the next night. When her phone had buzzed that final time, she'd read the message, then reread it in disbelief. It was like someone had taken Jasper's phone and written it to her as a joke. Because how could *that* Jasper be the same person? He'd called her his muse.

Her insecurities flared. Maybe he'd been full of shit. Another f-boy after all.

He's not into you. His career is what's important to him. If you were enough, then he'd stay. Actions speak louder than words. He ran for the literal hills when he could've holed up in his apartment to write because he didn't want you showing up on his doorstep. It's those texts you sent him, whining and complaining about your platform and how you need to get your followers' support back. And that viral video! Enough already. You call it venting, but he calls it crazy.

And to think you already took down your Hinge and Bumble profiles. Rookie mistake.

She'd waited several hours to respond. Then she'd simply sent k. She hoped he'd interpret the one letter as disappointment and reconsider. But he'd liked it and gone dark.

The window of jubilance she'd felt had slammed shut.

All week, she had been letting Jasper live rent-free in her mind, and now it was time to get back to *her work*. Like right now. As she sat on this panel about confidence.

On her right was twenty-eight-year-old Annie Jacobs, who'd gained fame with her podcast *Me, Myself, and I Can Do This* and had recently published a book with the same name. She commanded the room as she pointed at the crowd and said, "There's no we in 'I can't.'" On Lily's left was twenty-four-year-old Sarah Carter, who'd started a foundation when she was nineteen called TweenTech, which taught tweens how to navigate social media. She spoke with the wisdom of a woman three times her age as she explained the hidden dangers of popular platforms.

"Lily?" the moderator asked again. "What does confidence mean to *you*?"

Nothing. You don't know shit about confidence, and everyone there knows it too. Look at those faces in the crowd, full of people who have seen your video, who think you're a fraud.

Lily shook her head to clear the voice. She forced her lips to turn upward and begged her eyes to come alive and reached for the words she knew she needed to say. "I want to address the video that was released about me. You might have seen it." She looked into the crowd and saw Blair mouthing "no" and shaking her head, but she pressed on. "I bring it up only because I want you to know that I'm human—we're all human—and sometimes we have our moments. But I still believe in my message. That no one, including influencers like me, can define what makes *you* feel confident. Only *you* have that answer." Lily saw two women in the front row nod, and her voice gained strength. "As for me, I believe that the core of *my* confidence is purpose—one can't exist without the other."

The moderator leaned in. "And what's your purpose, Lily?"

Lily blinked. What was her purpose? She said the words she'd preached for so long, but she wasn't sure she believed them anymore. And it wasn't only because of the viral video. Jasper's rejection had also highlighted how much she needed external validation.

She looked at the moderator. Shit, what was her name? Jen? Judy? She glanced at the screen over her shoulder with the panel details.

"Jen," Lily began and started picking the hangnail again. *Flick, flick, flick.* "My purpose is to help people tap into what drives *their* confidence so they can achieve their goals, whatever they may be." Lily smiled.

That wasn't too bad, Lily thought. No one noticed she was off.

"You were off," Blair said before shoving a chip heavy with guacamole into her mouth. She blinked at Lily and waited for her reply. They were at a small Mexican restaurant near UCLA.

Lily's stomach swirled. She'd hoped her lackluster performance on the panel had been in her head.

She'd spent so much time in her own mind recently that it was hard to separate her negative thoughts from reality. Her mom called them devil thoughts and had been begging Lily to ignore them. *Listen to* me, *someone who loves and wants the best for you,* her mom had said yesterday. *You are worthy. You deserve to help women find their path to where you are. And your worthiness and ability to help others are not contingent on some guy texting you. Do you hear me?*

Yes, Mom, Lily said, but she was only half listening.

As Blair crunched her chip like her life depended on it, Lily felt tired. It was exhausting, trying to convince everyone else *they* were worthy when she didn't feel it for herself.

She looked at Blair. "Sorry I didn't deliver on the panel. I'm not feeling like myself today. Maybe I'm coming down with something." Lily touched her throat.

"Is this still about the video?" she asked. "Because, like I said the other day, I think we can use it. It will play nicely into your platform. It shows you can overcome adversity, which will get more people on Team Lily."

"No. It's not about that," Lily said, but her inner voice disagreed.

It is.

"Good. Because You Fest is a big deal, and you need to show that you can consistently hold your own on a stage." Blair pointed to Lily with a tortilla chip. "That will help when Marketing is deciding on your book-tour budget." Blair tilted her head. "Speaking of, have you figured out how to weave in the viral video yet? I haven't seen a draft in a while . . ."

Lily hadn't opened the document in days. Every time she considered it, the voice in her head said that nobody wanted to hear what she had to say. "I think I'm getting closer," she lied. She wished she could ask Jasper to read it and give some feedback, then pushed the thought away.

"I know it's been hard, but closer isn't finished." Blair leaned in and her mahogany beach waves grazed the top of the table. Lily noticed she'd added extensions since the last time she'd seen her. "I worry we'll lose our window. As it is, your original TEDx talk was almost a year ago, and then you didn't make the Thirty Under Thirty list." Lily started to say something, and Blair held up a finger. "But! People love a good comeback, and I feel confident the publisher is still excited about the project—especially with your thirtieth birthday on the horizon."

Lily rolled her eyes. "Can I get an extension on that?"

"The deadline?"

"The birthday," Lily said wryly. "Do you think anyone would notice?"

"I'm going to pretend you didn't say that," Blair chastised, before pointing a finger. "We need to figure out how you want to celebrate, by the way. It's going to be here before you know it."

Before Lily could answer, the server swapped out the empty basket of chips for a new one and Blair grabbed a handful. "I saw some reel on Instagram that four of these chips equals one tortilla so if you eat a basket of these, you're eating like a billion tortillas." She laughed. "Why do people figure that shit out, then feel compelled to tell everyone else about it?"

That made Lily smile. She picked up a chip and held it out to Blair. They toasted with them.

"Listen, girl, I know you can do this. Dig inward and finish that book on time. Get your head in the game."

Lily's inner voice chimed in. *Blair is right. You're going to blow this by staring at your phone, waiting for a text from some guy who is obviously not thinking about you.*

Blair leaned in. "Okay, I'm taking off the agent hat right now," she said, tipping an imaginary hat off her head with her forefinger. "Let's change the subject!"

"Please," Lily said.

"What's going on with the hot author?" Blair took a large gulp of her water. "I looked up his sales in BookScan, by the way. He wasn't kidding when he said only five people bought it."

Lily pushed the rice and beans around on her plate with her fork. Jasper was the other subject she didn't want to talk about. She'd been complaining so much about what happened with him to her mom that her mom had finally said, *I love you, honey, but you're in a cul-de-sac with this. Maybe talking about it so much is making you feel worse.*

And then the voice in her head said, *That's a lie. She's sick of hearing you talk about it.* Lily wasn't about to do the same thing to Blair.

Lily sat in her car after lunch. She zoomed in on the picture she'd taken with the panelists and moderator and analyzed herself. She was smiling, but her eyes were tense. She'd wanted to be invited to You Fest for so long, and then she'd let her devil thoughts prevent her from shining on the panel. She'd fulfilled her own prophecy.

She wasn't good enough.

She posted the picture on her socials and let her finger wander to the search button on Instagram. She hesitated before typing @jaspercrosswrites. She'd stalked his page constantly since he'd left for the mountains. So far, there'd been nothing. Which had made Lily feel better. Maybe she should believe what he'd said. That he'd gone there because he needed to write.

Maybe it wasn't about her.

Lily's heart raced as she spied a new photo on Jasper's grid. It was a picture of a glass of bourbon with a shot of the lake and the sun setting in the background. He captioned it: *Thinking.*

Lily stared at the glass of brown liquid, the sunset casting an orange glow on the photo. She struggled to identify what was going on inside her. Was she confused? Pissed? Sad? All the above? What was Jasper *thinking* about? Her? Their night together? He'd had time to drink whiskey and obviously turned on his phone to post so why hadn't she heard from him?

"Why did you leave me on *read*?" she asked out loud.

Because he's not into you. He's not thinking about you. *He's moved on, and so should you.*

Lily's eyes burned with tears, and she was instantly mad at herself.

She couldn't argue with her inner voice anymore. She turned on her car, cleared her head of Jasper, and drove home to work on *her* future.

Dr. Peakstone
Session with Jim Smith
May 24th

Dr. Peakstone: How are you?

Jim Smith: I've moved up five spots on the leaderboard. I'm *finally* beating Rich in Eldercare!

Peakstone: Congrats. But we've had several sessions and your ranking at work is all we've discussed. Tell me something about *you*.

Jim: I'm obsessed with the leaderboard.

Peakstone: Something that has nothing to do with work.

Jim: . . .

Peakstone: Okay, let me try another approach. How are you feeling today?

Jim: I'm fine.

Peakstone: Tell me more. You can open up to me.

Jim: But you record everything I say.

Peakstone: This is all confidential. I can't reveal anything from our sessions unless I worry you're going to harm yourself or someone else.

Jim: I wouldn't kill a spider.

Peakstone: This is a safe space. You can share anything.

Jim: I do have this friend who's been experiencing . . . new feelings.

Peakstone: Go on.

Jim: He has a crush on a coworker. It's not mutual, but that's okay with my friend, because it's not about the crush—it's how the crush is making him feel. He recently danced while stirring his spaghetti sauce and whistled while he walked to work! This crush has given him hope that life doesn't have to be one dimensional.

Peakstone: It sounds like your friend is having feelings of positivity. You look shocked.

Jim: Will my friend be sent to the Island? He has two kids . . .

Peakstone: I can help.

Jim: Help me—I mean, my friend—go back to feeling negative?

Peakstone: No. My job is to help everyone be their best selves no matter what that looks like.

Chapter Thirteen

Naysayland

"Someone has that *I have a new client* glow," Megan said to Ben as she wheeled her suitcase toward the hotel's registration desk.

She refreshed her tablet again, even though she knew the leaderboard would remain unchanged. Karla had strategically frozen the lead whisperers' public rankings a week ago, so they had no idea if they'd climbed to success or plummeted to the bottom of the board until the final results were unveiled at the closing ceremony at the off-site conference they were attending that weekend. According to Ben, anything could happen in seven days. He'd once witnessed Frances from the Midlife Crisis department climb seventeen spots because she convinced one of her clients to throw his wife an Old Bags, New Tricks–themed sixtieth surprise birthday party where everyone held fat heads of her unfiltered face on a supermodel's body and she kicked him out of the house. But Frances still hadn't surpassed Ben, he'd been quick to add.

Megan looked at her tablet.

#1 Ben Shaw

#2 Megan Lowell

She sighed heavily as Ben overenunciated his words into his headset, clearly putting on a show for her and the rest of their colleagues waiting to check in. He'd taken on a new client in the final week of the leaderboard competition, which had never been done before. He'd stood on his desk in the bullpen and made the announcement. *It's like I've given you all a life jacket in a water-treading contest while I go without. You're welcome.*

Soraya walked up wearing a backpack that was so oversize, Megan worried it was going to pull her backward. Megan leaned toward her. "Please tell me you're in."

Soraya shook her head. "Not yet. I hit another firewall. Access denied again. But I'm not giving up. I know someone left a back door somewhere, and I'm going to find it!"

Megan had tasked Soraya with hacking into Naysay Inc.'s computer system in order to access the latest rankings. She knew it was a risk; they'd both be fired if caught. Soraya promised she was covering her tracks, clamoring about brute-force attacks and social engineering, and how encryptions and VPNs would protect them, whatever that all meant. For her part, Megan had slept at the office almost every night leading up to the conference, tag teaming her clients with Beth and even allowing Soraya a few trial runs on the mic when Megan took a power nap or went to the bathroom (turns out Soraya was a natural!), so none of her charges were free from whispering for more than a few minutes.

But had her efforts been enough to beat Ben?

Before the leaderboard had ceremoniously gone dark at eight p.m. seven days ago, as the entire bullpen looked on, Megan had been only 0.005 percentage points behind Ben. They were two horses, racing neck and neck as they charged down the final stretch. As far as Megan knew, even though Ben had taken on an additional client, he and Carlos had still managed to leave at seven o'clock one evening to watch a basketball game at a local bar, leaving their fate in the hands of the overnight whisperer, whom Ben hardly ever utilized. When Megan chided him about this, Ben loved to remind her how he'd won every year for the past six with the same approach, so why should he change things now?

Because I'm here, she'd said.

He'd offered her a patronizing smile. *That's cute you think that,* he'd said.

She looked over at him now in his *It's Hard Being A Champ* T-shirt that hugged his biceps, and she vowed to beat him at every contest at this conference. Their departments would be going head-to-head in several competitions, and if her numbers came up short at the end, at least she could say she and her team had been victorious in events like the office chair races, the escape room challenge, and the ropes course.

"The thriller you wrote is a joke," Ben said into his headset "Everyone is going to figure out who did it by page fifty—and that's being generous. That's why no agent wants you. Your writing is as tired and predictable as you are. Delete the manuscript and go back to shopping for that overpriced litter box, Nancy." Ben raised his eyebrow at Megan, removed his headphones, zipped them into their case, and placed them inside his messenger bag. "I brought my client Nancy to tears in under a minute. That has to be a PR!" Ben grinned. "I think *I* get a shot of dopamine every time I whisper. Maybe I'm in love with my job?" he joked.

"And yourself," Megan quipped.

"And myself," Ben said with a shrug.

"Nancy is a new client so that means she's extra emotionally fragile. I wouldn't give yourself too much credit for her tears, being fresh off her AMOV and all," Megan said, crossing her arms over her chest. "What was her AMOV anyway? Give me the scoop!"

"You and your AMOVs. You're obsessed." Ben gave her a playful shove.

A tingle ran up Megan's arm, but she chose to believe it was because the air-conditioning was blasting and not because his hand had touched her skin. She needed to stay focused, get Ben to let his guard down, reveal something she could use against him when their teams competed this weekend. Maybe he was scared of heights or terrible at solving riddles! "Call it what you like, but I believe AMOVs are the best part of this job. Sometimes I read client point-of-engagement forms for fun."

"Really?"

Megan nodded. "Give me a glass of wine and a folder full of client origin-point stories, and I have all the entertainment I need. There's something about their acute moments of vulnerability that intrigues me. How did they get there? I like going back through their profiles and dissecting the different low points in their lives that led them to that moment."

"Okay, Dr. Peakstone," Ben teased, and Megan blanched. She hadn't told anyone, but she enjoyed her sessions with the Naysay Inc. psychiatrist, even admired the doctor, often imagining a world where the two of them would get coffee and *really* talk.

Megan looked at Soraya and tilted her head toward Ben's tablet. "So are you going to tell us about Nancy's AMOV?"

"Where to begin. She's a has-been chick-lit author. Had some *New York Times* bestsellers in the early 2000s. Rode the whole *I'm a thirty-something white female protagonist who wears stilettos and falls in love* wave until her sales plummeted and her agent and publisher said buh-bye. Now she's trying to get back in the game with a thriller starring an author protagonist. Get in line, Nance." He made a face. "As for her AMOV, she had a breakdown after she was rejected by the fifteenth agent while teaching one of those painting-with-wine classes. She started throwing paint everywhere and smashed the wine bottle on the floor. Want to know the worst part?"

Megan popped her eyes wide. "It gets worse?"

"The rejection email was from her original agent, who'd repped her for *two decades*. Told her that she was too busy to take her on."

Megan winced. "How old is Nancy?"

"Sixty-eight. She should cash it in. Play with the grandkids—plan her funeral." He laughed. "The art studio looked like a crime scene." Ben smiled.

"Show me."

Ben swiped the screen on his tablet. Nancy was curled into a ball, blowing her nose, a pile of used tissues next to her on the couch.

"Is that an empty wine bottle on the floor? That's ironic. And it's Vivo Vines. I hate to admit it, but I'm impressed," she said.

"Well, I had to take her back to the scene of the proverbial crime and all," he said. "And please the sponsors along the way, of course. All while maintaining my lead over you."

"Your very slim point-zero-zero-five-percent lead, you mean."

"Someone's counting."

"Like you're not."

"I've slept like a baby since that leaderboard went dark. Unlike someone I know."

"She's slept!" Soraya said.

"How cute! Your researcher is sticking up for you. And also whispering for you, I hear."

Megan waved him off. "For someone so confident, you seem pretty focused on what *I'm* doing."

"Or not doing, *rookie*," he said. "This weekend, I'm going to prove that I win everywhere, inside and outside the office." He stepped toward her. "I know you've stalked the website since this weekend's competitions were announced and have probably even started practicing."

She and Soraya *had* looked up the contests when they were posted last night at 11:59 p.m., and she *had* practiced for some of them. But she would never admit that. "What contests?" She held his gaze and took a small step forward.

"I think you're bluffing." Ben stepped closer to her, the gap between them closing even more.

"Think what you want, but I was too busy packing to be bothered," she said, inching in his direction.

"So, then you have *no idea* if there's, say, a mystery-song lip-sync battle?" He took another step toward her.

"Nope," she said, but she'd already started memorizing lyrics. You didn't know what song you'd be given with only five minutes to prep. So she'd pulled random tunes like "Bad Romance" and "No Scrubs" from the Real World's internet and practiced in the mirror while getting ready this morning.

"And you have zero clue if there's a PowerPoint battle?" He took another step, their faces now only inches apart.

"What's that?" Megan asked, even though she knew full well what it was. They'd be given a silly slide deck they'd never seen before and have to confidently present it.

"I think you know," he said.

"Sorry, totally in the dark over here," she said.

"Trivia contest?"

Megan shook her head. "Nope." They were now so close she could see that there were tiny flecks of gold in his brown eyes. "But those all sound like things I could do in my sleep. I can't wait to kick your ass."

Ben's eyes flicked over her. "Careful. You have no idea how *hard* I can bring it."

"I can't wait to find out," Megan said, her heart thumping so fast she wondered if he could see it.

Soraya cleared her throat. "*Anyway*, Megan will be quite busy attending the many panels I've signed us up for. Which are far more important to us than some three-legged race."

"That's right," Megan said and pulled up the agenda on her tablet and started reading. "'Nurturing Negativity Bias' at ten a.m. followed by 'Judge and Jury: What You Whisper Is the Law' at eleven fifteen and then, oh, this one is going to be good, at three thirty: 'Play Them like a Symphony: How to Orchestrate the Perfect Downward Spiral.'"

"Makes perfect sense for *you* to retrain on the foundational blocks of whispering. *I* don't need any help trashing my clients' egos."

"That's right," Carlos said, breezing into the conversation. He was holding two glasses of beer and handed one to Ben. "The only reason we're here is to collect your leaderboard award when they announce your name, *again*. Here's to lucky number seven."

They clinked their glasses.

"Sorry, Soraya. I would've bought you a drink, but they were out of Shirley Temples." Carlos half smiled.

"It's okay. My mom taught me to never take a drink from a strange man anyway," she said and high-fived Megan.

Megan said, "I'll grab you a drink at the reception later."

"Appreciate it. Can't wait," Soraya said. "I'm going to head up to my room and tackle that thing you assigned me," she said, then side-eyed Carlos's beer. "Some of us are actually taking this meeting seriously." She turned and headed for the elevator.

"Text me the second you get anything," Megan called after her, silently willing her to successfully break into the system. Three more days of Ben's inflated ego might actually be unbearable.

Carlos set his beer on top of a trash receptacle. "I also have work to do, contrary to what *she* might believe," he said and walked in the opposite direction.

"They are totally into each other," Ben said.

"What? Why do you think that?" Megan asked.

"It's so obvious. The jabs. The competitiveness. The way they look at each other . . ."

"Just because two members of the opposite sex banter occasionally, doesn't mean they like each other," Megan said.

"Doesn't it?" Ben asked, and she felt her insides go hot.

"So you won't be at the reception?" she said, changing the subject.

"Nope. I'm skipping it. You know you don't get points for going," Ben said.

"That's fine—I *want* to go," Megan said. "In fact, I *can't wait* to go." What Megan really wanted was to go to her room, put on her sweatpants, and prep for the contests the following day.

"You *want* to drink watered-down cocktails, eat rubber shrimp, and make small talk with people like Jim? Really?" He leveled a hard look at her.

"I do. I'd *love* to get to know Jim better," she said sarcastically, before adding, "Maybe he'll hold my waist during the conga line."

"I think Jim would love that. He has a thing for you."

"Jim does not have *a thing* for me," Megan said, giving Ben side-eye.

"Did I hear my name?" Jim made his way over. Megan noticed that underneath his rumpled blazer, he was wearing the neon Naysay Inc. T-shirt from the swag bag.

"You did. Megan was just talking about you," Ben said. "Tell him why, Megan. Something about a conga line, I think it was?"

"I, uh—" Megan stammered. She sent Ben a pleading look, but he met it with silence.

Jim looked at her like he was waiting for a punch line.

"You know, I can't remember."

"That's okay. I can't remember what I did five minutes ago." Jim laughed. "How are you, Megan? I haven't seen you since the COC. That was rough."

"I'm fine," Megan said.

"I'm doing great since the COC, too, Jim. Not that you asked," Ben said, his gaze sharp and unblinking.

Megan frowned at Ben, but he pressed on.

"I hadn't seen Karla that upset since Britney Spears worked up the courage to get a new lawyer and end her conservatorship," Ben said. "She threw her tablet at the wall and sent Theresa to HR."

"Who's Theresa?" Megan asked.

"Exactly," Ben said. "She was sent to HR and then to god knows where."

"And she was never seen again?" Jim asked.

"Nope," Ben said. "But the rumor mill swirls, and apparently, to this day, she still maintains that it was impossible to naysay against the #freebritney movement."

"I don't disagree," Jim said. "Those Britney fans are intense."

"Makes me relieved to have authors for clients. No one's out there forming movements for them. Most just fade into obscurity without anyone really noticing—or caring."

"Like Nancy?" Megan asked.

Ben nodded. "She'd been an auto-buy author for a huge percentage of women, a book club darling. They even made a movie out of one of her books that starred some actress named Catherine Zeta-Jones. But as soon as Nancy had a few mediocre releases, everyone forgot about her." He rubbed his hands together. "Makes my job easy."

"Does anyone know where Theresa is now? Or Abby?" Megan asked, wondering again if Soraya got caught hacking the system, what would happen.

Jim motioned for Ben and Megan to come closer. "You didn't hear this from me, but Jennifer in Stepparenting told me that if they don't get sent to the Island, they get reprogrammed and are given a new role at Naysay Inc."

"Reprogrammed? Like robots?" Megan asked.

Jim shrugged. "I don't know, but I hope I never find out. It sounds worse than both of my divorces."

"Then I suggest you be a better employee than you were a husband, *Jim*." Ben didn't blink as he said it, his head tilted to the side.

Jim flinched before smoothing his expression.

Megan felt something stir inside her and felt compelled to change the subject and take Ben's focus off Jim. "You guys, has one of your clients ever talked *to* you?"

"What do you mean?" Jim asked.

"Lately, my client Lily has been telling me to go away."

Ben pressed a fist into his mouth to stifle a laugh. "I can relate. I want to say that to you every day."

Megan swatted him with her tote.

"Why is she telling you that?" Jim asked.

"Why do you think, *Jim*?" A sharp sigh escaped Ben.

Megan widened her eyes at him, hoping he'd take the hint and ease up on Jim. "I think what Ben means is, we attack our clients' mental health every day, so they want a reprieve. And since the C-oh-C, I've been extra hard on Lily."

"How did she know to do that? Is she reading self-help books?" Jim asked.

"Worse. Her mom's been listening to a podcast hosted by some woman named Mel Robbins, who wrote a book called *Let Them, Let You*. She told Lily that Mel says she can take the voice in her head's power away by letting it say what it needs to say but then letting herself know it's not true and telling it to *go away*."

"Sounds like we need to get that Mel Robbins woman into the Fund," Jim said.

"Soraya looked into her—she'd never go for it. She has several *New York Times* bestsellers and a number-one-rated podcast. She won't want to hire a shady consulting firm. Plus she seems to actually want to help people." Megan made a face.

"Regardless, you need to figure this out," Ben implored. "If you don't, it will impact Lily's relationship with Jasper, which will impact me!"

"You could be a little less selfish, Ben," Jim chided.

"Hey, *Jim*, don't you have somewhere to be? Some panel about how to talk a two-time divorcée onto the ledge? That should take about ninety seconds, and then you can go up to your hotel room and eat your feelings."

Jim rolled his eyes, but Megan saw a flicker of something in them again.

She shot Ben a look like, *was that necessary*.

Ben shrugged.

Jim looked at Megan. "For what it's worth, Lily's probably trying to get rid of you because you're doing a good job getting under her skin. I know you'll come up with a solution because you're the best," he said, giving Ben a look. "Anyway, I'd better go. Will I see you at the reception later?"

"Sure. Save me a watered-down vodka cranberry." Megan eyed Ben as she said it.

Jim buoyed. "Will do."

When Jim walked away, Megan noticed a spring in his step. She turned to Ben. "Why are you so hard on him?"

Ben shrugged. "Why do you like him so much?"

"I like most people," she said, struck by her own statement. Did she? She pushed away the thought before she could come up with the honest answer.

"Since when?" He laughed. "And does that include me?"

"Looks like you're up." Thankful for the interruption, Megan pointed to the reservation specialist waving Ben over.

Ben grabbed his weekender leather bag off the floor and walked to the desk. Megan heard him tell the woman that he wanted a room with the least amount of light possible. In the middle of the exchange, he glanced at Megan over his shoulder and smiled.

A surge of heat tore through Megan's body. It swirled and tingled and radiated. She took a deep breath, willing it away, telling herself Ben was a narcissist, nothing more. And also, it was hot in the lobby.

◆ ◆ ◆

Megan had just checked into her room and sat down with her tablet and the latest notes on Lily—she hadn't texted with Jasper at all, which was good, but she was working hard on her platform, which was bad. She sighed.

Her phone buzzed. She grabbed it, hoping for a message from Soraya, but it was Ben.

Meet me at the bar for a real drink?

Megan had planned to stay in the hotel room and work until the reception in a few hours, but a cocktail did sound good.

Another text from Ben: Unless you're waiting until your date with Jim.

She forced the smile from her face. I can't she typed but didn't hit send. She wrote instead: I need to work. Remember berating me about figuring out how to stop Lily? What happened to that guy?

Sorry I was in a mood.
You think?
Let me make it up to you.
You can make it up to me by working! Do I need to remind you about Karla's threat?
I'm trying to block out that meeting.

Karla had called them into her office yesterday to discuss Lily and Jasper. Megan had expected it to be positive (if there was such a thing at Naysay Inc.) because their clients' vulnerability scores had increased slightly, a direct result of implementing Megan's research on brain chemistry to get Jasper to blow off Lily for Big Bear and Lily to ghost Jasper in response. She'd emailed that research to Karla and cc'd her mom, but neither had responded.

Megan and Ben took seats in the matching uncomfortable chairs opposite Karla. Megan smiled.

Why are you smiling? Karla barked. *I'm not happy with your clients' vulnerability indexes. They're trending down.*

I thought they were going up?

They did spike up temporarily before dipping back down. Totally unacceptable.

Lily and Jasper haven't communicated with each other in a week thanks to us! Ben said, then looked at Megan in solidarity. Which she appreciated after how he'd treated her in the COC meeting. *Give it a minute to show itself in their numbers.*

Their relationship might be on ice at the moment, but they're both thriving at work. Which means you aren't whispering the right things to them, yet again, Karla said. *Jasper has written thirty thousand words! And Lily has run two successful social media campaigns and gained ten thousand new followers. They seem to have forgotten about her viral meltdown! Looks like all you did was succeed in getting Jasper to drive two hundred miles away, but as a result, they've both been more productive.* She shot a hard look at Megan. *Maybe your Real World study wasn't so foolproof after all?* She scoffed. *As if their world could have something beneficial to offer ours. Be happy you didn't mention anything like that to me in your interview, is all I have to say.*

Megan started to speak, but Karla cut her off.

Get it together in the next two weeks, or I will think about moving both of you to departments where your skill level might be more appropriate. There are openings in Parental Pseudoactivism or Freeloading Adult Children. Can't imagine why they've had such a high turnover rate. She laughed.

Megan had sat in silence, frustrated that Lily and Jasper were like a seesaw. If you pushed one part of their lives down, the other went up. She stared at that painting above Karla's desk, of the man screaming, and wanted to join him.

Megan's phone vibrated again.

Maybe we do working drinks?

Working drink, maybe.

Or I could come to your room and we could work there.

Megan's heart started to beat in an off-kilter way. It sped up, then slowed down, then sped up again. She took a drink of water and stared at Ben's text. She looked around. She'd pulled off her bra and flung it on top of the dresser as soon as the heavy door had closed behind her. Her suitcase was open, and clothes were spilling out from when she'd grabbed a pair of sweats and put them on, the outfit she'd been wearing in a heap on the floor.

Having him in this room would feel too personal. Too intimate. Too many things.

She replied, I'll meet you for one drink. And I'm bringing my tablet!

Twenty minutes later, she walked up to the bar.

"I ordered you a dirty martini, three olives. That's your drink, right?"

"How did you—"

"I overheard you tell Beth once."

"Overheard or—"

"Eavesdropped." He threw his hands up. "Guilty." He grinned like he was happy to be caught.

She held out her glass, and they toasted. "To making our deadline," she said, giving him a stern look.

"Of course," he said. "But first. Do you know what a cat orders at the bar?"

What?

"A *meow*-tini."

Megan laughed a little. "I think you've been spending too much time with your new client, Nancy."

"Her cat, Raspberry, is kind of a stud," Ben said, then puffed out his chest. "Do you know what he says after he takes a dump in his *eight-hundred-dollar* litter box?"

"I have a feeling you're going to tell me."

"How do you like me *meow*?" He laughed.

Belinda walked up and ordered a screwdriver. She gave them both side-eye as she grabbed her drink and left.

"That woman stresses *meow*-t!" Ben said.

That time, Megan laughed until her ribs pulsed.

Four hours and just as many drinks later, with no plan in place to ruin their clients' careers, because causing a social media blackout and convincing Jasper to throw his computer in Big Bear Lake sounded like unrealistic ideas even while drunk, Megan fell into bed with all her clothes on, a little tipsy and a lot giddy.

She'd had a lot of fun with Ben. And she wasn't even mad about it.

Chapter Fourteen

Naysayland

"Megan, over here. I saved us chairs," Beth called. She was about fifteen rows back from the stage where the opening general session would be commencing. On each cushion next to Beth was an item that had clearly been pulled from the bowels of her handbag. A hairbrush thick with her black hair, a set of wooden chopsticks, a pocketknife, a roll of duct tape, a travel toothbrush, and a pair of socks. Megan had so many questions.

"Thanks for the seat," Megan said and meant it. She and Beth had been texting a lot and not just about their clients. Beth had confided that working the graveyard shift was wearing on her and that sometimes she felt lonely. Megan had shared that lately, when she came home to her empty apartment at night, she felt the same way.

Megan had also shared this with Dr. Peakstone, and she'd expressed concern that almost all Megan's time was being spent at work. She'd stopped cooking dinner for herself, eating takeout at her desk instead.

You need balance, Megan, Dr. Peakstone had said.

Megan had balked. Wasn't that counterintuitive to the culture at Naysay Inc.? Wouldn't they frown on a new employee who'd already made a big-ass COC mistake leaving the office early so she could prepare linguine with clam sauce?

That's why I'm here, Peakstone said. *To make sure you're not burning the candle at both ends, which will make you less productive. I know you like your studies, and experts do say having work-life balance will make you a more efficient employee. So try doing something social this weekend—maybe with Beth?*

So Megan had asked her to grab a drink and was surprised when she'd agreed. When Megan told her as much, Beth had confided, *I come across a little standoffish, but that's by design—it spares me a lot of nonsense.*

Surprising herself, Megan told Beth she also knew a thing or two about crafting work personas. She explained how she dressed in all black to avoid revealing any clues about her real personality, and why she rarely shared private details of her life—afraid they might one day be used against her. To which Beth had replied, *No shit.* That had made Megan laugh—hard.

She wouldn't elevate Beth to friend status yet, but it had felt good to be able to relate to someone.

Beth groaned, pulling Megan out of her reverie. "Somewhere between the conga line and my fifth (or sixth?) margarita, I promised Joan I'd save chairs for our department. She texted me at six a.m. to ask if I was already down here. I was like, no, I'm still in bed, because the meeting doesn't start for another *two and a half hours.* Then she sent me a bunch of texts in all caps, worried that we were going to end up in the back row and Karla would think our department wasn't taking this meeting seriously. That if Wanda from Aging Parents had better seats, she was going to have me sent to the Island."

"Hope you have your resort wear packed." Megan pointed to Wanda and her department, who were all front-row center.

Wanda flashed them a grin.

"Ugh! This is why I love the night shift. I get to avoid all these office politics and people—except you, of course." Beth dropped her voice. "I drunk whispered Lily last night."

Megan gasped. "That's a thing?"

Beth nodded. "I've done some of my best work after a couple shots of tequila." She leaned closer. "I put it in my energy drinks."

"What did you say to her?" Megan asked.

"She was scrolling way back through Jasper's Instagram feed—like *years* back—and there were pictures of him with a girl. I used the info you gave me about how Real Worlders get all obsessed when they're into someone, and I said a lot of things that would make Lily jealous, like maybe Jasper was hanging out with the girl again, maybe the girl was up in Big Bear with him, even though I had no idea if that woman in the pictures was an ex or a friend."

Another reason Megan was relieved Naysayland didn't have social media: She'd felt numb when she'd come face-to-face with her ex and his fiancée and her huge diamond ring in the grocery store. Probably just the shock. But the ability not only to *see* photos of his proposal, but to zoom in and characterize them? That might have stirred up emotions she wasn't ready to feel.

"So what happened?" Megan asked, praying whatever it was had caused Lily's vulnerability numbers to go up.

"She cried herself to sleep," Beth said, amusement glinting in her eyes. "But I'm not sure after that. I passed out too."

Megan sighed. "Great."

"Yeah, I know, drunk whispering has its flaws," Beth said. "Speaking of drinking, I saw you and Ben Shaw getting cozy at the hotel bar last night."

Megan blinked, startled. "We weren't *getting cozy*. We were talking about work."

"Uh huh," Beth said. "*Work* must be funny as hell then, because you couldn't stop laughing."

"We were blowing off steam. You know, like Peakstone suggested?" Megan wasn't ready to talk about Ben with Beth. Although she wasn't sure what there was to say anyway. Maybe their relationship had crossed over from adversarial to friendly, but that was it.

"Your eyes were all sparkly."

"He was making fun of his client's cat"—Megan waved her hand—"actually, it doesn't matter. I'm *not* interested in Ben. Besides, that would be against company policy."

"Easy, girl. I'm just playing around. I don't see you two together anyway."

Megan wondered why not. And then she wondered why she cared.

"I'm going to find some coffee. I'll need something to keep me awake during this boring-ass meeting," Beth said and took off.

Megan scanned the room for Ben and found him several rows up, talking to Karla. She hoped he wasn't telling her about their terrible whispering strategy ideas from last night—that was all they needed.

She sent him a text. You're not telling Karla about the laptop in the lake idea I hope?

He looked at his phone, then back at her and smiled. Nope. Just kissing her ass. Who thought of that lake thing? Probably me. You're the one with the good ideas.

Had she read that right? There must be a joke coming. But . . . ?

But nothing. You do research. You think. You might have inspired me to think about whispering differently. Do not tell Eddie I said that! I will deny it!

She laughed. What? How?

ChatGPT! Told Jasper it could do a better—and faster—job of writing a book than him. That the thirty thousand words he wrote were shit that AI could've written in five minutes.

That's good!

Also told him he should quit being an author and look for a job writing click bait headlines instead.

Nice.

He's on a nature walk right now.

Good work!

What about Lily?

She cried herself to sleep last night. Hoping she's too depressed this morning to do any work on her platform.

Perfect!

Your ChatGPT thing gives me an idea. Lily needs to get a REAL job. She brags about being almost thirty but has she thought about what happens after? Won't she be too old to keep influencing?

Love it! We make a good team-who knew?

I agree. Let's meet after this session and sync up our plans. We need to keep these two miserable and apart.

Ben added an exclamation mark to her text bubble.

A voice boomed from backstage. "Please welcome your fearless leader, Jacqueline Lowell!"

Jacqueline confidently took the stage to "Another One Bites the Dust," a popular song from the Real World that she had commissioned a local band to record. She'd told Megan the lyrics were exactly how she felt each time they took a client down, so she could overlook that they were written by a Real Worlder.

Joan tugged on Megan's elbow to join their standing ovation, then gave her a funny look, obviously confused why she wouldn't stand for her own mother.

She slowly stood and joined the applause. Her mother had hardly spoken to her since that night at Genevieve's. At their most recent dinner, a stilted meal where they'd mostly discussed whether her grandmother should replace her carpet with tile or wood floors, it was clear Jacqueline was still smarting that Genevieve had sided with Megan.

Megan studied her mother as she commanded the stage, amazed at how such a slight woman could fill the large space with her confidence alone. Unlike Megan's grandmother, there was no deviation between Jacqueline Lowell the CEO and Jacqueline Lowell the mother, something Megan had always accepted because she didn't know anything else. She'd then adopted the same trait. But after watching Lily with her mom, Megan had begun to wonder if there should be a middle ground between the two personas.

"Thank you, thank you, you may be seated," Jacqueline said, motioning her hands downward for almost a full minute until the crowd complied. "We've got a lot of territory to cover so let's get started. Profits are up, but we're still behind on plan. Our shareholders expect us to grow twenty percent. That's a ton of ground to make up, and we have less than one month left in this quarter to execute. So how will we do it?" she asked as she crossed the stage. "We lean *harder* into the chaos in the Real World. Upcoming elections, AI fears, and the peaceful regions that have become destabilized. Not to mention the tremendous bias in news reporting that continues to keep Real Worlders outraged and divided." She stared out at the crowd. "Shout out to our news department on that one," Jacqueline said and was met with a series of woo-hoos.

"Right. Yes, yes, news has been outstanding and is driving our bottom line, but it's not enough to hit these stretch goals. We've outlined a twenty-point plan that we think will get us there." Jacqueline glanced at the screen as bullet points appeared.

Megan's tablet vibrated in her bag. She grabbed it, ignoring Joan's side-eye. There was an urgent text from Soraya, who was surveilling Lily's clients during their sessions.

Lily needs urgent attention. She and Jasper are back in contact!

Megan tucked the tablet under her arm and ducked as she made her way to the back door and into the hallway.

Ben burst out a moment later. “Jasper and Lily are texting again.”

“I know.” Megan pulled up the surveillance feed, and she and Ben huddled over her tablet. “Looks like Lily sent Jasper a thirst trap,” Megan said.

“A what?”

“Hasn’t Carlos helped you with the Gen Y vernacular?” She stared at him. “Never mind. Soraya made me a manual—I’ll share it with you later. We need to focus.”

Megan studied the picture. Lily was in her clean kitchen; her elbows were resting on the sparkling countertop. Her hair was straight, her makeup soft—a palette of barely there pinks. The neckline of her white top was low, but not too revealing, a hint of something more. She looked beautiful.

And natural.

Megan sighed. “The research shows that people act erratically when they’re in the attraction phase, and this definitely tracks. Looks like she texted him right after, claiming it was a mistake. That it had been meant for her agent. There’s no way he believed that, is there?” Megan asked.

“Looks like he responded in seconds. Said he was happy he’d received it because he’d been thinking about her and wanted to come back from Big Bear to see her.” Ben rubbed the back of his neck. “I thought he left his phone in the cabin when he went on his walk.”

Megan shook her head. “One photo, and it’s back on. He’s been rewarded with one picture of her, and the dopamine and oxytocin are pumping like crazy.” She zoomed in on Lily’s photo. “It was a shrewd move on her part. I mean, wouldn’t you want to run home too if you got *this*?”

“Uh, I—” Ben stuttered. “She’s not really my type.”

“She’s everyone’s type, Ben. *I’d* make out with her.”

Ben's face flushed.

"I'm mad at myself for letting this happen. For agreeing to go to drinks with you last night *to work*. And we got zero work done! I woke up late and didn't surveil Lily this morning. I left it to Soraya, who's usually spot on, but maybe if I'd done it myself—"

"But you had fun with the person who kept you out late, right? Right? Laughing at his jokes?" He offered her a bemused smile.

"Yes, but that shouldn't be our focus right now," Megan said, ignoring the nervous energy his grin was creating inside her.

"*Meow* you're talking," Ben punned.

"Come on, Ben. Be serious."

"Okay, so what should we do to fix it this time?" he said. "Let's put our thinking *cats* on."

"Ben!"

He threw his hands up in surrender. "Okay, okay. Sorry."

Megan started pacing. "I need to think." She considered Beth's jealousy angle. Maybe Ben could use it with Jasper. She went back to the photo that Lily sent and pointed to it. "I think we can agree that this picture is only intended for someone you want to have sex with."

"And I have to make Jasper think that person is *not* him."

"Right. You cannot let him leave Big Bear."

"I won't. I got this."

"And I'll hit Lily with facts. Jasper bailed after sleeping with her and gave her some thin excuse about *needing to work*." A look passed between her and Ben because that had been their thin excuse last night. "It was only after she sent him a sexy photo that he says he misses her and wants to come home. Which is total bullshit. He just wants to get laid. Blah, blah, blah." Megan swiped her tablet. "We only have thirty minutes until the karaoke contest, and I've barely rehearsed—another thing I'm blaming you for."

Ben smirked.

"What?"

“I feel bad for keeping you from rehearsal, so I’ll make it up to you—I’ve got the perfect song for you.”

“Oh yeah?”

He leaned in. “Anything by Doja Cat.”

A laugh slipped out before Megan could stop it. She gave him a playful push, then yanked her headset out of her tote bag. “Let’s end this thing between Jasper and Lily once and for all. We are not getting demoted to Parental Pseudoactivism!”

“Why do we have to wear this?” Beth said to Megan later in the restroom as she tugged on the tight black T-shirt with *Social Media Makes a Splash* in white lettering across the front. “It was bad enough that they made us dress up for karaoke.”

“At least we beat Jim. He was the front-runner, and then he blew it on ‘Ex’s and Oh’s’—he was completely off-key when he went into *oh oh oh*; I was like *oh oh oh no*!” Megan laughed. “And you and I had the crowd on its feet during our duet of ‘Summer Nights.’ Our costumes were amazing.”

“You did look hot in your spandex, Olivia Newton-John.” Beth nudged her. “I saw Ben drooling over you.”

“Stop. You lie!”

“I would never lie. Anyway, I think you could win this thing.”

“I don’t know. Ben’s team won the egg toss, the three-legged race, and the paper-plane contest.” She paused. “Although I wish we’d had video playback because he definitely stepped over the launch line when he threw his!”

“At least they ate shit at the PowerPoint showdown, which was worth a lot more points. We killed that contest.” She high-fived Megan. “I thought they were joking when they said we’d be selling actual Real World products that made millions. Wearable blankets? A stuffed doll that supposedly comes from the North Pole at Christmas and moves to a different location in the house each night?"

"Pet rocks!" Megan joined in, shaking her head. She checked her watch. "We have the ropes course at three fifteen," she said with a reluctant groan.

"What? Are you nervous? We've got this."

Megan shook her head. "It's not that. Did you read the fine print?"

"Oh, that we could die. Yeah, I saw that."

"No, the part about the blindfold and having to *trust*." Megan had volunteered, hoping she could secure a win for their department. Beth would be her guide.

"You think I'm going to let you fall? I've got your back! Literally. You know that, right?"

"Of course," Megan said, managing a smile. But inside she was conflicted. It wasn't about trusting Beth; she did—at least a little. And for her, that was a lot. It was about giving up control. How could she let herself be defenseless, even with an *almost* friend?

"Great. Let's go kick some ass," Beth said, a huge grin on her face.

Megan nodded as she finished washing her hands. "Let's do this."

Outside, each department stood together in their matching shirts. Megan spotted Jim in a *Second Time's the Charm* tee. She scanned the area and located Ben and Eddie looking like two dogs about to be let loose in the park in their bright-red *Creatives Create Anxiety* T-shirts. Jacqueline was with her leadership team, her *C-suite equals D-feat* shirt stretched over her black dress.

Megan gazed up at the pulleys, ropes, and planks hanging in the trees.

"We *need* to win this," Joan said to Megan, her brow pinching. "The losers have to clean out the fridge in the break room every week for a year."

"That doesn't seem like a big deal."

"You haven't seen what Eddie leaves in there," Joan said, gagging. She nodded toward Eddie, who was running in place and chanting "three-peat" with Ben and the rest of their department. "Creatives have won the last three years. We have to crush them. Karla uses this competition as a barometer for each department's efficiency."

"Joan, take a breath. You run our department very well. Karla is Karla. She motivates through cruelty. Don't let her get to you."

Joan blinked at Megan several times. "Thank you. I needed to hear that."

Had she just given Joan a pep talk? She really would do anything to win.

The woman running the competition blasted the rules and information to the group through a bright-yellow bullhorn. There were two identical ropes courses set up so two departments could compete head-to-head. On each course, one team member would be blindfolded while another member attempted to lead them safely from one plank to the next. They'd be seventy-five feet in the air and had over one hundred feet to traverse from one side to the other. The team across first would win.

Megan caught Ben sidling up to her out of the corner of her eye.

"You ready to get beat?" Ben asked as the first two teams competed.

Megan didn't turn so she could hide her smile. "I'm not sure if you heard the news, but your winning streak ends today."

"The only thing that ends today is your misguided confidence. We're about to beat your asses," he said matter-of-factly, but she didn't miss the lilt in his voice.

Jim lost his balance and fell, his harness catching him before he hit the safety net below. His team was disqualified. A cheer erupted from Trainers, the competing department. Buoyed by Jim's fall, Bernard moved faster across his ropes. Megan was surprised at how agile he was for being such a tall man.

"Up next, Creatives versus Social Media," the woman with the bullhorn called out.

"That's a little tight," Megan said as Beth tied the knot of her blindfold.

"It's supposed to be. Hold still," Beth said.

Megan could hear Ben and Belinda arguing over who would wear the blindfold. It sounded like Belinda had lost the battle. The whistle was blown, indicating the clock had started.

Megan slid her right foot off the platform, searching for the rope.

"It's right there," Beth said. "The rope is below your foot, just step—"

"*Where* do I step? How far?" Megan said. She hated this feeling. Not knowing up from down. Not being in control. Dr. Peakstone would have a field day with this one.

"Step out straight."

"How far out?"

"The plank is about six inches in front of you."

"Thank you—you might recall that I *can't see anything*," Megan said as her foot contacted the board. It swayed underneath her as she put her weight on it.

"Creatives are passing us. Belinda is moving fast," Beth said.

"I'm going as fast as I can."

"Are you?" Beth said. "Try to pick up the pace. I won't let you fall. I got you."

Megan held her breath and extended her left foot, hoping taking larger steps would satisfy her. "Like this?"

"Yes, like that. But *faster*!"

Megan lunged her right foot forward and missed the rope. She started to fall, a surge of panic ripping through her. She hit something hard, the impact above her eye. Her harness finally caught, and she sprang upward, then bounced up and down for a moment until she finally settled. Stunned, she took off her bandanna and touched her head above her eyebrow where a lump was forming. Her fingers were damp, and when she looked at them, they were covered in blood.

The woman who'd been holding the bullhorn earlier helped Megan out of her harness. "Here." She handed her an alcohol wipe and a couple of BAND-AIDs. "We're short staffed today. The medic called out sick and his replacement isn't here yet." She rolled her eyes. "The irony, right? Anyway, I think you can clean it up yourself. I heard the face bleeds a lot even when the wound isn't serious. The bathroom is that way." She motioned to the right.

Megan's forehead was pulsing. "Okay."

Beth rushed over. "I thought the plank was closer to your foot," she said, then jerked her head back. "Oh my god, your eye—I'm so sorry! There's blood everywhere."

"It's not your fault," Megan said, her eyes watering from the pain. "Can you walk me to the bathroom?"

Beth looped her arm through Megan's. "Come on."

Megan examined her face in the bathroom mirror. There was a deep slash in her skin through the center of her eyebrow. She wet several paper towels and held them up against the wound. She winced.

Beth was fumbling through her fanny pack. "I think I might have some ibuprofen in here."

The bathroom door swung open. "Megan!" Jacqueline said.

Megan felt the tension release from her body.

"I heard you fell and got hurt," she said, rushing over. "Let me see."

Megan gently pulled the paper towels away.

"Wow, look at that gash."

Megan felt lightheaded. She needed to sit down. "I think I need to—"

"How did this happen? People are talking."

Megan sighed. Her mom wasn't concerned with the wound, only the optics.

"It was my fault," Beth said. "I was guiding her and—"

"Clearly. If you'd done your job, this wouldn't have happened." Jacqueline gave Beth a long look. "I can take it from here. You should get back to your team. But maybe don't volunteer to be the guide again. Not. Your. Strength."

As Beth left, Megan caught her eye and gave her a small smile. Why was Jacqueline so hard on people? It had never occurred to Megan to question this—probably because she was accustomed to such behavior, especially in their relationship—but seeing her mom reprimand someone else like Beth hit different.

"Do you think I need a doctor? I guess the one that was supposed to be here is sick."

Jacqueline leaned in. "Doesn't look like it needs stitches."

"Really? How can you tell?" Megan couldn't remember a time her mom had helped her with so much as a scraped knee. Now she was an expert on stitches?

Jacqueline didn't answer as she ripped open the alcohol wipe Megan had set on the counter and applied it to the skin around the gash. Megan gritted her teeth as her mom firmly pressed two BAND-AIDs over the wound.

Megan squinted at the mirror. The bandages turned from nude to dark red as the blood seeped through. "Are you sure this is all I need?"

"Don't act like one of those Real Worlders who wants crutches for a sprained ankle. It's not how us Lowell women conduct ourselves. You need to pull it together and get back out there," she said, the door slamming behind her.

Megan's eyes welled with tears. She splashed water on her face before heading back out. Maybe her mom was right. Maybe she was getting soft. Making friends with coworkers. Wanting first aid for a small cut. What would be next? Asking for a trigger warning on her next read? Begging for a second-place trophy?

Megan pushed the door open, startled to find Ben on the other side. "What are you doing here?"

"I wanted to make sure you were okay. The woman in charge of the race said you had a scratch, but I heard you hit your head pretty hard.

I hated that I was stuck up there on the platform while that happened to you. It felt like it took me forever to get down."

"I'm fine," Megan said, swallowing down a fresh wave of nausea. "Did you get your win?"

"We did, technically, but only by default."

"Because I fell?"

Ben nodded. "Beth refused to race with anyone else—even when Joan pushed. Said you were her teammate, and she'd rather forfeit."

Megan couldn't help but smile. Beth meant what she said about having her back. "So . . . you didn't really win then?"

"Guess not, but we'll beat your ass fair and square next year," Ben said, with a teasing glint in his eye—until his face tightened. "You're bleeding through your bandages. Can I take a look?"

"My mom wasn't worried, so I'm sure it's fine."

Ben bit his lip. "Will you let me check anyway?"

Megan tried to nod, but the horizon tilted slightly.

"Hey—are you okay? You're swaying."

Another wave of nausea rolled through her.

Ben slipped his arm around her shoulders and guided her to the nearest bench. "You need to sit down. And I am checking this."

Ben peeled the bandages back carefully, but even the light touch of air to her wound made her flinch.

He sucked in a breath. "Yeah, no. You need to get this looked at now—I think I can see the cartilage."

Megan swallowed hard. "I'm sure Beth will go with me."

"No," Ben said, pressing the gauze gently back into place. "I'm going with you."

A loud cheer erupted from the direction of the ropes course. "But you'll miss the awards ceremony," she said.

"Who gives a shit. Here." He guided her hand to the bandages. "Hold this. I'm going to grab some paper towels"—he pointed toward the bathrooms—"and then we're heading to the hospital. It will take me less than a minute." He looked at her closely. "Will you be okay while I'm gone?"

Megan's throat tightened. She didn't know what to say—still trying to reconcile this Ben with the one she'd met less than two months ago, the one who never missed a chance to collect a win no matter how it was earned.

◆ ◆ ◆

"That should do it," the physician said as she placed the butterfly stitch over the glue she'd used to close up the wound.

"Nice fashion statement," Ben teased from the corner of the triage room of the hospital.

Megan tapped her head. "How bad is it?" she asked the doctor.

"It's fine. You're lucky it's not worse."

"Am I able to leave now?" Megan asked. She had three missed calls and four texts from her grandmother since they'd arrived, asking if she was okay, and two from Jacqueline asking why she hadn't come back.

"I want you to stay a few more hours for observation so we can be sure you don't have a concussion. I'll check on you in a bit," she said and abruptly left the room.

Megan lay back in the bed and sighed. "I shouldn't be here. My mom—"

"You heard what the doctor said."

"And you know how my mom is."

Ben looked like he wanted to say more but didn't. "Does it hurt?"

"Yeah." Megan's head pulsed hard. "Thank you for bringing me, but I'm okay now. You're free to go—you might still make the awards after-party."

"It's not like I was being held against my will. I wanted to be here. I don't care about that."

"Really?" she asked and peered at him. His brown eyes popped against the ice-blue sweatshirt he'd thrown on, but his face was a mask of concern and wariness. For her? For missing the awards announcement? She wasn't sure.

"Yeah. That's what the whole exercise was about today—we're supposed to look out for each other, right? And we're buddies now, aren't we?"

Buddies. Of course that's all this was.

"Right," Megan conceded. "I guess I don't totally hate you."

Ben smiled. "I will consider that a victory."

A barrage of alerts burst from Megan's tablet, buried in her bag. She yanked it out and swiped the screen to check the incoming messages. She let out a gasp.

"What is it?" Ben asked, worry creeping into his voice.

They'd just announced Megan had finished at the top of the leaderboard. She'd come from behind to beat Ben, ending his multiyear reign. It was exactly what she'd wanted. Why she'd worked so hard. But as she searched Ben's earnest face in this hospital room, her stomach queasy, Megan felt an emotion she couldn't describe.

She eyed the tablet as a message from her mother popped up. Nice job living up to the expectation I set for you. Let's meet as soon as we get back to go over your action plan to win again next quarter.

"Is everything okay?" Ben pressed.

Megan cleared her throat. "I won," she said quietly.

Ben's eyes vacillated through a series of emotions. Megan saw the flash of surprise, then anger, followed by something else. Sadness? Jealousy?

"Ben—"

"It's okay, Megan. You can gloat. You know you want to."

Although she'd spent the better part of the last few weeks imagining this moment and all the petty things she'd say to Ben if she won, she didn't want to gloat. She wanted to make Ben feel better about losing to her. She wanted him to understand that beating him didn't make her feel like she thought it would.

Megan stared at him until Ben broke their silence. "It's making it worse that you're not talking."

"I tried to warn you I'd catch you," Megan said meekly.

"You did."

Megan blushed, remembering the day they met. "What can I say? I keep my promises."

A text came in from her grandmother. I knew you could do it! Congrats!

Megan smiled and then quickly fixed her mouth in a straight line.

"I'm happy for you, Megan," Ben said.

"No, you're not. You're pissed about losing."

"Can both things exist at once? Can I be happy for you and pissed for myself?"

Megan considered his words. "I guess I've never really thought about it."

Ben held her gaze. "Maybe you should."

He was about to say something else when Megan got another text. She swiped and saw a message from Soraya that Lily's vulnerability score had dipped again and read Soraya's explanation.

Megan sighed.

"What is it?" Ben asked.

"Lily and Jasper have been texting *again*," she said. "Where's your tablet?"

"I must have left it at the ropes course," he said.

"I don't think I've ever seen you without that thing." She laughed.

"I should probably go find it," he said and started to head toward the door. He turned and looked at her for a moment. "Will you call me when they release you?"

Her heart thudded. "Okay."

"I can pass along an update to the group—let them know the woman who topped the leaderboard is coming back."

"Right, of course," she said as he left.

What had she thought he was going to say? That he wanted to personally know she was okay? That he'd take care of her once she got back to the hotel? She shook her head. He'd already dedicated enough of his time to her hospital visit, not to mention he clearly had to swallow his disappointment about losing to her. What more did she want from him?

She wasn't sure.

She texted Beth and asked if she could come pick her up. Beth sent a thumbs-up emoji.

Megan scrolled back through Lily and Jasper's text exchange that had started around the time Megan's name had finally been called and she'd gone from the hospital waiting room to a bed in the back to see the doctor.

Jasper had started it off, texting Lily that he was sorry he'd been acting like an idiot. He'd let that obnoxious voice in his head get to him again. He wasn't jealous of her and some guy from three years ago.

Lily had fired back that her voice had been after her, too, but had finally dimmed over the past few hours, which had given her clarity. She had every intention of working on her book but admitted she couldn't stop thinking about Jasper and how she'd screwed things up with him. She said she was tired of playing games, games she didn't want to be playing in the first place.

Jasper agreed. Then asked if he could take her on a real date.

She'd said yes.

Megan knew that was her cue. She pulled her headset out of her bag. She needed to make her voice heard again.

Lily wrote back and asked Jasper to FaceTime. Megan heard the FaceTime ring. She saw Lily fluff her hair and angle the phone to answer.

Megan hesitated.

Maybe it was because she had a head injury. Maybe Ben's unexpected kindness and graciousness had softened her. Or maybe she was exhausted. But Megan Lowell decided not to whisper anything.

Dr. Peakstone
Session with Megan Lowell
June 6th

Dr. Peakstone: Are you seeing anyone? In a relationship?

Megan: I'm sorry, but how is that relevant to work?

Peakstone: We can talk about more than your job in our sessions. I'm curious about you.

Megan: Okay. Well, I'm single.

Peakstone: Are you dating?

Megan: No. My focus is to be successful at this job.

Peakstone: Fair. When was your last serious relationship?

Megan: College. Although I'm not sure I'd call it a relationship.

Peakstone: Why not?

Megan: Is it still a relationship if you know from the start you won't let it go anywhere?

Chapter Fifteen

Naysayland

"Want a glass of wine?" Megan asked Ben after he set his backpack on one of the chairs around her glass-top dining room table.

"Should we?" he asked, glancing at the bottle she'd already placed beside two glasses.

"They're having one." Megan pointed to her tablet, which was propped on the kitchen counter in between a stack of her most used cookbooks and the spice rack. Jasper and Lily had sat down to dinner at a new Asian fusion restaurant and ordered a bottle of Vivo Vines Cabernet.

It had been Megan's idea to have Ben over. She'd reasoned that they couldn't afford to let their temporary whisperers surveil Lily and Jasper's date. That they needed to be the ones to make sure their clients' vulnerability scores stayed high—especially because they'd both slipped a few notches on the leaderboard since the company conference.

Megan hadn't minded that her numbers had dropped and wasn't entirely bothered by the ensuing pressure from Leadership. The celebration over her big win had been surprisingly difficult to savor, her mouth twitching slightly anytime Karla or Joan brought it up or when Belinda used Megan's victory to shame Ben. Even her mother's accolades hadn't tasted as sweet as Megan had imagined they would.

Her crisp *That's how it's done* in the elevator a few days later had barely registered.

Megan knew it was a risk for Ben to be in her home. It would be hard to explain why they'd needed to monitor their clients after hours *in her apartment*. She didn't have an answer for that. Not one she wanted to admit anyway.

Excitement had bubbled up in Megan's chest as she watched Lily get ready for her dinner with Jasper. Lily carefully applied a face mask as "Just Give Me a Reason" by P!nk played in the background. Megan sang along, now knowing most of the words to many Real World pop songs. Megan approved of the jasmine-green maxi dress Lily chose to wear. She imagined herself telling Lily how flattering it was on her. Every time Lily glanced at her phone, Megan felt her own anticipation level up.

Megan ducked out of the office at five o'clock, keeping her head down as she hurried past Karla's office, a lie prepared should she get stopped—that she was taking a walk to clear her head. But really, she was making dinner for Ben, and she wanted to have plenty of time to shop for ingredients at her favorite bodega. She took pleasure in picking the ripest tomatoes and the freshest garlic for the bruschetta. She planned to examine the spinach with extra care and take time to sample the ricotta cheese that she would stuff her homemade ravioli with. She selected one of her favorite bottles of merlot on her way to the cashier and imagined sharing it with Ben.

"Well, it would be rude to let them drink alone," Ben said, pulling Megan out of her thoughts.

Megan poured Ben a glass and began to chop the garlic as they watched Lily and Jasper's conversation unfold. Lily was telling him that she was making headway on getting her book ready to turn in to her publisher, having written constantly for the past two days.

"It's funny what happens when there's no chatter," Lily said.

Ben pointed at the monitor with his glass. "She means you."

"No shit," Megan said, grabbing the dish towel off her shoulder and then swiping him with it.

"So where have you been, Ms. Chatter?"

"Silence has been my strategy. I wanted her to focus on her work, not him."

Ben rolled his eyes. "But yet, she's with him now. And you're still quiet."

Jasper toasted Lily. "I agree. I also had a productive weekend. I sent more pages to my agent—and he loved them!"

Megan grabbed a tomato and sliced it. "You were saying?" she teased.

"He used what I suggested," Ben countered. "I practically ghostwrote what he turned in." He lifted his chin, clearly proud of himself.

Megan rolled her eyes and opened the oven. She pulled out the bread she'd cut and toasted, set the pieces on a platter, heaped the tomato and garlic onto each one, and drizzled them with olive oil. Then she grated some parmesan across the tops. She pushed the plate toward Ben while she got to work on the ravioli.

He took a bite. "Delicious," he said. "You definitely cook better than you whisper."

"Debatable," she shot back as she laid out the pasta and put small dollops of her ricotta spinach mixture across the length of each. She put another layer of pasta across the tops, then cut them into squares and pressed the pasta together to make her ravioli.

"How long have you been cooking?" Ben asked.

"For as long as I can remember," Megan said. "When I was a child, one of my nannies used to let me help her in the kitchen."

"So this is what you do when you're not working. I had no idea," he said.

"Most people don't. It's my thing. Kind of like a ritual. I haven't been able to cook as much since taking this job, which sucks. Don't tell anyone because I'll deny it, but it grounds me, so I've been trying to make more time for it lately, if that makes sense?"

Ben nodded, a shadow of a thought crossing his face. "It does."

"Do you have anything like that?" Megan pressed.

Lily laughed and scooted closer to Jasper. They were sitting in a booth in a dimly lit restaurant, candlelight flickering, casting a warm glow across their faces. Megan could practically smell the garlic and butter wafting from the basket of bread on their table.

"Should we interject?" Ben asked, his hand hovering over the talk button on his headset.

"Probably," Megan said but was distracted by the boiling water on her stove, which was close to overflowing. She needed to start dropping the ravioli in. "Maybe try to make him feel insecure that her book might be published before his?" she offered as she turned down the heat a little. "That she didn't care about being an author but would probably outsell him?" Megan said, carefully dropping the ravioli in the pot.

"That's not bad. I'll try that, maybe after one more of these," Ben said, taking another bite of bruschetta.

Megan stirred the pasta as Lily and Jasper moved on to another topic. "Looks like the moment has passed now," Megan said.

"Darn," Ben said, his mouth full.

Megan and Ben sat down to dinner, the tablet between them, although neither was paying it much attention.

"This food is delicious," Lily said as she savored a bite of grilled octopus.

"This is also delicious," Ben said, pointing at his own plate.

Megan smiled. She hadn't cooked for anyone since her ex. He hadn't been a pasta guy—too many carbs. She wondered if that was why she'd chosen to make it tonight.

Jasper and Lily were served their entrées. Jasper asked about Lily's parents, and she was telling him how close she was with her mom. "She really is my best friend. I don't have any siblings, so it's always been my parents and me."

Ben looked at Megan. "Must be nice, right? To have a mom like that?"

"I guess," Megan said, feeling a slight pang. "Can I ask you something?"

"Anything."

"We talk a lot about my family, but I don't know anything about yours. Are you not close with your parents?"

Ben took a deep breath. "My mom got too attached to me. She was sent away to the Island."

"Oh my god! How old were you?"

"I was a baby. My dad raised me. He passed away a few years ago."

Megan's chest fluttered as she imagined Ben all alone. She'd grown up with a mother, but Jacqueline had always been detached. And in Megan's mind, Jacqueline's behavior was far more sterile than what was considered normal for mothers in Naysayland.

Observing Lily and her mom's relationship had given Megan a new perspective. The other day, Lily's mom had left a care package on Lily's doorstep, *just because*. Megan had felt her temperature rise as she'd watched Lily open her favorite organic chocolates—the expensive ones that she couldn't afford herself. Megan's eye had twitched as Lily held a delicate cream scarf to her cheek, recognizing it as something she'd admired in a shop window when they'd had lunch together the week before. Megan had thrown down her headset and went to the bathroom to splash some cold water on her face, not understanding the emotional storm inside her. Was it envy? Jealousy? Sadness? Or all of them at once? What was happening to her?

"I'm sorry," she said now to Ben, realizing she was sorry for them both. Because neither of them had experienced a mother's love.

She let that thought marinate for a moment. It was something a Real Worlder would think. But did that make it wrong? She wasn't sure anymore.

"Me too," Ben said. "And I've realized one of the reasons I can be so intense at work is because I'm trying to prove I'm nothing like her, you know?"

"Ironically, I started working at Naysay Inc. to prove I *was* like my mom, but now, I don't know. Maybe it wouldn't be so terrible if you were like yours."

Ben held her gaze. "You think it's okay to be sent to the Island? You could get in a lot of trouble for talking like that." He gave her a teasing grin and leaned his mouth toward hers.

Megan's breath caught, her head swimming as she stared at his lips. "I—"

Her phone rang, breaking the moment.

"It's my grandmother," she said. "Let me tell her I'll call her back—"

"No, that's okay." Ben stood up. "I should probably go."

Megan's heart plummeted. "Wait, Ben—"

He grabbed his backpack. "See you tomorrow," he called over his shoulder as he headed out the door.

She watched him walk away. "Okay," she said softly and answered the phone.

"I think something is wrong with me," Megan whispered to Joan the next morning as she waited for the coffee machine to dispense her latte. They'd been talking more since returning from the conference, Joan taking Megan's pep talk to mean she wanted to listen to Joan's problems. Joan had recently shared that her baby had colic, and she was starting to think there was a voice *in her head* because she hadn't slept through the night in months. Megan hadn't known what to say to that.

"I was going to ask what was up when I saw you wearing *that*." Joan made a face like she'd smelled garbage.

"What's wrong with this?" Megan asked. But she knew why Joan was confused. Megan's shirt was pink—and she *never* wore color. When she'd gotten dressed that morning, she'd put on her usual black pants, but then she'd done something radical. She'd gone to the back of her closet and pulled out the light pastel blouse her grandmother had given her years ago, which she'd never worn because it looked like a Real Worlder's Easter egg.

"Why aren't you in your usual *someone just died* outfit?"

"Something compelled me to put this thing on." Megan looked over her shoulder to make sure no one was coming into the break room. "I don't feel like myself."

"You have been acting off the past few days." Joan gave her a sideways look.

"Can we keep that fact between us, please?"

"If your leaderboard numbers continue to sink, I'm going to have no choice but to talk to Karla. You know that." She looked up at the board, which took up an entire wall of the break room where Megan's name was at number thirty-one. "You *won* the Top Whisperer Award last quarter, and now look at you."

"It's temporary. I'll build back, Joan."

"With your new so-called strategy?" She eyed her.

Earlier, Joan had raised one of her unruly eyebrows when she overheard Megan coo *you got this* into her headset. Megan had put her hand over the microphone. "It's all part of a master plan," she explained. "Sometimes you have to lift them up before you crush them. I read a study about it in the *Pessimistic People Journal*," Megan lied, and she could tell Joan didn't believe her. Megan knew it was a risk talking that way to her client in the bullpen, but it was almost like she was on autopilot. The lies to cover her actions kept tumbling out of her.

"Do I have a fever? Maybe I'm coming down with something?" Megan asked.

Joan expertly placed the back of her hand on Megan's forehead. "I don't think so—what are your symptoms?"

"Racing heart, sweaty palms, and my stomach tingles." Megan didn't say the rest. That she'd also been *thinking* differently. That morning, she'd gazed up at the gray, cloudy sky and imagined it clear and blue.

Joan stepped back.

"What?" Megan asked.

"If it's the flu, I don't want to get sick. Or get my baby sick. That's the last thing I need."

"That's the thing, I don't feel sick." *Not physically anyway.*

"Menopause?"

"What? I'm only twenty-six."

"Oh, I thought you were older than that."

Megan ignored her and sipped her latte. It tasted bland. She searched the cupboard until she found a packet of sugar. *Since when do I sweeten my coffee?*

"I'm sure whatever it is will pass. Stay hydrated," Joan said, then looked around. "We've already been talking for too long—I need to get back to work. And so do you."

Megan followed Joan into the bullpen, thinking about how her work had also been affected by the way she'd been feeling. The last time she'd signed on to get in Kristopher's ear, he'd learned that the network had committed to eight more episodes of his show because the pilot had rated so well. Megan knew it was the moment she needed to pounce—to bring him down from the cloud he was floating on—but she couldn't do it. She literally could not do it. She turned on her microphone and froze as she watched Kristopher and his wife jumping up and down in their bedroom after the producer had called with the news. Kristopher had kissed his wife and said, *Finally, I've done something right!* Then he'd called his dad who'd told him he was proud of him. *He's never said that to me before,* he said to his wife after, tears sliding down his cheeks.

Megan lost herself in the moment. She removed her headset, replaying Kristopher's tears and what he'd said about his father. It was almost as if she could *relate* to him because she had a parent like that too.

"Hey," Ben said.

Megan's heart started beating harder at the sight of him. Ben's thick blond hair was as unruly as ever. He was wearing his usual dark jeans with a white dress shirt tucked into them. He looked the same, but something was different. Was it him? Or her?

"I wanted to explain why I left last night. I—"

"No, no, it's fine. No need," Megan said, not sure she wanted to know. There was something in his eyes that she couldn't read. Did he feel sorry for her? Had she gotten it all wrong—was his concern at the hospital only pity, nothing more?

She took several deep breaths. Her stomach felt peculiar. Was this a delayed side effect of her head injury? She looked around like someone could be reading her mind. If anyone had the technology to do that, it was Naysay Inc. She almost laughed. Now *she* was paranoid.

"You okay?" Ben squinted at her.

"I'm fine. Thinking about a problem with a client," she said, which was partly true. She had also been thinking about how she'd failed to whisper to both Tatterson and Lily during critical moments.

She didn't recognize herself anymore. What had happened to the Megan Lowell who was valedictorian of her high school class? Dean's list every semester of college? Who was so prepared to work at Naysay Inc. that she'd made a spreadsheet of the best ways to make people feel anxious *before* she was hired?

"Which client?"

"Tatterson," she said, keeping her eyes off Ben.

"I thought he was your easy one?"

He *had* been her easy one. She could've sliced in half the joy he felt about his show getting picked up with a simple sentence: *It's only a matter of time before you let your dad down again.* Soraya had uncovered that Tatterson had borrowed money from his father to open his tattoo shop. Then COVID hit. He'd lost all his dad's money and respect, but Megan hadn't said a word.

She looked up at Ben. "He was—he is. I don't know." Should she level with Ben? Tell him how off-balance she felt, like a car with a flat tire? Maybe he'd gone through something similar. He could suggest a pill she could take. A book she could read. Or would he only be disappointed in her?

Maybe she needed one of those support groups that could rid you of your "positivity" or "empathetic tendencies." They met in basements and were anonymous. It was a twelve-step program that often worked, according to someone who'd had a sister who'd gone through it. Megan was shocked that converted Naysayers walked among them. But with her history of working at Naysay Inc., Megan knew such a group wouldn't be an option for her even if she wanted to go. She'd messed with their clients' unhappiness, and there was zero tolerance for that. She'd signed an employee contract agreeing to as much.

Joan popped her head over Megan's cubicle. "Karla wants you in her office—now," she said, two deep lines forming between her eyes.

The sessions between lead whisperers and their clients were recorded, but they weren't monitored. Only Karla or those higher than her could summon the transcripts. And they would only do that if they were suspicious.

Was Karla suspicious?

"I'm sure everything is fine," Megan said, despite the pit of dread forming in her stomach.

"Update me after, please," Joan said and walked toward her office, pausing. "I have to call Beth. Apparently, she's been consuming alcohol on the job—started a drinking game with another temporary whisperer where they took a shot every time the client won a live auction item on Poshmark they couldn't afford."

After she'd gone, Ben stepped closer to Megan. "Do you think Karla knows we were together at your place last night? I should go in with you, help explain."

Explain why you couldn't get out of there fast enough?

"Whatever it is, I'll handle it. I promise."

"Megan—"

"I have to go," she said and hurried to Karla's office.

◆ ◆ ◆

"Come in and shut the door," Karla said to Megan without looking up from her tablet.

Megan sat in the stiff chair and picked at her thumbnail nervously.

"Holy hell," Karla said when she raised her eyes. "What are you wearing? Is that *pink*?"

Megan feigned disgust. "I know, I know. All my black was at the cleaners. Forgot to pick it up." She tugged at the fabric. "It's more of a light pink than fuchsia, don't you think?"

"What's fuchsia?" Karla's face bunched up into a ball. She walked around the front of her desk and took a closer look at Megan. "What's wrong with you? You're glowing. Are you ill? Pregnant? *In love?*" She laughed. "Just kidding. We all know *that's* not possible—you're a Lowell." She shifted her tone. "Your numbers are still trending downward. I'm concerned. You're behind Martin from Luxury Hotel Concierges, and he only whispers part-time! His clients are already berated on a daily basis by elitist guests. The other day one of them was verbally abused because apparently all the fruit on the property was too hard. His client was forced to go off-site and search for soft papaya to put in a smoothie!"

Megan was still stuck back at the words *in love.*

She took a shaky breath.

Was she?

In love?

With *Ben*?

Was that why she felt like she was floating? Speeding up and slowing down at once? The reason she'd been experiencing empathy for others?

She thought of the study with the Real Worlders and their brains firing when they looked at photos of their love interests. What would her brain do if she looked at a picture of Ben? She gagged.

"Are you going to throw up? If so, please exit my office."

Megan swallowed down the bile. Maybe she *was* sick.

Lovesick.

The room turned upside down. Love infected the weak. It was a disease.

Wasn't it?

"I'm sorry," Megan said, heading for the door. "I need to use the restroom."

Karla wrinkled her nose. "I expected more from you. The flu is for losers."

"Can we table the discussion about my numbers? I'll fix them *and myself* right away. I promise," Megan said as she rushed out the door.

She leaned against the wall outside Karla's office. She had one priority, and it wasn't improving her numbers. She needed to gather her scientific research and figure out how to use it on herself. She literally stopped people from catching feelings for a living. Surely she could whisper herself out of the mess she'd created.

Every positive thought about Ben would need to be replaced with a negative one. Each time she caught herself staring at the deep dimple in his left cheek that peeked out when he smiled only a certain way, she'd think about the time she saw him spit in his trash can. Whenever she got lost in the moment listening to him whisper to a client from her cubicle, she'd remind herself what a competitive jerk he could be. And when he was kind to her, she'd make sure to not reciprocate.

In short, she needed to fall out of love. Stat.

Dr. Peakstone

Session with Megan Lowell

June 14th

Dr. Peakstone: I heard you have interesting theories on love.

Megan: How?

Peakstone: Don't worry about that. I'd love to hear more from you directly, if you'll enlighten me.

Megan: They aren't *my* theories. They're from the Real World. I learned that love isn't about the heart. It's about the brain. When someone desires another person, their brain releases hormones that make them giddy, energetic, and euphoric. And they'll do almost *anything* to keep feeling that way.

Peakstone: Has the research been helpful?

Megan: I believe it has helped us better control our clients, yes.

Peakstone: I mean, has it been helpful to *you*?

Megan: To me?

Peakstone: Has it helped you better control yourself?

Chapter Sixteen

Naysayland

Megan pumped her arms harder, her legs kicking up behind her as she raced Ben. It had been a week since Karla called Megan into her office, and she still hadn't found a way to unlove him.

She recalled their text exchange from last night. They often messaged after hours about work issues, but since that night at Megan's apartment, they'd shifted to more personal things. Ben told her about how he'd tried to make his own bruschetta and failed miserably, his tomatoes bland and hard as a rock. They weren't ripe, she'd teased. Then she'd revealed that her Taylor Swift obsession had reached new levels when she'd done a deep dive on the singer's dating history, matching each relationship to a song on her latest album. Which was so poetic, by the way. Last night, they'd agreed how spectacular a sunset was that Jasper and Lily had watched. The sky was streaked with bursts of reds and yellows.

Megan kept to herself that she wished she and Ben could watch one together in Naysayland. If only the clouds ever lifted.

Despite her plan to use the information she'd compiled about Real Worlders to make herself fall out of love, she seemed to be falling more into it. Her research told her what she already knew. Her brain had decided, and there wasn't a whole lot she could do about it. But the real question was, did she want to?

She'd called her grandmother while walking to work that morning. Genevieve had answered on the first ring, like she'd been waiting for the call. Megan made small talk before asking her the question that had been on her mind.

"Did you ever question if the Real World truly needs Naysay Inc.?" Megan said, her hand cupping the phone. As if that would make the inquiry less scandalous. "If we are really helping?"

Several beats of silence followed before Genevieve spoke. "*Help* is a relative term. Look how many times one Real World country has invaded another to *save* it. Real Worlders and their savior complexes have been destroying lives for years. The key is convincing yourself you're on the right side of it."

"You didn't really answer my question."

Genevieve laughed. "Why are you asking, Megan?"

"I think I need to know what side I'm on. They tell us our work is compelling and righteous, but sometimes it feels like it's more about the money—that we only exist to benefit the Fund."

"Why can't it be both? Look at the Real World's pharmaceutical companies—they help millions of people with their innovation but also are incredibly profitable."

Megan chewed her fingernail. "We aren't exactly curing cancer here."

Genevieve let out a long breath. "No, we're not. But this is what we do. And at some point, you're going to have to decide if you're cut out for it."

"And if I'm not?" Megan's hands began to shake slightly at the thought.

"Then you aren't," her grandmother said, her voice soft.

Megan hung up a few minutes later, her grandmother's words bouncing in her head like a pinball. She wondered which side she was on.

Now, as she collapsed onto the track after beating Ben to the finish line, their chests heaving and their hands grazing as they caught their breath, Ben rolled onto his side to face Megan. He'd peeled off his shirt, and she was so close she could see beads of sweat clinging to his chest. Her heart was still beating hard after several minutes of rest as she watched a bead roll toward his navel.

That was the thing she'd realized with each passing day. Ben made her heart race when they *weren't* running together. It would spike each time he walked by her cubicle, casually running his hand through his hair or looking at her over the lid of his favored thermos. Her pulse elevated as she felt his eyes on her as she presented at a meeting last week, her hands moving animatedly as she discussed the fine line between being condescending and patronizing, which had been part of her demoralization thesis in college. She worried her heart would fly out of her chest when she caught his eye and he let his mouth slide into the smallest smile. When he looked at her that way, it was as if everything around them disappeared.

And she found herself experiencing another new emotion. Worry. If he didn't return her text right away. If he was late meeting her for their runs. And right now she felt it because he was unusually quiet. She wondered what his silence meant. Megan had never worried what a man thought of her before or how his actions would impact her. This feeling was new and uncomfortable, but yet, she didn't want to stop whatever *this* was with Ben.

"Hey," he said, breaking their silence. "Can I talk to you about something?"

"Of course," she said, her arm brushing his as she leaned closer, sending an electric shock through her.

"I've been feeling—"

The door to the track opened, and her mom and Karla walked toward them.

Megan leaped to her feet. "Hi, what are you guys doing up here?" Megan asked, her voice not sounding like her own. Had they seen anything between her and Ben? Although what had there been to see, exactly? They'd only been talking.

So why did Megan feel so guilty, like she'd been caught?

"I need to come up with fresh tactics for berating the staff when their numbers are down because I can only call someone worthless so many times before it loses its punch. I thought a change of scenery might help. I convinced Jacqueline to join me because she's excellent at brainstorming new approaches to condescension," Karla said.

"She is *the best*," Megan said, her jaw tight.

Jacqueline flashed a smug smile. "Although this change of scenery doesn't seem to be helping Megan solve *her* low-numbers problem. She's up here constantly with Ben, running in circles, and it shows on the leaderboard. She's lower than everyone in Conspiracy Theorists. I hate to say *I told you so*, Megan, but *I told you so*. Looks like your research and theories on love didn't hold with your clients, just as I predicted. You chose the wrong horse when you bet on your grandmother's advice."

Megan bit her lip until she felt pain. From her mother's point of view, she'd failed because of the faulty research and her untested theories. But Megan knew the truth. She'd failed with Lily because she'd stopped trying. And it was only a matter of time before she was found out. Unless she changed something, *fast*.

"It's a shame, really. No matter what you do, you can't keep your client away from Ben's client. You two can't seem to stay away from each other either. My sources tell me you are up here *a lot*. Which I find interesting." Jacqueline stared hard at Megan.

Megan couldn't think. Her thoughts were jumbled.

"It's my fault," Ben said. "I've been pushing Megan to strategize with me about how to handle our client situation. Since I run, too, I show up when I know she's here. She was just telling me to leave her alone so she could think."

Megan shot him a look.

He'd taken the fall for her.

She wanted to hug him. She imagined wrapping her arms around his neck and breathing him in, holding the embrace for several beats. And she was *not* a hugger.

"Then why don't you take a hint, puppy dog?" Karla said. "What's gotten into you?" She leaned in. "Where's the guy from the COC meeting, the one who threw Megan under the bus? I know I got on you for that, but I'd prefer him over whatever *this* is. Because you're not yourself. Your numbers suck too. You're worthless." She took a beat. "I still really think that word works." She turned to Jacqueline. "Maybe it's time to do those client realignments."

"No, Karla, don't do that," Megan argued. "It will take too long to bring other whisperers up to speed on everything. We're in a critical window right now with Lily and Jasper—"

"You've seemingly been in a critical window since the COC weeks ago," Jacqueline interjected. "And you have nothing to show for it except a few sharp spikes in their vulnerability indexes here and there." She turned to Megan. "I was hoping the head injury you suffered would've literally knocked some sense into you."

"I agree," Karla said. "She's been *worse* since the injury. I accused her of being pregnant!"

"Pregnant?" Ben swiveled his head at Megan.

"I'm not. It was a stomach bug."

"Just as bad," Jacqueline said.

"Perhaps Eddie, Belinda, or even *Jim* should take a crack at whispering to their clients," Karla said.

"Please. I promise you we'll fix this," Megan pleaded. "And using only the tried-and-true techniques Naysay Inc. is built on." She locked eyes with her mother.

Jacqueline tilted her head in thought. "Consider this your final warning—I should've reprimanded you already. I'm sure your coworkers think I'm giving you special treatment," she said and grabbed Karla's arm. "I've lost my desire to brainstorm up here. Let's go," she said and started power walking toward the door.

◆ ◆ ◆

An hour later, Megan was freshly showered and had done her best to shake off the interaction with her mother and Karla. Despite what she'd told her mom, she had no clue if the situation with Jasper and Lily was fixable. Or if she *wanted* to fix it.

"Hey," Megan called to Ben.

He was sitting at his desk, monitoring his client Nancy as she cleaned out a kitty litter box that looked like a spaceship. "Hey." He smiled, and Megan's heart flipped a little. "Did you know there's an app that monitors how often your feline takes a dump?"

"That's an odd thing to remark on," Carlos said.

Megan looked around. She hadn't noticed him walk up.

Ben shot Carlos a look. "Something I can help you with, Carlos?"

"As a matter of fact, there is. I came over to make sure you saw my notes because you didn't respond to my last three emails. I'm concerned with some of the developments in your clients—including *her*," he said and turned up the volume on the monitor.

Nancy was calling for her cat, Raspberry, saying she wanted him to check out his clean bathroom. The cat trotted over, and Nancy picked him up and carried him to it. "What do you think, my little furry fruit?"

Ben laughed out loud.

Carlos pressed his lips into a tight line and crossed his arms.

Megan moved away to her desk, swiped through her tablet, and pretended she wasn't listening.

"Anyway," Carlos continued. "I stayed late last night to dig into their profiles. I wanted to capture some insights that could help."

"I'm sorry I haven't had a chance to read your emails yet, but it's next on my list," Ben said.

"This is serious, Ben. Especially Jasper's numbers. We need to turn these vulnerability scores around, or Karla is going to reassign us. I don't want to work in Boomers." Carlos lowered his voice, and Megan strained to hear. "Soraya told me Megan's been acting bizarre—seems distracted. And so do you."

Megan felt her heart catch.

"You're both overreacting," Ben argued.

"Are we? You two have been spending a lot of time together, and I'm worried her behavior will make you, *and us*, look bad. I thought we were competing with Megan?"

Ben shushed him.

Carlos's next words came out so low Megan could hardly make them out. "Soraya heard her humming a Taylor Swift song the other day—and not a sad ballad, one of her upbeat anthems. What is she, a Swiftie now?" he said with heavy snark.

"You have to admit, her stuff is catchy, for a Real Worlder," Ben said, and Megan smiled.

Naysay Inc. had been trying to get in the singer's ear for years. She fit the profile: a famous young woman whose every move was publicly scrutinized. Megan had come to respect how Swift didn't let Real Worlder trolls dictate her self-worth and loved the way she thrashed her suitors in song.

"Let me guess, she was humming 'Cruel Summer.' No, wait. 'Anti-Hero.'"

Megan suppressed a laugh. She'd introduced Ben to Taylor's music after the conference.

"I need to ask you, Ben. Whose head are you trying to get into? Your client's or Megan's?"

Megan held her breath, waiting for his answer.

Ben laughed, but it sounded hollow. "You're being ridiculous. What Megan is doing is Megan's business, not ours. You don't need to be concerned that she's rubbing off on me. Now walk me through what you're thinking with our clients."

Megan's stomach swished at his nonanswer answer, her face burning hot as he casually began discussing Nancy and the progress she was making on her thriller, despite several stale plot devices.

"I think we need to stall Nancy," Carlos said. "She's scheduled to attend a writing retreat this weekend with her best friend, Sarah May, who is one of the most popular romance writers in the Real World. I do not think she should be going. But since she's already signed up and her flight is first thing in the morning, it might be hard to stop her, so I came up with a plan."

"Can you send me an email detailing that?" Ben said dismissively. "I should get back to this."

"Wait, we also need to talk about Jasper."

"What about him?"

Carlos narrowed his eyes. "We could start with the fact that he's almost done with his book."

"First drafts are always trash. I'll get him doubting himself on the edit."

"Okay. But why is he spending time with Lily again? Soraya said they have sex so much that the feed cuts out constantly!"

"Yeah, that has made it challenging," Ben agreed.

"I blame Megan. It's her fault."

"What's my fault, Carlos?" she called out.

"We're discussing Lily Union."

"Why are you discussing my client? She's not your concern. If Soraya needs to—"

"I've spoken with Soraya," Carlos said. "And we both agree that Lily and Jasper's relationship is a huge problem."

"I've got it under control."

"She's excelling in other areas too. Do you want to talk about how she's most likely going to meet her writing deadline? And she reached out to the @ShapeKing yesterday and congratulated him on making the Thirty Under Thirty list! Said he deserved every success! Then she called her mom and said she was over not making the list. That she was done making online social comparisons."

"The @ShapeKing message was just a minor setback. It will take me seconds to make her do a one-eighty on that stance," Megan said.

"Totally," Ben agreed.

"Plus, she's still upset with @CallieCleanMyChaos for that video. It wasn't that long ago that Lily hate-watched reels of Callie cleaning all the vents in her house with a Magic Eraser," Megan added, hoping she sounded convincing. "There's a reason I do what I do and you do what you do. Sometimes you have to play the long game."

"It's true," Ben interjected. "Let Lily and Jasper have their moment. It will make them fall harder when we smash their spirits."

"They're having the best sex of their lives!" Carlos put his hand on his hips. "That's not okay."

Belinda whipped her head around. "Who's having the best sex of their lives?"

"No one," Carlos, Ben, and Megan said in unison.

"All righty then," Belinda said.

Megan put her hand on Carlos's arm. "You need to take a breath."

"They're talking about you guys. Upstairs."

"What? How do you know that?" Ben asked.

"I hear things. Do you think it's a coincidence Jacqueline and Karla were at the track this morning when you were both there?"

Megan shook her head. "How did you know—"

"I told you—I hear things," Carlos said. "There's also a rumor you two had dinner at Megan's last week."

Megan averted her eyes.

Carlos pressed on, glaring at Ben. "I don't care what you say. You have been off. And I can't, with you and your odd behavior." He shook his head at Megan. "If you two don't get it together, you're going to get us all sent to HR."

"Oh, come on," Ben said, but Megan heard worry in his voice.

Carlos looked around. "You two need to *stop*"—he pointed at them—"doing whatever this is, and *start* making our clients miserable again," he said and stormed off.

Megan turned to Ben. "What if we can't fix this? What if this current is too strong to swim against?"

"What do you mean?"

"What if our clients' free will is too much for us to overcome? Or worse, what if they're meant to be?"

"*Meant to be?* Have you been watching that Real World channel again?" He paused, trying to think of the name. "Hallmark?"

"No, I haven't been watching the Hallmark Channel. I'm just saying—maybe there's nothing to be done. It's possible . . ." Megan trailed off.

"What's possible?"

Megan hesitated. "I'm just saying, maybe we got the science wrong. Maybe soulmates do exist, and if they do, it's not something we can influence."

Ben chewed on the tip of his pen, crushing the plastic. "Have a drink with me tonight," he said, his eyes boring into hers.

Megan's heart thumped. "So we can strategize about Jasper and Lily?" She matched his stare.

"Meet me tonight and find out—I'll text you the address."

She bit her lip. It would be a risk to hang out with him again outside work.

"Do you trust me?" he asked.

"I do," Megan said without hesitation.

"Then meet me."

"I'll be there," Megan heard herself say.

Ben and Megan sat tucked into a cozy high-walled booth in the back of a dimly lit pub just down the street from Naysay Inc. A bartender washed pint glasses behind the bar, and a couple browsed songs at a battered jukebox in the corner, but the place was otherwise quiet. The wood-paneled walls muffled most of the noise from the street, making their booth feel like a private alcove, hidden from the world.

Their knees brushed beneath the table, and Megan's heartbeat quickened. She'd lied to Joan about why she was leaving work at four, claiming she had to meet the super about a leaky faucet, ignoring the twist of her boss's mouth as she'd hurried out the door. At home, she'd changed her outfit three times, not wanting to look like she'd tried too hard—finally settling on a green blouse and jeans she hadn't worn in years. As she touched up her makeup, she'd studied her reflection in the mirror feeling something she hadn't in a long time: pretty.

"So, what's your idea?" Megan asked, popping a french fry in her mouth, then smiling as she remembered the joke Lily had made to Jasper the night they met.

"I don't have one."

"What?"

"I mean, I was going to suggest we convince Jasper and Lily to take a trip this weekend. Traveling together can make or break a couple—sometimes you find out stuff about each other that's hard to unsee."

"Speaking from experience?" Megan asked.

"Maybe," he said, flashing Megan a coy smile, and she found herself wondering about his dating past. He'd once mentioned a woman named Daphne. Had he taken a trip with her that had ended badly? "Anyway, my idea involved Catalina Island, tourists, cruise ships, glass-bottom boats . . . So many awful things that would make two people want to kill each other."

"It sounds perfect."

"I know." He grinned, then his expression turned serious. "But maybe we should stop trying to ruin their relationship."

"Is that even an option? Giving up?"

"I'm not giving *up*. I'm giving *in*."

"To what?"

"Fate," Ben said, holding her gaze.

Megan froze, her breath hitching.

"You said it earlier today. What if that's why we can't keep them apart—because soulmates are real? What if, sometimes, people find each other, even when their *entire world* is rooting against them?" he asked, meeting her gaze, the silence feeling electric. "Do you know what I mean?"

The air between them seemed to tighten, suddenly heavier. "I think I do," Megan said, her voice raw.

"Do you think fate could really be a thing?" he asked, looking away for a second, then back, like he might be afraid of her answer.

A quiver of something rose through Megan. Fear and hope tangled in her chest. She nodded, because no words would come.

"Me too."

Something deep inside her swayed, like the axis of her world was slipping.

Ben stared at her lips. They locked eyes. Ben's flickered, like he was asking permission for the inevitable.

Megan edged slightly toward him, a rush of heat warming her chest. "What changed for you?"

"I met you," Ben said before leaning in, cradling her chin, the air between them charged. He pulled her closer, and their lips met.

A spark buzzed through her, like a jolt of electricity hitting her veins. Megan finally let go, surrendering to the feelings her body had been trying so hard to fight.

He stayed close, his breath tickling her lips. "You have no idea how long I've wanted to do that," he said. "That's why I left your apartment last week. I freaked out. Not because I didn't want you, but because of how much I did."

Megan tucked her head into his neck. She couldn't understand how so many different emotions could exist inside her at once—elation and dread, hope and panic, desire and apathy.

"Ben, we can't."

"I think we already did," Ben said with a sly smile.

Megan laughed. "True. But if work finds out. They already know we were at my place and—"

"They won't find out." Ben glanced around the pub. There was now only one woman at the bar, nursing a glass of wine, her back to them. "We're practically the only ones here. But if you want to stop—"

"Shut up," Megan breathed, hungrily pulling him back to her mouth.

This time the kiss was urgent and raw—no inhibition or restraint. Their hands meshed as they gave in to the free fall between them, neither of them noticing the ant-size drone floating above the table, recording everything.

Chapter Seventeen

Naysayland

Megan couldn't shake the feeling that she was being watched. She glanced over her shoulder as she walked the short distance from Ben's apartment to hers, but no one was there. What did Megan think—that someone from HR was following her? That a man in a dark suit was going to jump out from behind a building and scream *gotcha*? She shook her head. No way they'd have the balls to surveil Jacqueline Lowell's daughter. She knew she was only being paranoid because Carlos had warned her and Ben that the *people upstairs were talking*.

But that could just be a rumor. And Belinda probably started it.

Megan and Ben had been careful last night. No one had seen them together in that bar. No one suspected a thing. She was sure of it. Megan had only recently figured out how *she* felt about Ben. What that feeling in her chest meant when she watched the muscles in his biceps flex as he carried boxes of paper to the printer. That the nervous energy she felt before their runs was fueled by sexual tension. That the flush to her cheeks was from her attraction to him.

But now that they'd slept together, how were they going to hide their attraction?

She and Ben had discussed it over coffee before she left. She'd been wearing nothing except one of Ben's polos, which hung to her knees. She bent her nose to the collar and inhaled his scent.

"We should talk," he said as he refilled her mug. "About us."

Megan stared at her coffee. *Us.*

"If we move forward, we'll be risking everything," he continued.

Megan's breath caught in her chest. "Are you saying we shouldn't? Move forward?"

"No. Of course not. I want this." Ben grabbed her hand. "More than anything. But I don't have a mother and grandmother in Naysay Inc. Leadership to answer to. There's more at stake for you, so I want you to be sure. Your legacy won't protect us if we get caught."

Megan gazed at Ben's bare chest and considered his question. Was she willing to risk the job she'd prepared for her entire life for Ben Shaw?

No! the Naysayer in her thought. *No, no, and no!*

Yes! her heart purred. *Yes, yes, and yes!*

Who are you? Megan said to her heart. *Have we met?*

I've been here all along.

But I had plans, Megan argued, *to eventually be invaluable to the company, like my grandmother was. If I fall in love with Ben, that won't happen.*

Her heart had nothing to say to that.

Megan's grandmother had texted her last night to check in. Megan's stomach hurt as she replied that she was at home, reading a book. She tried to imagine what her grandmother's and mother's reactions would be if they knew where she really was—lying naked in Ben Shaw's bed. Megan knew, at the very least, Genevieve and Jacqueline would agree that her emotional tryst with Ben was a weakness. A failure professionally. Ben was a coworker, and that made their union forbidden. Naysay Inc. would not stand for such treason. And neither would Megan's family.

So, was Ben Shaw worth it?

He was.

"I'm sure, Ben," Megan said.

Ben brushed his lips across hers. "Me too."

"You're right, though," Megan said, running a finger along Ben's arm and watching goose bumps appear. "If anyone finds out, the man in the black suit from HR will come for us like he did Abby. He'll drag us out of our cubicles like common criminals."

"I can picture Belinda's reaction. She'll be like that emoji with the *O* face as she watches them get rid of us."

"She'll finally finish at the top of the leaderboard," Megan deadpanned.

Ben laughed.

"I'll give Belinda a show. I'll scream *it was worth it to sleep with Ben Shaw!*" Megan asserted, then waited for a beat. "All three times."

A smile danced across Ben's lips. "Which time was your favorite? I think for me it was number one."

"Number one for sure. Although there was a spring in your couch doing a number on my lower back." Megan giggled.

"Been meaning to get that fixed," Ben said, then wrapped his arms around her.

She looked up at him. "Just think—if Jasper and Lily hadn't met at that party—"

"Then *we* never would've happened. Thank you, Jasper and Lily!" Ben called out. "For refusing to let us split you up and making us fail!"

Megan looked at Ben. "I've never failed at anything before this job."

"How does that make you feel?"

"Content. Which is bizarre."

"I know, right?" Ben agreed. "Turns out you don't want to destroy peoples' lives when you're content with your own. It explains a lot. You know I sang in the shower the other day?"

"I complimented a stranger on her outfit."

"I petted someone's dog!"

"I danced in my living room . . . without music!"

They dissolved into laughter.

When the room fell silent again, Megan let Ben's words sink in. Was discontent the source of Naysay Inc.'s culture? And did they naturally project that on the Real World?

"What are you thinking about so hard?" Ben asked, tapping her forehead.

"Oh, just pondering the core of Naysay Inc.'s entire existence."

"That's all?" he teased. "Glad to see you haven't lost any of your intensity."

"It's still there. Just redirected," Megan said.

Her first week at Naysay Inc. felt like a lifetime ago. Her alphabetized notebooks, her rainbow display of highlighters, her list of goals. She'd wanted to blast through the office, leaving nothing but a string of Naysay Inc. employees in her path. Now she considered Beth a friend and found herself seeking out Jim just to say hi. The last six weeks had split her from the person she was destined to be and the one she was meant to be. Megan now understood the difference. One was a life sentence. The other was a choice.

"There's something I want to show you, but I'm not sure what you'll say when you see it." Ben searched her face. For what, she wasn't sure. Understanding?

"Okay," she said and followed him to a door he hadn't opened during the apartment tour he'd given her last night. He put his hand on the knob, and she took a deep breath as he opened it. "Wow," she said as she walked in.

"See?" Ben said. "You're concerned, right?"

Megan absorbed her surroundings. There were a half a dozen easels with painted canvases of fruit, landscapes, and flowers strewed about the room. The floor was covered with a giant paint-splattered drop cloth. On a table were brushes and other supplies.

She walked over and touched one of the canvases, the fabric rough beneath her touch. "Someone's been keeping secrets," she said.

"What do you think?"

"The old Megan would judge the hell out of what's in this room."

"And the new Megan?"

"She'd say these are pretty good. If the whole whispering thing doesn't work out . . ."

They laughed.

"Does anyone know about this?" she asked.

He shook his head. "I've kept it from everyone at Naysay Inc. for obvious reasons. If they knew I had a hobby like this, it could get me flagged. Especially if they knew *why* I paint."

"And why do you paint?"

"My first year at Naysay Inc., I would feel so heavy when I got home. It was like the things I whispered would stay with me." Ben pointed to an easel with a half-finished surfscape. "So I started painting. Every time I felt bad about something I'd said, I'd pick up a brush. I guess I was hoping it would counterbalance what I was doing at work."

Megan thought back to her first impression of Ben. "I never would've guessed. You seemed so . . . committed to naysaying. Not to mention all the leaderboards you've won."

"Being great at your job and having it fulfill you are two totally different things. Deep down I knew I was different from the other employees. Sometimes it took a toll."

"Did this help ease that burden?" she asked.

"Only temporarily. That's why there are so many." He swept his arm across the room.

Megan walked to the far wall where there were several canvases leaning against it. She bent over to examine one of them, her breath catching when she saw her image.

"Do you like it?" Ben asked, his voice tentative. He crossed the room slowly and paused behind her.

Megan studied the portrait. Although it was clear he was an amateur, Ben had captured a softness that Megan now realized she'd been trying to hide.

She turned and snaked her arms around his neck. "I love it."

"I love *you*," Ben replied, his gaze steady. "I think I knew it all along, but when I painted your face, there was no denying it any longer."

"I have never, nor will I ever, attempt to paint your face, but I can say with certainty that I love you too."

"Look at us, with all these *feelings*." Ben kissed her neck. "Speaking of, I think we have time to feel things one more time before you go."

Megan glanced at her portrait. "As long as we don't do it here. I'm not sure I can relax if she's watching me." She grinned.

As Megan got dressed for work, she thought about the plan she and Ben had made before she finally left his place and came home. They'd work hard to ignore each other and would half whisper their clients to get by. But something nagged at Megan. Could she make herself whisper half-terrible messages to Tatterson or partially mean-spirited killjoys to Lily?

Most of all, she wondered if she could pretend that she wasn't in love with Ben. She felt like it was written all over her face. As if her heart was split open on the conference table for everyone to see. She was no longer the person who'd strode into Karla's office for an interview. She had shed that skin like a snake, and the layer below it felt soft and vulnerable.

Megan's phone rang as she sat on the edge of her bed and slipped on her black kitten heels.

"Hi, Grandmother," Megan said, bracing herself to lie again. She didn't want to, but there was no way she could tell her the truth about Ben.

"Megan," her grandmother said, her tone urgent. "We need to talk."

"What is it? Is it Mom?" Megan shot to her feet.

"No, no. Jacqueline is fine."

"Are *you* okay?"

"Yes, I'm fine. But we need to meet immediately."

Megan's grip on her phone tightened. "Could you tell me now? I need to get to work."

She heard Genevieve sigh, long and heavy. "So, it's true then."

"What's true?" A chill crept up Megan's spine. She knew what her grandmother was about to say.

"Ben Shaw."

Megan held her breath.

"They know, Megan. *They. Know.*"

"Upstairs knows?"

"Yes."

Megan hurried to her living room and looked out the window. Maybe she'd been followed home from Ben's. She jerked the blinds closed in one swift motion, her thoughts scattering. "What do I do?"

"Do *not* go to the office. They are waiting to intercept you. Pack a bag, get your boyfriend, and meet me immediately. I'll send a car for you and Ben, which will take you to a location where I'll be—I don't want to give the address over the phone."

"Okay," Megan said. "Does my mom—"

"She knows. Do not take her call. Do not text her. Do not tell her where you are or that I called you. Do you understand?"

Megan was silent as she processed that her mother was part of the team wanting to bring her in.

"Megan, say it out loud. Say you understand you cannot communicate with your mother."

"I understand," Megan said, her voice small.

"And Megan?"

"Yes?"

"When they realize you aren't going to show up to work, they'll be sending drones to find you. We don't have a lot of time."

Megan looked to the gray sky, her heart racing. Were they watching her right now? Were they on the way to her apartment?

She raced back to her bedroom, her black heels clicking on the hardwood floor, sounding like the timer on a bomb.

Chapter Eighteen

NAYSAYLAND

Megan rang Ben's doorbell, bouncing on the toes of the Riptides he'd surprised her with last week. She'd changed into black joggers and a matching sweatshirt, pulling the hood tightly around her face and then slipping on a pair of oversize dark sunglasses, worried someone might recognize her.

She banged her fist against the door and was mid-swing when Ben opened it.

"Megan?" Ben stared at her. "That you under the hood?" He let out a laugh. "What are you doing back here? Not that I'm complaining—I was about to shower, and now you can join me."

The elevator chimed behind her, and Megan jumped.

"Hey, are you okay?" He reached for her, but she brushed past him into his apartment. Pulling down her hood and then removing her sunglasses, she revealed a flushed face, her skin hot and her hairline slick with sweat.

"Did you run here?"

"Close that," she said, ignoring him and rushing to the bay window. She dropped the black nylon backpack she was carrying. It landed with a thump.

"What's going on?" He picked up the pack. "Holy shit, this is heavy. What's in this thing?"

Megan's back tensed. How did you ask someone to leave their life?

She glanced down to the street below. The sidewalks were bustling with Naysayers walking briskly to work, refusing to make eye contact with one another. Shopkeepers were heaving open the gates of their storefronts. The streets were gridlocked with cars, a symphony of horns blaring. Everything seemed normal. It was anything but.

"Ben." She faced him, tears sliding down her cheeks. "They know."

He stepped closer to her. Put his finger to her damp face. "*Who* knows *what*?"

"HR knows. About *us*."

"How? There was no one from work in the bar last night, and when we left, we weren't followed. We were careful." He pointed to the backpack. "Are you going somewhere?"

"*We* are," she said, then dropped her eyes. "At least I hope you'll come with me. But we need to leave right now because they'll find us if we don't, and—"

"Okay, okay, slow down . . ." He wrapped his arms around her.

She leaned into his shoulder for a moment, then tensed and pulled away. "I promise I'll explain everything once we get out of here, but right now, we have to hurry." Megan jogged into Ben's bedroom and began rummaging through his closet. Shoving hangers to the side. Crouching down to see what was on the floor. She looked up at him. "Where's that duffel bag you put your running stuff in? You can't pack a suitcase—we don't want it to look like we're leaving town."

Ben ran his hand through his hair. "Slow down for a sec. Why do we need to leave?"

Megan tried to keep the tremble out of her voice. "Because they're waiting at the office to take us to HR. What about this?" She threw a backpack on the bed. "Only bring what you absolutely need."

Ben froze. "Where are we going?"

"I'm not sure yet. My grandmother called and said we can't go anywhere near Naysay Inc., or they'll apprehend us. They could come here. She wasn't sure."

"Genevieve called you?" Ben sank onto his bed. "We finally figured out how we feel about each other, and now we're running away together? Abandoning our jobs? The only lives we've known?" He rubbed his temples. "What if we go in and explain? I'm sure they'll be upset, maybe demote us, but maybe they'll understand," he said, biting down on his lower lip.

Megan sat next to Ben. "Have you forgotten what happened to Abby? She was taken to HR simply because she wasn't a good-enough assistant to Karla. Our situation is a lot worse. We slept together."

"They couldn't possibly know that."

"They know *everything*." She put her hand on his, hoping he couldn't feel it shaking. "My grandmother is sending a car, and it will be here any minute. Please, Ben," she pleaded. "I know I'm asking you to pack your life into a backpack, but we have to go. Do you trust me?"

Megan's chest froze. As she'd raced to Ben's apartment, there was never a question in her mind that he'd leave with her. That they were a team. But now, as she stared at the panicked look on his face, she wasn't sure.

Ben touched her chin, his features shifting into something tender. "I trust you. I'm coming with you," he said.

Megan let go of the breath she'd been holding. She watched as he stuffed his pack with two sweatshirts, a few T-shirts, a pair of pants, socks, underwear, and a toothbrush.

"That's all you're taking?"

Ben nodded. "I've always been a light packer. Didn't realize it might come in handy one day."

Megan's phone pulsed with a new message. "The car is here—we should go."

Ben zipped his backpack closed, grabbed Megan's, and reached for the handle of the front door.

"Wait." Megan pulled him into her. "I don't know what will happen from here on," she said. "But I don't care as long as I'm with you."

"Well, if that wasn't like a line out of a Real World rom-com," Ben joked. "What the hell, I'll roll with it. Let's go make a bunch of bad decisions like two Real Worlders in love." He laughed.

Her heart soared. "We're pathetic, aren't we?"

"Maybe," Ben said. "Or maybe we're the smartest people in Naysayland—I guess we're about to find out," he said as they headed into the hallway.

They hurried to the elevator, Ben clasping Megan's hand as it opened and then slid shut. She grasped his in return, tight like a knot, willing the bond to hold strong for whatever was coming.

Chapter Nineteen

Naysayland

A black SUV with tinted windows was waiting at the curb, and Ben and Megan climbed in quickly. The two rows of back seats faced each other, and they sat opposite Megan's grandmother. Her jaw was clenched.

The driver sped off before Megan had her seat belt on, and she fell into Ben. He held her steady as she yanked the belt across her chest. He helped her latch it. Genevieve studied him with curiosity.

"Thank you so much for helping us," Megan said to her grandmother.

"Yes, thank you," Ben said.

Genevieve tightened her mouth and shook her head. "I can't believe it, Megan. You fell for a coworker."

"I can explain—"

Her grandmother held up her hand. "I don't need your explanation—it's written all over your faces. You both look positively lovesick," she said, her face rigid.

"How did they find out?" Ben asked. "We were careful."

"Oh, were you now?" Genevieve laughed and put her hand to her chest. Her fingers grazed the black crow brooch on the lapel of her black tweed jacket. "You work for a company that surveils Real Worlders. How could you think they wouldn't notice? Your morning runs? The dinner at Megan's? Letting your clients fall in love?" She sighed. "You might as well have taken out a billboard on Naysay Boulevard." She looked at Megan. "I don't understand. This was the career you worked your entire life for."

Megan stared at her lap, and Ben squeezed her hand. "I know. But I realized it wasn't what I wanted," Megan said. She lifted her eyes to her grandmother's. "What did Mom say? You said she knows . . ."

Genevieve gave Megan a long look. "She doesn't just know. She's leading the investigation."

"What?"

"She blames him." Genevieve nodded at Ben. "Says he tricked you. And that it's due to his poor lineage."

Ben started to speak, but Megan put her hand over his. "What does that mean?"

"She blames his mother. Thinks what he has is hereditary."

"What I *have*?" Ben said sharply. "Like a disease?"

Megan gave him a look to calm him.

Genevieve's eyes softened. "Jacqueline is upset. This doesn't reflect well—"

"On *her*," Megan said.

Genevieve nodded. "And she's not going to stop until she brings you both in."

"But I'm her daughter."

"She doesn't want to appear impartial or worse, *weak*."

"I can't believe she could do this. Or maybe, I *can*." Megan looked out the window, her heart twisting.

Genevieve leaned over and put her hand on Megan's knee.

"Why are you helping us?" Ben asked.

Genevieve sighed. "I had a Ben Shaw in my life once."

"You've been in love too?" Megan whipped her head around to face her grandmother. "No way."

"I could've been," she said. "It was a man I worked with in the eighties, when I was a lead whisperer. He was my researcher. One minute we were stoking free market economics, the next he was professing his love for me in the break room."

"What did you do?" Ben asked.

"What I was supposed to do. I reported him to HR and never saw him again." Genevieve rubbed her bare ring finger. "I've never forgotten the look in his eyes when they came for him."

Megan put her hand over her mouth. "Grandmother—"

"I see a lot of myself in you, Megan. You may look like your mother, but inside? You favor me. I've often wondered what would've happened if I'd let myself fall in love. Correction, if I'd *admitted* I was in love. So, I've been keeping a close eye on you. I recognized the signs. I've seen your flushed cheeks at our dinners. How distracted you've been. Not returning my calls. I'm not the old fool you think I am. I know you weren't reading a book last night." She gave Megan a look.

Megan blushed. "How did you discover they found out about us?"

"Your mother called me—she obviously thinks I feel the same way she does."

"Does she have any idea you're with us now?"

"Of course not."

"But how were you able to circumvent their surveillance?" Ben asked.

"Oh, Ben, you have no idea the power I have," she said. "After I drop you off, I'm heading into the office to help *deal with you*," she said. "I know how to play both sides. How do you think I successfully instigated the Watergate scandal? Without me, it would've been nothing more than a robbery!"

"Where are we going?" Ben asked.

"My dear, you're going to see your mother."

"You're sending us to the Island?" Ben asked. "We're leaving forever?"

"Forever . . . for now," Genevieve said.

"What about Jasper and Lily? What will happen to them?" Megan asked.

"That's not my concern at the moment. And it shouldn't be yours either."

Megan nodded. "Can you—"

"Yes, Megan." Genevieve sighed. "I'll check on them for you."

"Thank you."

The car pulled up to a private dock with a boat waiting. "Here we are. This is the straightest channel to the Island. It's surrounded by scientifically designed low cloud cover to hide it from view. But don't worry, once you get there, the skies literally part and the sun appears."

They exited the car into a frigid wind. Ben shivered and looked toward the water. "How long does it take to get there?"

"Not long. Once you get out past the skyline, there's a portal that helps expedite the journey," she said and winked.

Ben shot her an alarmed look.

"Trust me, it's the only way."

Megan pushed aside the rising panic she felt and hugged her grandmother goodbye. "Thank you," she said and tugged on Ben's hand. "Come on. We have to go." She looked to the east for drones. It was clear, but she knew they didn't have much time.

"Ben, promise me you'll take good care of my only granddaughter," Genevieve said.

Ben looked at Megan and squeezed her hand. Her body flooded with relief.

"I promise," he said, jumping onto the boat and then holding his arm out for her. She clung to it as he helped her on the swaying vessel.

As the speedboat pulled away from the dock, they stared at the life they were leaving behind until it disappeared.

Chapter Twenty

Naysayland/The Island

The engine of the speedboat screamed as it journeyed toward the Island. Megan wanted to scream too—releasing her own swell of anger into the salty wind.

The boat's captain had given them blankets to protect them from the bitter breeze whipping off the ocean. Ben's arms were wrapped securely around her, yet her insides still felt ice cold. Megan hadn't expected her mom to be *happy* she'd fallen in love—Naysayland, or Nay*gray*land as the locals called it, would see blue skies before something improbable like that happened—but for her mother to head up the alliance that was chasing her down? That was hard to accept.

Why hadn't she called Megan and asked her to explain?

Megan shook her head. It wouldn't have mattered. Megan would've spouted several Real World platitudes like *I know we're supposed to be together* and *it feels right*, and that would've just enraged her mom more.

Megan had come to realize something that she was barely prepared to admit to herself, let alone Jacqueline: Falling in love was worth risking everything.

Ben squeezed Megan's knee. "How are you?" he called over the sound of the high-pitched propellers.

She shrugged, and he nodded like he understood.

"How are *you*?" she asked.

He shrugged, and she nodded like she understood. That morning, they'd woken up in Ben's apartment, with no idea they'd be departing the only lives they knew in a matter of hours.

Megan laid her head on Ben's shoulder and breathed in the salty ocean spray. She wondered what the Island was going to be like. It had been a bullying tactic in school—*you're strange. You belong on the Island.* She'd seen it as the title of an online dating profile—*No Island Vibes Here*. And it was a joke on late-night talk shows—*did you hear about the islander who was so desperate to return to Naysayland that he tried to get there on a pool floatie? They might get tanner on the Island, but they don't get smarter.*

But what was the Island, really, aside from a place to cast off people like her and Ben? To rid Naysayland of those who didn't conform to the rules of negativity?

Megan understood on paper how love could complicate, destroy, unsettle, and disrupt. But love had done only positive things for Megan. She felt better (who knew comfort could feel so good?), she looked better (her skin glowed), and she saw the world in a different light (shades of color instead of gray). If other people, like Megan's mom, could discover love, wouldn't it soften their sharp edges the way it had Megan's? Wouldn't everyone feel better?

Megan wondered if she'd feel at home on the Island or if she'd become so desperate to leave that she'd try to float back on a pool toy. She looked at the wake the boat was kicking off as they moved farther away from Naysayland and mused how quickly her homeland had turned on her. Or had she turned on it? It was hard to say who had betrayed whom.

An hour later, the Island started to take shape in the distance. When the boat slowed as it approached a harbor, she felt Ben tense.

"Do you know what you're going to say to your mom?" Megan asked.

"I have no idea. At this point, she's as much of a stranger to me as your sperm donor father is to you."

Megan squeezed his hand but knew it wasn't quite the same. Ben's mom was sent away for caring *too* much. Megan's biological father had handed over his DNA, knowing he'd never meet his child.

"Have you ever thought about what you'd say to him?"

"The guy who donated his sperm?" Megan asked. "No, but I do wonder what he's like—what qualities I got from him. If he's, you know"—Megan dropped her voice—"*positive*."

"I'm a little worried my mom might be *weird*."

"Well, *you're* weird, so it's entirely possible!" Megan laughed.

"Ha, true."

"But seriously, maybe *positive* and *weird* are labels we need to let go of for now because we don't know what we don't know, right? Maybe we're going to seem *weird* to them. Whose definition do we accept?"

Ben brought his face close to hers. "Did you just philosophize?"

"Oh my god, I did," she said. "I haven't stepped foot on the Island's soil, and I'm already sounding—"

"Like one of them." He kissed the tip of her nose.

Megan felt her body start to thaw and twisted her windswept hair into a knot at the base of her neck as the boat inched toward the dock.

A giant billboard read: **Welcome to the Island! Or Should We Say, Welcome Home?**

Home? Was the Island Megan and Ben's new home?

Megan pulled out the phone her grandmother had slipped into her pocket wordlessly as Megan climbed out of the car. "To stay in touch," she'd whispered in her ear.

Megan read a text from her grandmother.

They're looking for you. Thousands of drones have already been deployed.

Megan's stomach dropped as she read the next message.

Your mom suspects you're headed to The Island, but I dismissed the idea. I wanted to give you time to get through the portal before she realizes you're there.

Megan felt a flood of relief. And another emotion—joy, maybe? Knowing her grandmother was also willing to risk everything for Megan made her feel less isolated.

And spoiler alert: You've both been fired! 😬

The emoji made Megan laugh.

"What?" Ben asked.

"We got the axe," Megan said to Ben.

"Wow, it's only been"—he glanced at his watch—"less than two hours? Surprised it took them so long."

"Do you think you can date an unemployed loser?" Megan asked.

"Only if you can."

"I don't know about you, but I could use a vacation. Maybe on a tropical island?" Megan said.

"Hmm. I happen to know a place."

The clouds had parted as they'd passed through the portal and cloud cover and entered the Island's waters, clearing the way for bright-blue skies. The sunlight made Megan squint.

The captain handed them each a pair of sunglasses. "You'll need these here."

Megan slid them on and felt instant relief from the light.

The boat approached the busy dock. Three young men wearing life vests were renting Jet Skis. A group of people were doing yoga on the grass. A couple was taking a selfie while kissing in front of an ice cream stand.

"Do you see that?" Megan pointed.

Ben pressed his lips to hers. "When in Rome."

Their sunglasses clinked, and Megan giggled.

An older man with a lined face and a thick mustache tied a rope around the cleat on their boat and attached it to one on the dock. "How's the baby, John?" he asked their boat captain.

"Good—she rolled over!"

"Got a picture?"

"Sure do." John thrust his phone at the man.

"She's a beauty!"

On the other side of the dock, a man was whistling while he cleaned his fishing boat. Two middle-aged women wearing *Island Hair Don't Care* trucker hats were power walking along the shore. Megan heard one of them say *today is such a beautiful day!* The other replied, *Everyday!* They laughed like they were sharing an inside joke.

The man with the thick mustache greeted Ben and Megan. "I'm Randy—Randy James, head of onboarding relations. But I always say it should be *offboarding*." He laughed as he swept his hands to indicate stepping off the boat. "Welcome to the Island! What took you so long?"

Megan stared at him.

"Sorry, my jokes don't always land."

He reached for Megan's hand to help her onto the dock.

"But seriously, you're safe now," Randy said, his eyes soft. She imagined he'd said those words hundreds of times before, but by the sincerity in his eyes, she suspected he'd meant them every time.

Megan saw on Randy's name tag it read: *Castoff since 1983*.

"If you don't mind me asking, why were you sent here?"

"I don't mind at all. I fell in love—like you. Although in my case, she didn't love me back."

"I'm sorry," Megan said, feeling a twist of pain for him.

"It's okay. Hurt like hell for a while, but as soon as I got here, I knew I was going to be okay. Because there were other people like me."

Megan looked over her shoulder. After her grandmother's text, she half expected to see her mom in the hull of a boat racing toward her.

"There's no one coming for you, don't worry," Randy said.

"How can you be so sure? There are some people back in Naysayland who are not very happy with us at the moment."

"Years ago, there was a treaty enacted that forbids them from these waters."

"Why?" Ben asked.

"Ultimately, they don't want anyone that belongs on the Island in Naysayland. Our positivity might influence others. So we agreed—we don't go there, and they don't come here. You two might be an exception to that rule, but regardless, they will not violate the treaty. If they do, it'd open the floodgates for more violation. And the mixing of positive and negative people could threaten the evolution of Naysayers, disrupting the entire ecosystem."

"But what if I"—she looked at Ben—"or *we* wanted to go back?"

Randy sucked in a long breath. "Not an option."

Megan felt an unexpected pang in her chest as she pictured never cooking in her kitchen again, the one place she experienced true happiness. "I can't believe we don't live there anymore."

Randy placed his hand on her arm. "You don't realize it yet, but living on the Island will give you peace. You'll make your own choices here."

Megan felt equal parts elated and terrified at the thought of being able to decide what her life would look like. Where would she work if it wasn't predetermined? What would she do for fun if fun was a common thing? How would she act if she knew she wouldn't be judged—especially by her mother?

"It all feels so final," Ben murmured.

Randy nodded but said nothing.

Ben stepped out of the boat with their backpacks slung over his shoulders. He shook Randy's hand. "Hi, I'm Ben—"

"Shaw. Yes, we know. We've been expecting you. Your mom is on her way."

Ben's face went pale. "Really? Already? How did she know—"

"That you were coming?"

Ben nodded.

"The Island is big, but it's small, you know? Word travels fast. Especially when it's *two* Naysay Inc. employees being picked up by Captain John. Your situation is quite unique—but I say bravo! Way to stick it to the Naysaying Man." He clapped. "That corporation is pure evil. You're my heroes."

Megan and Ben traded a look.

"Thank you?" Ben said, but it sounded more like a question.

"And here she is now—your mom." Randy pointed to a woman who was running up the dock, holding the hem of her coral dress in one hand and waving at them with the other.

"She looks so young," Megan said.

"It's the Island air, I tell ya," Randy said. "I'm ninety-five!"

"Really?"

"No. I'm seventy-five years young."

Megan would've guessed he was in his sixties. She decided it wasn't the worst thing if the Island was going to keep her looking youthful.

"Ben!" His mom called out.

Megan could immediately see the resemblance between them. Their chocolate-brown eyes were identical. His mother's hair was more of a strawberry-blond color, but its coarse texture was the same as Ben's. His mom was also tall and thin. Megan wondered if she was a runner too. If she also pulled on the skin of her chin when she was deep in thought. If she charted things meticulously, the way Ben did.

"Oh my god, is that really you?" His mom squinted at him. "When they told me you were coming, I didn't believe it. After all this time." She wiped at the tears streaming down her face. "I'm so happy to see you."

Ben was frozen in place.

Megan gave him a small nudge. What she would give to have her own mother be this happy to see her.

"Hi, I'm Megan Lowell." She extended her hand toward Ben's mom, but she bypassed Megan's hand and gave her a coconut-smelling hug instead, Megan having no choice but to fall into her embrace. A surprising rush of warmth spread through her. She couldn't remember a time her own mother had hugged her. Ever.

"I'm Catherine. Are you—"

"Ben's girlfriend," Megan said. They hadn't discussed labels, but Megan thought leaving your life behind for someone constituted making things official.

"It's such a pleasure to meet you. I didn't know if I'd ever see my boy again. If he's here because of you, thank you so much." She wiped at her wet cheeks.

Ben stepped forward. "Hi, sorry. I don't know what to say. I guess I'm a little shocked. It's all happened so fast, and it takes me a while to—"

"Process things?" Catherine offered, and Ben nodded.

"I'm the same way with decisions too. I really take my time weighing my options," she said.

"Me too—usually." Ben looked at Megan. "Deciding to come here in under ten minutes is a record for me. I couldn't weigh any pros or cons." He laughed.

Catherine smiled. "I'm so glad you made an exception."

"Me too," Megan said.

Ben turned to Catherine. "What should I call you?" he asked.

"You can call me whatever you want." She bit the inside of her cheek. "I wouldn't blame you if you had some choice words."

"Maybe."

"Ben!" Megan reprimanded.

"No, it's okay." Catherine waved Megan off before turning to Ben. "I'll tell you everything you want to know. But first, let's get you settled. A hot shower? A cup of tea? Stiff drink? There's a guesthouse on my property where you can stay until they assign you your own bungalow, but only if you're comfortable. I could find an alternative if not. Maybe Randy's house. We don't have hotels here because—"

"No one only comes for a visit," Ben said, a distant stare in his eyes.

"Right." His mom's chin trembled.

Ben looked at Megan. She wasn't sure how she felt about them staying with his mom. She seemed nice enough, but she worried Ben might need a little space to unpack his emotional baggage. "It's up to you," she said.

"Your guesthouse is fine. Thank you."

His mom gave him a weak smile. "My golf cart is over there," she said, pointing to a lime-green buggy with a *5'oclk Smwhr* license plate.

They climbed in and began the winding trek up the hill, Megan's emotions as bumpy as the dirt road leading to Catherine's electric-blue bungalow.

"That was excellent, thank you," Megan said as she finished the kale salad with vegetables that Catherine had served, everything fresh from the community garden.

Megan's hair was still wet from the shower. Her tears had blended with the hot water. She didn't want Ben to see her cry—he had enough of his own emotions to consider—but Megan was struggling with all the change. In a matter of hours, she'd left her entire world behind, and it was just starting to hit her. Despite her mom's myriad flaws, Megan was still mourning her loss—she didn't know if she'd ever be back or if that life and everyone in it was now behind her forever. It made sense to Megan now how Real Worlders' vulnerability indexes could spike and then dip, like trend lines on a graph.

After dinner, Megan and Ben sat with Catherine on the back patio of her home and looked out at the sea. Ben had been quiet since they arrived, and she had let him be, but Catherine was staring at him, like she was afraid if she looked away, he'd disappear.

Megan concentrated on the horizon, trying to locate any evidence of her old life.

"You won't be able to see it from here," Catherine said, as if reading her mind. "I had the same urge to feel a connection—to see Naysayland, even though I knew it wasn't possible. I stared in that direction for quite a while, longing for Ben, until I was forced to accept that I could never go back."

Ben smiled sadly. Catherine put her hand on top of his.

"How did you get through it?" Megan asked.

"I think I'm still getting there." Catherine released a hollow laugh. "But the Island and the people here helped me. And the sun. That vitamin D, that warmth, we all need it."

Megan remembered the sun feeling like a warm blanket when they'd arrived. To think they could have that every day.

"Naysayland is so gray. The sun is always hidden beyond the clouds." Catherine shook her head. "You grow up with it, so you don't know anything else, but after being here only a few days, I realized that's part of what keeps people in Naysayland in a permanent state of negativity."

Megan nodded. It made sense.

"Why were you sent away?" Ben finally asked his mom the question Megan knew he'd been mulling all evening. Maybe the one he'd been asking himself his entire life. "Dad told me it was because you loved me too much."

"That's what *they* decided, yes," Catherine scoffed. "Imagine that—being punished for loving your child too much? You were a baby—a few months old—and they took me away from you." Her voice caught.

"How did they find out?" Ben asked.

"Your dad had been talking to a colleague at work about how I'd said I didn't want to go back to work after you were born. That I planned to stay home with you. I wasn't told anything by my mother about raising a child—what it would *feel* like. She was a cold woman. When I held you for the first time and looked at your tiny face, you wrapped your finger around mine, and I felt this powerful connection that I knew instantly must be real love. I'd cared about your father, but I was never *in love* with him.

"Your dad didn't mean to get me in trouble. He only told his colleague because he didn't know what to make of the relationship he said I had with you—most women didn't sing to their babies, didn't hold them constantly. Your father thought he could trust his coworker, but the man reported me. The authorities showed up at our doorstep, interviewed me, then told me to pack my bags."

"How could you let them take you away?"

"I tried to stop it. I fought. I kicked. I screamed. I hit. I begged to stay. I asked if you could come with me. They laughed at that. They ripped you from my arms and gave you to your father, who kept telling me how sorry he was while you wailed. It was"—Catherine took several shallow breaths because she was sobbing—"the worst day of my life."

Megan grabbed Ben's hand.

He squeezed it back hard, as if trying to anchor himself. He leaned forward, his voice low. "I'm so sorry they did that to you."

Catherine let out a shaky breath. "Me too."

"If you could go back in time, would you change anything—maybe act like you loved me less?" he asked, his eyes wet.

Catherine swiped her tears with the back of her hand and took several deep breaths. "I've asked myself that same question a million times," she said, a faraway look coming into her eyes. She turned toward Ben. "I could've faked it, but for how long? I plotted ways to get back to you, treaty be damned. I asked Captain John's father—who's retired now—to hide me on his boat and take me back when he went to pick up the next banished Naysayer, but he refused. John had just been born, and he couldn't risk never seeing him again. If he'd been caught, he would've been dumped in the Real World. The irony, right? I was desperate to get back there to be with my baby, and he was desperate to stay here to be with his. I was devastated. I tried, Ben. There wasn't a way."

Ben let out a long exhale.

"I decided if I had to choose between loving you and leaving or staying and pretending I wasn't capable of real love, I'd choose loving you every single time." Her lips quivered. "Because as you both now know, loving someone is not a choice. It happens even if we push it away. It doesn't matter if we tell ourselves we can't. Love lives in all of us. It just takes the right person to activate it."

Megan nodded, then gazed at Ben. He'd already been looking at her, his eyes soft, like he was waiting for her to turn. They shared a small smile of understanding.

"Did your father do okay?" Catherine asked. "Was your life good?"

Ben took a long time to answer. "Dad did the best he could. He supported me. Made sure I had a roof over my head. Paid for me to go to college. I think he did what he was capable of. He passed away five years ago. Heart attack."

Catherine's eyes softened. "I'm really sorry to hear that. He was a good man."

"Thank you," Ben said stiffly.

She stood and reached her hands toward Ben. "You activated my love, Ben, and I wouldn't change that. I know it's a lot to ask, but I hope one day you can forgive me. And then maybe I can forgive myself."

Ben shifted his weight but didn't move toward her.

Megan held her breath, waiting for any sign Ben might soften. Open his heart to his mother's apology. To let her know she did the best under the circumstances she was dealt. Megan wondered what she would do if Jacqueline stood in the same spot, asking for her forgiveness. Catherine hadn't been given a choice. In contrast, Jacqueline had clearly pledged loyalty to a company, a culture, over her only child.

But deep down, Megan knew she'd forgive her if she asked.

"Ben," Megan whispered. They locked eyes, and she pleaded silently for him to lower the walls he'd built so high. Not only for his mother, but for Megan too. She gave his hand one last reassuring grip and gently released it.

Ben cleared his throat and stood, his legs seemingly unsteady beneath him. "I forgive you," he said, his voice shaking.

He embraced his mom, who held him like she might never let go. Behind them, Megan noticed a star shooting through the sky before falling into the ocean with grace and felt of stab of hope that she may have found a place to belong.

Chapter Twenty-One

The Island

One Month Later

"Will you pass me the sunscreen?" Megan asked as she tucked her legs under the shade of the blue-and-white striped umbrella. "I'm starting to burn." A corner of Megan's mouth quirked with amusement. "Filed under things I never thought I'd say before coming here!"

"We should make a list," Ben said as he tossed her the bottle of SPF 50.

Megan laughed. "Good idea. I have *a lot*." There were so many for Megan. She never thought she'd defy her mother and run away from Naysayland to the Island with a man, let alone one she *loved*. (Maybe that counted as three?) She was curious about what was on Ben's list. "You start," she said.

"Okay . . ." He looked down. He was reclined in a low tropical-print beach chair. "I never thought I'd . . . get sick of only wearing swim trunks," he said, patting his bare chest.

Megan pulled down her sunglasses to gaze at him. "No complaints over here," she said as she rubbed lotion on her calves.

"Your turn," Ben said.

"I never thought I'd . . . keep a daily gratitude journal." Megan shook her head. "I've already filled five pages. Dr. Peakstone would be proud—she always wanted me to write my feelings down."

"Am I listed in there?" Ben asked, motioning to the notebook peeking out of her beach bag.

Megan leaned over and kissed him. "Of course."

Often, she'd muse about Ben's moods, which ranged widely from day to day. Megan wondered if the swings stemmed from his refusal to truly forgive his mother. He'd said the words that first night, but Megan could tell he didn't quite mean them yet. He was often short with Catherine and, when Megan called him out on it, with her as well.

"Your turn," she prodded.

"Let me think," he said, running his hand over his chin. He'd grown a short beard. It suited him.

"You can't think of anything else? Your first one shouldn't count—it was kind of negative," she said, giving him a playful nudge.

Ben glared at her. "I meant that I wear these *every single day*. Because we come here *every single day*. I'm not complaining."

"Right. Because how could you complain about seeing this *every single day*?" Megan sighed. "It's paradise. We finally have sun! It literally *never* rains here. We're in some vortex or something."

"Would a little rain hurt anyone?" Ben asked.

"Coming from the man who lived in Naygrayland? Do you want that back?" *Do you not like it here?* She wanted to ask but wasn't sure she wanted the answer.

He was right—they did come to the beach daily. But Megan couldn't imagine that ever getting old. She couldn't get enough of the cool ocean water tickling her ankles as the waves washed ashore, or the way the soft sand felt beneath her feet.

"I like the sun," he said, with less enthusiasm than Megan would've liked. "What I meant is, the days can be monotonous."

"Why don't you try painting? Your mom bought you that easel and those brushes."

"My mom also bought me tighty-whities, socks, and undershirts. I'm thirty-one years old, not six."

"I think she's trying to be nice."

He rubbed his hand over his face and opened his mouth to say something but closed it. He was silent for a few moments. "I don't want to paint," he finally said.

Megan's face fell, and she dragged her fingers through the warm sand. *He didn't want to do the one thing he'd always loved? What did that mean?*

Ben looked at her and grabbed her hand. "Maybe I'll try again. I could paint that house you love—the pink one with the white shutters?" he said but didn't sound convinced.

"Don't do it for me—I want you to paint because *you* want to paint," Megan said.

"I know I haven't been the easiest to be around. I've never lived with anyone before—not even a roommate," he said and smiled. "I'll get better about the toilet seat, I promise."

She gave him a sad smile. "It's not about the toilet seat."

"I know," he said. "I'm not navigating this whole Island experience very well. But, in my defense, coexisting with people who *only* wear Island Vibes T-shirts and walk around with coconut drinks like they have nowhere else in the world to be, ever, is *a lot*! If I never hear one more Bob Marley song, it will be too soon."

Megan laughed. "Fair—although you'll probably hear 'Buffalo Soldier' in the next five minutes." She thought for a moment. "But it is remarkable, isn't it—to live one life and not understand there's a whole other one waiting for you? We both said we never wanted to fall in love with anyone, never wanted to work anywhere else . . ."

Ben nodded as Megan's stomach swirled. She wished she could see his eyes beyond the dark lenses that masked them.

He took his thumb and wiped a smudge of sunscreen off her cheek. "I do know one thing for sure. As long as I'm with you, I'm okay." He wiped sand from his legs and stood, offering Megan his hand. "Do you want to head to the bookstore and see what new thrillers they have?" he asked, then broke into a wide smile. "I never thought I'd read thrillers," he added, before she could.

"Okay. Your mom isn't expecting us until five," she said, then caught the look on his face. "But we could cancel . . ."

"No, it's okay, let's go."

"You sure?"

"No," he said and laughed. He looked at his bare wrist. "I'm still in the habit of checking my watch. What time is it anyway?"

"Don't ask me—I still can't do the whole sundial thing. We'll have to ask someone—*again*."

Electronics of any kind—even watches—were frowned upon on the Island. They felt an abundance of innovation led to apathy and unhappiness. Megan kept the cell phone Genevieve had given her tucked in a bedroom drawer, grateful it was picking up a weak signal from a cell tower her grandmother had told her was built on the far end of the island. Only a select group of Islanders were permitted a phone for emergencies.

Megan and Ben had also learned that the Island, which was approximately six hundred square miles, was mostly self-sufficient, the food coming from its own crops and animals. They had manufacturing plants that produced household items, and the things they imported—like books—came monthly on a ship from the Real World, which was impervious to radar.

Catherine told them the shipping operation was run by former Islanders who'd gone to the Real World by choice in an effort to try to make it a better place. Many of them became teachers, were activists, or ran nonprofits. Those Islanders passed down their secret from generation to generation to ensure there would always be a group of people in the Real World that understood the importance of controlling your own narrative. Megan had never considered that there could be a quiet movement of people like her in the Real World, former

Naysayers—some of whom were rumored to have worked at Naysay Inc., according to Catherine—who were now trying to fight against it.

Ben and Megan grabbed their towels, umbrella, and chairs, and hopped in their golf cart. Ben navigated through the downtown past Positive Pizza, known for its pleasant pepperoni calzones, and Happy Hawaiians, a boutique where Megan had purchased two bold floral-print shirts for Ben along with a sarong covered in pink plumerias for herself. As they passed the gym, Endorphins, Megan waved at the owner.

They drove by the grocery store run by Raphael and his wife, Amber, a couple who'd met and fallen in love on the Island. They'd each been identified as *positive* when they were eighteen and were sent to the Island because their empathy scores were off the charts. They decided to lean into their compassionate natures by naming their store Empathy Grocery and hanging signs throughout that asked questions like *How are you really doing today?*

Last week, when Megan popped in to get some Honeycrisp apples, Amber, who'd been running the cash register, had pointed to the sign, her deep-blue eyes wide and focused as if she had all day to listen to her answer.

Tears welled in Megan's eyes. She hadn't realized how much she needed to confide in someone. "Honestly, I'm not doing great."

"Come with me to the stockroom. I will listen—maybe offer some advice too?"

As soon as they walked into Amber's office and she shut the door behind them, Megan broke down. "I thought no one cried on the Island!" Megan said through her tears.

"You aren't the first, and you won't be the last. The transition can be hard."

Megan thought of Ben. "But it hasn't been hard for *me*."

"Hasn't it? You're in a relationship, aren't you? With a man you love?"

Megan nodded. "He's struggling. He reconnected with his mom after thirty years, and she's clinging to him for dear life."

"And that probably affects you, right?"

"I guess."

Amber smiled. "Have you ever been in love before?"

Megan shook her head, the tears falling. "Never really cried much either."

"Love will do that to you," Amber said. "Want my advice?"

"Yes, please."

"This is going to sound counterintuitive, but you need to stop thinking so much about him and a little more about *you*. You left a family behind, didn't you? You have a mom who's pretty upset you left? That must be hard to deal with."

"How did you—"

She winked. "The Island is smaller than you think."

Megan had arrived back at the Pepto-Bismol-pink bungalow she shared with Ben, her eyes swollen but bright. She'd felt lighter.

"Where are the apples?" Ben asked, surveying her.

The Honeycrisps had been forgotten at the register.

"I unloaded on Amber, the woman who owns the grocery store," Megan said, shaking her head in disbelief that she'd cried about her truth to a perfect stranger. She missed her sessions with Dr. Peakstone more than she'd expected and had looked for a therapist on the Island. There were plenty of spiritual gurus, but no psychologists.

No one really needs therapy here, Ben's mom had said. *We don't have any real problems.*

But Megan was beginning to realize that Islanders *did* have problems—the ones they brought with them to the Island. Their baggage amounted to more than their luggage.

"You could go to the store."

"To get the apples?" Ben asked, confused.

"Yes, for that, but also to talk to Amber. She really helped me. I guess she was going to study psychology before she was shipped off."

"What did she help you with?"

"To see that I have some things I need to process. That coming to the Island didn't mean all my issues with my mom went away."

"Makes sense," Ben said.

"Maybe you could talk to her about your mom," Megan offered.

"So we both have mommy issues now?"

"*Now?*" Megan gave him a pointed look. "I think they've probably always been there, don't you?"

She wasn't putting their moms into the same category by any stretch, but Catherine was still *a lot*. She meant well, but she was trying to make up for thirty years of missed mom moments, and buying him the underwear had only been the beginning. She constantly drilled Ben with questions and comments about his past that came across as judgmental and nitpicky. Why hadn't he played an instrument? He'd seemed musical as a baby. Why hadn't he joined a sport in high school? The pediatrician had told her he'd be tall—and he was—so why not basketball? What had made him want to work at Naysay Inc., when there were so many better companies? Had his dad pushed that?

But she didn't stop there. She also wanted to be involved in everything he was doing now. Had he eaten breakfast? When he told her no, she'd shown up with a giant platter of bacon and pancakes, despite him explaining if he did eat first thing, it would only be a small piece of fruit. The list went on—had he been to see a doctor on the Island yet for his annual physical? Even though he was young and healthy, things happen. And it had to be Dr. Sherwin, not Kloss.

She also wanted to know his plans for the future. What was he going to do for a career on the island—obviously his Naysay Inc. skill set wouldn't be useful here. Would he go back to school?

And she wanted to be with him constantly, like every day could make up for one she'd lost. Cards on Tuesday nights, walks on Thursday mornings, and she'd convinced him to try her Zumba class. There'd been even more invitations that Ben had ignored or made excuses to not accept, and Ben wasn't dealing with how any of it was making him feel.

"Maybe it's my mom who should go see her," Ben said, his voice hollow.

"Maybe she should. But you could go first?"

"Why do we constantly have to be getting in touch with our feelings? It was hard enough with Dr. Peakstone. I keep a journal now. Can't that be enough?" Ben stared out the window, squinting. "I heard you talking to my mom about me last week."

"What do you mean?" Megan asked. But she knew exactly what he meant. She'd been helping Catherine with the dishes after dinner and thought Ben, in the other room, couldn't hear them over the running water.

"You told her how I don't appreciate her. That I don't understand how lucky I am to have a mom who cares."

Megan dropped her gaze, avoiding his eyes. "You don't."

"I can't flip a switch, Megan. She's a stranger to me."

"And as long as you refuse to let her in, that will never change," she said, thinking about how her talk with Amber had helped her figure out how she felt about the dysfunctional relationship she had with her own mom. "Do you know how much I would give to have my mom want to know me in a real way?"

"This isn't about you!" Ben shouted, his eyebrows knotting and his skin firing red. "If you want a mom so badly, you can have mine. It's clear she prefers you!"

Megan recoiled like she'd been slapped. He'd never yelled at her before.

I guess people yell on the Island too.

"Do you regret coming here?" Megan blurted, surprising herself. She'd been so afraid to ask him the question that had been sitting on her lips for weeks, that it had finally sprung out of her before she could stop it.

He stared at her, but his gaze was empty, like he was looking through her.

Looking for a way out?

"Because I don't have any regrets," she said, thinking of her mom, wondering if that was completely true. "I love it here."

"I think what you love is feeling safe. But that's not the same as living a balanced, productive life."

"What are you saying? That you think there was more balance in Naysayland?"

"I don't know, maybe."

"*Maybe?* Seriously?" A hot wave of anger flashed through Megan. "You want to go back to putting negative thoughts in people's heads? Because you're sick of the beach?"

"I worry this lifestyle doesn't work long term. People aren't meant to live in the place they go on vacation. I had a client, a political memoirist, who was so stressed he thought he was having a heart attack. Turned out it was just indigestion, but his therapist—not one of ours—told him to take his wife to the Caribbean to relax. I was able to talk him into going back to his home in Manhattan three days early, but my point is, if he'd *moved* there, it would've defeated the purpose of *relaxing* there."

"You're saying people need to live in a place that drives them to a near heart attack so they can enjoy a vacation?" She blinked at him hard.

His rejection of the Island felt like a rejection of them. In her head, she knew—she hoped—it was more than that. That it was also his mother's suffocation and his trouble adjusting to the new lifestyle the Island presented that were making him reconsider his choice to come here. But it didn't make her heart hurt any less.

She swallowed her tears, not waiting for him to answer her. "Forget I brought it up," Megan said.

"I'll go. You need the apples," he said, grabbing the keys off the counter and then storming out.

Megan's heart sank. "I don't want you to do something you don't want to do," she said to herself as he drove away, not sure if she was talking about going to therapy at Empathy Grocery or staying on the Island.

Now, as Ben and Megan arrived home from the beach, shaking out their towels on the front porch and hanging them on a hook to dry, Megan wondered if they'd ever be able to emotionally settle here. He'd come back from the store last week with the apples but said nothing more. Megan had no idea if he'd talked to Amber and wasn't going to ask. She was going to take Amber's advice and concentrate on herself. Since then, Megan had already filled two journals about her mom.

Megan went to pull her gratitude journal out of her beach bag, feeling an urge to capture her thoughts when her phone buzzed from the dresser drawer where she kept it hidden. She gasped as she read the message.

Dr. Peakstone
Session with Karla Yang
July 13th

Dr. Peakstone: We've spent the last three sessions on your anger at Ben and Megan for leaving. I think we should start talking about you.

Karla: But they broke promises to me.

Peakstone: It might be time to discuss your ex-husband. He broke promises too.

Karla: He got what he wanted—a hot young wife and new baby. I've moved on.

Peakstone: By becoming an insufferable boss? Your new assistant, Tania, went to the ER with chest pains after you yelled at her last week.

Karla: She forgot to alphabetize my emails!

Peakstone: I know you sent flowers to her hospital room.

Karla: That's a lie! I hate live plants! I would never—

Peakstone: There's footage of you at the florist.

Karla: Please. I can't get fired. Without this job, I'll have nothing.

Peakstone: I won't tell anyone if you do something for me.

Karla: Anything.

Peakstone: Agree that we can start exploring

the part of you that clearly has sensitivity and compassion.

Karla: Why? It was one moment of weakness.

Peakstone: Or an indicator that you're not all negative. And maybe that's a good thing.

Chapter Twenty-Two

The Island

"Megan?" Ben said as he hurried into the bedroom. "What happened?"

"My grandmother just texted me an update. Lily and Jasper broke up!"

"What? How? I thought they were in love?" Ben said, a shattered look on his face.

"They were," she said, then corrected herself. "They probably still *are*. But the new lead whisperers that replaced us *literally* live at the office—they sleep on the couch, shower in the gym." She sighed. "It's some sort of new regime of whisperers Karla has brought on as a response to what we did. They practically whisper nonstop."

"Nonstop?"

"As in we're going to beat this messaging into your skull until you are so tired of hearing it you accept it."

"Wow, that's brutal, even for Naysay Inc.," Ben said. "I can't believe it. I thought they couldn't be broken up."

She wondered if Ben was thinking what she was. If Lily and Jasper could break up, maybe they could too.

Megan shook her head. "That's not all," she said. "Lily says she's giving up her socials and stepping away from her Worthy by Thirty platform because her thirtieth birthday is in a week and Genova, that's her new whisperer's name,"—she made a sour face—"convinced her she hasn't achieved anything even close to be considered worthy. Lily also called her agent and might back out of her book contract. And she's been refusing to take her mom's phone calls. I'm worried about her!"

Ben winced. "That's terrible. And Jasper?"

"He finished his book but is having trouble with the edit notes Arnie gave him. He might scrap the whole thing and start over because his whisperer, Frederique, told him to!" She looked up at Ben. "He's considering taking a job helping kids write college essays. The breakup gutted him."

"Damn it."

"Oh, and Frederique also convinced Nancy to let her frenemy, Jan, beta read her thriller, and Jan panned it. Nancy threw her cat's eight-hundred-dollar litter box across the room and broke it."

"Oh, Nancy, not the litter box," Ben said. "I hope Raspberry is okay."

"The cat is taking it hard, apparently—he's now peeing in her bed. She's gone through six sets of sheets." Megan scrunched her nose.

Megan also filled him in on her other former client, Kristopher Tatterson. He'd made an appointment to get all his tattoos removed and had a meeting with producers to quit his show.

"Everything we did has been undone." Ben sat on the bed and put his arm around Megan. "We had to give up our lives for nothing."

"It wasn't nothing. We didn't want to be those people anymore. Those lives weren't worth living," she said. "Right?"

"Of course," he said quickly. "I guess I'm just having a hard time knowing Naysay Inc. won."

"What if we don't let them?" They couldn't allow Naysay Inc. to succeed. Lily and Jasper's love was the foundation Megan and Ben's relationship had been built on. If that crumbled, what did it mean for them?

Ben tilted his head to the side. "I don't understand."

"I have an idea. Let's get changed and head to your mom's. I think she can help us—in a way that won't annoy you." She smiled at him.

◆ ◆ ◆

"We want to go to the Real World," Megan said to Catherine.

Catherine's face crumbled. "Why? I thought you were happy here? You seemed like you were finally settling in. I know from our talk the other day that Ben has struggled to adjust—"

"It's not me," Ben said.

"Then what is it? We just found each other again," she said, her eyes wet.

Please don't cry, Megan thought.

"The whisperers who took over for us at Naysay Inc. have broken up Jasper and Lily," Megan said.

She'd confided in Catherine about how much it bothered her that she'd left Lily and her other clients behind. When she worried about Lily and Jasper, she'd told herself that they were still Teflon, that if she and Ben couldn't break them up, no one could. That their love would protect them and lower their vulnerability scores so much that they'd be immune to whispering. And Tatterson was tough—she figured he'd fight off whatever voice came next.

"I know you see your relationship in theirs, but you can't save them," Catherine said.

Megan's eyes blazed. "I have to try. I left Lily there unprotected, alone." Megan's voice caught as she imagined Lily curled into a ball on her sofa.

"You didn't have a choice."

"Didn't I?" Megan said, her insides twisting. It was almost impossible for her to remember when she didn't feel empathy because right now, it consumed her.

"Well, you chose yourselves, which isn't a bad thing. You gave up a lot to be here—are you sure you want to risk that?"

"I love your son, and I love it here, but I don't know how I can continue here, knowing my clients' lives have been destroyed."

Catherine turned to her son. "What do you think?"

He took a deep breath, and Megan's own breath caught. When she'd told him her idea earlier, he'd said he agreed, but what if he'd changed his mind after seeing his mother's reaction?

"I agree. I have a lot of guilt for the way I treated Jasper. If there's a way I can help him now, I want to do it."

"I would love to see you both undermine Naysay Inc.'s work, but it was so dangerous getting you here. If your mother finds out—"

Megan put her hand on Catherine's. "I know."

"We'll be careful," Ben said.

Tears welled up in Catherine's eyes again. "I just got you back. I don't want to lose you again."

"You won't," Megan said. "Ben will be back in Zumba class before you know it," Megan said, then locked eyes with Ben. She wondered how much of his motivation to help Lily and Jasper was to get off the Island. Would he be willing to come back with her after they made things right?

"There *might* be a way for you to get to the Real World," Catherine finally said. "But there's only one person who can make that happen." Catherine picked up her landline and made the call. After she hung up, she looked at them. "Randy said he'll hear what you have to say, but he probably won't do it."

"I'll convince him," Megan said, knowing she would do whatever it took to get to the Real World. They couldn't let their clients' lives stay this way.

Catherine grabbed a sweater from the chair. "You ready?"

Megan searched Ben's face. Were they ready? Once they convinced Randy and stepped off the Island, there would be no guarantees. If they pushed through with this plan, it might be the end of their own story.

Ben grabbed her hand and intertwined his fingers through hers like a promise. Her heart soared. "We're ready," he said.

◆ ◆ ◆

"You two really want to do this?" Randy smoothed his white mustache and leaned back in his chair.

Megan, Ben, and Catherine were all crammed into Randy's small, windowless office at the dock. Megan looked at the waist-high stacks of documents and folders that surrounded them and thought of her tablet back in Naysayland. If Islanders refused technology that could help them digitize their paperwork, at the very least, they could use some help getting organized. Maybe she'd start a business when they returned.

If they returned.

"We do," Megan said. "How soon can you get us there?"

"But you just arrived. Are the toxic positivity people driving you away?" Randy's eyes twinkled. "They need their own island if you ask me."

Megan forced a smile. *This guy really is on Island time,* she thought.

"In all seriousness, I meant what I said to Catherine. I'm going to need some convincing. Helping you get to the Real World would be a big risk for all of us."

"We recognize that, we do," Megan said. "But we really need your help. Going there is our only option. Our former clients were broken up by whisperers that took over for us after we left. They are meant to be together. They love each other. And they deserve their happy ending." As Megan said the words, she realized she wasn't only talking about Jasper and Lily.

She looked at Ben. She was also talking about them.

Randy smiled at Megan. "You don't lack determination."

"Nope," Megan said.

"I understand what you two want to do—more than you know—so I'm going to help you."

"Thank you," Megan said.

Catherine asked, "If they do this, will it be safe?"

"Mostly."

"Mostly?" Catherine blinked several times.

Randy pushed some folders to the side so he could rest his forearms on the desk. Megan noted the paper on top—a man named Peter Sloane was being cast off from Naysayland tomorrow. Printed under his picture in red ink: *Running underground Positivity, Anonymous meetings.*

The stories he must have, Megan thought.

"There's a ship arriving at five a.m. tomorrow with cargo. I've got a guy who can help me smuggle you on board." He stared hard at Ben and Megan. "This isn't something we advertise to Islanders. Not that they'd want to leave here, but people do get bored. They wonder what else is out there sometimes. I don't want to put this idea in their heads."

Ben nodded, and Megan wished she could read his thoughts.

"Anyway, once you arrive in the Real World, our people on the ground will do their best to keep you hidden. But because of the drones, and who knows what other technology they have, it won't take your mom and everyone at Naysay Inc. long to realize you're there. And once they find out, they'll be looking for you."

"They'll take them back?" Catherine's voice shook.

"Yes," Randy said. "You need to understand, Naysay Inc. won't stop until they capture you and bring you to HR. They'll want to set an example."

Megan's mouth was suddenly dry as she thought of Abby being hauled out of that conference room and never seen again.

When Megan and Ben arrived at the Island, one of the first things Megan asked Randy was if Abby was there. But after searching through his files, he'd shaken his head no.

"Then where is she?" Megan had asked, and Randy shook his head.

"If she's not here, she's most likely been reprogrammed and reassigned," he'd said.

Randy drew his eyebrows together now. "I hope the people you hurt naysaying are worth the risk of trying to save them."

Ben squeezed Megan's hand. "They are," he said.

Megan looked at Ben. She hoped he thought they were worth saving too.

Early the next morning, Megan and Ben said a tearful goodbye to Catherine and headed to meet Randy.

As their golf cart approached the dock, Megan squinted in the darkness. "Is that—?"

"No way—it couldn't be," Ben said.

Megan strained to see until she was certain. She'd recognize that rigid stance anywhere.

As soon as they parked, Megan ran toward her grandmother and threw her arms around her neck. "I'm so happy to see you!"

Genevieve stepped back and studied Megan under the light of one of the lamps on the dock. "You used to be so pale. And now you're so . . . *tan*."

"I know, right? The sun here is amazing."

"Huh," Genevieve said.

"What are you doing here?" Megan swallowed. "Is Mom okay?"

"As negative as ever. And still wants you to return home to answer for your actions."

Megan shook her head. Even after time away, her mom's disappointment in her still stung.

"As soon as I got your text saying you were planning to go to the Real World, I got on my helicopter. Don't worry, I covered my tracks—no one knows I'm here."

"If you came because you think you can talk me out of going, you can save your breath." Megan put her hands on her hips.

"That's not why I'm here, my dear," her grandmother said, a smile playing on her thin lips.

"Then why are you here?" Ben asked.

"Because I'm going with you." She motioned to a small bag sitting on the dock.

"Absolutely not," Ben said. "It won't be safe for you."

"And it will be for *you*?" Genevieve laughed. "I understand the Naysay Inc. systems, technology, and intelligence. I know how they'll track you and how to keep you from being found. You need me."

Ben looked at Megan. "She's right."

"Genevieve?" Randy said as he walked out of his office. "My god, is that really you, or are my old eyes playing tricks on me?"

Genevieve put her hand over her heart, covering the black crow pin on her lapel. "Randy?"

"What are you doing here?" Randy asked.

"Megan's my granddaughter." Genevieve's eyes brimmed with tears.

Megan's mouth fell open. Was her grandmother about to cry?

"Now's the part where you ask *me* what I'm doing here. But you already know that, don't you?" He let out a light laugh, but his body stiffened.

"I never thought I'd see you again," Genevieve said.

"Wasn't that the point?" Randy asked, his lips pinched tight.

"I'm sorry," Genevieve said. "If I could go back and change things, I would."

"Wait. *You're* the man who professed his love for my grandmother at Naysay Inc.?" Megan asked. "That's why you said you understood more than we knew. You were also a Naysay Inc. employee."

"Genevieve told you the story? That she loved me too but pretended she didn't?" He smiled, but his eyes didn't join in.

Megan nodded.

"I think I convinced myself I didn't love you because I was scared," Genevieve admitted. "My mother, as you know, was very high up at the company, and wouldn't have understood."

"Hmm, I wonder what that's like." Megan smiled a little.

"I lied to everyone, including you, Randy. I did care. It took seeing Megan and Ben fight for their love to make me understand what I did to you—*to us*—was wrong. That's why I'm here helping them."

"It was a lifetime ago. And I've been happy here, really," Randy said, but Megan could see he was trying to hide the hurt in his eyes.

Genevieve opened her mouth to speak but closed it.

"How did you get here? I run this dock—I would've seen your boat come in," Randy asked.

"Helicopter. They're monitoring the dock on the other side now. It was the only way."

"I know you two have a lot of catching up to do, but we should get going," Megan said.

"True. Maybe we can grab a coffee after we get these two on the ship, before you head back to your neck of the woods."

"That's a lovely offer, but I'm going with them," Genevieve said.

Randy squinted at her. "I'm not sure I can let you do that."

"And how do you think you're going to stop me?" A playful glint sparked in Genevieve's eyes.

"Same old Genevieve," Randy said and laughed. "Now I see where this one gets her fiery spirit." He nodded toward Megan.

"We do need her help, Randy," Megan said.

"If I've learned anything in my seventy-five years, it's to not argue with women—right, Ben?"

The horn of the incoming cargo ship blared through the thick darkness.

"Saved by the bell," Ben said.

"All right, it's time to get the *three* of you on that freighter." Randy winked.

Megan, Ben, and Genevieve waited in Randy's office while he coordinated things with his Real World contacts on the vessel.

"What a mess it is in here!" Genevieve said, brushing her pants as if they'd gotten dirty during the short time she'd been sitting there. "I don't remember him being such a slob."

"Maybe you can help him get organized when we get back." Megan gave her grandmother a sideways glance.

"Nonsense. I know I had a moment of contrition back there, and it was quite shocking to see Randy again, but I blame the island air. I must return to Naysayland after we go to the Real World. My koi fish need to be fed."

Megan rolled her eyes. "Uh huh. There wasn't a part of you that thought you might run into Randy—that knew he worked this dock and did onboarding for the Island? Wouldn't have been hard for you to find out something like that."

"I don't know what you're talking about." Genevieve looked away.

Randy swung open the door to his office. "Ready to go?" he asked, then caught their amused expressions. "What did I miss?"

Genevieve cleared her throat. "Nothing. When does the ship head out to sea?"

"*Schooner* or later."

"I see the bad jokes haven't changed," Genevieve said.

Randy escorted them to the boat. He held on to Genevieve's arm with the excuse that the dock could sway unexpectedly, but no one believed him.

"Thank you for everything," Megan said to Randy before they boarded. "We'll see you when we get back."

"You're not going to have to wait that long," Randy said. "I'm coming with you, too—Captain John is going to cover for me while I'm gone. That's the thing I was handling while you were in my office."

"Who said you were invited?" Genevieve asked.

"No one, but I wouldn't be able to live with myself if I let you go again and something happened. Well that, and I've heard the Shake Shack burgers in the Real World are amazing."

Genevieve turned her face away, but not before Megan caught the distinct glow that had appeared on her grandmother's cheeks.

"Plus, you'll need someone to connect you with the resistance movement on the ground there."

"Has anyone else tried this to help a former client?"

"No one has been that foolish so far," Randy joked. "But the timing is good. The resistance has been gaining steam, and I think they're finally ready to make some real headway. Maybe this mission will be the catalyst."

The sun had begun to rise, casting a warm, shimmering light across the water in the harbor. A man named Enrique with a wiry mustache and a beanie pulled low hurried them below deck.

As the ship raised its anchor and started its engine, Megan leaned her head on Ben's shoulder and nodded off. She slept soundly for the first time in days.

Chapter Twenty-Three

The Real World

The Real World wasn't at all what Megan thought it would be.

Megan decided, as first impressions go, the Port of Los Angeles, where their ship had arrived, was not doing the Southern California tourism industry any favors. By the confused look on Ben's face, she suspected he agreed.

First off, it was loud.

Horns from the vessels sounded like whiny children as they blared in a continuous loop to signal their arrival. Longshoremen shouted expletives as freely as *hellos*. And the engines of the eighteen-wheelers roared as they idled in a long line, waiting for their cargo to be unloaded.

Also, it was brown.

Well, the sky, anyway. Megan had expected it to be bright blue. Instead, there was a layer of muddy haze that floated below the clouds.

And the birds. They were everywhere.

They were squawking and swooping high, then low, as if protesting the activity around them.

I'm with you, birds. Megan sighed. She missed the zen of the Island already.

"This port is the busiest in this part of the Real World," Randy said. "It brings in almost forty percent of the nation's imports and twenty-one percent of its exports. Not pretty to look at and very different from the Island, but it's essential. I've never disembarked so I'm curious to find out what's beyond these docks."

"Well, for one, there's a manhunt for us," Ben said. He meant it as a joke, but no one laughed. Not even Randy, which Megan found ironic.

"I'm a little nervous now that we're here. How does the size of Naysayland compare?" Megan said. It looked so different through a video monitor.

"The entirety of Naysayland is about the size of the Real World's Manhattan. But don't be intimidated—it's nothing we can't handle," Genevieve said.

"Your grandmother's right," Ben said. "If we could handle Karla's precaffeinated morning tirades, we can do anything."

Megan noted how tired her grandmother looked. Their journey had been long. The ship was freezing, and they'd slept on cots with only light blankets to cover them. Her own back was sore. She couldn't imagine how Genevieve must feel.

Megan yawned and stretched her arms over her head. She wasn't just physically exhausted, but mentally depleted too. She, Ben, and Randy had shared stories of past clients as they crossed the Pacific Ocean. Genevieve had only listened, but Megan could see the wheels turning in her head. She knew her grandmother had more skeletons than all of them combined and wouldn't blame her if she never opened the box where she kept those memories.

To Megan's shock, after more than forty years away from Naysay Inc., Randy still had guilt over many of his charges, in particular, a mechanic named George who'd divorced his wife and moved to a commune in the desert at Randy's urging. The revelation only made Megan more resolute in her conviction to reunite Jasper and Lily.

After a few minutes, Randy's contact, Tanya, arrived. Her long dark hair had silver streaks running through it, and her expression was pinched as she stared at Randy. "You sure you want to go with them?"

Randy looked at Genevieve and nodded.

"You brought more than we normally allow," Tanya said, two deep lines forming between her tiny green eyes. "They aren't thrilled."

"I know. But it's a special circumstance. I owe you one," Randy said.

"And if you don't come back, they know what to do on the Island?"

"There's a plan in place, yes," Randy said.

Tanya grunted. "Your life."

Randy had told them on the ship he was an old man now and if he ended up having to live out the rest of his years in the Real World or was caught by Naysay Inc. and had to go to HR in Naysayland, it would be worth it if he was able to help Megan and Ben make things right with their clients. But Megan, now the eternal love optimist, hoped there was a version of Randy's story where he got his happy ending with Genevieve.

Tanya clapped. "Okay, everyone, we need to be fast. You cannot be in open air for longer than one minute or you could be seen by drones. Put these on—they're all I could find on such short notice, left behind by some tourists on one of the cruise lines." She tossed a pile of baseball caps at the group's feet.

Ben grabbed one that read *Lost, Please Return to Hotel.* Megan selected *Resting Beach Face.* Randy snatched *Professional Tourist.* Genevieve took *I May Be Gray but I Slay* and then laughed and muttered, "I guess that can have more than one meaning."

"Now listen up. You will follow me in a single file line, heads down, and whatever you do, do *not* look up! Naysayland has facial recognition software and will detect you!" she bellowed, sending a chill up Megan's spine, the tone of her voice eerily close to Karla's. "Am I being clear?"

Everyone nodded, pulling on their caps.

As they hurried behind Tanya, Megan's heart was beating so hard she felt like she'd run the one-hundred-meter dash. A large black SUV with tinted windows was waiting at the foot of the gangway.

"Get in," Tanya demanded. "Now!"

Once they were all seated inside the vehicle with their seat belts on, as the burly driver in a crisp black suit had demanded, Megan looked for Tanya out the window. But she'd already disappeared into the crowd of people on the dock.

Megan stared out the window as their car passed in and out of sunlight every few feet. Observing the sky in the Real World was like an in-between of the Island and Naysayland. Depending on where the clouds were, it could appear dark or light.

"It's been a while since we've had your kind here in the Real World," the driver said. "The last guy I picked up like you didn't—ah, never mind that. You guys want some tunes? What are you into? How about reggae? Bob Marley's grandson is pretty good. You know him?" He pressed the screen next to his steering wheel and some music like what was popular on the Island played.

"Excuse me, sir, what were you going to say? The last guy you picked up didn't what?" Megan asked.

"He didn't come back, Megan," Genevieve said and made eye contact with the driver in his rearview mirror. "But *we will.* Staying here is not an option."

Randy's eyes lit up.

"I have things to do at my home in Naysayland. Not on the Island," she said and looked directly at Randy.

"Understood," Randy said and looked out the window.

Megan's heart sank. Couldn't her grandmother give him another chance?

"So, subject change . . ." Megan said.

"Please," Genevieve said.

"What existed first, the Real World or Naysayland?"

"Legend has it that Naysayland was formed in response to the modernization and evolution of the Real World. Others think they originated at the exact same time—that, at a certain point, one couldn't exist without the other."

"What do you think?"

Genevieve sat up a little straighter in her seat as she answered Megan. "I'm not sure about the timing of the creation of the worlds, but I do believe that there might have originally been a legitimate need for Naysayland to balance out the Real World as its civilization became more modern. The fact that Naysay Inc. profited off the Real World's misery ensured there would never be proper guardrails to how far they could go."

Their SUV slowed to a crawl, and the driver pressed his palm to the horn for several seconds.

Ben winced.

"Are you okay?" Megan asked.

"All the visual and audible stimulation in the Real World is making my head throb. The Island might be slow and monotonous, but I must admit there was something to be said for the quietness of it," he said, rubbing his temples.

Megan pressed her hand on his thigh but said nothing.

They passed a Coffee Bean & Tea Leaf, and Megan remembered the vanilla frappé that Lily had often ordered from there, musing that their combination of sugar and caffeine helped hype her up for her live stream. Megan had reprimanded her for drinking them until Lily had finally stopped. She shook her head. She had a lot to make up for with Lily.

Megan turned back to her grandmother. "So, what would happen if Naysay Inc. ceased to exist, Grandmother? Would it end the suffering that Real Worlders endure because Naysayers wouldn't be controlling their thoughts?"

"That's the million-dollar question, as far as I'm concerned," Genevieve said.

"I think it's normal to have a range of emotions," Randy chimed in. "To question yourself. Experiencing pain or sadness or angst but then pulling out of it is part of being human, but Naysay Inc. has gone too far. They've plunged the Real World into emotional chaos and that must stop—as far as *I'm* concerned."

"Are they having their first fight in forty years?" Megan whispered to Ben.

"I think so," Ben said but couldn't keep the smile off his lips.

The driver spoke into his earpiece as they turned onto a street called Sunset Boulevard. They passed a sign with *Bel Air* printed in script, and as they ascended a winding road, Megan was amazed at all the mansions set back from the street, each one more opulent than the next.

When they pulled up to a large gold gate, their driver punched in a series of numbers and it swung open, revealing a long driveway lined with palm trees, manicured flower beds, and rolling hills of green grass. The driver waited for the gate to close behind him and kept his eyes trained on the rearview mirror the entire time before accelerating again.

At the end of the road was a large marble fountain. Behind it, an estate. Naysayland consisted mostly of skyscrapers, and the Island was filled with colorful and quirky bungalows. This modern structure was painted white and was all angles and glass—an architectural masterpiece.

The driver made a call, and the giant front door opened, revealing the clean lines of a foyer.

There was no turning back now, Megan thought as she hurried from the vehicle and ducked inside, Ben's hand slipping from her grasp.

Chapter Twenty-Four

The Real World

"What is this place?" Megan whispered to Ben.

After being offered sandwiches, salads, pastries, and a charcuterie board piled high with meats and cheeses, they were escorted to a room that looked like a control center by a woman in a sleek coral dress named Gloria. On the wall, there were dozens of video monitors and electronic equipment with lights, buttons, and levers that reminded Megan of the soundboards she'd seen Eddie's clients use in their recording studios.

She still wondered how he of all people had seen their attraction before they had.

Genevieve stared at the red dots that littered a map on one of the large screens above them. "I'm impressed," she murmured.

"It means so much to get your approval, Genevieve." A man that looked to be in his forties, tall with dark hair that matched his skin, had entered the room. He wore an immaculate gray suit, his salmon-colored tie peeking out from beneath his fitted jacket.

"Anthony—it's been a while. I wondered where you'd ended up," Genevieve said. "What I meant is, I'm impressed that you have such a high-tech setup here. We had a control room like this one over a decade ago, but I'm sure you'll eventually catch up."

"I see you haven't lost your charm, Genevieve." Anthony laughed. "I know you would've preferred they'd locked me in that prison you call HR, but here I am in the Real World leading the resistance against Naysay Inc."

"That you are." She pursed her lips.

"I was surprised to hear you were helping these Naysay Inc. fugitives. I haven't seen a manhunt like this one since I joined the resistance. You've come a long way since breaking up Crosby, Stills, Nash, and Young."

"Ah! I wish I could take credit for that, but it was a colleague of mine who did the world a huge favor. No one needed to hear the song 'Carry On' again."

"Speak for yourself." Anthony glared at her. "What are you really doing here, Genevieve? Are we supposed to believe you're on our side now? Because you don't sound sorry for the things you—or your colleagues at Naysay Inc.—have done. Is the matriarch of the biggest Naysay Inc. family joining the resistance, or are you here for a dick-measuring contest? Because if it's the second one, I'm pretty sure I'm going to win."

"Is that so?"

"My boyfriend has no complaints."

Genevieve tilted her head. "I'm not here to measure genitalia, Anthony. I'm seventy-five years old and probably incapable of being rewired when it comes to how I remember the decades I put into Naysay Inc. But what I can tell you is, after I saw the company through the lens of my granddaughter and her boyfriend, I've had a change of heart."

"Funny," Anthony said. "I didn't think you had one."

"Turns out it was in here the whole time." She tapped her chest.

"You really think we can trust her?" Anthony asked Randy.

"Yes. She would never double-cross her own granddaughter."

"Just her daughter?"

"Come on, Anthony. She's trying to do the right thing."

Anthony twisted his mouth in thought. "Fine," he said to Randy, then turned to Megan and Ben. "Congratulations. You flipped the great Genevieve Lowell." He golf clapped and looked them both up and down, his gaze lingering on Ben's Hawaiian shirt. "Gloria?" he called out. "We're going to need to handle this." His finger made a circle around Ben. "I'm thinking a crisp striped button-down," he said. "Now, let's talk game plan. At best you will have seventy-two hours to achieve your goals."

"Seventy-two hours?" Megan asked.

"Yes, that's our guesstimate for how long it will take Naysay Inc. to discover you're here and mobilize a team to intercept you," Anthony said, then snapped his fingers in quick succession. He gestured toward the electronic map on the wall and pressed a few buttons. "Okay, so we're pulling up Jasper's and Lily's locations." He pointed to the screen.

Genevieve leaned in to take a closer look. "How were you able to figure out where they are?"

"Who has the advanced technology now, girl?" Anthony flashed Genevieve a satisfied smile.

"Touché," Genevieve said. "So aside from *how* you discern who's who, are you willing to explain how the resistance counteracts what we—I mean, what Naysay Inc. does?"

"We try to create scenarios that lower the clients' vulnerability indexes. We help them get a job they desire, remove someone toxic from their lives, or help them move on from victim mentalities. We encourage therapy, medication when needed, and holistic healing. But because we're not in their ears like some people"—he narrowed his eyes—"it's harder to evoke change. We do have some former Naysay Inc. employees on the payroll and are still working to build our network—if you know anyone who might be interested."

Megan thought about that job—it would be something she'd be good at. She could probably spot a Naysay Inc. client from a mile away. But she couldn't imagine living here.

Anthony pressed another button, and two dots came into focus. "This is Jasper, and that one is Lily. We're tracking their locations so you can make contact with them." He looked at Ben. "What's your plan?"

"We were going to talk to them," Ben offered. "Tell them the voice in their head isn't their own."

"I thought you said they knew what they were doing?" Anthony snapped at Randy.

"Calm down. Their intentions are in the right place," Randy countered.

"Intentions will get them nabbed by Naysay Inc. the minute they step outside. This isn't amateur hour."

"So why don't you help us, Anthony," Ben said. "We're here, we're willing to take the risk, but you're the expert. Tell us what to do."

Anthony looked from Megan to Ben, then back up at the map. "Okay. But it won't be easy."

"Nothing worth doing ever is," Megan said, squeezing Ben's shoulder.

Anthony pulled up a new screen. "This is what I'm thinking. Pay attention. You'll have only one shot at this. Go time is tomorrow at 0500 hours."

The next morning, after a restful sleep in a few of Anthony's many guest rooms, Genevieve, Randy, Megan, and Ben rode over with Anthony to the café where Megan would attempt to connect with Lily. Ben would go on to find Jasper. Anthony and Genevieve, who'd stayed up late the night before sipping from large mugs of hot coffee and sharing intel from both sides, had decided Randy would stay back at the house and fashion prosciutto into roses for that night's charcuterie. (No one, including Anthony, had the heart to tell him he couldn't offer much else in terms of helping.)

As their sprinter van drove down Santa Monica Boulevard, Megan took in the world with fresh eyes. When she'd watched her clients on the feed from Naysayland, she'd only seen them as pawns in the chess game she was playing. Watching from a distance, it had been too easy to dehumanize them all. And it made sense, really. She'd noticed the more time Real Worlders spent online, watching the world through their tablets and smartphones, the more their empathy, arguably their greatest weapon against naysaying, would bleed out.

People breezed down the street, hardly looking up from their devices. Headphones on or earbuds in to shut out the humanity around them. A tall man in a tracksuit knocked into another person without acknowledging the bump. Several teens sat at a table, bent over their phones, not speaking to each other. An unhoused man perched on the corner, a leashed pit bull sitting obediently at his side, a sign asking for money on his blanket, the busy people of Los Angeles stepping over him as they rushed to their next destination.

"It's wild being here, seeing them," Ben said to Megan.

"Did we make them like this?" Megan asked. "They're so—"

"Disconnected," Ben finished. "Maybe. Real Worlders have become increasingly apathetic, but free will exists here. Everyone gets to choose how naysaying affects them."

"Exactly my point yesterday," Genevieve interjected.

"But we're interfering without them knowing. I'd argue that negates their free will," Megan said. "They assume the thoughts we place in their heads are their own. How is that fair?"

"It's not," Ben said.

Genevieve shrugged. "I suppose you have a point."

Megan seized the opening. "So without us intervening right now—"

"There's no hope for them," Ben interjected, offering Megan a smile.

"We're almost to the coffee shop where Lily is," Anthony said. "A man named Everett will be outside. Megan, he'll be your protection in case Naysayland locates you. Because they're surveilling Lily, they will most certainly make the connection that it's you. But I think it will take them at least an hour to mobilize."

"No pressure," Megan mumbled to Ben.

"Now remember, if you let the clock go over sixty minutes, it will leave you vulnerable to being discovered by her lead whisperer, who will flag it and start trying to figure out who you are."

He'd done his homework. That was standard protocol at Naysay Inc. Anyone who engaged your client for a lengthy period was instantly on their radar.

Anthony's phone rang. "What? Are you sure? Send me everything you have." He hung up.

"What's happening?" asked Ben.

"We're hearing that Jacqueline is going to come to the Real World."

"What?" Megan's eyes popped. "Grandmother, did you know this?"

"No, which means she's keeping me in the dark. She must suspect I've been helping you. I knew my cover story of nursing a migraine wouldn't hold up for long."

"Can you stop her?" Megan asked.

"Not from here. And she's probably told them I'm a traitor. They'll never listen to me now."

"So, what do we do about my mom?" Megan asked Anthony.

"We stick to the plan," Anthony said. "I will make sure Everett has a description of Jacqueline, just in case."

"In case of what?"

"Well, if she's on her way to the Real World, it's likely that she'll travel to Lily's location, as she will expect you to do the same."

"How long will it take her to get here?"

"Seconds. As head of the company, she has access to a portal from Naysay Inc. to the Real World," Genevieve said.

"That's a real thing?"

"Yes. She'll have to get the combination to open it, which won't be easy. But if she makes a strong-enough case, the board will give it to her."

The sprinter van idled at the curb next to the coffee shop. Lily was sitting at a table inside by the window.

"There she is," Ben said to Megan. "You've got this."

“We’ll be around the corner,” Anthony said. “The wire you’re wearing and the hidden camera in your lapel will allow us to watch and listen to the conversation through these monitors here.” He pointed to the wall of the van, which looked like the control room at the estate. “If anything goes wrong, we’ll alert Everett.”

Ben swallowed. “Are you sure I can’t go with her?”

“There’s not enough time—especially if Jacqueline is on her way. We need you to get into the van behind us and go to Jasper immediately. Tanya, who helped you at the dock yesterday, will be your security.”

“I love you,” Ben said to Megan.

“I love you too,” Megan said. “I’ll see you later.”

“You’d better,” Ben said, before hopping out of the van.

“Listen to me, Megan. You can do this. Don’t let your mother coming here intimidate you,” Genevieve said.

“I don’t want to let you down, Grandmother. You’ve risked so much for us,” Megan said, reaching forward to squeeze her hand.

“You’ve risked a lot too. You’ve shown me that feeling love is okay, and for that, I’m grateful.”

“Does that mean you and Randy—”

Genevieve held up her hand. “Too soon.”

“Noted,” Megan said.

She yanked the van’s door handle, deciding that this was her moment to own her mistakes—to fix the lives she’d broken. Not just Lily’s but all the clients targeted by Naysay Inc.

“Wish me luck, Grandmother. I’m going to need it,” she said as she stepped out and slammed the door shut behind her.

Chapter Twenty-Five

The Real World

Megan took a deep breath and walked into the coffee shop.

A cool breeze from the air-conditioning struck her as she entered. She spotted Lily and made her way to the counter. *Order something with a latte in the name, and make sure you ask for an alternative milk,* Anthony had warned. *Everyone in LA is either lactose intolerant or vegan, or pretends to be, so you'll blend in better that way.*

Megan got her drink and sat at the table across from Lily. She pulled out the laptop Anthony had given her and stacked her notebooks neatly next to it, making sure the copy of *How to Write a Book* was in Lily's line of sight. Anthony had insisted pretending to be a writer would help her gain Lily's trust, and from what Megan knew about Lily, she agreed. *Do not lead with the truth,* he'd warned. *If you tell her that you're from a place called Naysayland, you might as well say you're an alien. People in Hollywood will believe a lot, but saying you live in an alternate world that plants negative messages in people's minds is taking it too far. Although now that I think about it, that's a great idea for a screenplay.*

Megan put her earbuds in and pretended to make a call. "Hi," she said to her fake literary agent and paused as if listening. "Yes, I got your email. I'm not done with the manuscript yet. I feel stuck."

Megan sipped her lavender-infused oat milk latte with a honey drizzle, which she had to admit was quite good.

She let out an exaggerated sigh. "I know you needed it last month, but I don't feel confident in my writing. I want to give you something good, something you can sell."

Lily looked over, and Megan rolled her eyes. Megan cupped her hand and made the motion to indicate her agent wouldn't stop talking. Lily smiled, and Megan returned it.

Bingo.

"I understand, but—"

Megan pretended to be cut off by her fake fiery agent. Megan shook her head at Lily. Maybe Hollywood was wearing off on her. She felt like she was nailing the role of *frustrated writer on the phone with a demanding agent.*

"Okay, okay, fine. I'll send you what I have by the end of the day. But it's not my best work. It's going to need *a lot* of editing." She paused again as if listening. "Okay, thanks. Bye." Megan hung up and blew a stream of air through her lips.

"I couldn't help but overhear," Lily said.

Megan pressed her lips into a grimace. "My agent just doesn't—"

"Get it?" Lily offered.

Megan nodded. "Exactly. You're a writer too?"

"Trying to be," Lily said.

Megan thought about some of the details about authors Ben had prepped her with. "It's hard, isn't it? Some days I'm in the flow and look up, and I have two thousand words, but other days, I hear this voice in my head that tells me I can't do it."

"Oh my god. Same. And it's so hard to block it out."

"Right?" Megan said.

Lily leaned forward on her elbows. "When I had a hard time ignoring the nasty voice in my head, my mom suggested I give her a name and talk about her like she wasn't me to help take my power back. So I called her the Devil Lady."

Megan tried to keep her face neutral. "Isn't it terrible the things we say to ourselves?"

"Totally. Maybe you could try that, giving yours a name."

How about Megan?

"Maybe," Megan said. "How did the voice in your head affect your life?" Megan asked, not sure why she wanted to hear it. Maybe she needed to?

Lily groaned. "I have this Worthy by Thirty platform, and I didn't make a list I really wanted—which sounds so long ago now that I cared about that." She shook her head. "I had a meltdown that went viral—*long story*—and I couldn't stop thinking about how I wasn't worthy."

Megan cringed.

"I think I let it really get me down. I'd lie in bed at night, questioning myself. Overthinking. Fighting with people in my head about things that hadn't happened yet. I'd worry about every little thing. I met a great guy and had a hard time believing I deserved him."

Megan thought of Beth and how they'd tag teamed Lily, with Megan whispering things during the day, then Beth doubling down at night. Megan shook her head. "I'm so sorry," she said. "That sounds awful."

"It was, but then my mind quieted. I don't know what it was that helped—my mom bought me this book called *Chatter*, I listened to a meditation app, I turned on brown noise." She looked off in thought. "Maybe it was all of it?"

Megan nodded. What happened was she fell in love with Jasper.

"Work got better—I was making a lot of new content for my socials. I felt like myself again. People seemed to forget about my meltdown. Or maybe I did? I started making progress on the book I sold."

"Congrats!" Megan said and meant it.

"Thanks. Life was good. I was hanging out with the guy again." She smiled—a wide grin that filled her eyes. "But . . ."

Megan knew how this story ended, but her heart still sank as she waited for the rest.

"I started doubting myself again."

"Your inner voice?"

"It came back. I pushed Jasper away. He did everything to make me trust him and the way he felt, and I broke up with him anyway. Now I just feel empty." Lily took a sip of her coffee. "I'm sorry to throw up on you."

"No. I want to know." Megan had lain in bed many nights on the Island after Ben had fallen asleep, listening to the waves crashing against the rocks, asking herself why she couldn't fully relax into her new life. Why she couldn't stop wondering which whisperer had taken over for her.

Why she couldn't forget *Lily*.

"I tried to stay positive, but the negative thoughts were nonstop. And I leaned into them. Started to think I should cancel my book deal because no one wanted to read what I wrote. To abandon my Worthy by Thirty platform. I thought I was low-key losing it. I made an appointment with a top therapist in Beverly Hills, and you know what she told me?"

"What?"

"That our inner voice is there to push us when we need to be pushed. That I should trust the voice."

Megan knew Naysay Inc. was in bed with select therapists throughout the Real World, but it was one thing to understand the synergy of Naysay Inc. and the Fund and another to see its destruction of someone in real time. How many people in the Real World had gotten rich off people like Megan placing these thoughts?

"I couldn't believe it. Like, aren't therapists supposed to lift you up? Why would she want to help tear me down?" She shook her head.

"It's not you, Lily."

"Hey—how did you know my name?"

Shit.

Megan scrambled. "You told me, didn't you?"

"No, I don't think so."

Megan noticed Lily's name was written on her cup. "It's there—I guess I saw that."

"Oh, yeah, right. Sorry I flipped out—sometimes I get a little jumpy because it feels like I'm being watched."

Because you are.

"When I say it all out loud, it does sound paranoid. You're probably thinking that therapist was legit, and I'm the batshit crazy one, right?"

"No, of course not."

Lily gave her a long look. "Have we met before? You seem so familiar."

"I don't think so. I'm new to town."

"Huh, it's strange. I feel like I'm having déjà vu."

Was it possible Lily felt connected to her? Megan supposed if a Naysayer was watching you day after day, whispering in your ear, a client could sense it. She'd never thought about it from their point of view. "Maybe I remind you of someone?"

"Maybe. What's your name?"

"Grace Potter."

"Doesn't sound familiar. Where are you from?"

"It's a place far away—you've never heard of it, *trust me*."

"A life you'd rather leave behind?"

Megan nodded. "Something like that."

It was surreal to be so far away from Naysayland, a place she never thought she'd leave. Now she was in the Real World sitting across from the woman whose life she'd strategically ripped apart for months and felt more at home than she ever had there.

"This town is full of transplants like you. You'll fit right in."

"I hope so," Megan said and glanced at the watch Anthony had given her. She needed to go soon.

"We've been talking about me so much. What are *you* writing—I'm assuming it's a novel?" Lily pointed at the copy of *How to Write a Book* in front of Megan.

"It is. Or it's trying to be, but I'm stuck in the middle. I bought this in a moment of desperation," Megan said.

"What's it about? If you don't mind me asking."

Megan couldn't believe she hadn't planned for this question. She took a drink of her latte to stall. Her mind raced until she remembered Anthony's comment that their lives would make a good screenplay. "It's about a parallel world that surveils this one and uses advanced technology to make sure people stay anxious and unhappy. They profit off of it. I'm calling it *The Naysayers*."

They do say to write what you know.

"Wow. No wonder you could relate to what I told you. That's a really good idea—it would make a good movie too."

"That's what I hear," Megan said, then pointed at Lily's computer. "What are you working on? I hope you didn't listen to the therapist and didn't abandon the book deal."

"My mom told me to get a different therapist, and my agent told me I'd be insane to give up. But I had already deleted everything I'd written one night when I couldn't sleep. It felt like I couldn't escape my own insecurities."

Megan's stomach hurt as she thought of all the hard work Lily had thrown away. "I'm so sorry," she said, surprised at the tears welling in her eyes.

"You don't need to be sorry."

Oh, but I do.

"Are you okay?" Lily asked.

"Yeah, I'm fine. It just sucks how we put ourselves down."

"I know. It's total self-sabotage."

"Whatever happened to the guy? You said you started things back up again?" Megan asked, but she knew the answer.

"I ended things. But I still stalk his socials. His name is Jasper," Lily said.

Megan smiled. "Do you miss him?"

"I do. But he's better off."

"Why do you think that?"

"We had an amazing first night together—a total connection. But then it was like we were never going to work out. He was overthinking us, then I was overthinking us. It was harder than it should've been."

I know.

"You sound like you miss him, though," Megan said.

"I do. He's a really good guy. We had this connection that I can't explain. Have you ever had that?"

Megan thought of Ben and wondered how it was going with Jasper. For Megan, there was no room for failure. She'd already faced that word enough times—she wasn't willing to again. The futures of both couples were intertwined. She hoped Ben still felt the same. "I have."

"Then you probably can't believe how I walked away from all of it. My mom thinks I had a serious case of impostor syndrome."

"Don't be so hard on yourself. If you miss him, you should let him know. And if Jasper's the guy you think he is, he'll want to hear from you. Because you deserve love *and* a career. They aren't mutually exclusive. You can have both."

"You're so positive and reassuring. I wish *you* were the voice in my head."

Oh, the irony.

Megan thought of her mom, possibly on her way to the Real World. She'd already been talking to Lily for a half hour. She needed to speed this along in case Naysay Inc. had people on the way. "Why don't you text him right now?"

"I don't know. What if he ignores me?"

"Do you think he would do that?"

Lily shook her head. "I don't—at least I hope not."

"Just do it. I'll be right here. Consider me your emotional-support stranger."

"All you need is the vest!"

"Right? If this whole writing thing doesn't work out for me, I can start a business."

Lily laughed, then her eyes turned serious. "You do seem like more than a stranger. I'm not normally so open with people I've just met, but there's something about you. I feel like I know you."

"Maybe we were meant to meet."

"I'm glad we did," Lily said and smiled.

"Okay, text Jasper. I'll be right here. Whatever he says, I'll help you deal with it."

"You really think I should?"

"I do."

Lily reached for her phone. She scrolled until she found his name. "What do I say?"

"Ask him to meet up tonight."

"Tonight?"

"Yes. You don't want to waste time," Megan said, glancing at her watch again.

"Won't I sound . . . desperate?"

"No, of course not," Megan said, hoping her instincts were right. That Jasper missed Lily as much as she missed him. "And you have nothing to lose at this point."

"I don't know."

"Here's what you do. Tell him you and a friend are having drinks and you'd love to see him. Make it sound super casual—he could bring a friend along too. I'll go with you. I know we don't know each other very well, but like I said, I can be your emotional-support person."

"Why not? Like you said, I have nothing to lose," Lily said, but then she set her phone down and shook her head.

"What is it?" Megan asked.

"The voice—it's back. Saying he'll reject me."

Fuck. Lily's lead whisperer had logged on.

"Megan, if you copy me, cough." Anthony's voice came into her earpiece.

Megan coughed and took a drink of her latte.

"You need to hurry up. We have confirmation that your mom is in Los Angeles. I'm sure they'll figure out you're talking to Lily any second now."

"Listen, Lily," Megan said. "Remember what I said before? You *do* deserve love. And after meeting you, I'm telling you Jasper *will* want to see you again. You're lovely and smart and funny. And you felt a real connection with him. Listen to *me*, not *that* voice."

"Okay." Lily wrote the text, her finger hovering after she'd finished.

"Hit send. You can do it. He's going to write back," Megan said, praying she was right. That Ben had already intercepted Jasper. Because if Jasper's lead whisperer was in his ear right now, that would not be good.

"I did it," Lily said.

"Listen, Megan, you have to get out of there right now," Anthony barked in her ear.

Come on, Jasper, respond.

"I see the three dots. I'm so nervous." Lily stared at her phone.

The door to the coffee shop opened, and Everett, a burly man with biceps the size of Megan's thighs, walked in and gave her a long look. "Excuse me, is that your van parked down the street? I think I saw you get out of it earlier." He raised one of his thick brown eyebrows.

"No. I mean, yes. Yes, it is."

"I think you're about to get a ticket."

"Oh no, okay. Thanks for letting me know."

"You'd better hurry—parking tickets around here are like two hundred bucks," Everett said.

"Okay, give me a second to say goodbye to my friend, okay?"

"You don't have a lot of time," Everett said.

"Okayyyy." She made eyes at Everett, who, in her opinion, was *not* acting like a typical Real Worlder. Hadn't he done this before? "Did he write back yet?" Megan asked Lily.

"The dots keep starting and stopping. I think he's trying to figure out how to reject me."

"He's not going to reject her. Ben is there, telling Jasper about his own true love. I hope."

"Who are you talking to?"

Shit, she hadn't realized she'd said that out loud.

"Just saying some affirmations for you," Megan said.

"Megan, you need to leave right now. Follow Everett out of the coffee shop immediately!" Anthony yelled, and Megan thrust her neck back.

"That was too loud." She turned her head and murmured to Anthony.

"He wrote back," Lily said. "It's long. I'm so nervous. What if he's saying thanks but no thanks?"

"I'm sure he's not," Megan said. "Right, Anthony?" she asked him under her breath.

Lily was bent over her screen and didn't seem to hear.

Megan's heart was hammering. Anthony wasn't responding. This needed to work. They didn't have a plan B.

Finally, Lily looked up, her eyes wide. "He said he's missed me too. He wants to meet and is going to bring a friend like you suggested."

Thank god. Her chest heaved. Ben had done his part. He was still committed to this. To her. "I knew it, Lily. See, you're special! Here's my contact info." She jotted it down on a piece of paper. "Text me, and we'll figure out where to meet tonight."

"You should really go check on your van, miss," Everett said.

"You're really taking this whole Good Samaritan thing to a whole new level," Megan shot back.

"Hey, Grace, why did you write Megan next to your cell phone number?" Lily asked.

Shit.

"That's it. The lead whisperer has positively ID'd you." Anthony's voice was sharp in her ear, and she winced. "Get out of there right now, or this entire operation will be compromised."

"It's a nickname," Megan said.

"How do you get Megan from Grace?"

"Long story. I'll tell you about it tonight." She shoved her laptop and books into her tote bag and rushed for the exit. "I'm so happy I met you," Megan said, surprised by how much she meant it.

She trailed Everett down the street to the waiting van. It screeched away from the curb, the engine revving as it sped the mile to another coffee shop with metal chairs and tables on the sidewalk. It pulled into an open space a block away, and Megan held her breath.

The van doors slid open seconds later, and Ben jumped in.

Anthony touched his earpiece and listened. "I think we're clear. Anyone on our tail?" he asked the driver as the van sped away from the curb.

"No, we're good."

"Mission accomplished!" Ben said, his eyes bright, looking once more like the man she fell in love with.

Chapter Twenty-Six

The Real World

When they entered the control room back at the mansion, they caught part of Genevieve and Randy's conversation.

"That's too dangerous," Genevieve said. "I won't let Megan do that."

"Let me do what?"

"Your grandmother heard about your plan to meet Lily and Jasper at the hotel bar and thinks it's too risky. That your clients will reconcile on their own. They don't need you there," Randy said.

"I agree with Genevieve," Anthony said.

"Well, I do believe hell has frozen over," Genevieve said. "Anthony and I agree on something."

"That we do," Anthony said. "What's next? We'll concur that the woman on *Love Is Blind* does resemble Megan Fox?"

"Never." Genevieve stood her ground. "That's a bridge too far."

"But we can't *not* meet them," Megan interrupted. "We've already let them down too many times."

"I told Jasper I'd be there, and I intend to keep that promise," Ben said.

He'd given the details of his intercept on the drive over as Megan gripped his knee. He'd managed to strike up a conversation with Jasper and convinced him to respond to Lily's text. But he suspected it had very little to do with him and everything to do with Jasper missing her.

"It was such a trip to meet him in real life," he'd said.

"Right?" Megan agreed. "It was surreal being right across from her, looking her in the eyes."

Genevieve was detailing how Jacqueline was in Los Angeles, but that's all they knew at this point. "She *will* find you soon. And if you go back out there, she could intercept you. I want you to understand the risk."

"I do." Megan crossed her arms. "And I don't care. We're going."

"I don't think we're going to change their minds," Randy said. "So maybe let's try to work together here—listen to what they have to say."

Genevieve huffed.

"We have to be with Jasper and Lily tonight because we know them better than they know themselves. Only we can ensure that their vulnerability indexes drop low enough to get Naysay Inc. out of their heads so they can get back together," Megan explained.

"I would bet Jasper's index dropped to a six from getting Lily's text. And because I was there, I could fight back when the whisperer tried to talk him out of meeting her," Ben said. "Their whisperers are likely attacking them now, convincing them to cancel on each other."

"We can only send so many texts today keeping them on track. We need to be with them face-to-face to make sure this works," Megan said.

"Are you going to let them do this?" Genevieve asked Anthony.

"I think we need to, don't we? Isn't this why they came here? Why *you* did?"

"Grandmother," Megan said. "We got this. I promise."

"But it's just one couple," Genevieve argued.

"It's so much more than that." Megan caught Ben's eye, and he nodded.

Genevieve looked back and forth between them, then nodded. "Okay."

Anthony snapped his fingers, and Gloria appeared. "Call in everyone you can."

"Everyone?" she asked.

"Yes. *Everyone.* Tonight is the night we take those Naysay Inc. assholes down. For good."

"What if he's not coming? Do you think he changed his mind?" Lily chewed her bottom lip. It was a tell Megan recalled from when she surveilled her. Her insecurity was spiking.

They'd been at Château Marmont for fifteen minutes, and Lily's lead whisperer was already at work. Anthony had set up an antidrone perimeter around the hotel so they wouldn't be able to enter, but he said they still needed to be vigilant. Naysay Inc. knew where they would be, making them easy prey.

Megan glanced at the time on her phone. It was only 7:59 p.m. "He's coming," Megan insisted. "It's not eight yet."

"Do you think this is okay? I was wearing it the first time we met, and he complimented me on it." Lily tugged on the hem of her burgundy sweater.

That sweater, Megan realized, was the beginning of it all. If Megan had done her job properly and convinced Lily not to buy it, would the night have turned out differently for Lily and Jasper? Or were they destined to meet anyway?

"I thought that wearing it would be like an icebreaker, but now I'm wondering if he'll think it's desperate."

"Lily." Megan put her elbow on the bar and leaned toward her. "I think it's endearing, and I think he'll love that you wore it."

"If he remembers it."

Megan recalled how Jasper had looked at Lily when they were talking at the Soho House that night. Like she was the only woman in the room. "Oh, he'll remember it. You look stunning now, and I'm sure you did that night too. It fits you perfectly, and the color really brings out your eyes—it's like it was made for you."

"Thank you," Lily said. "I'm so happy I met you, Grace."

"Me too," Megan said and meant it. If they'd met under different circumstances, she thought they could have been friends.

"I wish I could take you everywhere with me. Every time my inner voice strikes with a negative thought, you say the perfect thing to squash it."

Megan smiled. *Take that, bitch!*

Over Lily's shoulder, Megan noticed Jasper walking toward the bar, his intense dark eyes scanning the room for Lily. Megan looked expectantly at the doorway behind him, but Jasper was alone.

Where was Ben?

Megan's mind started to go to worst-case scenarios to explain why Ben wasn't there. Did he change his mind? He seemed pumped earlier, but Megan knew he'd been struggling with where he might belong—with his relationship with his mom, and to an extent, Megan. Her thoughts raced with all the things that could go wrong. Was this how a Real Worlder felt when a whisperer was in their head?

She never wanted to find out.

She started to tell Lily that Jasper had arrived, but remembered *Grace* didn't know what he looked like. She took a sip of her martini.

"Lily?" Jasper said her name, and Lily swiveled on her stool to face him. "Hi," Jasper said, his face instantly relaxing as he absorbed her. Megan had seen Ben look at her the same way.

It was love.

"Hi," Lily said, and to Megan's delight, she threw her arms around him. The earlier Lily—the one who'd been worried he wouldn't show—had disappeared. Megan could practically feel Lily's vulnerability-index score lowering and Naysay Inc. losing its grip.

Jasper wrapped his arms around her waist and held on like he never wanted to let go. "It's so good to see you," he said.

It was like Lily had forgotten she was there. Megan couldn't be happier.

"Oh my gosh. I'm so sorry, Grace—" Lily turned toward Megan, her eyes twinkling. "This is Jasper. And Jasper, this is my new friend, Grace."

"It's a pleasure to meet you," Megan said, starting to shake his hand.

Jasper waved her off. "I think a hug is in order. I mean, if you don't mind?"

"Oh, right, of course," Megan said, feeling slightly awkward at the embrace. She accepted Jasper's arms around her and patted his back.

"I hear I have you to thank for the text message I got from Lily this morning."

"I can't take all the credit—"

"No, it was all her," Lily said, then caught Jasper's raised eyebrows. "I mean, I already wanted to talk to you, of course, but she helped me realize it."

"I had a very similar thing happen to me today. I met this guy, Jake Taylor, and he helped me get my head out of my ass."

"Is that the friend who was going to come with you?" Megan asked, her heart starting to beat a little faster with every second that Ben hadn't walked into the bar.

"Yeah, where is he? I need to give him a big hug!" Lily said.

"I don't know where he is. He said he'd meet me in the lobby, but he wasn't there. I waited for a few minutes, but I didn't want to be late."

"Have you texted him?" Megan asked, then realized she needed to back off when she saw the confused look on Jasper's face. Why would Grace Potter care where Jake Taylor was? "Let's get you a drink," Megan suggested, motioning to the bartender, who Megan knew was part of the resistance. The bartender gave her a slight nod of recognition as he asked for their order.

"So, how did you two meet?" Megan asked as the bartender started making their drinks. She knew from her surveillance days that Real Worlders loved telling this story. She hoped it would help lower Jasper's and Lily's vulnerability scores more.

As she listened, nodding with enthusiasm and laughing as if she'd never heard it before, she couldn't stop thinking about Ben. He was over twenty minutes late, which was not like him. Fifteen minutes early was late for Ben.

Did Ben bail on her?

Megan wasn't wearing any comms. The antidrone technology made them obsolete. She was going to excuse herself to go to the ladies' room so she could call Anthony to find out where the hell Ben was, but Lily launched back into the story. They weren't leaving out a single detail. Megan forced herself to keep a smile on her face.

"Another round?" the bartender asked, and Jasper and Lily nodded. "And what about you?"

Megan shook her head. "I'm good." She needed to keep her head clear so she could think.

"You sure? I make a mean mojito." The bartender turned his torso away from Lily and Jasper and started muddling mint in the bottom of a glass. "We're trying to figure out where Ben is. Anthony will figure out a plan B, but for now, he said not to freak out."

"*Not to freak out?*" Megan said, her voice rising.

"Everything okay, Grace?" Jasper asked.

"Yeah, fine. I was saying I'll freak out if his mojito is as good as he's promising."

"It is," the bartender said. "It's one of those drinks that makes you feel like everything is going to work out, you know?" His eyes bore into Megan's.

"Then I'll take one too!" Jasper said.

Lily's face flushed pink. "Make it three," she said.

Megan wanted to scream. How was she supposed to continue standing here when Ben was a no-show? Did he decide the risk wasn't worth it?

"I have to use the ladies' room," Megan said. She needed to think. Splash some cold water on her face. Something.

"I'll go with you," Lily said.

Megan took a deep breath as Lily got up and followed her.

"You okay?" Lily asked as she touched up her lipstick. "Were we being cringy? Is that why you checked out during our story?"

"No, no, I loved your story. Sorry if I didn't seem like I did."

"Is it the voice in your head?" Lily asked. "I know how you feel—it's happened to me in bars when I've felt alone. I'm sorry, I should've tried to bring you into the conversation more."

"No, it's not that. I'm fine, really."

"You don't seem fine," Lily said. "I can tell something's wrong. Out with it, girl!"

Megan was touched by Lily's concern, which made her feel more terrible about when she'd whispered to her. Megan scrambled for a cover story but realized she didn't have any more lies in her. "Listen, Lily, I haven't been honest with you."

"What do you mean?"

"I need to tell you who I really am."

Lily blinked. "What do you mean, *who you really are*?"

Megan ushered Lily outside the bathroom. "Okay, so I don't want you to be upset, but my real name isn't Grace."

"What? What are you talking about?"

"Let's go back to the bar—I'll explain everything to you and Jasper there."

"Thought you guys left me," Jasper joked when they returned. "You okay?" he said to Lily. "You look a little thrown."

"Grace, or whatever her name is, apparently has something to tell us," Lily said.

"What?" Jasper asked.

"You guys liking your drinks?" the bartender said. "Can I bring you anything else? We have some excellent appetizers. Our crab cakes are amazing. Of if you'd like a vegetarian option, we can—"

"The drinks are excellent and we're not hungry," Megan said. "Now if you don't mind, I was about to tell my friends a story."

"You sure you want to do that?"

"One hundred percent."

The bartender held up his hands as if to say *your life*.

"What was that about?" Lily asked. "Do you know him or something?"

Megan ignored the question and took a deep breath. "Okay, so this is going to sound odd, but I need you to hear me out. The guy who was supposed to meet you here, I know him."

"Wait, what?" Jasper asked. "How do you know Jake Taylor?"

"I know him as Ben Shaw."

"And your name isn't Grace Potter?"

"No, it's not. I'm Megan Lowell."

"What is this? Are we on some kind of hidden-camera show? I won't sign a release so you can stop now," Jasper said.

"That's not what this is," Megan said. "I'm not from here, or anywhere near here. I'm from another world called Naysayland."

"Naysayland, like in the book you're writing?" Lily asked.

"Yes, but it's not fiction. It's my life. Or it was, anyway," Megan said. "Ben—or Jake Taylor—he's from there, too, and he's my boyfriend. We worked at the same company, Naysay Inc., and our job was to be the voices in your heads."

"What the fuck?" Jasper said.

"Look, I know this is going to sound insane, but Ben and I fled Naysayland because we didn't want to be those awful voices anymore. We came here, to the Real World, to help you get back together. Because we're the reason you broke up originally."

"So, let me get this straight. You're aliens who destroyed our relationship by planting bad thoughts in our heads, but now you've come to Planet Earth to get us back together? And you're writing a book about it? Spoiler alert: It's not going to sell. And FYI: You need to work on your elevator pitch."

"I know about your aunt Louisa, Jasper. I know about Monopoly. The shoe was always your piece," Megan said.

Jasper got quiet. "I've never told anyone about those games. How do you know that?"

"Ben told you to go to the cabin—to ghost Lily—because you guys were vibing. You really liked her, and at that time, he didn't want that relationship to work out. Ben suggested she was a distraction—that you needed to get your book to your agent and if she was in your life you wouldn't finish."

Jasper went silent again.

"See? How would I know all that?" Megan asked.

"You could've hacked my phone or my email."

"But that's not what we did. We surveilled you from Naysayland. Watched you through drones that are so small the human eye can't see them."

"Creepy," Lily said.

"I know," Megan said. "But it's true."

"So, what does the inside of my aunt's cabin look like? I've never taken anyone up there, so you should be able to describe it."

"He didn't tell me that, but if he was here, he could."

"But he's conveniently not here, is he?" Jasper's face was tight.

"He's not, but he wanted to be. He meant to be. I swear." Megan's voice caught. "Lily, please believe me. I was your inner voice."

"So now you're going to use something I told you in confidence?"

"That's what con artists do," Jasper said.

"I'm not a con artist."

"Aren't you?" Lily shook her head at Megan. "Because if your story *is* true and you *are* my inner voice, then that's exactly what you do. You manipulate. You control. You con."

"You're right, I fit that definition. But I've changed. I want to make up for the things I said to you, but I didn't think I could approach you with the truth in the café. You would have never believed me."

"Sort of like right now." Lily pinched her lips.

"I understand why you don't trust me, but I want you to know that I'm sorry. I'm sorry I got into your head and made you feel lesser than. I'm sorry I told you you'd never be worthy by thirty and that you didn't deserve love." The tears rolled down Megan's face. "That I made you play Taylor Swift to drown me out. She's talented, but a person should only have to listen to 'Cruel Summer' on repeat so many times, you know?

"I feel terrible that I told you your mom gave terrible advice. You're so lucky to have her. And now Ben is missing, and I don't know if he left me on purpose or if something happened to him. Either way I'm afraid I'm going to lose him forever. And I guess I deserve that."

Lily didn't speak for several seconds. "I've never told anyone about Taylor Swift."

"You blasted her in the Jeep after you bought the sweater you're wearing tonight. I tried to convince you to go back to the store and return it, but you blared the *Lover* album. Which, for the record, I thought was a brilliant move."

Lily's eyes widened slightly at the revelation, but she quickly hardened her stare. "If your goal was to break us up, why do you want us back together?"

"Because I fell in love too. I realized love was amazing and that Ben and I stole that from you."

"And that's why you disappeared?"

"Exactly. Ben and I became distracted with one another. And as we fell in love, it became harder to keep you apart. Our work performance became inconsistent."

"I do remember there was a period when the voice in my head wasn't there. I called mine *Mom*, because it was such a nag. That was amazing. My writing was flowing. Everything was working," Jasper said, his gaze alert.

"You're right. And then it came back, harsher than before. That wasn't you, was it?" Lily said as she connected the dots.

"It wasn't. When they found out about how Ben and I felt about each other, we had to flee Naysayland. But we came here, we risked it all, to make things right with you. We were hoping that if we could help you get back together, it would lower what we call your vulnerability index scores to a point that your whisperer would be kicked out of your head, permanently. You'd be free. I know how far-fetched this all sounds, but it's true. I swear to you," Megan said.

The tears continued to fall. Was this why Real Worlders cried so much? She had to admit the release of intense emotion felt good.

"I can vouch for her," the bartender interjected, as he shook a martini. "She's not making it up."

"Wait, so you *do* know each other?" Lily asked.

"We don't, but I'm part of the resistance—an organization trying to undo all the things she's talking about. I used to live in the same place she did, and she's telling the truth."

"Thank you—" Megan realized she didn't know his name.

"Eric."

"Thank you, Eric." She turned back to Lily and Jasper. "Even if you don't believe me, please believe how sorry I am, for everything. I hope you realize you love each other and keep each other close always because you are meant to be together. I have to go now. I have to try to find Ben." Megan got off the stool and started to leave.

"Wait!" Lily said. "I believe you."

"You do?"

Lily nodded, then looked at Jasper.

"I do, too, pending Ben's description of the cabin, of course." He smiled.

"That's very gracious of you." Megan started to leave again.

"Megan," Lily said. "Don't go."

"I have to."

"Stay and tell me a little more about how your world works. I think I have an idea of how I can help you."

Chapter Twenty-Seven

The Real World

Ben stared at the dark desert sky as the SUV sped past a town called Barstow. The image of palm trees and rolling hills under the glow of the full moon was breathtaking. The juxtaposition of the beauty he was witnessing outside the car and the ugliness inside it wasn't lost on him. There was a time he wouldn't have seen the light, so to speak. Now, despite the fact he was being forced back to Naysayland, he wouldn't change a thing.

He'd walked into Château Marmont at 7:45 p.m., knowing Megan was already seated at the bar with Lily. He waited for Jasper and watched Megan sipping a martini and laughing at something Lily said.

God, he'd been such an ass lately. Working with her again to save Jasper and Lily had made him realize how good they were together. Why had he been mourning his life in Naysayland instead of being present with Megan? He hated that he'd made her question him. He couldn't wait to tell her that the only life worth living was the one with her.

"I'm sorry," he said to Megan, even though she couldn't hear him. "I'll make it up to you, I promise."

"Aw, how sweet," a gruff voice had said. Ben was yanked by the collar, pulled through a hallway, out a back door, and pushed into the black SUV where he was now.

Jacqueline glared at Ben. Her dark hair was wrapped into two tightly knotted braids. Ben thought she looked like that Real World movie character Princess Leia.

She was really leaning into the whole space travel thing.

Abby was seated beside her. Her red curly hair was slicked back into a severe bun, her large black framed glasses were gone, and her eyes were empty, like her life had been sucked out of her.

"Hi, Ben," Jacqueline said, her eyes hard and cold. "You remember Abby? She now heads up the Naysayer Reprogramming Department in HR."

"Hello, Ben. I'm looking forward to our transformation sessions. Shouldn't take long to get you back to square one," Abby said, a slow grin curling on her lips.

Ben put his hand on the door's handle and jiggled it. It was locked. So was the control for the window. He had to get the hell out of there.

"Oh, Ben, where are you trying to go? We're taking you home, where you belong," Jacqueline said. "Anyway, the doors and windows can't be opened from the inside, and our security guards have a higher level of training than this world's Navy SEALs. So, if I were you, I'd sit back and enjoy the ride to the portal that will launch us back to Naysayland. Unless you want to answer to Sam, who hauled you out of that hotel like you were a sack of potatoes in under ten seconds." She laughed.

"What do you want, Jacqueline?"

"My daughter. She needs to be reminded of who she's meant to be."

"And why do *you* get to decide that?"

"I'm her mother."

"I'm not a parent, but being someone's mother doesn't give you license to control them."

"Doesn't it? I birthed her. She wouldn't be here without me. So, yes, Ben, I get to decide what happens to her."

"I think she's made it pretty clear what she wants her life to look like. Spoiler alert, it's not with you."

"Don't be ridiculous. Free will is for Real Worlders." She laughed. "I have a strong feeling that after we get you back to Naysayland, you'll have a change of heart."

"I'm done with that life."

"I bet Megan is doubting that right now. Wondering where you are. Why you bailed. That's what I'll tell her anyway."

"She'll never believe you."

"Won't she? I heard you weren't one hundred percent sold on the Island."

"How do you—"

"You don't think we keep tabs on the place we export our rejects to?"

"It's true I was having a hard time adjusting to the Island, but it didn't have anything to do with Megan."

Jacqueline laughed at that.

Abby's phone pinged, and she showed the screen to Jacqueline, who gave her a stoic nod. "Ben will be happy to hear that."

Ben noticed a Route 66 sign on the side of the highway. He remembered one of Eddie's clients did a cover of the song with the same name, and they'd laughed at the ridiculousness of driving across the country for pleasure. But now Ben could see the appeal of taking the time to appreciate the world around you.

"Let me guess." Ben tapped his chin. "You've decided to stay in the Real World? To get your kicks on Route 66?"

"That's funny, but no. Turns out the sad little Real World couple that you and Megan threw your lives away for left the Château Marmont *together*. Holding hands." She turned to Abby. "I will never understand the appeal of pressing sweaty palms together for pleasure."

Abby rolled her eyes in solidarity.

"It seems Lily's and Jasper's vulnerability indexes are too low for us to monitor any longer. A surprising development, since Megan's replacement orchestrated fifteen mental breakdowns last quarter alone while in the Teenage Competitive Sports Department, and Jasper's Naysayer had ended a record-breaking two hundred and fifty nuptials while running the Marriage Department." Jacqueline scowled. "Abby, make a note to call them into my office when we get back. They need to explain how Lily and Jasper were still able to overcome their crippling insecurities."

Ben smiled. Megan had done it. She'd convinced them to be together. "You mean they overcame the insecurities that Naysay Inc. *gave* them," Ben said.

"That Naysay Inc. *drew out of* them. There's a difference. We didn't create the negative feelings they were having. We *enhanced* them."

"Semantics."

"If every Real Worlder was satisfied and happy, there would be no progress. Evolution comes from struggle. Creativity rises from anxious minds."

Abby's eyes glowed. "Without us, they'd still be using VCRs."

"And floppy disks."

"Dot matrix printers."

"Don't forget pagers." Jacqueline and Abby laughed.

Ben balked. "Are you two done? You have no way of proving there's a link between Naysay Inc.'s whispering and Real Worlders' productivity. That's something you tell yourself so you can sleep at night."

"I do sleep soundly every night, Ben, knowing that we're improving the lives of Real Worlders."

"Naysay Inc. isn't helping them. It's destroying them whisper by whisper for profit."

"That's where you're wrong. They're destroying themselves," Jacqueline said. "How else do you explain the popularity of Crocs?" She shook her head. "Walking around in gardening clogs and calling it fashion?" Jacqueline sneered. "You're kidding yourself if you think sparing Jasper and Lily from our influence will make a difference. You can't stop us. Naysay Inc. is still in the ears of millions of Real Worlders and always will be."

Ben hoped she was wrong. That Lily and Jasper getting back together was the beginning of real change. That the resistance could continue its mission, one person at a time.

"But I do have to hand it to you, Ben. You managed to poison an entire bloodline. *My* bloodline. My mother and my daughter both turned against the cause. Who would've thought? Bravo!" Jacqueline clapped loudly, and Abby parroted her.

"I wish I could take the credit, but they made their own choices. And so did I."

"Megan belongs at home with me. After she's reprogrammed, she'll settle back into the life she was meant to live and the legacy she was meant to continue. She's rebelling because she *thinks* she's in love with you."

"She'll never go back. And we *are* in love."

Jacqueline waved him off. "Love doesn't last. People are selfish."

"You don't know the first thing about love, Jacqueline. You've obviously never felt it."

"Hallelujah." She held her hands up in prayer. "What if you and I make a deal?" Jacqueline leaned toward Ben. "Help me bring Megan home, and I'll let you return to Naysayland and your career there or to the Island to be with your mother. Or even here! Your choice."

"No thanks. Not interested," Ben said.

"Is being with Megan worth losing everything?" Jacqueline lowered her voice. "I'm offering you your life back, Ben. Take it."

Ben tightened his fists. The only place he knew he wanted to be was by Megan's side, wherever that might be. Jacqueline had it all wrong. Love had saved him. Given him purpose. He'd rather spend the rest of his life in Naysayland as a converted man than offer up Megan.

Ben put his hand over the phone in his front pocket. Hopefully Anthony was tracking his location, and they'd find him before they reached the portal.

"What is *that*?" Jacqueline peered at Ben. "Do you have a cell phone? Sam, didn't you pat him down?" She sighed.

"He put up quite a fight when I grabbed him."

"You're pathetic. Do I have to do *everything* around here?" Jacqueline seethed. She leaned across the seat and yanked the phone out of Ben's front pocket, then threw the phone out the window. "If they were tracking you, they're not anymore." She and Abby shared a laugh.

"I don't care if they can't save me. I'll never help you," Ben said.

Jacqueline made a gagging sound "This isn't one of those ridiculous Real World television shows where you get to be a hero in the end. We won't be wrapping up this story in a pretty bow before the credits roll. You're heading back to Naysayland to be reprogrammed, and it might take some time, but we will also reclaim Megan and Genevieve. Your bravado will mean nothing."

"We'll see about that," Ben said and gazed back up at the sky filled with stars, letting their brightness fill him with hope.

◆ ◆ ◆

"We're twenty minutes out, Ms. Lowell," Sam said as a blaze of lights came into view.

Ben recognized the view from a trip his client Nancy Sawyer had taken with her friend last year. "Las Vegas," he said out loud.

"Someone knows his Real World geography," Jacqueline said. "But we won't be gambling or taking in a show—although I hear the Sphere's worth a visit, if you're into the whole immersive LED video thing Naysayland has been doing for over a decade. We'll be traveling through one of the portals back home. It's located in the basement of a casino."

"A portal in a casino?" Ben scoffed.

"There are several located throughout the Real World. The one we'll be taking was the first, placed here because it was in the middle of nowhere. Then in the early 1900s, developers came sniffing around so we bought the land around it and built a casino, which turned out to make perfect sense for our business," Jacqueline mused. "People who come to Las Vegas often have high vulnerability indexes, and when they get drunk and lose their rent money?" Jacqueline grinned. "It's almost too easy. Not to mention the casino funds most of Naysay Inc.'s operations. Fun fact," she said, a gleam in her eye. "Our casino was the first to offer free alcohol to people while they gamble. It was genius, really. Real Worlders are willing to lose hundreds of dollars playing blackjack while waiting for their complimentary vodka sodas." She shook her head. "But you think they're all worth saving."

"I do," Ben muttered.

"Fool," Abby said.

"What happened to you?" Ben looked at Abby. "You used to be so—"

"Unconfident? Insecure? Hesitant?"

"Well, yes, but also—"

Jacqueline put her hand up. "She also no longer trembles or hesitates." She gave Abby a once-over. "Or wishes people a happy birthday. Or tries to resuscitate dead houseplants. God, that was so annoying."

"But there was something human about you, Abby. Something *real*."

"This is who I was meant to be," Abby said simply.

"I could see she had promise, which is why she's here and not on the Island. She benefited greatly from reprogramming, and so will you."

Ben closed his eyes. He didn't want to be the old Ben Shaw again. But if that was the price that he had to pay to protect Megan, he'd do it.

"Anyway, let's cut the small talk, shall we? We need to get back to business. I've called ahead to arrange our transfer back to Naysayland," Jacqueline said as a man stumbled out into the street, almost getting hit by a passing cab, his yard drink splattering a blue liquid across the asphalt. "There's so much good work to be done here. Maybe I'll suggest doubling our efforts in this city. Abby, could you make a note?"

Abby pulled out a tablet and clicked. "Noted, Ms. Lowell."

The SUV pulled into a parking garage marked EMPLOYEES ONLY and backed into an empty loading dock. Sam got out and opened Ben's door. "Don't try anything stupid. This entire place is filled with Naysay Inc. surveillance and security. You won't get far."

Sam led them into a dimly lit hallway and waited for Jacqueline to use her thumbprint to open a door marked NO UNAUTHORIZED ACCESS.

"After you," she said to Ben.

Ben entered the room and shivered. On the back wall was a large steel door with another keypad. After so many years of hearing hypotheticals about the portals to and from the Real World, it felt daunting to be standing in front of one.

Ben heard a loud click as the door swung open, revealing a dark tunnel.

Sam pushed him. "Let's go," he said.

Ben stared at the bleak pathway and thought of Megan. Of Randy and Genevieve. And of course, Jasper and Lily, and his other clients. He paid a silent tribute to all the people who would benefit from his sacrifice, and this gave him the light he needed as they walked into the darkness, back to his former life.

Chapter Twenty-Eight

The Real World

"Where is he?" Megan pointed to the place on the screen where Ben's beacon had been flashing. "Is he *gone*?" She grabbed the edge of a chair, her eyes darting around the control room.

Lily touched Megan's arm but didn't speak.

"Anthony, say something, *please*," Megan said, clutching her chest, hoping Ben's tracker might reappear, even though it had been almost twenty minutes since it had disappeared off the grid.

Anthony pressed several buttons. "I don't think we can get his signal back. I've tried everything. We've lost contact," he said. "Either his battery died, they removed his SIM card, or—"

"They're in an area with bad cell service. It can be spotty in the desert, right?" Megan suggested, knowing it was unlikely. But she didn't want to accept that Ben had gone through the portal and was on his way back to Naysayland.

With her mother.

"Megan," Genevieve said, her eyes sad. "I think we need to accept he's gone. At least for now."

"*Or* the system is glitching. Can't you turn it off and back on?" she asked Anthony, her voice choked with emotion. She remembered her Real Worlder clients would often restart their electronics when they weren't working.

Anthony shook his head. "This isn't a laptop," he said, a condescending tone to his voice.

"How far from the portal were they?" Megan asked, tears in her eyes.

Anthony softened his tone. "About twenty miles outside of Las Vegas. There's no way to get there in time."

"If you knew the location of the portal, why weren't we there waiting for them?" Megan rubbed her temple.

"There are multiple portals in the Real World," Genevieve said.

"There are?"

"Yes. And there was more than one that your mother could have reached by car from Los Angeles," Genevieve said.

Megan slumped into a chair. "Maybe I should turn myself in. Tell my mother I'm coming back. Then maybe she'll let Ben go."

"I don't recommend that," Genevieve said.

"Why not? She doesn't want Ben. She wants *me*," Megan said, noticing again how tired her grandmother looked. She should be feeding her koi fish right now, not on some mission in the Real World. What had she pulled her into?

Genevieve pursed her lips. "If I know my daughter, she'll trick you. Agree to an exchange, but then she'll have both of you. After everything we've been through, I can't let you be *converted*." Genevieve's voice broke. Randy grabbed her hand, and to Megan's surprise, she let him.

"I'm sorry I brought you into this, Grandmother," she said. "You should be enjoying retirement."

"In Naysayland?" Genevieve scoffed. "I'm not sure I want to go back to that place."

"Really?" Randy and Megan said at the same time.

"Don't get all excited, Randy. I'm only saying I'm not sure." She lifted her chin. "Or if I could go back, at this point."

"I know a place where it's sunny all day. I'd love to see you with a tan," Randy said, wiggling his eyebrows.

"I'm not sure I'm ready for bikini weather quite yet," Genevieve said with a light laugh.

Randy put his hand over his heart. "I'm willing to wait until you are."

Genevieve looked at him, her eyes misty. "You'd do that for me—*again*?"

Randy smiled at her. "A million times over."

They locked eyes.

"Okay, Boomers," Anthony interjected. "If we're going to try Lily's idea, we need to start now." Anthony's fingers tapped the keyboard. "If HR still operates the way it did when I was at Naysay Inc., Ben could have already started reprogramming therapy."

"Already?" Megan's lip trembled. "How long does it typically take to kick in?"

"It's different for everyone."

"If anyone can fight it, it's Ben."

Anthony tilted his head and looked Megan in the eye. "They all do. Until they don't. Naysay Inc. is relentless."

"Luckily, so are we," Megan said. "Lily—will you walk everyone through your idea?"

"Sure," Lily said, making her way to the front of the control room.

Megan was struck by how poised and confident Lily seemed. Like the woman she used to be, the one who'd given the "How to Be Worthy by Thirty" TEDx talk.

"It occurred to me after the voice disappeared from my head that its ability to live within us is driven by ignorance." Lily looked at Genevieve. "Because as soon as Jasper and I knew the truth, the voice no longer held any power, and poof! It was gone." She glanced at Jasper, then turned to Megan. "So, what if we gave *everyone* back their power? What if we set everyone free with the truth about Naysay Inc.?"

"What if no one believes you?" Randy asked when she finished.

"Has the Island frozen over? Is the eternal optimist questioning things?" Genevieve teased.

Randy laughed. "You got me there, Genny."

Genny? Megan thought.

"It won't matter," Lily said. "That's the thing about the internet and social media in our world. Sadly, whether your content is true or not isn't relevant. You only need it to be heard. What we need is for the video to go viral. If it does, it will get people talking about it. Plant the seed. It can start with my followers."

Lily pressed on. "If I can help one person know they can fight the voices—that they don't have to live with a *Devil Lady* in their heads—we will have won."

"Or *Jackhole Rat Bastard Asswipe Shithead*," Jasper said, then caught Megan's stunned face. "That's what I called my voice when I was really mad at him. Sorry, I'm sure Jake slash Ben is a great guy *now*, but do you know how many nights I spent with a frozen dinner, a bottle of Jack, and a blank laptop screen because of him?"

Megan offered him a sad smile.

"How will making the video take away Naysay Inc.'s power?" Anthony asked.

"Power is in the truth. If we can get enough people to listen to what we're saying and then make their own videos and posts on the subject, the voices will disappear. Like they did for us." She turned to Megan, biting her lower lip.

"What is it?" Megan asked.

"I don't know how this will help Ben."

"One step at a time. First, we free the Real World. Then we save Ben."

"What do you need to execute this, Lily?" Anthony asked.

"Just my phone, someone to film us, and some reliable Wi-Fi," she answered.

"What about ring lights? A cozy chair? A blanket? Candles?" Megan asked. She thought back to Lily's apartment and the many things she used to portray her Worthy by Thirty messages to her followers.

"We don't need any of that. We aren't going to hide behind filters or soft lighting or props." She squeezed Megan's hand. "We're going to be *us*," she said. "Anthony, what's your Wi-Fi password?"

"Bagofdicks1234."

Everyone turned to gape at Anthony.

"What?" he said, a proud smile clinging to his lips. "Long story, long night is all I have to say to any of you."

Lily pulled up her Instagram account, clicked the live button, and handed the phone to Tanya. "Hey, y'all," she said, her face filling the screen as the number of people joining the session began to climb. "Everyone come close. It's story time. I'd like you to meet my friend Megan. Well, we just became friends. She tried like hell to ruin my life first. But then she saved it. And she can save yours too."

Lily pulled Megan into the frame. "You're on, girl. Release the truth to the world."

Chapter Twenty-Nine

Naysayland

The commotion in the hallway was so loud it drowned out the reprogramming video Ben was watching. Not that he was complaining. It was hour number eight—or was it nine?—of relearning the history of Naysay Inc.'s influence over Real Worlders.

Ben was so bleary eyed and exhausted that the current lecture was starting to make sense. Naysay Inc. claimed to be a vital part of advancing the Civil Rights Movement because they'd whispered all races and cultures equally.

Ben shook his head to clear the thought. How had he ever bought into these theories?

He leaned back in his chair and strained to listen to the voices on the other side of the door, almost falling over when Abby burst into the room. Her eyes were wide as she spoke in hushed tones into the instructor's ear, a stout man named Donte with a bushy mustache.

Ben exchanged a look with the only other person in the room. She was an elfish woman named Eden, who Ben recognized from the IT department.

Donte jutted his chin, glancing at the restraints on the table and then back at them, as if trying to decide whether he should tie them up in his absence.

Ben heard Abby call Donte's name urgently.

"Stay here!" he said.

Where would we go? Ben thought.

When Ben had been brought into Naysay Inc. yesterday, he'd planned to escape. But not only did they have him wearing an ankle bracelet—there were also guards at every exit. Not to mention the restraints that could be used at any time. And the blinking red lights from security cameras in every room, the hallway, and—to his horror—the bathroom, reminded him he was under constant surveillance.

Ironic, he'd thought. But also, *I deserve this.*

Abby and Donte rushed out. As the door was closing behind them, Ben spied several people gathered around a large monitor in the hallway, watching a woman speak. He couldn't see her face, but he'd know that voice anywhere.

Megan.

The door slammed shut.

Eden was staring at him. "What was that all about? Must be serious for them to leave us here unattended. Not that we'd get far." She kicked out her leg with the ankle bracelet attached.

Ben looked up at the blinking light on the surveillance camera and spoke through clenched teeth. "You still have your credentials, right?" He tilted his head slightly toward the camera, so she'd understand he didn't want them to be overheard.

She nodded. "I think so."

"I need you to break into the Naysay system." He shifted his eyes toward Donte's tablet that he'd left behind. "I'm pretty sure I saw Megan on the video they were watching."

"Ben, you're losing it. I know you miss her, but you have to accept you've lost. It's over. We're prisoners who are undergoing a slow-burning naysay lobotomy. Before long you won't remember her anyway, so you might as well let her go now."

Ben had accepted he'd never see Megan again in person. But if she was on a video—right now—he wasn't going to miss the chance to watch. "I *know* it was her. Will you help me or not?"

"Fine. It's got to be more interesting than that." Eden indicated the reprogramming video that was still playing. "Grab Donte's tablet," she commanded.

Ben hustled to the front of the room and picked up the tablet, clinging to it as he held his breath. If anyone had noticed, they'd be rushing in any second to reprimand him. He didn't want to find out what that would look like.

But no one came.

"Here." He handed it to Eden.

Her fingers swiped at record speed.

"Anything?" Ben said, his eyes trained on the door, his heart hammering.

"It's been like two seconds, Ben. Slow your roll," she said, her face pinched in concentration. "Wait, here, I think I found it. It's a live stream from a social media platform in the Real World." She turned the tablet toward him. "There she is."

"Yes," Ben said, his body flooded with adrenaline.

Eden turned up the volume.

"Hi, my name is Megan, Megan Lowell, and I'm from a place called Naysayland—"

Lily pushed into the frame. "You guys, I'm going to keep it real for you. What we're about to tell you is absolutely legit," she said, smiling at Megan. "Naysayland is a parallel world, and there are people there who monitor our emotional states. You know those voices we hear in our heads? They're not ours. We aren't the ones putting ourselves down, making ourselves feel less than, doubting ourselves. Please share this and ask your friends to join right now because everyone needs to hear this. And, after, we'll also post the video from this live on all my socials."

Ben blinked hard. Lily and Megan were together? And Lily knew the truth? And now they were telling everyone in the Real World about it? He looked at Eden in surprise.

The number of people joining the live ticked up furiously. Forty thousand, fifty thousand, seventy-five thousand. But Ben knew that was only a fraction of the Real World's population.

"They need more eyes on this," Ben said.

"Hold on," Eden said as she clicked out of the screen. "I have an idea." She typed furiously for a moment, then sat back, a huge smile spreading across her face. "Handled."

"What did you do?" Ben asked.

"I projected their feed onto every screen in the Real World. Times Square in New York City, every sporting event, concert. Basically any television or computer that's on and connected to the internet is now playing this," she said proudly.

"How did you do that?" Ben asked.

"I have top clearance to every system—that's why they're trying to reprogram me. I know way too much for them to let me sail off to the Island." She laughed and clicked one more key. "I also locked the system so they can't make any changes."

The fervor had increased in the hallway.

"I'm sure that's what they're freaking out about right now," she said. "I covered my tracks, but it still won't take them long to figure out it originated on this tablet."

Ben drew Eden into a tight hug. "Thank you for taking the risk."

"If it's the last good thing I'm able to do before they reprogram me, I'll take it." She pointed toward the screen. "Now that Megan has the audience, I hope she can convince them."

Me too, Ben thought.

Megan continued. "I used to be one of those voices you hear. I worked for a company called Naysay Inc. and was paid to infiltrate the minds of people like Lily. She was one of my clients."

Lily put her hand up. "But here's the thing. I didn't know it." She turned to Megan, "It's absurd that you called us clients. We didn't hire you. We didn't ask for this."

"I know. And I'm sorry," Megan said, then stopped, biting her lip hard.

Lily put her hand on Megan's. "It's okay. Now you're exposing the company and what it was doing." She looked into the camera lens. "They slide into your thoughts at your most vulnerable moment and then don't leave. For me, it was a very public and embarrassing meltdown that I'm sure many of you remember. I was obsessed with the shame for much longer than I should've been. Now I understand why.

"I want you all to think about a rock-bottom moment of your own. Was there a voice that wouldn't let you get past it? That's *them*. That's what they do. If you want to break up with that voice once and for all, listen to what Megan has to say."

Ben could see Megan's eyes filling with tears. "You got this, Megan," he said. "Tell them everything. Expose the shit out of this place. Take Naysay Inc. down with the *one* weapon it can't defend: *the truth*."

"Amen," Eden said.

Megan looked into the camera. "They tell us in training that we're helping you. That you need us, or your world would erupt in chaos. But that's a lie. It's for the money. Naysay Inc. is paid by companies in your world, or the Real World as we call it, to make you feel insecure about your choices. To make you question everything."

"Tell them how you profit," Lily said to Megan before turning back to her followers. "Wait until you guys hear this. It's nuts!"

As Megan explained how the Fund worked, Ben wondered if Real Worlders would believe what Megan and Lily were saying. An alternate world where people implanted negative thoughts in your brain? That was asking a lot.

Voices in the hallway were growing louder and more intense.

Ben looked at the door. Did they realize they were watching the live broadcast too? His heart started to pound. He didn't want them to take this away from him. It might be the last time he ever saw Megan.

"That nasty voice in your head? That was me. I'd be sitting in my cubicle in Naysayland, sipping my morning coffee and ruining your self-esteem."

"I'd insane obsess over the smallest things," Lily said. "I couldn't deal when a nice guy liked me. I was a mess."

"But something happened when you met that nice guy, Lily. I fell in love with the voice in *his* ear. He was my coworker. And once we understood what love felt like, we couldn't bring ourselves to ruin your relationship."

Eden looked at Ben. "Someone's all gooey in the center now." She rolled her eyes.

"Hey. Don't knock it till you've tried it."

Comments began to roll in.

> I don't believe you.
>
> You clearly have your own agenda.
>
> This is fake news.
>
> This is worse than AI!
>
> You're a troll and everyone should stop watching this nonsense.
>
> I'm turning this shit off.

Megan looked at Lily. "I'm not sure this is working. Look at the comments. The whisperers are still in their heads."

Ben's heart sank. He walked over and opened the door carefully. Everyone was staring at the screen. Jacqueline stood closest.

"They are thrashing her in the comments. It's not working," she said. "These Real Worlders are too far up their own asses to recognize the truth for what it is," she added, high-fiving Abby. "I knew my daughter didn't have it in her. She thought she could take down generations of

Naysaying with an Instagram video, of all things?" She let out a shrill laugh. "The audacity."

Ben clicked the door shut and stared at Megan's eager face on the screen. "Come on, Megan," he said, willing her to find the right words.

"Tell them," Lily pleaded. "Like you told me."

Megan took a deep breath and stared into the camera, her eyes blazing. "Here's the thing. Your minds are beautiful, but they are also complicated. And because your world embraces technology in the wrong way, you are also losing your grasp on humanity. Social media has made the Real World smaller, and while there are some benefits to that, it also is sending your collective anxiety through the roof. It's become too easy to compare yourselves to others. You say awful things online that you'd never say in person. You use memes to express your opinions on complicated political and social issues instead of having live conversations. You hide behind your screens. You don't pick up the phone anymore.

"I'm here to break the bad news—it's slowly eroding away the Real World's greatest weapon: your empathy. How you relate to others, and to yourself, is changing rapidly. That makes Naysay Inc.'s job so much easier because they thrive on you pulling away from the people around you. They want you to forget that you're all connected. That humanity is a collective. They count on filters and clickbait to make you feel like crap about yourselves. Doomscrolling is one of the best things that's happened to their business. They've convinced you the truth is subjective."

Ben could see Megan glance at the comments as she paused to take a breath.

Yes!

This makes so much sense to me!

My head is clear now! Thank you! Keep talking! Set us all free!

"She's doing it," Eden said. "She's actually lowering their vulnerability indexes with the truth."

"That's my girl," Ben said.

"They want you to think that because love makes you vulnerable, it also makes you weak," Megan continued. "But it's the opposite. Love is the strongest bond. It's what will save us all. And I know because it saved me." Megan paused. "If you're watching this, Ben, I love you. I'd make the same choices over and over again because loving you saved me from myself."

"I love you, too, Megan," Ben said, touching the screen.

"If anyone listening right now wants the voice to leave, you must start trusting the thoughts that build you up, not the ones that knock you down. Stop *thinking* and start *doing*. Put your screen down. Take a walk. Listen to music. Dance in the rain. Have coffee with a friend. That's how you bring down Naysay Inc. You reconnect and plug back into the people around you. But most importantly, you get to know your true self. I have a feeling you're going to like who you are."

Megan wiped a tear from her eye as she finished. Lily hugged her.

"Holy shit. Vulnerability indexes are lowering so quickly that it's crashing the entire whispering system," Eden said.

"So, no one is whispering in Real Worlders' ears, whether they were watching or not?"

Eden shook her head. "No. Looks like the system is down. For now, anyway."

Abby burst into the room, her eyes wild.

Eden and Ben jumped away from the tablet. Ben braced himself for his punishment.

"Did you see that?" Abby asked as she peeled off her white coat.

Ben took a breath. This was it. They were going to give him that surgery for sure.

"It was amazing," Abby sang.

"Wait, what?" Ben asked and stared at her in disbelief. "Did you say, *amazing*?"

"I sure did."

Had collectively lowering Real Worlders' vulnerability indexes and crashing the system changed the hearts of Naysayers themselves?

"Come, follow me," Abby said. When neither of them moved, she pulled on Ben's arm. "It's okay, I promise," she said, the light back in her eyes.

They followed Abby out of the room. Everyone, including Jacqueline, stood at the floor-to-ceiling windows, staring at the gray clouds as they parted to reveal a bright-blue sky. Sunlight filled the room.

"What is happening?" Eden asked. "What is that?"

"That's the sky," Ben said.

"I don't understand."

"When Naysay Inc. lost its collective purpose, it must have balanced the scales. That's what the sky looks like in the Real World sometimes."

"Only some days?" Eddie asked.

Everyone in the room was intently listening to Ben. He found Jacqueline's face before continuing. "In the Real World, they have balance. Or at least they try to. That means some days are sunny, some cloudy. It's like a metaphor for their daily lives too. Some days are good, some are bad. Some people are kind. Some are awful."

Ben raised his voice to reach everyone. "Naysayland and the Island operate in isolation from each other, and that's why they live in such extremes. The Real World is how humanity was intended. *Without* our intervention," he added, and a few people looked to the floor.

"I feel lighter," Jim said, then tapped his stomach. "Well, metaphorically speaking," he said with a chuckle. "I can't believe I'm up here. In HR!"

"While I was in the system, I may have also sent an email asking every employee to come to this floor immediately," Eden said. "I wanted them all to see what really goes on up here."

Jacqueline stared at the clear skyline. "I'm feeling *things* from your little speech, Ben." She tapped her chest. "This area feels warm. What is that?"

"Understanding that we can all be a part of making people's lives better, not tearing them apart, and in turn our lives will improve. It's a collective optimism."

"Oh, gross? Really?" Jacqueline cleared her throat. "Sorry. Hard habit to break. It actually doesn't feel completely awful. I guess I could get used to it." She looked back at the screen, where Megan was still answering questions. "My daughter did all this?"

"She did," he said, smiling up at the screen.

"I didn't know she had it in her," Belinda called out.

"Shut up, Belinda," Ben and Jacqueline said, and everyone laughed.

"Well, some things won't change," Ben said. "We can still hate on Belinda."

"Thank god," Jacqueline exclaimed.

Belinda huffed.

Karla popped her head through the crowd. "Do we still have jobs? Will Naysay Inc. cease to exist?"

Ben paused. The entire company needed a new purpose.

Ben looked to the sapphire sky, to the eager faces that surrounded him, and then to Megan on the screen, the woman who started it all. A thought landed in his head as if she'd whispered it.

"Let me tell you how we move forward," he said and began to speak, his voice strong as he outlined their future.

Epilogue

One Year Later

"Good morning, Ms. Lowell. Beautiful day today, isn't it?"

Megan removed her sunglasses. "It certainly is, Donte. How's the baby?"

He let the heavy glass door he'd opened for her shut and pulled a picture up on his phone. "Smiled for the first time last week."

"He's precious," Megan said as she stared at the infant with the gummy grin.

Megan's bright-pink skirt swung as she glided toward the elevator.

"Twenty-fourth floor, Ms. Lowell?" Belinda asked, looking sharp in her royal-blue bell uniform.

"Yes, please," Megan said, and moments later, the doors opened to reveal a spacious reception area with a living green wall, plush sofas and ottomans in soft pastels, and a neon sign with the company's name.

"Yaysay Inc., how may I direct your call?"

Megan paused at the front desk, waiting for her mother to finish.

"Yes, please hold while I transfer you to him." Jacqueline pressed a button and pulled off her headset. "I don't understand why Eddie's fiancée can't dial his direct extension," she said, rolling her eyes. "And that squeaky voice! Can you imagine what it sounds like when they—"

"Mom, that's not nice," Megan interrupted. "Remember our motto."

"We put the yay back in your day," she said with forced enthusiasm.

"The more times you say it—"

"The more I'll start to feel it?"

"Exactly," Megan said. "It's why we started you off answering phones instead of—" She pointed to the rows of cubicles filled with people promoting cheer.

Yaysay Inc. was established after *the Change*. That's what former Naysayers called the day Megan's message to the Real World altered Naysayland as they knew it. With help from Anthony and Genevieve, Ben and Megan upended Naysay Inc.'s business model and used its advanced technology to raise people up, not down. Yaysay Inc. was born with one major distinction—Real Worlders would now *choose* when they wanted a Yaysayer in their ear.

If they were nervous before a first date, worried about a job interview, or having a bad day, they could swipe a screen, click a mouse, or log into an app and instantly be yaysayed.

And the best part?

It was free.

Yaysay Inc. had changed its designation to a nonprofit and accepted donations from thankful patrons in both worlds. There was also the pile of money Naysay Inc. had made in the past hundred years. The new CFO had confided in Megan that it was enough to keep the company in business for the next hundred years.

Jacqueline wasn't the only former Naysay Inc. employee who wasn't suited for yaysaying even after their (literal!) change of hearts. Belinda and Donte had also been assigned jobs that didn't have a direct line to people requesting positivity. But many former whisperers, like Beth (who'd stopped drinking alcohol and had a side hustle selling a line of mocktails she'd created called Night Shift Spirits) transitioned easily, enjoying their impact on a variety of people's lives. Never knowing if they'd get a politician wanting a pick-me-up, a teenager requesting a pep talk, or a parent needing praise.

Others, like Eddie and Jim, requested to work with the same group they'd naysayed before, wanting to absolve themselves of their guilt. Eddie was proud to report he'd convinced James Blunt, Daniel Powter, and Snow Patrol to tour together. He was considering starting a company that managed bands. He'd call it Comeback Corporation.

Jim, who was on track to win Yaysay Inc.'s Bright Star Award (turns out he could've secured top whisperer status, but he'd strategically hidden his true competitive nature under his rumpled blazers) was back with his ex-wife and kept a spreadsheet of the people he'd already saved from divorce. (1,102!)

Soraya and Carlos had been promoted to lead whisperers and had requested to work as a team having been inspired by Megan and Ben. From the way they'd been looking at each other lately, Megan wouldn't be surprised if they were also hoping for their own happy ending. (Megan had been adamant with Bernard that it would *not* be against Yaysay Inc. policy to date coworkers.)

Yaysay Inc.'s services weren't limited to the Real World. Islanders and Yaysayers in Yaysayland (they'd voted to change the official name) had access to them too. Amber from Empathy Grocery had made an appointment after a huge fight with her husband over inventory and was thrilled to discover Megan, who still occasionally donned the headset, pop in her ear with some encouraging words.

Megan settled into her office that overlooked the sea of skyscrapers and sighed.

"All okay?" Karla glided into the room holding an iced-coffee drink and a tablet. They'd given Karla a shot at yaysaying, but when Eden, who ran the company's IT, discovered Karla had sent an inappropriate picture of herself to one of her clients, she'd been reassigned as Megan's assistant. Megan could never unsee the picture of Karla in the lace bustier, but she had never been more organized.

"I can't believe it's been a year since we started this company."

"A year? Today?" Karla asked. She looked out to the skyline. "Wow."

"Do you ever miss naysaying?" Megan asked.

The change of heart had affected each person differently. Which made sense, of course, because they were all individuals. Naysay Inc.'s biggest flaw had been expecting its employees to think and feel singularly, and if they didn't, they'd be sent to HR. (Which did exist at Yaysay Inc. and was run by Bernard, but only to do traditional things like support recruitment, employee relations, and performance management.)

Yaysay Inc.'s internal mission was to develop and hone the positive traits of each employee. The external goal of Yaysay Inc. was to help people connect to their humanity. To serve as a reminder they were never alone.

"Sometimes I miss my old life," Karla said. "But when I do, I crank call your mother from my old burner phone. It's incredibly satisfying." She laughed, tucking a strand of hair behind her ear. She'd grown out her blunt bangs and sharp bob, and Megan thought it suited her.

Megan smirked. "I bet."

Karla set the iced drink on the desk. "Here's your latte. And this," she said, waving the tablet, "has the updates you asked for."

Megan stared at the screen. "How are they doing?"

"See for yourself," Karla said. "Oh, and I like the new painting," she said, pointing to the wall where *The Scream* used to hang. Megan had immediately returned it to the Real World and replaced it with a mural of a bright sunset that Ben had painted. More recently, Jacqueline had taken to joining him in the art studio. She said it helped quell her negative nature.

Karla shut the door behind her, and Megan clicked on the first file folder. Every few months, she checked in on her and Ben's former clients to see if they'd dug themselves out of the hole their naysaying had created.

There was a picture of Kristopher Tatterson holding a golden statue. His show *Tatty, Tatt, Tatt* had recently won a Daytime Emmy. It looked like he'd requested to be yaysayed a handful of times, often before tape days to remind himself to enjoy the ride. That the success or failure of the show didn't define him. He still struggled quieting his own intrusive thoughts and self-sabotaging tendencies, but his self-awareness and a well-intentioned therapist who had never paid into the Fund had helped him learn how to push them aside.

Dismantling the Fund had been Megan and Ben's first order of business. They'd exposed all those who'd participated in it. The physicians and therapists had lost their licenses, lawyers were disbarred, and most of the companies had either been restructured or gone bankrupt. Not surprisingly, all the political candidates continued to thrive despite the negative publicity.

The next file was for Nancy Sawyer and included her new author headshot. She was holding her cat, Raspberry, both displaying an identical sly smile. To Megan's and Ben's surprise, Nancy had never procured Yaysay Inc.'s services. Karla had included a note that said *Author=Sadist*, meaning it was possible that Nancy's experience of constant rejection in the publishing industry made her more tolerant of her own negative thoughts. Some could argue that grit is what gave writers their edge. It had certainly worked for Nancy. She'd thrown out that thriller and written a cozy mystery about an older woman and her cat, Pineapple, who solved cold cases. It had been billed as *Murder, She Wrote* meets *Puss in Boots* and had sold at auction. The TV rights were already secured, and the project had been rushed into development, with Kathy Bates slated to headline and executive produce. Her former agent had emailed Nancy, apologizing for not taking her back, and urged her to reach out if she ever changed agents again.

Nancy had found great pleasure in deleting that email.

Megan couldn't wait to show Ben. They still mused about Nancy's cat, Raspberry, and his litter box, which was more expensive than many people's beds. It was comforting to know Nancy could now afford his pricey toilet.

There was a quick knock, and the door opened. "I have your grandmother on video call for you."

"Okay, transfer it over," Megan said, running her hand through her hair before clicking on the tablet.

Genevieve's tanned face appeared. "Hello, my dear," her grandmother said. "How are you?"

Megan cocked her head. "Are you wearing a muumuu?"

Genevieve laughed. "This is called a *nap dress*."

"Do you nap in it?"

"No, but I *could* if I wanted to," she said proudly. She stood up and twirled. "Randy loves it."

"How is he?" Megan asked. "And are you still enjoying the Island?"

"Randy's good. The dock has gotten so busy since *the Change*. So many new residents since we let people choose where to live."

After *the Change*, some inhabitants from the Island, like Ben's mom, had returned to Yaysayland to be reunited with the families they'd been forced to leave, and some former Naysayers, like Joan and her baby, had left to live a quieter life on the Island.

"I do like it here, but I can only play beach-blanket bingo so many times. And Randy means well, but if he signs me up for one more seashell jewelry-making class, I'm going to lose it. Lord have mercy!"

"Sounds like you have a bad case of island fever, Grandmother." Megan laughed. "Good thing you're coming here next week for the board meeting."

"Yes. I cannot wait to see you. Randy is going to stay back and hold down the fort."

"Need a little space?"

"I love the man, but I was single for seventy-five years, so I need a little space here and there."

The Yaysay Inc. board consisted of Anthony, Genevieve, Megan, Ben, and Abby (who had also commissioned the living green wall in the reception area and drew great pleasure from watching Jacqueline water it between answering phone calls). They met every few months to reevaluate their business model, understanding that the world they served was in constant flux and they couldn't afford to wear blinders.

"Tell Anthony not to order from that bagel place again. They were stale last time," Genevieve huffed.

"Why don't you tell him yourself?" Megan smiled. Although they'd quite possibly saved humanity together, her grandmother and Anthony still had a beef with each other. He'd taken to calling her Island Girl, playing "La Isla Bonita" as she'd walked into the last board meeting. Genevieve had not been amused.

"How's Ben? How are you two doing?"

Megan glanced at the emerald-green dress hanging in the corner of her office. "He's great. We're great. Heading to the wedding soon."

"Please give them both my best. I'm happy they figured it out. And what about you two? Feeling inspired?" she asked, smirking.

"We're happy and taking one day at a time, Grandmother," Megan said as Ben walked in wearing a black suit with an emerald tie that matched her dress. "Speak of the devil."

"You're not dressed yet?" Ben asked, looking at his watch. "We need to leave in—"

"I know, I know," Megan said. "I got caught up with some old friends," she said, pointing to the tablet.

Ben came around and waved. "Hi, Genevieve!"

"Hello, Ben! How's your mother? Is she enjoying her job in the training department?"

Ben nodded. "She loves it. But she still misses the Island's ocean breeze."

"Well, tell her I have a guest room, and she is welcome anytime. Ahem. That offer stands for both of you too." Genevieve gave them a pointed look.

"I promise we'll visit soon. I can't wait to see your new koi pond. How are the fish holding up?"

"The transfer was successful; they seem right at home—I'm the one still settling in." She smiled.

"You'll get there," Megan said. "Okay, I have to run. See you next week. I love you."

"Me too," Genevieve said, still not comfortable saying the words, but Megan knew she loved her, and that's all that mattered.

Megan sent a quick email to Dr. Peakstone confirming their session for next Wednesday. *Whether they're naysaying or yaysaying, people will always have problems I can help with,* she'd said to Megan when she'd asked her to stay on as their staff psychologist to keep the staff—especially her mother—from backsliding into their naysaying ways.

It was discovered later that Dr. Peakstone had been a member of the resistance for years, working hand in hand with Anthony. When Megan thought back on their sessions, it made sense. How Peakstone had encouraged her to understand the *why* behind her feelings and relationships. And that thing about finding balance! Could she have been more obvious?

A few minutes later, Ben and Megan clasped hands as the elevator headed toward the basement, Belinda at its helm.

"A Real World wedding, huh? Isn't the divorce rate there still like fifty percent? Maybe wait on sending a gift," Belinda mused.

"Stick it, Belinda," Ben said as the doors opened, and they walked off the elevator into the chilly room that housed the portals to the Real World.

Ben turned to Megan. "Did I mention you look stunning in that dress?"

"Only about a dozen times. But I'm not complaining."

"I love that Jasper and Lily wanted to get married today, of all days."

"Me too."

"Do you have the gifts?"

Megan nodded at her bag. "In here."

They'd had the Monopoly shoe crafted out of silver as a reminder of Jasper's beloved aunt Louisa, and an artist had hand painted Lily's book cover on a canvas. Megan had sent pictures of them to Lily's mother, Sophia, who'd agreed they'd love the thoughtful gifts. Megan was looking forward to meeting her for the first time in person that night.

Although there were still strict guardrails set up between the two worlds, and travel between them was rare, Megan and Ben had felt it was important to make occasional exceptions with Lily and Jasper.

Megan was one of her first calls when Lily walked away from her *Worthy by Thirty* book deal and pitched a different book: *How to Wrangle Your Own Voice*. The Real World no longer had *uninvited* voices whispering in their ears, but they still needed to learn how to manage their own internal judges.

Lily had sent Megan an advance copy, and she'd made it required reading for all incoming employees at Yaysay Inc. It would be published in the Real World next month, and Lily had speaking gigs lined up all over the country. She'd decided to interview @CallieCleanMyChaos at a few of her events. It turned out she'd had a whisperer in her ear that had driven her to record and post the video.

Lily had also turned thirty last year without much fanfare, and that was exactly the way she'd wanted it. Megan was proud of her friend.

"Jasper sounded good when I spoke to him last week," Ben said.

"He likes the new teaching gig?"

"More than he thought he would."

Jasper had shelved his second manuscript, but he still owed the publisher another on his contract, and Megan had joked to Jasper over a recent video call that it was too bad the Real World wouldn't want to read Grace Potter's book idea because she'd gladly let him have it. Jasper thought once things had settled, a tell-all might be the move. He could hear his aunt Louisa's voice again, and she'd reminded him to slow down. For now, Jasper had pivoted to teaching a creative-writing course at UCLA. He was surprised to discover how satisfying it was to help develop someone else's talent. Jasper had told Ben, who would be his best man in the ceremony, that he was marrying the love of his life and that was the real win.

Megan approached the portal and lifted her hand to the keypad that would transport them back to Las Vegas, where Jasper and Lily were getting married on the top floor of the casino's grand ballroom. "Such an easy commute," Megan said.

Ben grabbed her hand before she could place her thumb on the keypad. "Do you ever worry we'll tip the scale of balance too far the other way? That all these happy endings in the Real World will seem manufactured and people won't know how to find their own sense of contentment?"

"I thought you'd be happier for Nancy and Raspberry," Megan teased, wrapping her arms around Ben's neck. "It's true what they say about pets and their owners starting to look alike," she said, thinking of the author-cat photo on the inside of the book's jacket.

"She did dye her hair to be the same color as his tabby fur." Ben laughed, then grew serious again. "Are you concerned people will become too reliant on being happy? Unwilling to feel any twitch of unease? Yesterday, someone requested to be yaysayed after their Botox wore off prematurely."

Megan smiled. "I think history has taught us that Real Worlders have a bad habit of overcorrecting," Megan said. "So, I say, let them. The scales will balance themselves out eventually. We've reminded them that they are all in possession of free will. What they do with it is up to them."

Ben nodded. "You're right. But I still worry."

"The fact that you're worried—that you care about what happens—makes me more than sure that it will all be okay." Megan kissed him.

She understood his concern. Although most of their former clients were enjoying streaks of success, that would eventually fade. New challenges would present themselves. And Yaysay Inc. would be there to help them through it—if they sought their assistance.

Life was a series of choices—some good, some bad, some terrible. Megan wanted Ben by her side for every single one because if she'd learned one thing, a life that was all good or all bad was not sustainable. The biggest joys of life hid in the in-between.

She typed the code into the keypad, and the metal doors swung open, revealing the dark hallway to a world not so different from theirs. Megan held out her hand. "Ready?"

Ben laced his fingers through hers. "Always."

They walked into the darkness, their hearts filled with the in-between.

ACKNOWLEDGMENTS

As authors, we constantly wrestle with that negative voice in our heads—the uninvited critic with way too many opinions. It shouts things like: *Girl, you're not writing a book—you're just aggressively typing and hoping for the best!* And *where's this story going anyway? Spoiler alert: nowhere fast!* But that Naysayer didn't only show up when we wrote, it also crept into our daily lives—lecturing us about our parenting, questioning our friendships, and zeroing in on every flaw in the mirror. We became intensely curious: Where do these thoughts come from? And what could we do to stop that negative self-talk? We turned our existential spiral into this novel. And in true Lily fashion, we found a way to talk back to the Naysayer inside us: *Sorry, girl, you don't get the final word.*

Catherine McKenzie, you're the voice we always want in our heads. Thank you for your pep talks, the (lovingly) pushy encouragement, and the expert agent matchmaking (we are in love—see below!). This book wouldn't exist without your tireless yaysaying. Naming a character after you wasn't nearly enough—and yes, we did banish her to the Island—but we still hope it made you smile.

Stephanie Kip Rostan, we adore having your whip-smart, funny, and calming voice in our ears. You're part agent, part editor, part wizard—and the reason we keep going. We're so lucky to have you.

To Selena James, our editor—you have one of the most positive voices we've ever heard, and that helps *tremendously* when you're working through an edit letter! Your ideas for improving this book did exactly that—and then some. Big thanks to you and the entire team at Little A for believing in this book—and in us.

Kristi Yanta, your editing skills are incomparable. Your sharp eye, smart solutions, and narrative instincts elevated this story in every way. Our characters thank you. We thank you.

PS: Our inner voices have no notes.

To our film agent, Ali Lefkowitz at Anonymous Content, we appreciate your hard work and enthusiasm to bring this book (and others!) to the screen.

Author friends, you're amazing! There are too many of you to name here—which, honestly, we love. One of the greatest gifts of this career has been the friendships we've formed with fellow storytellers. You've made the hard parts easier and the good parts even better.

Readers, *you* are the reason we keep writing! When that nasty inner voice makes us question ourselves, we picture you holding this book and enjoying it—and that keeps us going.

You make it all worth it.

Mike and Matt, you've stood by us through *nine* books (and at least *nine thousand* writing crises!). Thank you for nodding patiently when we let our Naysayers get the best of us—and for pretending it was the first time every time. We truly don't know how you do it, but we're glad you do.

About the Authors

Liz Fenton and Lisa Steinke have been best friends for over thirty-five years and survived high school and college together. They've coauthored nine novels, including *The Good Widow*, which is an Amazon charts bestseller, and *Forever Hold Your Peace*, which is optioned for film. They both reside with their families and several rescue dogs in San Diego, California.